$10

THE
AVALON
COLLECTION

Web of Magic, Books 4-6
by Rachel Roberts

D1613556

red sky
publishing

cds BOOKS
New York

For information please address:

CDS Books
425 Madison Avenue
New York, NY 10017

ISBN: 1-59315-147-0

Orders, inquiries, and correspondence should be addressed to:

CDS Books
425 Madison Avenue
New York, NY 10017
(212) 223-2969 FAX (212) 223-1504

Printed in the United States of America

First Edition
10 9 8 7 6 5 4 3 2 1

The Secret
of the Unicorn

Chapter 1

*E*mily Fletcher danced.

Swirling through soft lights that surrounded her like snow-white silky curtains, she moved to the sound. The melody wrapped around her, carrying her away. It was like no song she'd ever even imagined — lyrical, dazzling, enchanting. Bathed in the sweet sounds, she twirled, longing for the song to go on forever. Snowflakes swirled, spinning faster. The melody curved, arcing like a graceful bird, then fell like the sea, crashing on the shores in timeless rhythm. Arms outstretched, Emily moved like a ballerina. Reaching for the dizzying notes, she felt the melody just out of reach, slipping away on gossamer wings. She ached for the music to find her again. Somehow she knew that she was the only one on the planet who had ever heard this song. The song was inside her, and she was the only one who could bring it to life. . . .

❧ ❧ ❧

The dream was still as vivid as it had been when she'd awakened that morning. Summoning

1

her memory of the song, she raised her flute and —

ScrooKK!

That sure wasn't it. Furrowing her brow, Emily placed her fingers against the keys. Taking a deep breath, she lifted the mouthpiece to her lips and blew into the instrument again.

A series of lovely notes wafted into the air. Gaining confidence, she replayed the melody in her mind as her fingers flew faster toward the final phrase.

SKEEoooWWW!!

Ahg! How horrible was that?

Emily wrinkled her nose. She turned the flute over in her hands. The cool metal felt smooth and sleek against her palms.

"That'll sure make an impression at the audition," she muttered, tossing a strand of loose, reddish-brown hair from her face. She glared at the flute, its clean lines and gleaming, polished surface catching sparkles of light from the large window in her bedroom. The beautiful instrument seemed to mock her weak and off-key attempts to play such an exquisite song. She glanced around her bedroom helplessly, wondering why she'd bothered to take out the instrument in the first place.

"Don't drop the music because of me," her father had said over the phone the evening before. *"That's really cool you're trying out for the jazz band."*

She hadn't bothered to explain that there was no jazz band at Stonehill Middle School, only a marching band — not that she'd thought one way or another about joining it. In fact, she hadn't even bothered to unpack her flute case until that very morning. Even though it had been almost a year since her parents had divorced and her whole world had broken apart, she still didn't feel much like making music. It was easier just to stick with everyday, necessary things — school, homework, helping her mother at the veterinary clinic — and now her involvement with the Ravenswood Wildlife Preserve.

How could she explain that to her father, though? An enthusiastic amateur saxophonist, he had been thrilled when he'd realized that Emily had inherited his gift for music — right along with her mother's knack with animals. She remembered those lazy afternoons playing music together. Dad riffing on the sax, dancing around like a rock star, Emily tootling along on the flute. Mom always covered her ears, but Emily didn't care what they sounded like. The important thing had been sharing those moments — moments now faded like remnants of a tattered dream. Trying to reconnect with those feelings, she had taken out her once-prized possession. But now Emily couldn't seem to find the right notes. Her mind could no longer wrap around the music and flow with it. She felt the loss piling up inside, even as she tried so hard to keep it at bay. Maybe she once had musical talent, but that had changed.

That wasn't the only thing that had changed lately.

Emily held up her wrist and eyed the rainbow-colored stone on its beautiful silver bracelet. Nobody would have guessed that it was anything other than a pretty piece of jewelry. Emily knew differently. The rainbow jewel had special powers. Her friends Kara Davies and Adriane Charday knew it, too. Together, the three of them had discovered magic — and that they each had unique magical talents that would someday make them mages, magic masters.

Emily was a Healer. Her special talent enabled her to connect with injured creatures, to help them heal by focusing her power with the magic of the rainbow jewel. Adriane was a Warrior. The gem she had found looked like a tigereye, but ever since it had bonded her with the mistwolf named Stormbringer, she had called it her wolf stone. With its magic, she was learning to shape and control the physical world around her. Kara was a Blazing Star — her gift was to act as a sort of magnifier for the magic of others, attracting, strengthening, and sharpening it.

As if in response to her thoughts, the rainbow jewel caught a ray of light through the window and sparkled.

Too bad I can't magically remember how to play the music, Emily thought, sighing.

She closed her eyes and let the warm sunlight dapple across her face as she thought about the dream. The notes of the song danced through her head again, haunting her like ghosts. Quickly, before they could slip away, she lifted the flute and played. The music poured easily out of the instrument, each note clear and shimmering. But as she neared the elusive end of the melody, the music faltered. She reached inside, trying to find the notes that would bring just the right ending. But the notes danced out of reach, and the melody faded. She paced her breathing, knowing what her father would say: *Follow the music, Em. Don't be afraid to really feel it.*

She couldn't let herself give up. She wasn't a quitter.

Closing her eyes tight, she followed the melody again, running her fingers through the combination of notes, moving to form a high C — no, not a C, it should be an *F sharp*! She hit the new note, blowing with all her might.

SooOOKKWHONNNGGG!

A deafening cacophony of sound burst from

the flute, like a dozen different chords being played at once on an enormous pipe organ.

Emily's eyes flew open. The notes hung in the air, vibrating and fighting one another, loud and jarring and clashing. Her flute was changing colors — gold, scarlet, amethyst, emerald flashed across its polished surface, one after another, so fast that they formed a prism effect. The colors expanded and filled the room, glowing brighter and brighter with every passing second, until dark spots swam in front of Emily's eyes. She leaped to her feet, letting the flute fall off her lap onto the thick blue carpet. Her jewel was flashing like a rainbow beacon.

And just like that, the colors blinked out and the sound stopped, as if someone had flipped a switch.

Emily blinked, trying to clear her vision.

"Emily?" A knock on the door broke through the sudden silence.

With a gasp, Emily jumped.

She hurried to the door. Opening it, she saw her mother standing in the narrow upstairs hallway, dressed in her veterinarian's lab coat, smiling wryly.

"Got the flute out, I hear." Carolyn Fletcher peered into the room curiously. "Sounded like a whole orchestra."

"Oh, uh, I was playing along with the radio," Emily lied breathlessly, sliding a long sleeve over her jeweled wrist. "Didn't realize it was so loud."

Carolyn nodded, handing Emily a sheet of paper. "My noon appointment's here, Em," she said. "I need you to check this delivery. This order doesn't seem right."

Emily gawked at the shipping slip as if waiting for it to turn green.

"Now would be a good time," Carolyn added sternly.

With a flash of guilt, Emily looked over at the clock on her bedside table. "I guess I lost track of time."

"You've been doing that a lot lately." Carolyn raised an eyebrow. "I can't always be available to back you up when you get off schedule. Our guests in the Pet Palace can't feed themselves, you know."

"I know," Emily mumbled. "I'm sorry. I'm on it right now."

"And make sure those dogs get walked!" Carolyn called out.

"Okay!" Hurrying past her mother, Emily took the stairs two at a time and then headed for the back door. The Pet Palace was located in an old barn behind the house. It had been Emily's idea, when they'd first moved to Stonehill that summer, to convert it into a kennel for boarding pets.

As Emily jogged across the short strip of lawn separating the house from the barn, she read over the delivery form. Two dozen bags of gourmet kibble, liver, beef, bacon, and mixed blend; eight boxes of special biscuits and treats; a box of mixed jerky strips; two dozen snuggle balls; a pet bed heater with heated cat cup; and a grooming kit?

That's a strange order, Emily thought. It looked like supplies for a pet *party*. Then she swung open the barn door, and her eyes widened in horror.

The kennel was a disaster. Large bags of pet food were flung everywhere. Near a row of open cages, Muffin, the Feltners' terrier, and Ranger, the Paulsons' shepherd mix, were growling at each other as they played tug-of-war with a strip of beef jerky. The rear paws of a spotted beagle stuck out of a giant bag of gourmet kibble. A very contented Persian cat stared out from inside a box of treats.

"These liver snaps are delicious," a voice said with a mouthful of food.

Emily looked at the cat, eyes wide. "You can talk?"

"Of course I can talk! Pass some of that jerky."

Emily stopped in her tracks. Oh, no! She flashed back to the wild colors that had danced across her flute, those bursts of weird sound and colors in her room. Was this mess connected to that? Had she accidentally released some kind of crazy magic? She and her friends had learned a lot about how magic worked, but they still didn't know everything. Not even close.

"Easy, Maurice," she called softly, taking a step toward the cat. "How long have you been talking?"

Maurice blinked big green eyes. "Ever since I was a little elf."

A small, bright-eyed, furry face popped into view behind the cat. Two ferret eyes went wide in astonishment as they surveyed the barn. "*Gah!* I told you guys to put the stuff away! I didn't mean literally!"

So *that's* who'd been talking! "Ozzie." Emily crossed her arms and glared at the golden-brown ferret. "What's going on here?"

Ozzie shook his head. Then he hopped out of the kibble pile and, standing on his back paws, brushed crumbs off his belly. He had a small silver comb stuck in the fur behind his ears.

"What do you have to say for yourself?" Emily asked sternly.

"*Uurrrp.*"

"Did you place this order?" She waved the shipping form in the ferret's face, forcing Ozzie to sit back.

Squeak!

"Scuse me." Ozzie removed two snuggle balls from under his rump. "You said you needed help with the supplies, so I ordered some."

Emily put her hands on her hips and glared at him. She should have known. This wasn't a magical mishap at all. It was an Ozzie mess.

Ozzie could pass as an ordinary ferret, as long as he didn't open his mouth to talk. He was really an elf from a magical world called Aldenmor. He had been sent to Earth by the Fairimentals, protectors of the good magic of Aldenmor, to search for three human mages — a Healer, a Warrior, and a Blazing Star. They were destined to help find a mysterious place called Avalon, the legendary home of all magic. Ozzie had been upset to find that the Fairimentals had disguised him as a ferret to help him blend in on Earth. But he still managed to enjoy exploring everything this new world had to offer — especially the edible parts.

"I asked you to inventory supplies, not order the entire catalog!" Emily said, bending over to pull the jerky away from the struggling dogs.

Ozzie shrugged and kicked piles of loose kibble into a half-empty plastic package. "I inventoried. There was nothing left. *Mmrrph*, these liver snaps are especially tasty."

Emily watched him shove more food into his

mouth. So much for having everything under control. As usual, control seemed to have slipped away from her when she was least expecting it.

"How am I going to explain this?" she grumbled, grabbing a broom. "Since you made this mess, the least you could do is help me clean up."

"*Stoof!*" Ozzie spit out a piece of loose kibble. "Sure, no problem." He leaned hard against Scooter the beagle, trying to push the dog's nose away from the bag of kibble. "Ugh — move it!" he mumbled.

"We have to hurry." Emily started picking up boxes and bags. "I'm supposed to pick up Kara at the football game, then meet Adriane at Ravenswood."

Ozzie had resorted to jumping onto the dog's back. Scooter stood up, and Ozzie slid off with a *whoa!* and scurried into a box, scattering more treats across the floor. "Hey! Who ordered the rice and lamb flavor?"

Scooter sat on Ozzie and licked the ferret's head.

Doof! Ozzie wriggled away.

Emily rolled her eyes. Obviously she was going to have to take care of things herself — and fast. If she didn't leave soon, she would be late meeting her friends.

Thinking about Kara and Adriane gave her an idea. She stared at her stone. "It's worth a shot, right?"

Could she do this? Moving objects around magically was Adriane's department, not hers. Still, what did she have to lose?

Emily stared at the jewel on her wrist, focusing all her attention on it. Her breathing slowed. She lifted her eyes to a big bag of kibble and pictured it moving up into the air and over to one of the open food bins against the far wall. Her stone began to glow softly as she worked to visualize every detail — the bag lifting, swaying, floating across the room.

At first she didn't think it was working. Taking a deep, cleansing breath, she willed herself to sink deeper into her own mind, concentrating totally on her goal. The room around her faded into a vague, misty background. Nothing existed except her and the bag.

The bag quivered, then slowly levitated a few inches into the air.

"I did it!" Emily cried. "It's moving!"

Psyched that her experiment was working so well, Emily refocused her energy. By using magic, she could have the whole place cleaned up in no time! The bag lifted higher . . . higher. . . . Soon it was floating five feet above the floor.

"Okay," she murmured. "Now to move you over to the bins."

She traced an arc in the air with her stone, trying to steer the levitating bag toward the wall. The bag shuddered and bucked.

At the same time, her head was suddenly filled with a jangling, discordant sound — awful, broken, painful notes just like her flute had made a few minutes earlier. These were stronger, though. The barks of the dogs added to the noise.

"Ruff!"

A chubby beagle floated by Emily's head.

"Uh-oh."

"Meow!"

There went Maurice!

Suddenly the barn was filled with flying animals, all three dogs floating around the room in a whirl.

"Down!" Emily yelled out.

KAPOW!

A bag of kibble under Ozzie exploded in a burst of rainbow light, so bright that Emily cried out and squeezed her eyes shut.

"Wheeeeuuuuuuuu!" Ozzie cried, tumbling head over heels from the center of the explosion.

Emily felt tiny, hard objects pelt her head and shoulders like hail. Looking up and squinting cautiously through one eye, she saw sparkling rainbow pellets raining down all around her. As they hit the floor, they popped and exploded, then turned back into ordinary dry brown kibble.

As suddenly as it began, it all stopped. The animals were on the ground, no worse for the wear. Kibble was everywhere.

What had just happened? What was that awful noise?

The weird, jangling sounds echoed in her mind. "Something is very wrong."

Chapter 2

The sound rumbled across the field like an incoming train. Lightning sparked, even though the day was clear. Three electrical bolts slammed together in an explosion of light and sound. An immense dark cloud swirled out of nothingness to hover in the air above the field.

The portal had opened.

Animals and creatures came tumbling out, falling over one another in a rush as they hit the ground.

"Warrior, come quickly!" Storm called to Adriane. The mistwolf was already bounding across the field to help the new arrivals move away from the portal before it could close and vanish.

Wails of pain filled the field. Adriane's breath caught in her throat as she ran in from the surrounding woods to witness the chaos and confusion. Bodies, furred and feathered, were scorched and covered with a sickly green glow — Black

Fire. The dreadful poison magic of the Dark Sorceress must be spreading. If it wasn't stopped, the magical world called Aldenmor would be laid to waste.

Lyra, the large spotted, winged cat, and Ariel, the snow owl, had been among the first wave of wounded creatures to arrive when the portal first appeared that summer. Since then, no new refugees from Aldenmor had arrived. Today changed all that. Now, dozens of hurt and dying creatures were struggling to reach the safety of Ravenswood.

Lyra, healed now, thanks to Emily, joined the fray, herding animals so more could make it through the swirling mists of the portal.

Just as the last few new arrivals were herded off to the side, the portal began to close. Suddenly another creature appeared in the shrinking, swirling hole. It screeched in fear, a wild, jumbled sound. Bright colors shimmered across its body as it darted from the closing portal, bolted into the woods, and vanished.

❧   ❧   ❧

"Heel, Scooter!" Emily cried.

The stout little beagle looked up at her uncomprehendingly, his pink tongue lolling happily out of his mouth. With a shrill *yip!* he bounced off in pursuit of a passing moth, tangling his leash around Ranger's legs. Muffin stopped suddenly, nose down, investigating a half-eaten hot dog.

"Aaaargh!" Emily tugged at the leashes, dragging the three dogs toward the playing fields behind the high school.

Just ahead, she could hear the cheers of a large crowd. Today was Stonehill Middle School's first big football game of the year, and it sounded as if half the town had turned out. It was just past noon. She hoped it was almost halftime. The sooner Kara's cheerleading was over, the sooner they could join Adriane at Ravenswood. Emily couldn't shake the feeling that something was wrong there — something magical — and every minute she had to wait was a minute lost.

As Emily and her charges got closer, she heard the marching band start to play. They sound pretty good, she thought. Not like the lame band at my old school.

Hurrying forward and peering through a gap in the bleachers, she saw the band standing in formation on the sidelines on the far side of the field. As she turned away to check on the dogs, the band finished their song and started another. The last one had been a fight song, but this new one sounded — different. Emily listened in surprise, rooted to the spot. The instruments sounded muted and exotic, the complex and sinuous melody slithering its way into her mind like a snake. She blinked, and her eyelids felt strangely heavy and slow. Why did she suddenly feel so funny, like she was moving through water instead of air? The music crept into her mind, taking root — beautiful, haunting, incredible music. It sounded so familiar. Swinging her head around with effort, she stared at the marching band.

Wait . . . a . . . second, she thought, the words flowing through her mind like molasses. They're not even . . . playing their instruments . . . right now. Where . . . is that music . . . coming from?

"Rrrrrowrf!"

Emily snapped out of her daze as Scooter leaped forward, yanking the leash right out of her hand. "Hey!" she blurted as the little beagle raced toward a tall woman who was just turning away from the nearby hot-dog stand. "Oh, no," she whispered as she recognized the woman.

Mrs. Beasley Windor let out a shriek as the beagle planted his muddy paws on her spotless beige slacks. "Off!" she yelled. "Get off me, you mangy beast!"

"Oops!" Emily gasped, lunging forward and pulling the dog back by his collar. Scooter panted with excitement and struggled to escape again. "I'm so sorry, Mrs. Windor," she exclaimed.

"Well, little Miss Ravenswood Tour Guide." The woman glared at Emily over the tip of her beak of a nose. "I should have known."

Emily felt her cheeks burning. Of all the bad luck! Mrs. Windor was an influential member of the town council. She thought the Ravenswood Wildlife Preserve was a menace and wanted to develop the land into a country club. Emily and her friends had led the winning fight to save Ravenswood from being shut down and had been appointed official tour guides for the wildlife sanctuary, much to Mrs. Windor's displeasure.

"I'm really sorry," Emily mumbled helplessly.

Mrs. Windor sniffed and said, "If this is how you watch those animals, it won't be long until someone gets hurt." She bent closer, her voice a cold hiss. "I know you and your friends were responsible for letting dangerous animals loose in the town. As soon as I can prove it, we'll just see how fast Mayor Davies changes his mind about your precious Ravenswood." She stood and scowled at Emily. "I'm keeping my eye on you."

With that, she stormed away toward the far end of the bleachers.

"Great. Just great," Emily muttered. The last thing she wanted to do was give Mrs. Windor any more ammunition in her campaign against Ravenswood. If the preserve was bulldozed, dozens of magical animals — quiffles, pegasii, jeeran, and many others — would no longer have a safe haven. Not to mention the fact that Adriane's grandmother lived there as caretaker, and if Ravenswood was shut down, Adriane and Gran would lose their home.

Emily shuddered as she remembered the wrath in Mrs. Windor's beady little eyes when Scooter jumped on her. Maybe bringing her Pet Palace clients to the football game hadn't been such a hot idea after all.

Keeping a firm grip on the leashes, she headed into the gap between the two closest sets of bleachers. The marching band was playing again — a normal song, no weird, snakelike melodies this time. She shifted her gaze to the faces of the spectators across the field. Where was Kara? A mass of golden hair fluttered. Was that her? Emily strained to look closer. The crowd seemed to fade away as one face crystallized and leaped out. Emily gasped — and all the breath left her body in a *whoosh*.

Pale skin, pale as death. Jagged, grotesque cheekbones. Skeletal shoulders draped in black.

And the eyes — Emily felt ice course through her veins as she caught a glimpse of two blazing pools of malice and evil. The ghoul suddenly looked straight at her — and smiled. A wide, red-rimmed, grinning mouth full of crooked yellow teeth.

Emily squeezed her eyes shut. Her whole body had gone numb and cold. She felt a wave of dizzying nausea sweep over her. She wobbled forward, throwing her hands out just in time to stop herself from falling.

"Hey!" The teenage boy whose shoulder she'd grabbed was staring at her suspiciously as she opened her eyes. "What's the deal?"

"Um, sorry," Emily blurted, her gaze wandering back toward the ghastly specter.

But it was gone. She blinked, staring up at the bleachers. All sorts of people were sitting there, watching the game as if nothing out of the ordinary had happened. The horrid skeletal face was nowhere to be seen.

Emily shot another cautious glance across the field. Had she really seen that thing, or was her imagination playing tricks on her?

This was getting really weird. The rainbow jewel on her silver bracelet pulsed a steady warm glow as feelings of dread tickled up and down her back. She had to find Kara and get to Ravenswood fast. She took a step forward when Muffin and

Ranger leaped out in front of her, nearly sending her head over heels again.

"Look who's here," a familiar voice said. "It's Ms. Dolittle, the animal girl."

Glancing up, Emily found herself looking straight into the grinning face of Kara's fourteen-year-old brother, Kyle. Kara's friends Molly, Heather, Tiffany, Joey, and Marcus were sitting with him.

"Oh." Emily gulped, disentangling herself from the dogs' leashes. She was suddenly way too aware of her flushed, sweaty face, her messy hair, and the dogs slobbering on her shoes. Stay calm, she told herself. "Um, hi, guys."

"More comfortable to *sit* and watch the game," Marcus commented, sliding over to create a space next to him and Joey.

"Thanks." Emily felt herself blush as she sat down on the bench. "Are you okay?" she asked, pointing to the splint on Marcus's right wrist.

"Sure. Just a sprain, but enough for Coach Berman to keep me out of play for a week," Marcus smiled.

"Just when Stonehill needs 'Marcus the Sharkus'!" Kyle slapped his friend on the shoulder. "Emily's the doc, maybe she can do her magic on you. Whatdaya say, Em?"

"I'm only good with animals," she responded, hardly paying attention. She anxiously scanned the field searching for Kara.

Joey broke out in a laugh, punching Marcus in the arm. "Exactly."

Emily smiled in spite of her worry. They weren't bad kids, just silly. She leaned forward to pat the shepherd as it sat down on her foot. The other two dogs sprawled on the grass in front of Marcus.

"Hey, Ranger," Marcus said, kneeling forward to tickle the shepherd behind the ears. Ranger gave the boy a big, slobbering lick. Kyle and Joey jumped down to play with the other dogs. The dogs barked in pleasure, crowding in for some petting time.

"Yeah, good dogs. They look great, Emily," Joey smiled at her.

Marcus was sprawled on the grass with Ranger. "You do a great job at that pet hotel."

"Thanks." Emily smiled, trying to hide the fear building inside.

"Who brings all their *pets* to a football game, anyway?" Heather asked snidely.

Emily bit her lip.

"Where's Adriane? Is she coming to the game?" Joey asked.

"She's over at Ravenswood," Emily answered.

Marcus snickered. "Dude, you are way too obvious." He winked at Emily.

As the others turned their attention to the game, Emily gazed across the field to where she'd seen that ghastly face. Or had she? After the way she'd spaced out just before Scooter started jumping all over Mrs. Windor, she wasn't too sure. She snuck a peek at her jewel. The stone now lay quietly on her bracelet. She frowned, remembering the flute and the flying dogs. Had she imagined all that, too? No way.

"Yeah, but Emily here, could save the day." Molly's voice broke into Emily's thoughts. "She's got enough animals for five schools."

"She's like a walking zoo," Heather sniffed.

"Yeah, smells like one, too," Tiffany muttered just loud enough for Emily to hear.

"Huh?" Emily belatedly realized that she had become the topic of conversation again. "Um, what did you say?"

Tiffany shrugged and examined her perfectly manicured nails. "Keep up, animal girl. We were just saying how lame it is that we don't have a team mascot," she explained lazily. "That's totally got to be why we're losing this game."

A glance at the scoreboard at the far end of the

field confirmed it. The home team was down by six points, with less than two minutes left on the clock before halftime. She looked at the person in a tiger costume dancing around on the sidelines near the end zone.

"Wait," she said. "If Stonehill doesn't have a mascot, what's with the guy in the stripes down there?"

Heather snorted. "That's the *other* team's mascot," she exclaimed. "They're the Thornbury Tigers. We're the Stonehill Sparks. Duh."

"Whatever," Emily muttered, sorry she'd said anything. Still, she could look on the bright side — a couple of weeks earlier, Heather and Tiffany wouldn't have bothered to speak to her at all. They had been best friends with Kara for years. And now Kara was spending so much of her time hanging out with relatively uncool Emily and Adriane. How would Kara explain it? *You see, the three of us are mages, destined to save the universe and find the source of all magic.* Right. That would go over *really* well.

Still, Kara had done an amazing job getting her old friends involved in helping out with the tours. Ravenswood needed all the friends it could get. Emily hid a smile as she glanced out onto the field, where both teams were huddling.

"How about the Sparky the Stonehill Beagle?" Kyle spoke up. "Go, Beagles!" He stood up and howled.

"Sit down, you goof," Molly commanded, yanking at the hem of his rugby shirt.

"His name is Scooter —" Emily's words were cut off as the marching band launched into a loud, rousing fight song. Kara and the other cheerleaders raced onto the field, dancing along with the music, their blue-and-gold pompoms tracing out patterns in the air.

Emily winced. Was it just her, or was the band's music painfully loud? A hard, sharp high note blared at her, seeming to travel directly from the trombone section to her eardrums. She shook her head as the flutes broke in shrilly, their unrelenting tones piercing through her consciousness until she couldn't think straight.

Glancing at the others, Emily saw that they seemed totally unaware of what was happening. Why couldn't they hear it? She cringed as a cymbal crash reverberated through her bones and made her teeth chatter. Only the dogs seemed to notice that anything was wrong. All three of them were sitting up, pressing themselves against the metal bench and whining nervously.

Emily was vaguely aware of a creeping feeling, pulling at the edges of her mind. Suddenly a saxophone punched out a series of harsh, off-key notes, sounding as if it was wailing directly in her ear, and she gasped.

"Em? Hey, you okay? You look kind of weird." Marcus stared at her.

Emily squeezed her eyes shut. The sounds were too painful for her to answer.

Everyone except Emily suddenly leaped to their feet. The kids were yelling as the Stonehill team pushed forward to the twenty-yard line.

The cheers echoed as if in a huge cavern. Emily shook her head again, trying to clear it. "I — I'm okay." But she knew she wasn't. Fear trickled up and down her back.

The others weren't even listening to her anymore. There was a sudden flurry of movement on the field, and another roar went up from the crowd.

A wave of pain lanced through her, but her scream was covered by the raucous cheers around her.

"Score!" Joey crowed, pumping his fist in the air. "Now all we need is a field goal, and we could actually win this thing!"

"Check it out!" Heather's voice was shrill with excitement. "Someone's starting the wave over there."

Emily gasped for breath. The band had

reached a fever pitch, and the cheerleaders were going crazy with excitement. As if in a dream, she saw Kara bounce into a high kick as some of the other girls started to form a pyramid on the sidelines.

"Kara," Emily whispered, doubling forward as sharp cramps wracked her body.

Kara jumped to a stop, startled. She looked around the stands, her long blond hair flying in the wind.

"Kara . . ." It was all Emily could do to keep from screaming out. "Help me."

Meanwhile, across the way, the crowd was cheering and hollering as it performed the wave, the people in each section of the bleachers standing and waving their arms in turn. The human wave traveled swiftly from the left end of the bleachers to the right, then jumped across the field to the far end of Emily's side. She could see it coming closer . . . closer . . . closer.

The band was playing faster and louder than ever. Emily clenched her hands into fists, her face wet with sweat and tears. Her heart beat faster and faster as her wrist burned fire. Her jewel was blazing in warning.

Marcus, Joey, and the others jumped up, shouting and throwing their hands into the air. But Emily couldn't move, bound by the oppressive weight of overwhelming pain. She swallowed hard, closed her eyes tight, and braced for the impact as the enormous tidal wave of magic energy smashed into her. The rainbow jewel exploded with color, and everything went black.

Chapter 3

"Emily, are you all right?"

"Is she dead?"

"You doofus, she fainted!"

Voices reached her from down a long hallway. Emily felt rough dirt and grass against her stomach. Then she felt hands lifting her as she opened groggy eyelids.

She looked into the concerned faces of Marcus, Joey, and Molly. Kyle, Heather, and Tiffany sat behind them, watching.

"Are you all right, Emily?" Marcus asked.

She could see why Kara liked this boy; he had such deep blue eyes, full of compassion.

"I — uh — fine." She tried to push away, but her hands didn't seem to understand her brain's command. Instead she clung tightly to Marcus's arm.

"Move it. Move it. I said out of the way!"

The sound of Kara's voice sent Emily's strange sense of serenity skittering away. The golden-haired girl pushed her way to Emily's side, taking half her weight from Marcus.

Emily shook her head, trying to gather her thoughts. That weird, snaky music was still dancing around somewhere in the far corners of her brain, distracting her and making her thoughts difficult to gather. She noticed other kids gawking with curiosity. Had the loud, clashing music actually knocked her out? The noise of the crowd suddenly flooded around her like a dam bursting.

"Man, you see that?"

"A girl passed out!"

"Give her some air."

"Is she all right?"

"Fine, fine." Kara replied to the gathered throng. "Bad hot dog."

Kara and Marcus gently settled Emily back on the bleacher seat. Joey handed her a drink.

"Thank you," Emily said, taking a sip.

"What happened?" Kara asked.

"She just fainted," Marcus told her.

Emily winced. Feelings of suffering washed over her. She recognized the feeling. Her mind raced back to one fateful August afternoon, only a few months ago. A cat had been so badly burned that Carolyn had thought it would not survive. But Emily had helped it heal, even before she had her rainbow jewel.

Suddenly everything became clear, the one possible explanation for what was happening: More injured creatures were coming through from Aldenmor. Their terror and distress pulsed at her like a beacon — a cry for help, for a healer.

"We have to get to Ravenswood right now," Emily told Kara, trying to stay calm in front of the other kids. "An animal is terribly hurt."

"Healing animals is your thing, I have a game to win," Kara said.

"We need you, too, Kara."

Kara looked back and forth between the cheerleaders and Emily's concerned face.

Ring, ring!

Kara whipped out a small blue cell phone from her waist cinch. "Hello?"

She listened for a few seconds, her sparkling blue eyes widening in shock. Then she snapped the phone shut and slid it neatly back in its case. "Adriane," she said to Emily. "You're right."

She turned to her friends. "Listen up, you guys. We have a Ravenswood crisis. I have to go."

"Is there anything we can do to help?" Molly asked.

"Tell the others I had to leave."

"We'll take the dogs back to the Pet Palace for you," Marcus offered Emily.

"Thanks," Emily said, handing him the leashes. She gave him a grateful look.

Marcus smiled at her.

Emily felt herself pulled away as Kara grabbed her arm. "Let's go."

The two girls raced down the sidelines heading toward the exit.

❧   ❧   ❧

Stormbringer's keen eyes spotted Emily and Kara as they pushed through a patch of woods toward the huge, grassy expanse where the portal had appeared at the Ravenswood Wildlife Preserve. As they emerged into the meadow, the giant silver mistwolf raced up to them, skidding to a stop in front of Emily. *"Healer. Come quickly."* Emily heard Storm's voice clearly in her mind.

Behind Storm, Lyra padded over to Kara. *"A new group of animals came through. They're in bad shape."*

Although Lyra was thinking her words to Kara, Emily could hear them, too. Fear gripped her heart. It was always this way when she got close to a creature that needed her. Its pain, fear, confusion, and frenzy became her own, taking hold inside her and connecting her to the injured one. It was the hardest part of being a healer — having to share all those terrible feelings. Now she stared out over the meadow, her feet rooted to the ground in shock and horror.

It was worse than she had feared. Creatures of various sizes and shapes lay sprawled in the tall grass, crying and shaking. A pegasus — a winged horse — stood forlornly, his hide covered with burns, one of his gauzy, butterflylike wings hanging at an unnatural angle, limp and torn. Two or three long-eared, deerlike jeeran staggered, their soft, green-striped fur charred and their skin oozing blood. There were many species Emily couldn't even identify — small red bearlike creatures, jet-black possum creatures — but their sounds and feelings and expressions of pain were all too familiar.

They were covered with patches of a sickly greenish glow, the unmistakable sign of the Dark Sorceress's hideous Black Fire. Its dark energy seeped into Emily's mind, making her feel light-headed.

A winged shape momentarily blocked the early afternoon sun as Ariel, the snow owl, swooped from the sky and fluttered onto Emily's arm, wings sparkling with magical highlights of turquoise and jade. *"Ooooh,"* the owl sighed sadly as she surveyed the scene.

Ariel had been the first creature Emily had ever healed by herself, and seeing the healthy shine of the snow owl's feathers bolstered Emily's courage. "I'm glad you're here," she said.

"Emily!" Adriane ran into the field, followed by Ozzie, Balthazar the pegasus, and Ronif and Rasha, silver-billed ducklike creatures called quiffles. These magical animals had proved valuable advisers to the girls over the past few months.

Baby quiffles poked their heads out of pockets in Adriane's down vest. "Tell us what to do," the dark-haired girl asked Emily.

Emily snapped out of her daze. She looked at the ring of friends waiting for her. It was time to help.

Her first instinct was to run to the nearest injured creature and dive right in. But a voice in her head — her mother's calm, cool, unhurried voice — warned otherwise. *Take the time to get organized. Don't move faster than you can think, or you'll end up working twice as hard and helping half as well.*

"Start figuring out who is worst off," she instructed her friends, working to keep her voice calm and assured. "Bring me those first. But keep the others near so I can get to them as fast as possible. Move the healed ones out of the way as soon as I'm done with them."

The entire group whirled into action. Within seconds, Kara was hustling back over to Emily, ushering forward a badly burned red koala-sized bear. "Start with him." She patted the small, furry bear before hurrying away.

"Easy, there," Emily said, calming the scared creature. "Any idea what it is, Ozzie?"

"A wommel. They live in the trees of the Moor-groves."

Emily stared at the creature. It was keening softly, its big, wide eyes glazed over with pain. Out of the corner of her eye, she spotted Adriane herding a small group of limping, burned jeeran toward her. Did she have the strength to do this?

"It's going to be okay, little one," she murmured, placing a gentle hand on its soft, furry chest. Her rainbow jewel flashed erratically, cycling through colors.

She took a deep breath and forced herself to be still, to allow the wommel's pain to flow into her. Her stone pulsed in time with her heartbeat, and after a moment she became aware of the creature's heartbeat, fast and panicky beneath her hand. She breathed deeply and steadily, and gradually its heartbeat slowed, locking onto hers. Emily focused on the wommel's injuries and concentrated on sending out healing magic. The rainbow jewel blazed with light, and soon she could feel the Black Fire's poison weakening, breaking up — and finally leaving the creature's body. The sickly green glow faded, dissolving into rainbow sparkles that floated away on the breeze.

Emily barely had time to point the healed wommel toward Ozzie before the next victim arrived — and the next, and the next. For a while she could hardly even think, which was just as well. She had never seen so much horror and heartbreak all in one place. It seemed that the parade of injured creatures would never end.

Finally, Emily found herself healing the last of the injured. Her knees wobbling, she sank to the ground, the dry seed heads of the autumn grass tickling her hands as she leaned back and felt the slight breeze cooling the sweat from her brow. Still, she couldn't quite seem to relax. A tiny nagging hint of *something* — a sound? — tickled the edges of her mind, like a teasing memory. But what was it? She wrinkled her nose and shook her head, but the vague sense of uneasiness remained.

Ozzie scampered up to Emily. "You did an amazing job. Who would have thought when I first met you that you would be the perfect mage I was looking for!" The ferret beamed with pride.

"Thanks, Ozzie," she said distractedly. Something was buzzing in her ear. Climbing to her stiff, tired legs with a groan, Emily glanced around the meadow once more, again trying to pinpoint where the sound was coming from. But nothing she saw gave her an answer, so she just shrugged and followed Ozzie over to where her friends were standing among a kaleidoscope of creatures.

"Does anyone hear that?" she asked.

"Hear what?" Kara panted as she jogged over with Lyra.

Another wave of frenzied, broken, tuneless noise swept through Emily, like needles of sound piercing her all over. "That!" she gasped. "Those sounds. Can't you hear it?"

Adriane shot her a concerned glance. "What does it sound like?"

"Like — like an instrument badly out of tune."

"You're probably just exhausted." Kara smiled briefly at Emily, then turned and clapped her hands for attention. "Is that everyone?" she called. "Does anyone else need help? Speak up, guys."

"We are whole again," the red wommel spoke. "Thank you, Healer!"

"Yes, thank you, Healer!" More creatures echoed the wommel's gratitude as a cheer rose up over the meadow.

"You were incredible," Adriane said to Emily.

"Yeah, really," Kara agreed.

Emily gave them a tired smile. A few worried mumbles from a handful of quiffles caught her attention. They were gathered around Ronif.

"You heard it, too?" one quiffle asked another.

"Where did it go ... must be really hurt bad ... too dangerous ..."

Emily stepped toward the quiffles. "What are they saying, Ronif?"

"There might be another wounded creature, Healer," the quiffle answered.

"Another?"

Ronif edged a little quiffle forward. "Tell them what you know, Waldo."

The quiffle named Waldo shrugged. "I think there was another, Healer," he said, flapping his rubbery silver beak. "It was making horrible noises and sounds."

"Sounds?" Emily echoed. She felt a chill trickle down her spine. Was this what she had been sensing?

"Ariel, did you spot another creature?"

"Something runs, hidden."

"What kind of creature?" Emily asked Waldo as Adriane, Kara, and Stormbringer walked over to join her.

Before the quiffle could say anything more, a newly arrived pooxim — a sleek little creature that looked like a cross between a songbird and a rabbit — spoke up in its singsong voice. "I *see*-saw it," the pooxim announced. "A *glim*-gleaming blue thing with *flish*-flashing, angry eyes full of magic."

"Did anyone else see this magic creature?" Adriane asked.

"There was something behind us, following us!" another wommel cried excitedly. "We barely got away from it. It tried to run us over."

"But it wasn't blue," Waldo said. "It was green. It nearly kicked my head off."

"You're both wrong," a pegasus piped up. "It was a big purple beastie."

"No, it was red," a quiffle disagreed. "And it was howling so horribly I almost lost my mind — and my eardrums."

"Wait a second." Emily held up a hand. "Waldo said the creature was green, and the pooxim said blue. But the one you saw was red? Are you sure?"

The pegasus shrugged his sleek, spotted shoulders. "It was so hectic when we crossed through the open portal. Maybe I can't be sure of the color, but the sounds it made were unforgettable."

"Maybe it was something evil," a wommel suggested nervously.

At that moment, the noise came again, filling Emily's head. She clenched her fists, her fingernails digging into her palms. Glancing down at her stone, she saw that it was glowing with soft, multicolored light. She chewed on her lower lip. Her uneasiness was growing. She didn't think it was evil she was sensing — just uncertainty and suffering. Could that be it? Could one or more magical animals be hiding somewhere, still unhealed?

"There's another creature out there," she murmured aloud.

Ozzie looked at her. "Sounds like a lot of creatures."

"And it — they — also sound wild," Adriane added.

"It's hurt bad and needs help." Emily took a step toward the forest. "I'm going to check the woods."

Adriane grabbed her arm. "You are not going out there by yourself."

"What am I, chopped rugamug?" Ozzie straightened up to his full sixteen-inch height.

"No offense, Ozzie."

"It could be dangerous," he said.

"Right," she agreed quickly. "That's why you're coming with me. It's okay, Adriane," Emily continued. "You stay and get things organized here."

"Take Storm with you," Adriane ordered.

The great silver wolf rubbed against Emily's side, her ears pricked alertly.

Emily cast a glance at the forest surrounding the meadow. Even in broad daylight, the thick, tangled woods looked gloomy and forbidding. "Thanks, Storm."

Storm nodded firmly.

"Four, five . . ." Kara was counting off a group of jeeran, making notes on a pad so the creatures could be logged into the Ravenswood journals. She looked up as Adriane approached.

"How's it going?" the dark-haired girl asked.

"Eight, nine . . ." Or was that the same one she'd already counted? "Aargh!" Kara cried as she completely lost track of where she was.

"Everyone is settling in," Adriane announced. "Thank goodness Emily got here in time."

"One, two, three . . . Hey, you! Stand still!"

Adriane was glaring at her.

"Six, seven . . . What?" Kara demanded.

"I think we should contact Zach."

Kara smirked. A few weeks ago, Adriane had followed Stormbringer through the portal to Aldenmor. She'd had an amazing adventure there. But since her return, she refused to talk about the time she had spent with the adorable sandy-haired guy she'd met there. Emily and Kara were dying for details.

"Need a last-minute date to the harvest dance?" Kara asked innocently.

Adriane rolled her eyes. "Get real, Princess Pea Brain," she snapped. "I just think we should try to find out what's going on over there. Something caused the portal to open again, and these injuries were really awful."

Kara had to admit she had a point. "Okay. I can do that." She grinned. "What would you do without me?"

"Just call them." Adriane frowned. "Though why they listen to *you* is anyone's guess."

"It's all in the training." Kara took a deep breath, picturing tiny, brightly colored dragonflies in her mind.

"Yoo-hoo!" she sang out. "Goldie, Barney, Fiona, Fred, Blaze! Come out, come out, wherever you are!"

A cloud of multicolored bubbles danced into sight. The bubbles burst in a sudden blizzard of flashing rainbow sparkles, turning into tiny, chirping, brightly colored flying dragons.

"Keee-keeee!" a golden one sang. It fluttered up and down happily before coming to rest on Kara's shoulder.

"Goldie!" As Kara scratched the little dragon's head, its golden, jeweled eyes glowed with pleasure.

Red Fiona, orange Blaze, and purple Barney vied for her other shoulder. *"Kee-keee!"*

"Dee-deee!" Blue Fred hooted gleefully, zipping around Adriane's head, leaving little trails of colored sparkles behind.

"Listen up, crew," Kara commanded sternly. "We have work to do."

The dragonflies perked up and sprang to attention.

"We need a little portal," Adriane said. "Like the one you made for me on Aldenmor."

"So start spinning," Kara ordered.

Moments later, the dragonflies had joined wingtips and were spinning in a perfect little circle.

"Good dragonflies," Kara said.

"Ooooo," Barney cooed.

"Show us where Zach is," Adriane said, picturing the boy's handsome face and warm smile, the way his eyes danced. "He has that dragon stone I gave him. Hone in on its magic."

"Ooookayy."

A swirling, wavering mist appeared inside the circle of spinning dragonettes. Adriane clutched her wolf stone with a look of intense concentration.

"Are you getting anything?" Kara peered into the small tunnel anxiously. The dragonflies could be restless and unpredictable, and this was strong magic that was being asked of them. She knew they only had a few minutes to make contact.

Adriane shook her head, looking frustrated. "Lyra, we need your help!"

The cat loped toward them. *"Rasha, Ronif, Balthazar, bring the others, too."*

The older pegasus and two quiffles came, as did a dozen other animals drawn by the urgency in Lyra's voice.

Kara gestured for them to come closer. With all their friendly magical energy joining in, Adriane's stone glowed brighter. She looked at Kara and held out her wrist. Kara reached out and touched the wolf stone, making it flare with amber light.

The mist within the portal swept away, replaced by a new, slightly hazy scene. The background details were blurry, like faded watercolors, but Zach's sharp-featured face stood out clear and unmistakable in the foreground.

"Adriane?" he asked uncertainly, blinking toward them. "Is that you?"

"It's me!" Adriane called. "How are you?"

"Fine. My dragon stone just went crazy," Zach said, holding up the bright red jewel on his wrist. Crimson facets sparkled like tiny flames. "I knew it was you."

"Hi." Kara's head pressed close to Adriane's.

"Hello."

Adriane glowered. "You remember Kara."

"Yes." But his eyes were on Adriane.

"How's the drake?" she asked, referring to the baby dragon Zach was helping to raise on Aldenmor.

There was a sudden thunderous, roaring sound

in the background. "What's that noise? Are you in trouble?"

"No, no, it's okay," Zach assured her quickly. "The drake is fine, but he really misses you. Did all those animals make it to you safely?"

"Totally!" Kara called back. "It was a regular Noah's ark."

Zach and Adriane looked at Kara.

"Oops, sorry," Kara whispered. "You two kids go right ahead. This is a long-distance call. Pretend I'm not even here."

"Just tell us what happened," Adriane said.

As Zach opened his mouth to speak, his face swam woozily and his voice suddenly faded, as if the volume on a radio had just been turned way down.

"Hey!" Kara said sharply to the dragonflies. "Keep spinning!"

"Kooo-koo!" the dragonflies sang excitedly, spinning faster and faster. *"Soooooo-reeeeeee!"*

Zach's face swam back into clear view. ". . . another explosion near the Dark Sorceress's castle," he was saying. "The biggest one yet."

"Is that how all the animals got burned?" Adriane asked.

Zach nodded. "Black Fire came down all over the place," he reported grimly. "But that's not all — whatever the Sorceress did made the portals here go wild. The one leading to Earth opened, and a bunch of others just suddenly disappeared — including all the ones to the fairy glen."

"Oh, no!" Adriane cried. This was seriously bad news. The fairy glen was the home of the Fairimentals and the magical heart of Aldenmor. "Have you tried to contact the Fairimentals?"

"Of course. But we haven't been able to find —"

His face wavered again. The dragonflies' bright wings were flickering wildly as they spun, letting out tiny popping noises and rainbow-colored sparks.

"Wrap it up," Kara muttered to Adriane.

Adriane bit her lip.

". . . you have to be careful," Zach was saying. "One of the mistwolves said he saw a suspicious creature go through the portal. He said it reeked of evil."

"Evil," Adriane breathed, tensing. "Did he say what *kind* of creature?"

Zach shook his head. "It went through too fast. Just be on the lookout."

"Okay, thanks," Adriane said.

"Adriane, I'm real glad to see you," Zach said.

"Me, too."

"I —"

"Me, too." Adriane smiled and blushed.

Zach grinned back.

"How cute is this?" Kara said with a sugary smile. "Just make sure she's home by ten!"

At that moment, the dragonflies flew apart in a flurry of squawks and chitters. The portal blinked out of existence.

"You ditz!" Adriane yelled. "Didn't you hear what he said?"

"Dragon stone, huh! How come *he* has a magic jewel?"

"Forget the stone! Something evil might have snuck in when the portal opened!" Adriane exclaimed.

"Oh, that."

"And it's loose out there," Adriane finished.

Together the girls turned their gaze to the edge of the glade. Beyond the tall firs that encircled the glade, an ocean of trees stretched forever into the blackness of deep forest.

A monster. And Emily was out in the woods tracking it down right now!

Chapter 4

*I*ve found another print, Healer."

Emily hurried to peer over Stormbringer's shoulder. A patch of sunlight illuminated a hoofprint pressed into the moist dirt near the edge of the path. The mistwolf had already discovered half a dozen similar prints, beginning at the edge of the woods back in the meadow.

"Same size and shape as the others," Emily mused, staring transfixed at the print. "Could be jeeran." She leaned closer as the faintest hint of sound flashed through her. Music? No, more like those off-kilter chords she'd heard earlier. She listened closely, but the sound was gone, leaving behind a lingering sense of anguish and defeat.

Ozzie stepped forward and peered at the print. "Jeeran are stupid herd beasts with little magic. I still say pegasus," he guessed. "Or maybe something like a demicentaur or even a large kelpie. What do you think, Storm?"

Instead of answering, Storm stood stock-still,

her limbs rigid and her eyes half closed. The tip of her bushy tail twitched slightly.

"What is it?" Emily asked anxiously.

Storm remained silent for several more seconds. Finally, she blinked her golden eyes and gazed at Emily somberly. *"The Warrior just sent me a message,"* she said.

Emily knew that Storm was referring to Adriane. Due to the strong magical bond they shared, the dark-haired girl and the mistwolf could communicate mind to mind across almost any distance. "What did she say?"

"She has contacted Aldenmor," Storm told her. *"Something evil may have crossed over with the others."*

Emily felt a chill pass through her as she glanced down at the print again. One thing they had learned since discovering magic was that evil could take many forms. Something horrible could be out there with them right now. Behind a tree, listening to them, waiting . . . She took a step closer to Storm, drawing comfort from the mistwolf's powerful presence.

Ozzie looked worried. "What if we're following a satyr?"

"A what?" Emily asked.

Storm snuffled derisively. *"A satyr hardly warrants 'dangerous,'"* she said. *"They are mischievous*

50

troublemakers, Healer, half goat and half goblin. More of a nuisance than anything."

"How about a nightmare then?" Ozzie declared excitedly. "Big steeds black as night, snorting fire. One can take out a dozen trolls all by itself and —"

"The tracks head this way," Emily broke in. "Let's keep going. Whatever it is, we need to find it."

"Right," Ozzie muttered, breaking into a jog to keep up with the much longer legs of the others. "Unless, of course, it's a basilisk, in which case our best plan of attack might be to run very, very fast in the opposite direction."

Storm shot the ferret a glance. *"Mistwolves fear nothing,"* she reminded him. *"Not even basilisks."*

"Oh, yeah?" Ozzie retorted. "Well, ferrets — er, I mean, elves — fear nothing, either. Cousin Brommy took on a golem all by himself — tricked it into falling down a ravine. And golems are much tougher than your average evil creature."

"Golems are strong, ugly, and brutal, but not very intelligent," Storm agreed. *"Werebeasts, on the other hand . . ."*

"Werebeasts! Now *those* are monsters!" Ozzie agreed. "And you don't die if one rips you to pieces — you just turn onto a creeping, howling, bloodthirsty were —"

"Do we really have to talk about this right

now?" Emily interrupted. Their conversation was starting to spook her. She was seriously hoping to avoid running into anything that fit into the evil, creepy, and larger than Storm category.

"It is best to know the enemy one is facing, Healer," Storm said, sniffing the air near a thick stand of trees.

Emily flashed on the image of the ghastly face she'd seen at the football game but shook it off quickly. "I just think we — *ahh*!" She almost doubled over as a sudden burst of magic energy barreled into her like a punch in the gut. Colored lights ignited in her brain like flashbulbs; blue, red, gold streaked across her vision like shooting stars.

Storm was at her side in an instant.

"Emily, what's wrong?" Ozzie's worried face looked up at her.

Wheezing, she glanced around. "Look!" She gasped.

She pointed to a break in the trees just ahead. *Flash!* A streak of bright blue flickered behind a cluster of evergreens.

"Over there!" Ozzie yelled, pointing in a different direction.

Flash! Emily whirled around. A short distance away, between two tree trunks, a burst of vivid red appeared. *Flash!* This time, clear yellow. Suddenly a screeching sound echoed off the rocks and leaves. It was all around them, coming from everywhere and nowhere. Emily slapped her hands over her ears. "That noise!"

Storm was tense, ears alert, tail straight out behind her, hackles rising.

The sounds built to a crescendo, piercing the woods like a hurricane, and then vanished, eerily echoing away into silence. Emily straightened up and took a deep breath.

"Which way did they go?" Ozzie cried, spinning around wildly. "Where are they?"

Emily spun around, too, trying to find the colors. *Flash!* A hint of emerald green disappeared over a hillock farther down the trail.

"That way. There's strong magic here," Storm declared, setting off down the path at a brisk trot. Ozzie followed, chattering about a color-changing enchanted gnome he'd once known.

Emily lagged behind, still breathing hard. The burst of magic she'd felt had been so sudden, so powerful. And that sound . . .

What *was* that sound?

Her steps slowed. Wrinkling her brow, she gazed around and strained to hear. Gradually she became aware of sweet tones singing in her ears, beautiful, exotic music that floated into her head as easily as if it had always been there, always belonged there.

Where . . . is . . . that . . . coming . . . from? Emily wondered, stopping in her tracks. She hardly noticed that Storm and Ozzie were almost out of sight. She had to hear more.

She started to turn, swaying as the music wrapped around her. Arms outstretched, she weaved from side to side. Streams of sunlight fell over leaves, dirt, and moss in patterns of shifting light and shadows as a sweet sound snuck into her head. Leaves tumbled around her as she danced through sunbeams. That melody, so enchanting, teasing, reaching out to her.

Something was moving with her. It was between two large trees. She couldn't put her finger on exactly what it might be — its face and body were vague. All she could focus on was its eyes. Deep, dark pools of bliss, watching her. They seemed to hold all the love, wisdom, and certainty of the world. Within those eyes, nothing changed — ever. All was still, calm, perfect.

Comme clllossssserrr . . .

The words were barely a whisper in her mind, a graceful counterpoint to the haunting melody that surrounded her. Feeling as if she existed in some wonderful, never-ending dream, Emily danced. Time was passing, each second seeming to take an eternity as she twirled closer to the magical sounds.

Come to me . . .

She spun faster, closer . . .

"Healer!"

Storm's urgent voice broke through the dream-like fog, pulling Emily to an abrupt stop. The creature in front of her reacted, too, its eyes narrowing and its mouth opening in a vicious snarl. Emily gasped as the world slid back into focus and she realized she was staring at a pale white skull and gaunt cheekbones. A ghoulish grin twisted under haunting, evil eyes full of malice. It was the nightmare face from the football game!

Emily screamed, the noise ripping out of her, shattering the last few strands of the eerie melody. Stumbling backward, she nearly lost her balance.

There was a whoosh of cold, dank air and a deafening explosion of noise, like every note in the world played at once. Then she heard the more familiar sound of rushing feet.

The wolf was at her side in an instant, standing protectively in front of her.

"Healer! What is it?"

"What? Did you see the monster?" Ozzie came running behind Storm. "I knew it! I told you it had to be a basilisk! See, she's frozen in place! Now what are we going to do?"

Emily tried to speak, to reassure them that she was all right. "Eerp" was all she could manage.

Ozzie quickly clambered up her pant leg and hopped onto her shoulder, to peer into her face. "Uh-oh," he said. "Not a basilisk. Looks more like the work of a mind-muncher. *Do you remember your name?*" he shouted into her ear.

Emily winced and pushed him off her shoulder. "Stop that!" she said. "I'm not deaf. And of course I know my name."

"What did you see, Healer?" Storm was staring at her seriously.

Emily glanced nervously toward the trees. But the spot where she'd seen the apparition was empty; only a few leaves and twigs hung there now. "It — it — I don't know," she stammered. "I mean, I think I saw — it was only there for a second."

She managed to point to the spot. Storm bounded over and circled the trees, carefully examining the ground with eyes, nose, and paws. *"There might have been something here, but it's gone now,"* she said after a moment.

Emily shook her head, trying to clear it of the lingering fog left by the monster's eerie music. She had seen this thing twice now, and she still didn't know what it was.

"Listen, you two," she began. "The thing I saw was — wait!"

A note rang in her ear, the faint hint of sound, clean and pure.

She slowly turned to a curtain of thick autumn leaves hanging between the trees. With Ozzie and Storm on each side, she carefully reached out and parted the curtain of colors.

Screeeeeeeeee!

Something large burst out of the woods straight at them, almost trampling Ozzie on its way. The explosion of sound was so sudden and overwhelming that Emily was knocked backward onto the ground. Off-key chords grated against one another, echoing through the woods and slicing into her head. Scrambling to her knees, she caught flashes of a horselike shape. It had a bright turquoise hide and a mane and tail that shimmered silvery blue. She pointed and shouted, though her words were lost in the cacophony of sound.

Storm was already after it.

"Storm! No! Wait!" Emily paused just long enough to scoop Ozzie up before following, running wildly through the woods. Ahead, the creature dove into a thick patch of brambles and disappeared.

"There!" Emily cried as the noise faded, leaving behind only faint, staticky reverberations. "It went that way!"

A flash of movement rattled the far side of the thicket. Then a patch of fuchsia caught the sun as a large shape crashed through the shadowy underbrush. A second later, Emily caught a glimpse of garish purple.

Storm started to run in that direction, but a huge, twisted wild rose shrub blocked her way. Panting, she darted around it. Emily shielded her face and followed.

"*Ahh!*" Ozzie shrieked, clinging to her for dear life. "Watch out for that branch!"

Emily ducked just in time to avoid getting smacked by a gnarled tree limb. Unfortunately she failed to notice the exposed root in her path. Her sneaker caught on it and she went flying, landing with a thud in a pile of dry autumn leaves.

"*Whoooo-aaaaah!*" Ozzie flew off her shoulder and landed a few feet away. "*Urfff!*"

By the time they managed to sit up and make sure nothing was broken, Storm had returned. *"Whatever it is, it has powerful magic. I couldn't get near it,"* the mistwolf admitted, panting.

Ozzie nodded, brushing a twig out of his fur. "I think it's safe to say we're not following a basilisk," he said. "My guess is pegasii."

Emily sat up, thinking back to the brief glimpse she'd caught of the creature. "I didn't see any wings. Why do you say 'it,' Storm? Seemed like several creatures."

"I could only make out one set of tracks," Storm answered.

"Are you suggesting it's *one* creature?" Ozzie asked. "They were all around us. How could one animal move so fast?"

Emily bit her lip. "One set of tracks," she said. "I could feel it — it's hurting bad," she whispered.

She looked up to see Storm sitting directly in front of her. They were almost nose to nose. The wolf's golden eyes glowed deep and warm.

"Perhaps you should open yourself to those feelings, try to follow them," the mistwolf suggested.

Emily looked at the ground. "I'm afraid."

"Fear is the worst enemy we face. I am here."

Emily knew the mistwolf was right, but she hesitated. She had just healed so many, felt so much fear and suffering. How much more did she have to give? Even Adriane and Kara didn't really know the toll it took on her.

Still, she had to reach inside and find the strength. It might be the only way to help the creature — or creatures — that clearly needed her. "Okay," she said. "I'll try."

"Hang on to me."

Emily reached around the wolf's neck and hugged the animal close. Doing her best to keep her mind clear and still, she closed her eyes and breathed in deeply, exhaling in a whoosh.

Soft fur against her cheek, Emily smelled pine and forests, clean and sweet. She felt the strength of the wolf against her like a wall, impenetrable and solid.

The rainbow jewel flashed brightly, and she reached out with her mind.

The emotions hit her with a wallop, making her cry out in shock and pain. Instantly she felt Storm's iron will bolster her. *"Steady, Healer."*

She stayed open, inviting the fierce pain, intense anger, and violent sorrow into her very soul. These feelings were stronger than those she had felt from the quiffles and jeeran back in the meadow. And a powerful undercurrent of magic throbbed along with these emotions, twisting them, making them stronger and more dangerous until Emily was gasping raggedly for breath.

"Don't run. I want to help," she said breathlessly. Her jewel glowed with an intense blaze of color. Then all was quiet.

Arms still wrapped tightly around Storm's neck, she opened her eyes. Ozzie was on her shoulder, arms wrapped tightly around her neck, his eyes shut, his ferret brow furrowed in intense concentration.

"You can let go now, Ozzie," Emily said, pulling away from Storm.

Ozzie's eyes flew open and he leaped back.

Emily gave each of her friends a kiss. "Thank you, both."

"No problem," Ozzie said proudly. "Did you get through?"

"I don't know." She got up and started into the forest. "This way."

Storm and Ozzie flanked her as she walked, following the trail of shifting emotions. Her rainbow stone gleamed steadily with dark, murky colors. Agony, dread, and desperation pulsed through her body, grabbing her heart and squeezing it, in and out, faster and faster, until it felt as though it would burst right out of her chest and —

"Wait." Storm's voice broke into her mind. *"Something is following us."*

At the sudden interruption, Emily's concentration faltered and the magical connection slipped. Her heart beating faster, she turned to see the mistwolf gazing intently at a dense copse of evergreens. The thick fur along Storm's spine was standing on end.

Ka-thunk. Ka-thunk. The sounds of heavy feet pounded the earth, heading toward them.

Ozzie and Emily huddled close together. "What is it, Storm?" she asked.

Stormbringer bared her teeth and a low growl rumbled in her throat. *"Stay behind me, Healer."* Her voice was grim. *"It comes."*

Chapter 5

*K*a-thunk. Ka-thunk.

The sound came directly at them, flat steps falling with a dull thud. Storm and Ozzie moved in front of Emily. The wolf tensed, growling low. Ozzie grabbed a stick from the ground nearby and held it up like a club. Nearby, leaves and branches rustled. Then the steps came to a halt.

Emily panicked, remembering that horrible, ghoulish face, those deep-socketed, soulless eyes. If that hideous specter stepped out of the trees, she would surely lose her mind. The branches parted.

A large, rotund creature hopped out.

Hopped? Emily raised her eyebrows in surprise. It looked like a giant frog. It had lumpy blue-and-purple skin, flippers for feet, and a wide mouth stretched across its face in a perpetual smile.

"Look out!" the giant frog screamed.

Emily, Ozzie, and Storm looked around, confused.

"A mistwolf!" It whispered, pointing a flipper at Storm. Its bulbous, crystalline eyes were wide with fear.

"What the —" Ozzie lowered his weapon. Storm stopped growling.

"She won't hurt you," Emily explained.

"She won't?" The frog creature was not convinced.

"Not unless you mean us harm."

"Me?" The creature slapped a flipper against its chest.

Ozzie stomped up to it, examining it carefully. "It's a flobbin!" he exclaimed.

"A what?" Emily stared at the newcomer, who was easily as tall as she was but three times as wide.

A long, ribbonlike purple tongue flicked out over Ozzie's head.

"Gah!" The ferret frantically wiped his head with both front paws.

"I didn't think any animals from this world talked," the flobbin said.

"I'm special." Ozzie kicked the big frog. "And I am not edible!"

"Oh. Well, thank goodness I found you," the flobbin continued. "I've been wandering around for hours in these forests."

"Flobbins are fairy creatures," Storm explained to Emily. *"They are made mostly of fairy magic."*

"Is it dangerous?"

"Not that I know of."

"Dangerous? Heavens, no!" The flobbin took a hop closer to Emily but stepped back as Storm walked between them. "I was on assignment for the Fairimentals, looking for magic blobs."

"What's a magic blob?" Emily asked.

"You know, pockets of loose fairy magic. Some blobs are quite large and dangerous. I track the blobs, map them out, and report to the Fairimentals for proper handling."

"You know the Fairimentals?" Emily asked him.

"Sure." The flobbin shrugged his sloping, warty blue shoulders. "The F-sters and I go way back. Say, maybe you can help me. I'm supposed to find an elf called Ozymandius."

"Gah! That's me!" Ozzie jumped up and down.

"Really?" Big, bulbous eyes looked Ozzie over. "You're awfully fuzzy."

"It's a long story. Trust me."

"My name is Ghyll," the creature announced.

"I'm Emily, and this is Stormbringer." Emily waved her hand to include the wolf.

"I was heading to the fairy glen when everything went crazy," Ghyll explained, keeping a wary

64

eye on the mistwolf. "The portals got all mixed up and I ended up here. At first I thought I was in the Moorgrove, near Dingly Dell."

"Dingly Dell?" Ozzie's eyes went wide.

"I have many elf friends there. Donafi, Brommy, Fernie —"

"Brommy's my cousin," Ozzie cried delightedly.

"Yes, he's the one who told me about you."

"How is that rotten little pointy-eared creep?"

"Oh, he's fine," Ghyll said.

"Do you know what's happening on Aldenmor?" Emily interrupted.

"All portals to the fairy glen have been closed. It's as if the fairy glen just vanished."

"*Gah!* That's awful!" Ozzie exclaimed.

"So I guess I'm stuck here," Ghyll said.

"You and all the others that got through," Emily pointed out. "Are you hurt?"

"No."

"Well, if you need anything around these parts, I'm your elf," Ozzie said.

"I've been hopping around in these woods for hours and I'm famished. What do you have to eat in this world?" Ghyll's long purple tongue snapped out.

"Now you're talking my language!" Ozzie grinned and patted himself on the chest. "Stick with me. They have the most incredible food here, you won't believe it —"

"Er, Ozzie?" Emily broke in, knowing that the ferret could easily discuss food all day long. "Why don't you take Ghyll back and get him settled in? Storm and I can keep going without you."

"Where are you going?" Ghyll asked, blinking big eyes.

Emily hesitated only for a moment before answering. After all, if Storm and Ozzie felt the flobbin was a creature of good magic, she had nothing to worry about. "We think some injured creatures ran away into the woods," she explained. "We're trying to track them down so we can help them."

"I'm a natural magic tracker. Perhaps I can help," Ghyll offered, puffing out his large chest.

Emily gave a quick glance at Storm, then asked Ghyll, "You haven't seen anything . . . peculiar around the woods, have you?"

Mistwolf, ferret, and flobbin looked at one another.

"That's a relative question," Ghyll answered.

"Come on, Ghyll!" Ozzie grabbed a flipper and pointed toward the trail. "I'll show you around Ravenswood."

"Excellent." Ghyll looked down at Ozzie. "Lead the way!"

Emily and Storm continued in the opposite direction. The sun angled on its late afternoon arc, sending bright patches gleaming off leaves and rocks.

"What do you make of Ghyll?" Emily asked Storm.

"I sensed nothing dangerous about the creature," the mistwolf answered.

"Something doesn't feel right. I mean, if he's a magic tracker for the Fairimentals as he says, he's not very good."

"How so?"

"There's enough wild magic flying around here to attract every creature on Aldenmor, and yet Ghyll didn't even mention he sensed any magic."

"He didn't say he didn't, either," Storm said.

"Yes, I suppose."

Emily turned her attention back to finding the hurt creature. She was afraid the encounter with Ghyll had wasted valuable time. How far had the magical creature gone?

"Why don't you try to reach out again?" Storm suggested.

Emily faltered. "Let's just check the clearing beyond those trees."

She pushed through the underbrush, Storm at her side. Suddenly she changed direction.

"This way," she said, heading across a small, nearly dry streambed. The signal had shifted;

whatever they were following was still on the move.

But what *were* they following? All she knew was that something was out there, and she had to find it. An all-too-familiar grinning skull face popped into her head, but she refused to consider it. What they were after couldn't be evil.

Still, Emily felt frustrated. "How are we supposed to help creatures that won't even let us get close?"

Storm shook her shaggy gray head. *"If a creature is too far gone to recognize help when it comes, it may be too late for any help to work."*

"No!" The word flew from Emily's mouth before she could stop it. "We can't give up. We have to keep going."

Storm gazed at her with patient golden eyes. *"Lead on, Healer."*

A slight breeze carried a light note. Listening closely, Emily picked up a fast swirl of faint static, like interference on a car radio. Within the jumble, she caught a flurry of notes. They reminded her of the crazy noise that had emerged from her flute that morning.

Storm was looking at her. *"Healer, let's head back now. Tomorrow is another day."*

All the energy seeped out of Emily. What was the point of continuing this ridiculous game?

Storm was right. The creature didn't want to be found, and wandering around in the woods wasn't helping anyone. They might as well go home. She felt the familiar wall of despair building, closing in, until she wasn't sure she could keep the tears at bay any longer.

She stopped suddenly. A wave of magic was building. Again. She felt it rushing toward her, sweeping through the trees, thundering past rocks and over streams.

"Storm, run!" Emily yelled. But there was nowhere to go.

Storm howled, turning to face an enemy that wasn't there. With a rushing roar, the magic peaked, crashing down around them like a tidal wave breaking against a rocky shore.

Emily braced herself for pain — instead, she was swept away into a dream.

She twirled and spun through snowy, shimmering mists, listening to music. Wondrous deep sounds echoed, rising and falling in the vast space, each note reaching into the depths of her soul. The mists parted to reveal a path of stars, twinkling like diamonds under her feet. The music echoed over streams of pathways spread out before her, a million lights as far as her eyes could see.

Ahead, the path began to break apart, dissolving in great bursts of fire. Emily panicked. The fire raced toward her. Burning, searing agony attacked every inch of her body. Horrible fear and guilt ripped through her. Terror stole her breath and squeezed her heart like a vise.

Emily realized she was feeling the pain of the wounded creature. She couldn't give up. As the dark feelings swirled through her, Emily fought to keep herself open to them. She had to stay strong and focused. She could feel her rainbow stone pulsing warmly with the unsteady beat.

Something flew at her. She caught the hint of a blade, the flash of steel. Fast and vicious, it sliced toward her.

She screamed, and her eyes flew open. She was standing in the forest.

"Are you all right, Healer?" Storm's voice in her head sounded worried.

Emily nodded, her breath coming in ragged gulps. "I don't know," she croaked, plunging off the path at an angle, straight through a thick tangle of underbrush. She hardly noticed as vines grabbed at her hair and brambles slashed her skin.

She rushed through a cluster of trees and stopped at the edge of a meadow. Bending over to catch her breath, she curled her hands into fists and pounded the air in frustration. What's the point? Even if we find the creature, there's no guarantee I'll be able to help it. Emily was becoming exhausted, and she wobbled on the verge of tears. She swallowed hard and tried to remain calm. *I might as well just turn around now and . . .*

Wiping sweat-streaked hair from her face, she stared in amazement. There, standing across the clearing, was the most beautiful creature she'd ever seen.

Chapter 6

Emily stood rooted, staring in awe at the creature. It looked like a delicately built pony mare. It stood about twelve hands high and had a finely chiseled head, round, polished hooves, and a lavish mane and forelock. In the reddish late-afternoon sunlight, the creature's coat looked magenta. It must once have been wondrously beautiful, before Black Fire had ravaged its colorful coat, leaving it charred and oozing and covered in patches of a sickly green glow. It was trembling in fear.

"Stand back, Healer," Storm growled, stepping out of the brush, her hackles up.

The pony snorted at the mistwolf's appearance, her eyes rolling back in terror. Kicking up her rear hooves, she spun and leaped — and vanished. A burst of loud, angry, chaotic sound followed.

Emily was stunned.

"Wait!" she cried desperately. The creature

couldn't run away again — not now that she'd finally seen it!

The pony suddenly reappeared at the far end of the clearing. It was gazing at Emily suspiciously, flanks heaving, breath coming in short, ragged bursts. Its coat was now a bright shade of reddish-yellow. Emily felt waves of fear emanate from it.

"Storm, she's afraid of you," Emily realized. "Stay in the woods for a minute. I'll call if I need you."

The mistwolf hesitated, then nodded. *"Be careful."* She melted back into the forest.

"It's okay," Emily whispered. She could feel pain and apprehension sweeping toward her. "I won't hurt you."

As she spoke, the creature's coat shifted to a shimmering pale aqua, then to a rusty orange, then to a swirl of deep blue and chocolate, before paling again and changing to a radiant red. That was one mystery solved, Emily realized. They hadn't been following a herd of different-colored creatures after all. Just one that changed color from moment to moment.

She stepped forward cautiously, her gaze fixed on the angry burns. The closer she got, the worse they looked. Her stomach churned. How had this wounded pony even survived this long?

"Easy," Emily murmured as the animal raised

its head and danced backward, its coat flashing reddish-purple. She forced herself to stand still and wait until the creature settled down again. "It's okay. I want to help."

The pony didn't run away, but it didn't come any closer, either. Emily bit her lip. Now what?

Patience. She heard her mother's voice inside her head. *Patience is the number-one rule when you're dealing with animals. The number-two and number-three rules, too.*

Emily knew that. But it wasn't easy to stand there doing nothing when the creature in front of her was wracked with pain that only seemed to grow with every passing moment.

She forced herself to remain calm. Freaking out wasn't going to help. The animal's gaze met her own, and in the soft greenish-gold eyes Emily could see the intense pain, fear, and sadness.

She took a step forward. The pony tensed and took a quick step back. Emily sighed and re-treated. Then it stepped forward, gold-tipped ears pricked toward the girl.

"It's okay," Emily said, and the creature jumped in surprise.

This wasn't working. Emily decided to try communicating in a different way.

She tried to fill her mind with soothing images. I'm your friend. I want to help you.

The animal cocked its head, staring at Emily suspiciously. There was a sudden blare of that jarring noise and a jumble of feelings.

Emily waited. Her hands were twitching, wanting to touch the animal and to try to heal its wounds. But she knew that wouldn't happen unless she could win its trust.

Pain. Fear and pain. Notes, emerging suddenly out of the white noise.

Emily listened. Was that — ?

She shook her head. She had to be imagining things, didn't she? She couldn't possibly be hearing what she thought she'd just heard.

Without quite knowing why, she hummed the first few notes of "her" song.

The pony stood stock-still and raised its head, and for a moment Emily was afraid she'd scared it again. Then the confusion of noise in her head cleared for a second — and echoed the same notes back to her!

Emily gasped. "You heard me!" she exclaimed out loud. "You understood!"

The pony creature repeated the first few notes — all at once — but the tune got lost in the chaos of white noise and jangled chords. Then it lowered its graceful head and let out a low, sad whine.

Emily pointed to herself. "I'm Emily."

She focused her thoughts again. *What is your name?* she asked.

Another burst of static. Then — a single word. *Lorelei.* The voice coming from the animal's mind was feminine and musical-sounding.

"Lorelei," Emily whispered. Was that her name or the name of a kind of creature, like a quiffle or a flobbin? She had no way of knowing, but somehow she was certain that it was the former. So then what *was* Lorelei?

She shook that question away. The important thing now was to stay connected so she could get close enough to heal Lorelei's wounds.

Taking another step forward, Emily held her breath. The creature gazed at her. Fluctuating, uncertain feelings flashed in the greenish-gold eyes — fear, pain, suspicion, worry — but Emily kept her own gaze steady.

Patience. Patience. Let her feel your good intentions, she told herself.

The creature stared back. A few notes danced through Emily's head, and she felt a shock go through her, like being struck by lightning. Through the shock she was aware that a connection had been made, a bond that was almost frightening in its intensity. What it meant, she didn't know.

She wasn't sure how much longer it was before she took another step forward, and another. Each time, she stopped the moment she sensed Lorelei tensing up and preparing to retreat. Each time, she waited for the animal's eyes to calm before moving again.

Finally, they were standing only two feet apart. "All right," Emily murmured, trying not to stare at the angry burns that seemed to swallow up her body. "Now it's up to you, Lorelei."

For several long, breathless moments, nothing happened. Girl and magic pony stood and stared at each other. The only thing that changed was the rainbow jewel at Emily's wrist, which cycled steadily — blue, gold, scarlet, indigo.

Emily waited. She could feel herself aching with the agonizing burn of the Black Fire. It was hard to stand there and look at the terrible wounds — hard to stand there and not rush to help. But somehow she knew there was no other way. Finally, Lorelei trembled and took a small, cautious step forward.

That was enough. Emily slowly reached forward and touched the animal on the shoulder.

Instantly, the forest tilted at a crazy angle and dropped away. And she heard it again, that dreadful noise blaring, screaming, frantic, oppressive — and the gleaming edge of steel flashed, cutting through flesh and bone.

Emily cried out and tried to pull her hand away. But she couldn't move. *Focus! Focus!*

Squeezing her eyes shut, she tried to make sense of what she was doing. She had to concentrate on the healing. That's why she was here.

The wild sound picked her up and she was carried forward, her heart racing crazily and her lungs gasping for breath. Then one tone leaped out at her, and she locked onto it. A note. One pure note in the pandemonium. It came again, pure and clean. Her own heartbeat. It slowed and steadied as she suddenly became aware of another heartbeat matching her own, pulsing raggedly but strongly. An image of Lorelei danced in front of her, her wounded coat bathed in a pure, clear, white light, familiar and yet — what was it? What was different about her? Emily shuddered as her focus wavered.

The Black Fire was strong. Stronger than she had ever encountered before. Was Emily strong enough to fight it? She didn't dare think about it. Instead, she focused on the matched heartbeats and on the melody that rose up to mingle and harmonize with them, growing louder and stronger with each beat. It was a familiar melody, and Emily found herself listening eagerly, aching to hear the last few notes that would make the song complete.

"What are you?" Emily asked.

Images of a first snowfall, clean and pristine, drifted into Emily's mind.

"I don't understand." She tried to reach deeper.

A family, mother, father, and three little ones, running, racing strong and sure along a golden thread of stars. Each of the creatures had a crystalline horn at the center of their foreheads. The music they made was heart-wrenching in its beauty.

Emily was awed.

The image burst apart with a blare of harsh, staticky noise, full of pain, shame, grief, sadness.

"No!" she cried desperately. She felt the connection rupture, and her eyes flew open. Lorelei was springing away, her eyes wide and rolling with fright. "Wait!" But it was too late. The creature leaped into the air and vanished.

"HEALER!"

Storm's urgent voice exploded inside her head, and Emily whirled around to see the mistwolf racing toward her, lips drawn back in a threatening snarl.

"No!" Emily cried, falling to her knees. She felt overwhelmed by despair — she had come so close, only to be wrenched back at the wrong moment. "Storm, no!"

Stormbringer skidded to a stop in front of her and let out a low growl. *"Did you not sense the danger?"*

Emily blinked, not sure at first what the mistwolf was talking about. Then she glanced around.

The ground was littered with branches, leaves,

and other debris. Several large boulders were scattered about like a giant's game of billiards. Furrows of fresh dirt crisscrossed the clearing, like gashes in the earth itself. An enormous, ancient oak tree had been ripped up by its roots and lay at a crazy angle across the clearing — one huge bough only a few feet from the spot where Emily was crouched.

"Wha — when did this happen?" she gasped.

Storm was gazing at her intently. *"When the two of you connected."* She didn't bother to finish, merely shaking her shaggy head and glancing around at the destruction in the clearing.

Emily buried her face in her hands. What was happening? She thought she had made a connection with Lorelei. But at the last moment, the creature had given up, run away. Why? She shuddered as she remembered the hopelessness and fear and something else — shame?

The last image floated back into her mind, fully formed and clear. She looked up, her eyes widening as she realized for the first time what had been different about the creature.

"Storm," Emily breathed. "I think I know what she is. Lorelei. She's a — a unicorn!"

Chapter 7

Emily poked at her oatmeal, feeling fuzzy and out of sorts. She had slept poorly, tossing and turning as disturbing dreams flitted through her mind. Now her head felt like it was stuffed full of cotton, her eyelids heavy. Her first waking thought had been of Lorelei, the unicorn. Could that really be what she was? The more she thought about it, the less certain she was. She and her friends had seen a unicorn before — Kara had even ridden one. That unicorn had been noble, confident, powerful. He hadn't changed colors. He hadn't made awful noises. He hadn't caused chaos wherever he went. He hadn't been afraid of them.

And of course, he had also had a long, beautiful, crystalline horn.

Carolyn entered the kitchen, already dressed in her white lab coat.

"Mom? How important is a good attitude for

your patients?" Emily asked, still thinking about Lorelei.

"What do you mean?" Carolyn headed straight for the coffeepot on the counter. "Like a good temperament? Is that Feltner dog giving you trouble again?"

"No, no." Emily shook her head, frustrated. "I'm talking about healing. Getting better. How important is it for an animal to, you know, *want* to get better?"

"Oh!" Her mother finished pouring her coffee. "Well, animals don't really want things the same way people do. And they're not aware of the future like we are, either, so of course they can't really foresee what it will be like to feel better. That's why supportive care is so important while they're recovering — pain medication, a peaceful environment, and so on."

Emily sighed and rubbed her eyes. Her mother wasn't getting it, and she wasn't sure how else to explain it — especially since she wasn't even sure what she was asking.

Before Emily could try again, Carolyn walked over to the table and gazed down at her. "Speaking of a peaceful environment," she said, "I was very disappointed when I stopped into the Pet Palace yesterday. The place was a mess."

Emily winced, recalling the kibble explosion.

She had done her best to sweep up, but she definitely hadn't planned on her mother seeing the place until she'd cleaned the rest. "I know," she said hurriedly. "I was going to clean that up when I got home."

Carolyn lifted an eyebrow. "Oh?" she said. "That's interesting, since as you may recall you didn't get home until after seven. Not only did I have to take care of the afternoon feeding for you, but I had to ask Rachel to leave her desk to help the Smiths pick up their dog."

"Look, I'm sorry, okay?" Emily frowned. She'd totally forgotten that Scooter's owners were coming to pick him up yesterday. Still, it wasn't as if she was the only one who could open a dog run. Why was her mother making such a big deal out of this? "I had stuff to do at Ravenswood, and it took longer than I thought."

"Ah, Ravenswood." Carolyn sighed. "It's great that you're so eager to help over there, but you can't just ignore the rest of your life."

Emily clenched her fists under the table. Her mother had no idea how important Ravenswood really was. Not even close.

"You were the one who wanted to start the Pet Palace," Carolyn went on. "And now I'm afraid you're going to have to adapt your lifestyle to the new responsibilities."

"Adapt?" Emily exclaimed, totally fed up. "*You're* telling *me* to adapt? What about *you*?"

Carolyn looked startled. "What?"

"First you tell me to go out and make friends. Then you tell me to stay home more." Emily's hands were shaking. She dropped her spoon, which clattered off the table onto the floor. "Meanwhile you don't even *try* to adapt. You just work all the time and pretend everything's all fine and dandy."

"That's not true, I —"

"Don't tell me it's not true!" Emily cried. "I'm not stupid." She waved a hand toward Carolyn's lab coat. "Where are you going right now? It's Sunday, you know. *Most* vets take a day off once in a while. When was the last time *you* took a day off?"

Carolyn frowned. "Lower your voice, Emily. And try to understand, I'm so busy —"

Emily didn't let her finish. "Yeah, like you were so busy back in Colorado that you let your family fall apart!" she yelled. Suddenly she couldn't stop the angry words from flowing. "That's the reason we're here — that's why I have to worry about adapting — because *you* couldn't make things work with Daddy, so *my* whole life got ruined! I had to leave my old friends, my old school, everything, and move to a whole new state! Ravenswood is the only really good thing that's happened to me here, and now you want to take it away from me!"

Carolyn's jaw dropped. "Emily," she breathed. "I — I —"

Before her mother could go on, Emily shoved her chair back so violently that her cereal bowl tipped over, splashing milk and Cheerios everywhere. She jumped to her feet.

"I'll be at Ravenswood, where I'm really needed." She turned and raced out of the room.

❦   ❦   ❦

Emily walked into the circular driveway in front of Ravenswood Manor. The grand building had been was more than a century old. When Emily had first seen it, she had been spooked by the strange Gothic castle, complete with gargoyles perched on the stone parapets. Now she welcomed the strength of its solid stone and seasoned wood. The big front windows watched her, looking down in welcome.

So many other things seemed so fleeting, she mused. How something so real, so close, could vanish in an instant, gone in the blink of an eye.

Emily blew out a frustrated sigh and shifted her backpack to her other shoulder. She followed the cobblestone walkway around the house and entered the first of many gardens that surrounded the great lawns. Her friends were probably already in the meadow. They had planned to meet there and discuss what to do about the portal. Somehow they had to figure out how to replace the dreamcatcher that had protected the portal from evil.

"Emily?"

Adriane's grandmother was working in the garden. Nakoda Charday — better known to Adriane and her friends as Gran — was the caretaker of Ravenswood. She had worked for its owner, Mr. Gardener, for many years before Adriane had come to live with her.

"Oh," Emily muttered. "Hi." Lowering her head to avoid the woman's wise, observant gaze, she started to hurry past. She just wasn't in the mood for dealing with adults right now. *Any* adults.

"What's the matter, child?" Gran asked. "Your face is as dark as a thundercloud."

"Sorry," Emily snapped without thinking. "I didn't know that being in a good mood was a requirement for coming here."

She immediately regretted the sharp words. Her face flushed with shame, and she stared at her feet. But Gran hardly seemed to notice as she stood up.

"Come," she said. "Walk with me."

Emily sighed and walked beside Gran across the great lawn toward the maze of gardens. Gran took a deep breath, looking around. "The world is full of colors today, isn't it, child?"

"Sure." Emily glanced around, too, suddenly noticing the brilliant, ever-changing autumn colors of the maples and the oaks, the dogwoods and the sweet gums.

Gran was watching her. "It's amazing what one sees when one's eyes are open," she commented. "What good is a rainbow, if we only focus on one color?"

"Gran," Emily began hesitantly. "Do you think someone who's injured has to *want* to get better?"

Gran nodded soberly. "If the spirit does not desire healing, no true healing can take place, even if the body seems to recover."

"But why would a person or animal just give up when there's still hope?" Emily pressed on. "Especially if there are people trying to help?"

"Hope means different things to different people," Gran replied. "And if you want to help, you have to be willing to give the kind of help that's needed, not just the kind you *think* is needed."

Emily wasn't quite sure what the old woman

meant. After all, her mother didn't ask each dog what it needed before she treated it.

Gran must have seen the confusion in her eyes. "Think of it this way," she said, leaning over to pick up a stick from the ground. "The physical and the spiritual often intersect. Like this." She scratched a figure in the dirt — one strong line going up and down, another crossing it from side to side. "Sometimes there is suffering on the physical line only, or on the spiritual line only. But when the pain lies right here" — she pointed with the stick to the spot where the lines bisected — "that is when healing can be most difficult."

"Oh." Emily nodded, thinking of Lorelei. The unicorn — or whatever she was — had been badly injured by the Black Fire on the outside. What if she had been just as badly injured on the inside? "But how can you help someone like that?"

Gran shrugged, dropping the stick on the ground. "By remaining open to all possibilities. If one way isn't working, try another. And another. And another after that, if necessary."

"But what if you run out of ways?"

Gran shook her head firmly. "There are infinite possibilities in this world," she said, "just as there are infinite shades within a rainbow. It's just a matter of opening your heart to them."

Emily chewed on her lower lip. "I guess," she said hesitantly.

Gran smiled at her. "Emily," she said, "you can never truly fail as long as you give all of yourself to the attempt."

❁ ❁ ❁

"Okay, guys, now do your thing! Go ahead! You can do it!"

"This isn't going to work."

Zzzzzinnnng! Pop! Buzzzzz! Sllllurrrrp!

"No! No! You're not supposed to *eat* the spaghetti, you goofballs!"

"Yummmmmmmmmmyyyyyyyyyyyy!"

"Aargh! Stop them, Kara! I have noodles in my hair!"

Even before Emily entered the meadow, she could hear the loud, excited voices drifting toward her on the slight breeze. What in the world was going on?

She stepped into the field just in time to see Adriane brushing frantically at her long, dark hair as Stormbringer circled her anxiously. Lyra was crouching in the grass, batting at Fred as the dragonfly flew about, skillfully missing the big cat's playful swipes. Nearby, the other dragonflies, Barney, Goldie, Blaze, and Fiona, and others Kara had not named, careened around the field, leaving trails of twinkly magic sparks everywhere. Kara was waving her arms around, obviously trying to control the cluster of dragonflies.

"*Emmupheee!*" Goldie flitted toward Emily, banking just in front of her face.

The little yellow dragon seemed to have something long, pale, and stringy hanging from her miniature beak.

"Hello, Goldie. What have you got?"

"*Magiccc noodilll!*" Goldie squeaked.

Adriane glanced at her and rolled her eyes. "We're testing another one of Miss America's lamebrained ideas," she explained.

"I don't see you coming up with anything better, Miss Crouching Tiger," Kara snapped back.

Emily held her hands up to avoid getting hit with a wet noodle. "Whoa," she said. "Somebody fill me in, okay?"

"Since the dragonflies wove the last dreamcatcher, I figured they could weave another one," Kara explained. "I even let them take a few strands of my hair, and that didn't work." She crossed her arms over her chest, then ducked as Blaze buzzed past, wobbling crazily under a mass of spaghetti strands.

Emily had to admit that the plan made some sense, but spaghetti?

"I like spaghetti. It could work," Kara said.

A few weeks ago, a wild burst of uncontrolled magic had caused Kara's hair to grow superlong and turn every color of the rainbow. Once her hair had been trimmed, the dragonflies had used the cut strands to weave a protective web over the portal. It had worked like a dreamcatcher, only instead of keeping nightmares away, it had covered the portal to keep nightmare *creatures* from coming through. That way, only good magical creatures had been able to pass through when the portal opened. But now the dreamcatcher was gone.

Emily glanced at Adriane.

The dark-haired girl grimaced. "We've already tried Kara's yarn, some ribbon, some socks, and now this."

"Yeah," Kara added morosely. "That spaghetti was supposed to be lunch today."

"Well, there's always more possibilities, right?" Emily said, remembering what Gran had just told her. "We just need to find something else with Kara's magic touch to give them."

Adriane stared thoughtfully at Lyra. "Hmm," she said. "What about —"

"Poooowieeee!" Fred went flying as Lyra batted him across the field.

"I don't think so," the cat interrupted before Adriane could finish, backing away warily.

Emily brushed away Blaze, who was buzzing

excitedly near her left shoulder, and pointed at Kara's feet. "Hey, what about those?"

Kara looked down at her pink sneakers. "You mean my shoelaces?" she exclaimed. "I had to search every store in the mall to find these! They match my pink baseball cap exactly."

"Fashion is so fickle, you know," Adriane commented. "I heard purple is the new pink."

"All you ever wear is black, so how would you know?" Kara rolled her eyes, but took off her sneakers. As she slid the laces out of the holes, she glanced at Emily. "Hey," she said. "What's happening with our mystery guest?"

"Pretty much what I already told you," Emily sighed. She'd E-mailed Kara and Adriane about Lorelei as soon as she'd gotten home last night. "I just can't seem to get through to her. How are all the new animals?" she asked instead.

"Fine. Most of them are over at the glade. Ozzie and some of the others are filling them in on this world and everything," Adriane told her.

Pink shoelaces in hand, Kara said, "Storm doesn't think Lorelei is a unicorn. And neither do I."

"Why not?"

"Think about it." Kara tapped herself on the forehead. "What do unicorns have that makes them so special? Duh. A *horn*."

"Yes, you're right, but still —"

Kara waggled her shoelaces in the air. "Yoo-hoo, guys," she called to the dragonflies. "I've got something else for you to play with."

The dragonflies buzzed over and eagerly grabbed the shoelaces, spinning them into small webs. Tiny, colorful sparks started to pop in the air all around them.

"This is nuts. The dreamcatcher has to be made from something stronger, some real magic!" Adriane said.

"We're waiting for your suggestions, Snow Black," Kara quipped.

Ignoring Kara, Adriane went on. "We know something has happened in Aldenmor and it most likely involves the Dark Sorceress. We need to think of something more effective to cover the portal if it opens again."

Emily bit her lip. She understood why her friends were so focused on fixing the dreamcatcher. As long as the portal remained unprotected, there was no telling what might come through when it opened again. But she couldn't seem to concentrate. Not while Lorelei was still out there somewhere in the woods, alone and scared.

"I'm going back out," she said as casually as she could. "See if I can find Lorelei again."

The other girls exchanged a glance. "I'm not sure that's such a good idea," Adriane said.

"She's right," Kara agreed. "It sounds like that nonunicorn of yours is pretty dangerous. What if it's the evil something Zach warned us about?"

"Evil?" Emily echoed in surprise. "Lorelei isn't evil."

Adriane ducked as two dragonflies swooped past, inches from her head, furiously trying to spin tiny pink dreamcatchers. "Well, knocking down trees and throwing around giant boulders doesn't exactly sound good to me."

"Lorelei didn't mean to do all that." Emily couldn't believe how her friends were reacting. They hadn't even been there! She whirled toward the mistwolf. "Storm, tell them!"

Storm met her gaze steadily. *The creature has very strong magic,* she said. *So strong that she seems unable to control it. That counts as dangerous.*

Glancing over her shoulder, Emily saw Ghyll hopping over to them. Ozzie was strolling next to the flobbin.

"Hey, Ozzie," Kara said, staring curiously at the giant froglike creature. "Who's your new friend?"

Emily realized that Kara must not have seen Ghyll the day before. She was about to explain.

But before she could say a word, Ghyll suddenly straightened up, his bulging eyes seeming to expand to twice their usual size. His warty blue skin glowed as his mouth opened in astonishment, purple tongue rolling onto the ground. "Well, hello there!" he cried out, leaping forward so eagerly Ozzie went flying.

"Hey!" the ferret cried. "Watch it!"

Ghyll didn't even seem to hear him. His gaze was pinned on Kara. He hopped up to her and stopped. "Most beautiful of creatures," he said breathlessly. "I am Ghyll, your most humble and adoring servant."

"Hey. Not so close." Kara brushed her blond hair back from her face, dislodging a stray piece of spaghetti as she did so. "I'm Kara Davies, *the* most beautiful of creatures."

"What ravishing beauty!" Ghyll hopped closer still, gazing at Kara adoringly. "Would you honor me with a kiss?"

Kara wrinkled her nose. "I don't think so," she said, taking a step backward. "I'm on a break."

Ghyll leaned forward eagerly. His bulging eyes were level with Kara's forehead. "Just one little kiss — to turn me into a handsome prince!"

He puckered his wide, rubbery lips and closed his eyes. Lyra stood up, her fur bristling, pushing her way between the flobbin and the girl. *"She said no,"* the cat growled.

She jumped as Ghyll planted a slobbery kiss right between her eyes. *"BLECCCH!"*

"Hey!" The flobbin's eyes flew open. "What's the big idea?"

Ozzie rolled on the ground, laughing. Even Storm looked amused.

"Is this frog for real?" Kara asked.

"He's a flobbin," Ozzie explained.

"Listen up, flubber, you've been reading too many fairy tales," Kara said. "I don't do magic kisses."

Kara took a few steps away from Ghyll as Lyra glared at the flobbin suspiciously. "Maybe the unicorn is a flipper, too —"

"Unicorn?" Ghyll broke in. "Is there a unicorn here?"

"No," Kara and Adriane replied, at the same time Emily said, "Yes. Maybe."

"There is a magical creature on the loose," Storm explained to the flobbin. *"Horselike, but with no horn."*

"Ah." Ghyll blinked his bulbous eyes. "No horn means no unicorn, right? It's probably an eqqtar — a wild Aldenmor pony." He glanced at Emily. "You should be careful," he added. "Eqqtari can be unpredictable at the best of times. And if this one's *pretending* to be a unicorn, well, who knows what it could be up to? You really ought to stay away from it. Far away."

Emily was about to respond when five despondent dragonflies plopped to the ground at her feet. "Uh-oh," she said, bending to pick up Barney. "I guess the shoelace thing isn't working, either, huh?"

The dragonflies squeaked helplessly, sparks shooting out in all directions, and popped out of sight.

Adriane turned to Kara. "So what do we try next?"

Kara glanced at her pink-strapped watch. "Nothing, for now," she said. "We have a tour in, like, ten minutes." As part of their agreement with the town council, the girls had agreed to lead public tours of Ravenswood Wildlife Preserve on the weekends. Tourists could see exotic animals, just not the magical ones.

"I will come, too," Ghyll said eagerly. "I want to help you, beautiful princess of Earth. I will earn your love and gratitude."

"Fine," Kara said. "Go stand over there and hide. Forever." She pointed to a spot all the way across the meadow.

"Your wish is my command!" Ghyll hopped away quickly.

Ozzie shook his head. "I'll make sure he stays out of the way," he murmured, scurrying after Ghyll.

"You guys probably don't need me for the tour, right?" Emily said to the other girls.

Adriane and Kara stared at her.

Emily shrugged stubbornly. "Whatever Lorelei is, she needs help. I'm not just going to abandon her."

"Just be careful," Adriane said.

"Okay." Emily watched as Kara and Adriane hurried toward the path leading back to the mansion. Storm and Lyra went with them.

Soon the meadow was empty except for Emily. She bent over to pick up her backpack. The top flap was half open, and she noticed something sticking out. Huh?

She reached in and pulled out her flute. How had that gotten in there? She had taken it out to practice for the band tryout, but she always put it back in its case when she was done. Didn't she? She must have stuck it in her backpack without thinking.

"Oh, well," she muttered aloud. She slung the backpack over her shoulder and walked into the woods, holding the flute in her hand. The smooth, cool metal felt somehow comforting, reassuring.

An hour later she stood at a crossroads in the trail, feeling stupid. What was she doing? She couldn't even *find* Lorelei, let alone help her. Meanwhile, her friends were stuck doing her share of things — not just the easy things, like leading tours of Ravenswood, but really important things, like trying to replace the dreamcatcher.

Glancing down at her magic jewel, she saw that

it was cold and dark. If she didn't know better, she would think it was just a pretty hunk of lifeless rock.

Still, she kept walking.

Somewhere nearby, a twig cracked loudly. Emily glanced toward the sound.

And there was Lorelei just ahead of her, coat swirling with colors that changed so fast Emily couldn't keep track.

Emily gasped. "I — I thought you wouldn't come," she blurted.

The creature jumped, startled by her voice. Backing away, she gazed at Emily suspiciously.

"No, wait!" Emily had an idea. Putting the flute to her lips, she played a few bars of her song. Lorelei cocked her head, her expression wavering between interest and wariness.

Emily kept playing. A moment later, a humming sound filled the air around her. She tensed, expecting it to explode into that horrible, jarring noise she had heard before. But this time Lorelei's "singing" was clear and pure, the uncanny music wrapping around Emily's notes and carrying them, expanding them into something perfect and whole and — magical.

Lorelei approached Emily and knelt down before her. Holding her breath, Emily slowly lowered the flute. She moved close, hand outstretched, and touched Lorelei's head, combing through the silky mane with her fingers. Lorelei closed her eyes. Emily ran her hand down the creature's neck and back up over her head — and stopped. There was a small nub, like a slightly protruding bone, in the middle of Lorelei's forehead.

"What's this?" Emily asked, feeling the bump. Lorelei hummed softly.

Images flooded Emily's mind. Twinkling stars, spread out in a pattern, like a city seen from a night-time flight. A circle of light, steady and beautiful.

Emily tried to send a few images of her own. Questions. What was she seeing? What was Lorelei trying to tell her? What had happened to her?

Lorelei's music grew hurried, almost frantic. The sounds were becoming different, darker. Anguished. Almost violent —

Crash!!!

A giant tree branch fell to the ground at Emily's feet. Startled, she jumped back, swinging her flute through the air. There was a glint of steel, a horrible blade cutting into bone —

Lorelei's voice erupted into a jumble of screeching, painful noise. She reared up, looking at Emily, eyes wide in terror.

"Wait!" Emily gasped. "It was an accident. Don't go!"

Too late. With one last burst of noise, Lorelei vanished.

Chapter 8

He's just the cutest guy on the entire football team. Plus he's an eighth grader, you know. Seventh graders can be so juvenile, don't you think?"

Emily sighed, not bothering to answer. She knew the girl next to her wouldn't even notice. The band audition had been easy, since Emily could read music and had her own flute. That was about it. And now here she was, actually at an afternoon football game against Evanston Junior High, sitting next to a chatterbox named Rae.

Slumping in her seat, she rested her chin on her hand and glanced out at the football field, where the players from both teams were huddling. What had possessed her to join the band anyway? It was just one more thing keeping her away from Ravenswood — and Lorelei. Not to mention her chores at the Pet Palace.

Thinking about the fight with her mother, she got a sick feeling in the pit of her stomach. When she'd arrived home last night, her mother had acted as if nothing had happened, and Emily had not brought it up, either. The two had pretty much avoided each other as much as possible all evening. This morning, Carolyn had left for the clinic by the time Emily had come down to breakfast.

Maybe that's the best way, she thought uncertainly. *We should both just forget about what happened.*

Pop!

Emily jumped, startled by the sound. She looked around frantically for any unidentified flying dragonflies.

Rae was staring at her from behind a huge bubble. She sucked it back into her mouth, then popped her gum noisily.

"Ravenswood has been there, like, forever," Rae chattered away. "Kinda too bad it'll all be gone soon."

"Ravenswood isn't going anywhere," Emily said firmly.

"My aunt says it's practically a done deal," Rae said in her loud, slightly nasal voice.

"Your aunt?" Turning to look directly at the other girl for the first time, Emily narrowed her eyes suspiciously.

Rae gazed back. The crisp autumn breeze lifted a loose strand of her dull brown hair and blew it across her cheek. For the first time, Emily noticed that the other girl's face looked strangely familiar. Who else had those beady eyes, those broad, flat cheekbones, that pointed nose?

"My aunt Bea. She's right over there."

Emily looked where Rae was pointing. Mrs. Windor was sitting in the wooden bleachers directly across from the band, her thin frame wedged firmly between Mayor Davies and his wife.

"Mrs. Windor is your aunt?" Emily asked through clenched teeth.

"Uh-huh." Rae didn't even seem to notice Emily's dismay. "Aunt Bea told my mom a golf course is just what Stonehill needs, not an animal preserve." Leaning into Emily, she whispered, "You know the animals there are dangerous."

Emily knew she should just ignore Rae. She knew all too well what Mrs. Windor thought about Ravenswood. Still, she felt anger bubbling up from deep inside her, hot and frantic. How dare Mrs. Windor decide what was best for the town? How dare she try to undo all their hard work, belittle Ravenswood's long history, and displace all those innocent animals?

Her gaze wandered to the field again, searching for the cheerleaders. Kara was standing in formation with the rest of the squad, watching the play on the field. Just behind the cheerleaders,

Emily spotted Molly, Heather, and Tiffany. Sitting near them, but obviously not *with* them, was an unhappy-looking Adriane. Emily felt bad. She knew Adriane hated these school games. She shouldn't have asked Adriane to come hear her play. But Adriane *was* here, and Emily wondered if she should try to send her a magical message about what Rae had just said.

No, better not, she decided a second later. With the way my luck is going lately, I'd probably mess it up and cause another magical explosion or something. After what happened at the last game . . .

A soft, insistent burst of music startled her. For a second she thought she had missed a signal, that the band director had started a song without her knowing it, and she grabbed her flute. But then she realized that nobody else was playing, either.

Then where was that music coming from? She half closed her eyes, listening intently as the melody wrapped its way around her brain. How could music like that exist? So mysterious, so strange, and yet so familiar.

Her head started to feel fuzzy. Rae's voice faded until it was little more than an annoying drone at the heart of the silky melody. Glancing down at the field, Emily noted with surprise that the players seemed to be running in slow motion.

The scene tilted, making her dizzy, and she grabbed at the hard bleacher seat to check her balance.

Wow, she thought. That's weird.

The only thing that wasn't moving in slow motion was her heart. It started to beat faster and faster. Her brain struggled to catch up.

This . . . has . . . happened . . . before, she thought. The music kept distracting her, confusing her, but somehow, somewhere at edge of her memory, she knew that something was about to happen. She could feel small eddies of magic swirling in the distance, building into a wave.

Oh, no! She tensed. Not again.

The rainbow jewel was throbbing at her wrist, its colors muddy: blood red, dirty green, sour yellow.

Yes, something was about to happen. Something bad.

Glancing around for help, she noticed the band director's shiny, bald head, which seemed somehow comforting all of a sudden. She forced herself to focus on it. If she just watched that, all this weirdness would go away.

The band director stood up. Lifting his baton, he turned around . . .

. . . and grinned directly at Emily with yellowish, crooked teeth. Gaping eye sockets leered at her, burning in dead white skin.

Emily opened her mouth to scream, but no sound came out. A nudge to her ribs made her turn.

"Come on, we're on," Rae whispered, already holding her flute to her lips.

Emily turned back to see the director's baton moving up and down, his normal, pudgy face concentrating on the trombone section.

Just breathe! she told herself.

Raising her instrument, Emily stared desperately toward her friends. Kara and the other cheerleaders were doing a routine, standing in a line and shaking their gold-and-blue pompoms over their heads, then down by their waists. As they lowered the pompoms, Emily looked for Adriane behind them. Her eyes scanned the crowd and stopped suddenly. There it was again. One horrible face — a gaunt, gruesome figure with dark, evil eyes.

She jumped to her feet, her heart pounding so hard it seemed it would burst out of her chest.

"Hey, what are you doing?"

Rae's voice sounded faraway and weak. Ignoring her, Emily stood on her tiptoes, trying to see over the cheerleaders' waving pompoms. The hideous monster was just a few rows behind Adriane and the others. Was it after her friends? She had to warn them! Emily's arms felt leaden as she tried to wave back and forth.

Was it her imagination, or was the monster one

row closer now? Its sly, menacing gaze was waiting to meet her own; it locked in on her — and nodded.

With immense effort, Emily managed to rip her gaze away. Taking a deep breath, she did her best to shake off the spell of the sinister music. She had to get a message to Adriane and Kara!

But trying to organize herself, focus her magic, was like wading through quicksand. The wheedling, mysterious music was pulling her deeper and deeper, and before long the struggle just didn't seem worth the effort. The ghoulish face had melted into the crowd, indistinguishable in the sea of faces. Emily felt heat at her wrist. She knew her jewel was pulsing a warning, but she didn't care. She sat down, listlessly holding her flute. Wherever she was being pulled, she should just give in, let it carry her wherever it would — even over the edge of the void into utter darkness.

Suddenly a pure, clear, high note cut through the fog in her mind. The crisp notes called to her. Emily sat up straight, almost dropping her flute.

All at once, the heavy, foggy feeling disappeared. The mysterious music had stopped, and Emily felt things snap into normal speed again.

And this time, she wasn't the only one reacting. All around her, people were murmuring and calling to one another.

"What is that?"

"Hey, check it out — down there on the field!"

"Is that a horse? What's it doing here?"

Emily glanced at her jewel, which was now pulsing with bright, clear light. Still clutching her flute, she pushed past Rae.

"Hey!" the other girl protested. "Where are you going?"

Emily ignored her. "Excuse me," she muttered, pushing her way forward. "Excuse me. I have to get through."

A chubby kid holding a trombone blocked her way. "Look at that thing! It's wild!" he said.

"Whoa!" one of the trumpet players cried. "What's it doing now?"

"I don't know, but looks like Coach Burton is going to kick its horsey butt!" another boy shouted. "Whoo-hoo, go, Coach!"

The call came again, frightened and panicked. Finally, one of the tall kids in front moved aside, and Emily had a clear view of the field at last. "Oh, no!" she breathed, astonished at what she saw.

It was Lorelei. At least she thought it was Lorelei. The creature stood at the edge of the field, near the visiting team's goalpost. Now, her coat was a dazzling, snowy white instead of a multitude of shifting colors. Her silvery hooves gleamed in the sunlight, and her mane and tail were pure white silken strands.

But Emily hardly noticed any of that. She was staring at Lorelei's head, where a long, graceful spiral of a crystalline horn jutted proudly from her forehead.

"I knew it!" Emily whispered in awe. "You *are* a unicorn."

The unicorn shifted her head, long, silky mane flowing, and looked around at the crowd, searching.

"I'm here," Emily whispered.

Both team's coaches and a dozen players were now running down the field toward the unicorn.

"No! Don't hurt her!" Emily yelled. She pushed her way to the playing field. The band members all turned to look at her.

"What's with her?" a sax player asked.

"Kara, Adriane!" Emily called.

Lorelei pawed at the ground, turning in a tight circle as more people surrounded her.

A flash of dark hair pushed through the crowd. Adriane stood face-to-face with three football players, yelling something and forcing them back. She was clearing a path for the unicorn to escape.

Lorelei was frantically looking left and right.

"Run!" Emily called.

The unicorn looked across the field to Emily, reared up, and raced through the break between the players.

"Hey, horsey! Stonehill can't win even *with*

you!" A large bird stood in Lorelei's path, waving its arms up and down.

"Go, chicken guy!" Kids from the visiting team were cheering on their mascot.

"I am the Evanston Eagle!" the chicken guy announced, bowing to the stands.

The student dressed as the Evanston Junior High Eagle wore an enormous round papier-mâché eagle's head. He moved toward Lorelei, dancing and flapping his arms, which were encased in fake wings lined with scraggly feathers that fluttered in the light breeze.

"Go, Evanston Eagles!" the visiting students cheered as the chicken guy did his chicken dance.

Stonehill students booed. "Go, Stonehill Unicorn!" they chanted.

Lorelei snorted and fixed her large, liquid eyes on the humans as they came up behind her. The chicken guy closed in, flapping its wings. "Evanston rules! For I am the chick — I mean, eagle!"

Chicken guy danced toward Lorelei, taunting her and trying to press her back toward the waiting players.

Lorelei reared on her hind legs, and for a moment Emily thought she was going to wheel and vanish as she'd done before.

"No! No magic, *please*!" Emily breathed.

Lorelei landed with a snort, lowered her head . . .

. . . and charged.

"Nice horsey." Then a muffled scream came from inside the giant eagle head. *"Ahhh!"*

Chicken guy turned to run, but it was too late. Emily gasped and covered her eyes as Lorelei's gleaming horn ripped through the garish yellow beak and pierced the bulbous head.

When she peeked out through her fingers a second later, she saw Lorelei dancing in place, shaking her head frantically, trying to free herself from the giant hollow orb impaled on her horn. The kid in the mascot costume — minus the eagle's head — was running in the other direction. His hair was a little messy and his face a little pale, but otherwise he looked okay.

The crowd cheered. "Go, Stonehill!"

Suddenly an undercurrent of noisy, confused sound slammed into Emily. She almost screamed.

As waves of emotional magic rolled over her, nearly buckling her knees, she could feel Lorelei's panic rising. Emily herself felt on the verge of hysteria. She had to get Lorelei out of there — now!

"Lorelei!" Emily pushed and shoved through the crowd, barreling out onto the sidelines. Lorelei had managed to free herself from the eagle's head at last. She was standing in the end zone, snorting

at the cheering crowd. Adriane was trying desperately to hold back several big players, but it was
only a matter of seconds before Lorelei would be
trapped. Why didn't she run?

Lorelei spun around, looking at Emily, waiting
for her.

"Go! Run!" Emily yelled, taking a step onto the
field.

A hand landed on her shoulder.

"This is the final straw, young lady!"

Emily whirled to find a wagging finger in her
face. "Your animals are finished, and so is Ravenswood!" Mrs. Windor said.

"Let me go!" Emily yelled. Pulling away, she
turned and sprinted across the field to Kara's side.

"Stand back, everyone," Kara said to the
crowd, allowing Emily to get through. "We're professional tour guides!"

Lorelei stood, nodding her head toward Emily.

"Get her out of here! Now!" Kara whispered.

"I need some time," Emily said, moving slowly
toward the terrified unicorn.

Kara saw Mrs. Windor grabbing some teachers
and pointing toward the girls. Even from here, she
could tell Mrs. Windor's face was flushed with
anger as the woman started across the field. "Here
comes trouble," Kara said.

She clapped her hands, grabbed her pompoms, ran into the field, and let out a whoop. "Let me hear you, people! Goooooo, Stonehill!" she sang out at the top of her lungs. "We all know Stonehill needs a team mascot, and this is your special halftime surprise. We brought a friend from Ravenswood, and with a little papier-mâché magic, she's going to bring Stonehill to victory. Yay!"

The stands erupted in wild cheers. "Stonehill, Stonehill!"

Mrs. Windor was forced to a stop as curious kids pushed forward, blocking her way.

"What's everyone think of the Stonehill Unicorn?" Kara yelled out.

"Awesome!"

"Yeah, that thing really showed the lame Evanston Eagle what's what!"

"Stonehill rules!"

Emily smiled. Yes! Kara was a genius. Nobody would realize that they'd just seen a real-life unicorn.

Unless, of course, Emily couldn't get Lorelei out of there in time.

Emily slowly walked to within two feet of the unicorn. "Easy. It's only me," she said as calmly as possible. Lorelei's frightened eyes darted back and forth between Emily and the surrounding football players. Then Emily realized she was still holding her flute. She stared at it. Could it work?

She had to try. Raising the instrument to her lips, she took a deep breath and blew the first few notes of her song.

The flute's music was soft and lilting, easily swallowed up by the hoots and hollers of the crowd. Still, Emily closed her eyes and played on, focusing on the music. As the gentle notes drifted out of the flute, Emily imagined them moving to Lorelei in slow, serene, rhythmic waves. Even with her eyes closed, she could sense that her jewel was pulsing steadily in time with the music.

Someone nearby shouted something about calling Animal Control. She thought she heard Rae yelling that *she* was supposed to solo, and for a second Emily's concentration wavered.

She forced down panic. Focusing her energy again, she tried to form her thoughts into a song, a lyric to go with the music she was playing.

Look into my eyes
Know that you can trust me
Listen to the sound
I'll always be around

Hear my words
Feel the magic in them
In friendship we are bound
I'll always be around

You and me
It's meant to be
We'll always be
Friends forever

Emily opened her eyes. Lorelei's head was lifted again, the breeze playing with her silky forelock. The unicorn's eyes locked on Emily's. Still playing, Emily took a step toward the exit. The unicorn stood stock-still for a moment, then finally took a hesitant step, following Emily. Surprised murmurs from the crowd surrounded her as Emily, like a modern Pied Piper, led the creature through the exit and out to the grassy area beyond the playing field. Behind her, she heard the crowd break into cheers as the game resumed.

Emily faced Lorelei. She raised her hand and gently stroked the creature's velvety cheek.

"You came to me," she said wonderingly, tears welling up in her eyes.

Lorelei nodded. *"Emily hurt."*

"No. I'm okay. You have to get out of here, now. Please."

Lorelei looked deep into Emily's eyes. *"Friends forever."*

With a last wild snort, the unicorn turned and raced away.

Emily stood and watched her friend vanish.

Chapter 9

How could a horn suddenly appear when it wasn't there yesterday?" Adriane asked as the girls made their way to the secret glade behind Ravenswood Manor.

"I don't know," Emily replied. "Unicorns have strong magic, right? So maybe they can do that. Just grow another horn, I mean."

Kara shrugged. "Okay, but what happened to her original horn? And why in the world would she decide to show up at the game like that? I doubt that unicorns — if that's really what she is — are big football fans." She snorted. "We're just lucky everyone bought that lame mascot story."

"That was quick thinking, Barbie," Adriane admitted, giving Kara a sidelong glance.

"Thanks, Xena." Kara looked pleased.

"She came because she thought I needed help," Emily told them.

"I thought you were helping *her*," Kara said.

"There's something I haven't told you guys yet," Emily said, slowing her steps.

Adriane and Kara stopped and faced Emily.

"Spill it, girl," Kara said sternly, crossing her arms.

"She came because, I — I guess she thought I was in trouble." Emily shrugged uncertainly.

"And why would you be in trouble?" Kara asked.

Emily gulped. "I — I think there may be something following me. Something bad."

"What are you talking about?" Adriane demanded.

Emily regretted not telling them sooner. Just ahead, the immense Rocking Stone rose up through the trees, its spindly peak pointing the way to the portal field. As they walked toward it, she quickly filled them in on the mysterious, ghoulish figure that had appeared at the football field, and the strange musical sounds she'd been hearing.

"You should have said something to us earlier," Adriane said angrily.

"I'm really sorry," Emily replied. "I didn't know if it was real or not."

"Especially after what Zach told us!" Adriane continued.

"Yes, yes, I know."

"Are you sure it was right there in the bleachers?" Kara asked. "I didn't notice anything."

"And just how many times have you seen this thing?" Adriane asked.

"Three." Emily looked sheepishly at her friends' startled faces.

Adriane and Kara exchanged glances.

"That's real enough," Kara said.

"Tell us more about the music," Adriane suggested.

Emily tried to explain what had happened, the magical explosion in her room, the waves hitting her in the field, the garbled noise turning to clear, crisp sounds from Lorelei. And the strange music that had hypnotized her, had made her feel so peaceful, without a care in the world.

"Let's summarize, shall we?" Kara took over. "Lorelei was changing colors and made loud, awful noises. Then she shows up with a horn, looking all beautiful and making sweet music."

"Right."

"Then the monster thingy starts making different music, like a spell," Kara continued.

"Yes, it was like being under a spell," Emily agreed.

"And then Lorelei shows up at the game and

saves you from this monster's spell," Adriane jumped in.

"I think that's what happened."

"So why is the monster after you?" Kara asked.

"I don't know. Maybe it's after Lorelei, not me."

"Let's say Lorelei *is* a unicorn." Adriane sighed. "How did she get here?"

"What do you mean?" Emily blinked. "She came through the portal with the other animals."

"First of all, unicorns don't need portals." Kara counted on her fingers. "Second of all, how come it's not coming to me?"

Adriane and Emily regarded her.

"What! I *am* the one with unicorn experience, you know."

"Jealous, Rapunzel?" Adriane teased. "Emily has a deep empathy with animals — she's obviously feeling the pain of this creature," she continued seriously.

Emily tried to explain. "It's like we feel each other's pain."

"How did she get past the Dark Sorceress?" Kara asked. "We know she's trying to get her hands on magical animals — trying to steal all their magic. She was after *my* unicorn, right? So why would she just let one leave Aldenmor?"

"Maybe Lorlelei escaped," Adriane suggested.

"Hiding with the others, she snuck through." Emily continued the train of thought. "And this monster is now after her."

"Makes sense," Adriane said.

"So what happened to her horn?" Kara asked.

"I don't know — it's part of the mystery."

Kara tugged at a lock of blond hair. "We need to be sure of what it is, and if it's dangerous," she said. "As president of the Ravenswood Wildlife Preservation Society, I hereby call an executive meeting. We need some magical opinions."

"Agreed," Adriane said. "Let's gather the troops."

The girls walked through the natural arch of trees to the Rocking Stone and on to the magic glade.

"I didn't know you played the flute," Kara mentioned to Emily.

"Yeah."

"Adriane plays guitar — maybe we should form a band."

"And what would *you* do?" Adriane asked.

"Lead singer, of course. La-*laa*!" Kara crooned.

Adriane covered her ears. "Well, we'd be a smash at the Pet Palace."

The three girls laughed. Kara and Adriane entwined their arms with Emily's and walked into the wondrous glade together. Emily felt better, at least for the moment. With her friends at her side, nothing could harm her.

❧ ❧ ❧

"This meeting of the Ravenswood Wildlife Preservation Society is now in session!" Kara declared, walking back and forth as she surveyed the large crowd of animals and creatures. Emily, Adriane, Storm, and Lyra sat on the bank of the small rippling stream that emptied into the still, glassy pond. A handful of quiffles perched on the delicate bridge that arched gracefully over the stream. Other creatures — jeeran, pegasii, quiffles, brimbees, and more — were sitting or standing on the leaf-strewn grass surrounding the water.

"Everyone's met the newcomers, and I'm glad you've all settled in," Kara continued.

"Beautiful princess!" a breathless voice sang out, interrupting her. Ghyll sprang out from behind a fir tree, followed by Ozzie. The flobbin hopped speedily over to Kara. "I'm here. I came as soon as I heard your call. Won't you please allow me to apologize for my tardiness with a nice big kiss?"

Kara brushed him away with a wave of her arms. "Not now, I'm busy."

"When would be a good time, O goddess of magic?"

"How about never? Does never work for you?"

121

Lyra stepped in front of Kara, leaving no doubt as to the time frame involved. The others all gestured for Ghyll to sit down and keep quiet.

Ozzie sat next to Emily. "You know," he muttered as Ghyll took a place by the pond, "I'm starting to think there's something a little odd about that guy."

"Quiet, please." Kara paced back and forth, hands behind her back. "How can I concentrate? We've got an evil creature that's here right now, you know!"

The crowd gasped. Murmurs of dismay rippled through the gathered creatures.

"Don't panic," Emily called out. "We just need to figure out what it could be."

"Right." Kara hopped up on a large, flat rock at the edge of the pond.

"What kind of monster are we talking about?" Balthazar asked.

Emily stood up and gave a quick description of the thing she'd seen.

"Could it be a banshee?" a brimbee asked.

"No, we know what those look like." Emily shuddered at the memory of the ragged, green-skinned, red-eyed hags that had attacked them not long ago. "This creature had pale white skin and black eyes and was sort of bony."

"A night stalker!" another voice cried.

Ronif shook his head. "No, no," he said. "They have dark eyes, and their skin is black as midnight."

"That creature who ran away, the one who made the horrible noise," a wommel called out. "We haven't seen it since we got here. *That's* your monster!"

"We think that creature may be a unicorn," Emily said.

"A unicorn. Here?"

Gasps of wonder broke out among the crowd.

"Surely with the magic of a unicorn, we need not worry about a monster," a brimbee said.

"They can travel freely on the web itself," another quiffle explained. "They don't need a portal or anything. Why would it be here?"

"We're not sure she *is* a unicorn, yet," Kara said.

"This monster made beautiful music. I can't explain it — it was hypnotic," Emily continued. "I forgot about everything else when I heard it."

"It has to be a harpy," a pegasus declared.

"Or a siren, creatures that use beautiful music to lure victims," Rasha added.

"There's a famous painting of the sirens of Waterknell hanging on the wall at my cousin Brommy's place," Ozzie said, excitedly. "I'm sure you must have noticed it, Ghyll?"

"Of course," Ghyll replied immediately. "It's quite striking."

Emily noticed a weird look cross Ozzie's face.

"Sirens always take the form of beautiful maidens; they're not ghoulish," Balthazar pointed out. "But they do use similar magic as harpies."

"Oh, no, a harpy is here?" an animal cried in a frightened voice.

"A harpy spirited my brother away."

"Calm down!" Kara's voice broke through the commotion. "What's a hippy?"

Once again there was an eruption of responses.

"Harpy."

". . . hideous beastie . . ."

". . . song that can lure anyone to their doom . . ."

". . . horrible, gaping eyes of death . . ."

"Harpies weave spells using musical enchantments," Balthazar explained. "They lull victims into a state of mindlessness and then take control of them — make them do their bidding."

"They use music as magic?" Emily asked.

"Music can be a potent form of magical energy," Balthazar continued. "The right sounds or combinations of sounds can have a strong influence on magic and those who use magic."

All around the glade, heads were nodding.

Ghyll stepped forward. "The harpy's music creates a beautiful vision, sort of a dreamtime state — disguising it just long enough to get close so it can attack. Only those with powerful magic of their own can see the harpy's true form." He nodded toward Emily.

A lot of things were starting to make sense now. Emily remembered the weird, dreamlike spell the music had thrown over her, the exquisite illusion she'd spotted briefly in the forest. "What are we supposed to do?" she demanded, pushing the images away. "What if this thing is after Lorelei?"

"You're the only one who's seen it. Maybe it's after you," Ghyll suggested.

"When the Dark Sorceress tried to get the unicorn last time, she tried to use *me*. Maybe now she's trying to use *you*," Kara put in, nodding.

"Catch it and send it back through the portal!" an agitated voice cried from the crowd.

"Yes! It's the only way!" someone else called.

"We can't send Lorelei back to Aldenmor and into the Dark Sorceress's hands," Adriane said sharply.

"Maybe we can," Ghyll said.

"Why do you say that?"

"Unicorns are at the top of the magic chain," the flobbin explained. "As the beautiful princess pointed out" — he gave Kara a little bow — "the Dark Sorceress couldn't get a unicorn on her own. If the creature *is* a unicorn, it should be able to

125

handle the Dark Sorceress just fine. If it's *not*, she won't pay any attention to it anyway. So everybody wins."

Kara blinked. "Unless, of course —" She stopped.

"Unless what?"

Kara paced back and forth again. "Unless the Dark Sorceress knows the unicorn thing is here." She raised a finger in the air. "What if she *sent* it?"

An anxious murmur swept through the crowd.

"No!" Emily cried. "The thing I saw — it's definitely evil!"

"Ribbit." Ghyll cleared his throat. "There is another possibility. If this harpy is particularly powerful, it might be able to shape shift."

"Harpies can change their shape?" Adriane asked.

"Some," Ghyll said. "If their magic is strong."

"Then maybe Lorelei *is* the harpy," Adriane concluded unhappily.

"No, no, no!" Emily shook her head.

"The Dark Sorceress would send only the most powerful of her magic trackers to this world," Ghyll warned. "It is possible that a powerful harpy could make itself look like a unicorn."

"So you're saying this so-called unicorn could be something else in disguise," Kara said. "Something evil."

"It's not just possible — it's likely," Ghyll replied. "You have seen a real unicorn?"

"Yes," Kara answered.

"Then you know this is not unicorn behavior. What kind of unicorn would cause this kind of trouble?"

"Good question," Adriane murmured, shooting Emily a sidelong glance.

"No," Emily protested, overwhelmed by all the new information.

"Then why did she just disappear?" a quiffle asked.

"Why is she hiding?" a brimbee added.

"I don't know," Emily replied, exasperated. "Maybe Lorelei is different." She was surprised and a little annoyed at the way her friends were acting. "It's not like we've met hundreds of unicorns. How do we know they all act alike? People don't. Just look at you two, for example." She gestured at Adriane and Kara.

Kara shook her head impatiently. "Whatever. The point is, unicorn or not, your new friend has been acting — well, odd."

"So what?" Emily argued. "The *point* is, I don't care what she is. I know she's in trouble, and I know I have to help!"

"We're the ones in trouble," Adriane said bluntly. "If any more magical creatures go bursting out in public, the Ravenswood Wildlife Preserve is history!"

Emily frowned and picked at the lush grass growing beside the stream. Adriane was right. If they couldn't control the animals at the preserve, how were they supposed to keep it from being shut down and Adriane from losing her home?

"It wasn't Lorelei's fault," she blurted. "She was just confused. She was trying to find me. Anyway, nobody got hurt."

"Just barely," Adriane said, her brow set in a stubborn line. "It's not like we don't have enough problems to deal with right now as it is."

She didn't go into detail, but Emily knew exactly what her friend was thinking about, because they were all thinking about it. They were running out of time to replace the dreamcatcher. Horrible images flashed unbidden through her mind — the gaping jaw of the monstrous manticore, the evil glare of the Dark Sorceress — and she shuddered.

"We can't control how the portal opens and closes," Adriane said, standing up and facing the crowd. "But when the dreamcatcher was there, at least it kept anything evil out. As long as the portal remains unprotected, we're all in danger from something else slipping through."

"If anyone sees anything unusual, it should be reported to Storm or Lyra right away," Kara said.

"But until we get some answers, we give Lorelei the benefit of the doubt," Adriane announced, giving Emily a smile. "One thing I do know," she continued, putting her hand in Emily's. "Whatever happens, we stand together with Emily."

Everyone voiced agreement.

"That okay with you, Sherlock?" Adriane asked Kara.

"Absolutely, Watson," Kara replied, folding her hand over Adriane's and Emily's.

Emily smiled gratefully, feeling the magic of friendship flow through her. Deep inside her, she also felt the bond tighten between herself and Lorelei. She knew something had happened to Lorelei, something terrible and traumatic. If only the unicorn would trust her enough to tell her about it.

Until then, they could only wait for the monster to make its next move.

Chapter 10

Sun streamed through the large windows of the library in Ravenswood Manor, illuminating the rich red of the mahogany shelves and the rows upon rows of leather-bound books. Emily paced back and forth, thinking. Adriane sat at the computer console, logging in the list of new arrivals and running through pages of E-mails that had backed up over the past few days. Even if the tours weren't making much of an impact, the Website had been a big hit, attracting friends from all over the world.

"Em, Meilin sends you her regards," Adriane called out. "Here's one from Max in Acapulco. He thinks his dog is talking again."

"That's silly — animals don't talk," Ozzie commented, lazily. He was sunning himself on the window ledge.

The door opened and Kara bounded in. "Hey, kids, I've got good news and bad news. The good news is everyone congratulated me on the cool mascot at yesterday's game, even if it was just a horse with a party hat on its head." She winked.

Emily winced. She was beginning to wish it *was* just a party hat and not a real unicorn horn.

"And the bad news?" Adriane asked.

"The bad news is Mrs. Windor — she's on a rampage. She wants an inspection."

"What?" Adriane was outraged. "That's all we need — Mrs. Windor snooping around out here!"

"What we need is the council's permission to set up the Ravenswood benefit concert," Kara reminded her. "The only way we get it is if she thinks we have everything under control."

Adriane sprang to her feet. "We've got harpies, wommels, and flobbins!"

Ozzie perked up. "Harpies, wommels, and flobbins? Oh, my!"

"The benefit concert will put Ravenswood on the map!" Kara pointed out. "Besides, she's coming whether we like it or not."

"Well, everyone is accounted for," Adriane said. Then she looked at Emily, adding, "Except for Lorelei."

"Emily, you've *got* to find her," Kara said.

"I know," Emily said.

❧　　❧　　❧

Emily paused at the treeline and glanced back. With a sigh, she turned away and continued on into the woods. She needed time to think, to process everything she'd learned.

At least they knew what they were dealing with: a harpy. That was what she'd seen. But was it following her, or was it after Lorelei?

Despite their support, her friends were not sure Lorelei was what she seemed to be. And who could blame them? Since coming through the portal, Lorelei had demonstrated complete lack of control over her magic. The unicorn had uprooted trees and flung rocks around, busted into a football game, and beheaded a mascot — not to mention leading Emily herself on more than one wild-goose chase. Still, nothing could erase the memory of the connection she had felt with the beautiful wild creature. Emily felt Lorelei's pain as the unicorn felt hers. There was no way she could be anything but good!

Emily sank down onto a boulder just off the trail, her head swirling with so many questions she couldn't think straight. She buried her face in her hands. This was too much for her. She'd have been better off staying in Colorado, better off if she'd never heard of the magic web or quiffles or unicorns or any of the rest of it. If only this wasn't so hard. . . .

Mmwwnngg.

A quiet chord, like a question, sang out from somewhere nearby. Emily lifted her head. "Hello?" she whispered uncertainly.

Mmmwwnngggg.

Emily stood up. Her jewel was glowing. As she watched, the rainbow colors grew brighter and brighter until they flowed together into a pale, almost clear white light.

When the chord came again, Emily turned toward it. For a second she hesitated, thinking of how deceptive the sounds of the harpy could be.

For some reason, her father's voice floated into her head — *Don't be afraid to really feel it.*

She *had* dared to feel, to connect with Lorelei, and now she had to follow through on that connection. Lorelei was calling to her, needed her. That was enough to convince her that the risk was worth it.

She stepped forward, following the music. It led her off the trail and through the woods. After a few minutes, she saw a brighter patch of sunlight ahead. She pushed through and emerged into a large meadow.

Lorelei was standing there, waiting for her. She looked magnificent. Her coat was white as snow; her long, silky mane was blowing in the breeze; and atop her forehead, her long, diamondlike horn sparkled in the sunlight. Emily glanced around quickly, realizing they were in the portal meadow.

Lorelei stared at her. Emily stared back, holding her breath, afraid that the unicorn would run away. Slowly she sat down in the tall grass, crossing her legs in front of her. It was up to Lorelei now. Emily had answered her call, but she wasn't going to chase her anymore.

For a long, breathless moment, the two stared at each other.

Then Lorelei stepped forward. She walked up to Emily and gazed down at her. She exhaled in a long sigh, and inside her head Emily heard a breath of tinkling bells, with a barely audible word wrapped inside the notes: *"Emily."*

"I'm here," Emily whispered.

Lorelei knelt down in the grass, then sank to the ground. With another long sigh, she lowered her head, resting it in Emily's lap.

Emily stared, transfixed by the beauty of the unicorn. The wondrous crystalline horn sparkled just inches from her face. Hardly daring to breathe, she raised her hand and stroked the unicorn's silky head. Lorelei trembled but stayed where she was. Tiny bursts of magical energy danced around the horn.

"What happened, Lorelei?" Emily asked.

Lorelei shuddered again. A burst of melody swirled from the horn, as bright, white-hot emotions seared an image in Emily's mind: pathways of stars, reaching endlessly into the distance.

Emily squeezed her eyes shut, her head pounding from the intensity of the feelings. "Tell me. It's all right."

Lorelei raised her head and gazed at Emily, her eyes filled with despair. This time the words floated into Emily's mind in somber harmony, like a dirge, a horrible, swirling mass of notes in a minor key, so sad her eyes immediately filled with tears.

"... *the circle is broken ...*"

In her mind, Emily saw a circular pathway of stars crumbling. Between smoking, gaping holes was the blackness of nothing. All at once it became clear. The map of stars was an image of the magic web itself, the system of pathways, connecting worlds, allowing magic to flow from one place to another.

This time the music was little more than a breath of melody.

"... *I am ashamed ...*"

Emily shook her head, more confused than ever. "I don't understand."

She waited. A second later, the images started to come.

Lorelei, dancing joyously along a circle of stars and gleaming threads. Music and magic radiating from her, from her beautiful horn. As she danced, magic from her horn wove the stars into patterns, creating new pathways, and joy filled her.

"You make the web?" Emily asked.

"Unicorns heal the web and keep it strong. Our magic weaves the strands."

The next image shook Emily as she watched a spiral of web collapse upon itself. Strands disintegrated, falling away, vanishing.

Lorelei trembled. *"I lost my magic."*

Emily hesitated, afraid that her next question would send the unicorn running off again. But she needed to know. "What happened to your horn?" she whispered.

She felt the unicorn's body tense. But Lorelei stayed where she was. Her limpid eyes closed, and she breathed out a long, weary, out-of-tune sigh.

A dark, sickly-green wave spreading, blotting out stars . . . darkness engulfing Lorlelei, covering the unicorn, trapping it in a net of green fire.

A tall figure in dark robes, long silver hair slashed by lightning.

Emily's eyes flew open. "The Sorceress!" she cried.

The web became weaker and weaker, damaged parts unraveling like a badly frayed rope.

Lorelei breathed out another sad, aching chord.

"It is my fault. Soon the destruction will spread all across the web. I have failed."

"How could this happen?" Emily blurted, still confused.

Lorelei hung her head in shame.

More images burst into Emily's mind, so fast she could hardly follow them.

An exhausted Lorelei, brought before the Sorceress in a dark place. Two monstrous ogres standing on either side of the unicorn.

The Sorceress giving a sharp nod. The beasts lifting a huge, savage-looking sword. The vicious blade caught the reflection of golden fire as it hung in the air, poised over the unicorn like a guillotine.

Emily squeezed her hands against her ears as an unearthly shriek filled her head. A scream of sheer anguish, terror, and humiliation as the blade slashed downward.

"No!" she cried. The unicorn's scream exploded inside of Emily's head, a deafening chorus of agony and defeat. Emily cried out along with Lorelei, falling to the brittle grass.

But the images kept coming.

Laughing triumphantly, the Dark Sorceress held up her prize — the gleaming, crystalline horn of the unicorn.

Lorelei, hornless now, running in wild-eyed terror, staggering hopelessly over the web, not seeing or caring where she was going, tumbling at last through a portal.

"Oh, no!" Emily gasped in horror.

She stared at the unicorn, tears streaming down her face. Lorelei was gazing at her sadly.

Emily gently reached out and touched Lorelei's horn.

"I didn't know it would grow back."

"But it wasn't your fault," Emily said gently.

"I must fix what is broken."

"You mean the web?"

"That is what unicorns do. I must repair the circle, or all will be in danger."

"But is that creature still after you?"

"It hunts me still, but I must fix what has become undone before it's too late."

Lorelei got to her feet. She stood back and raised her head high. Music spun from her horn, sparkling in the air, shimmering and glittering.

A sudden wind whipped Emily's curly hair around her head. The sparks of sound flared, bursting into bright lights. She shielded her eyes as the light grew brighter and brighter, filling the meadow, and finally exploding into bolts of lightning.

Vvvzzzzzzzzzzzzzzzzzz!

The air itself seemed to rip apart as a huge,

dark opening yawned where a moment ago there had been nothing but fallen leaves and empty air.

Emily braced herself against the wind.

She got to her feet, staring transfixed into the tunnel of swirling stars — the magic web.

"*I must go back.*" Lorelei's voice was frantic, terrified.

"No!" Emily shouted above the wild, zinging sound of the spinning vortex. "It's too dangerous!"

The unicorn shuddered, sending out music that filled Emily's head with fragmented and off-key chords and words that were little more than broken cries. "*We must go on.*"

"Yes," Emily said. Her heart constricted with fear, but she stood firm.

Something tickled at her mind. A snaking sound penetrating into her very being. Music, so calm, so soothing . . .

Lorelei snorted and took a step back.

Emily turned and faced the monster.

The harpy stood not three feet away, its ghoulish face white as death. Blazing eyes glowed like dying embers.

Run, Lorelei, Emily wanted to cry out, but she couldn't. She couldn't move.

"Thank you for bringing me the unicorn," the thing said, smiling through broken yellow teeth.

Lorelei looked at Emily, her liquid eyes stricken and confused.

"No," Emily cried to Lorelei. "I didn't know! I didn't know it was following me."

"I will take the beast now," the harpy interrupted in its silky, slithering voice. "We have work to finish." The creature's arm emerged from under its cloak, revealing a glittering horn. It shone with a dull green glow.

Lorelei stepped back in horror, transfixed by the magic of her own horn, now diseased by the poison of Black Fire.

"Emily!"

Emily turned toward the shout and saw Kara and Adriane running toward her. Ozzie, Storm, Ghyll, Lyra, and dozens of other creatures were right behind them.

"You were right, Kara. The portal's opened!" Ozzie cried.

"We saw it open on the computer," Kara yelled. "We have to —"

Wreeeeeeaaaaaaaaaarrrrrrnnnnn!

A burst of chilling, bone-rattling music exploded over the meadow, drowning out the rest of Kara's words. Emily turned and saw the harpy waving the green unicorn horn.

Lorelei reared, terrified.

"You've got to stop it!" Emily shouted to her friends. "The monster is taking Lorelei!"

Stormbringer was the first to react. With a savage growl, the mistwolf leaped after the monstrous harpy, teeth bared.

The harpy turned, its mesmerizing eyes focusing on Storm. Its wild song changed suddenly, becoming softer, eerily hypnotic. Storm skidded to a stop right in front of the creature. She stared at it for a long moment. Then her tongue lolled out of her head, and she sank down onto her haunches. Her golden eyes glazed over, and she stared at the harpy adoringly.

Emily realized what was happening. "Wake up!" she screamed at Storm as the harpy glided closer, still singing. "Don't listen to the music!" When the mistwolf didn't respond, she turned toward her friends. "You've got to help her!"

To her horror, she saw that her friends were standing in place, staring trance-like toward the harpy. Kara's mouth was hanging open slightly, and Adriane was swaying unsteadily to the rhythm of the creature's song. Ozzie and Ghyll were leaning on each other, their eyes half closed, while Lyra purred loudly and rolled onto her back.

Oh, no! Emily felt her own heartbeat slowing, matching itself to the beat of the harpy's captivating song. Her friends were already bewitched, and now she was falling under its evil spell, too.

Maybe I should . . . just . . . give up, Emily thought fuzzily. Easier . . . just to . . . go along with it.

"Lorelei," she cried, summoning one last ounce of resolve. Her voice, too, seemed overtaken by the harpy's powerful musical magic, and she sang out, "Lor-e-lei."

Music exploded in a painful jumble of noise as the unicorn struggled to express herself. *Emily, focus on my voice. Stay awake.*

The monster's music changed rhythm, becoming quicker, almost violent, yet still beautiful.

Lorelei's voice in Emily's head broke through the fuzziness, and she managed to shake off most of the effects of the spell. However, the others were still entranced. The harpy hovered in the air between Emily and the portal, grinning as it continued to sing.

The unicorn was trapped. She snorted and tried to bolt, her eyes rolling back with fear. Magic crackled and popped. It formed a ring of shimmering blackish-green energy around her.

Emily watched as the harpy swept toward Lorelei, skimming just above the grass. Its shadowy dark cloak billowed around its gaunt shoulders, and its yellow teeth formed a hideous grin as its eyes bored into Emily. The unicorn backed away and reared up, her silvery hooves flashing. But the harpy didn't slow. It reached out its arms and wrapped Lorelei in its evil embrace, sweeping her into the portal.

Chapter 11

Wake up!" Emily screamed, running toward her friends. "You've got to fight it!"

She shook Kara by the shoulders. The blond girl stared listlessly, as if looking right through Emily.

Behind them the animals came running into the field.

"Everyone!" Emily called out. "I need your help!" She pointed to Adriane, Kara, Ozzie, Storm, Lyra, and Ghyll. "Form a circle around them."

Emily raised her jewel and concentrated on drawing in the magic of the animals around her. The rainbow jewel flared blue, and Emily held it before Kara, bathing her in bright light.

Kara's eyes cleared, and she looked at Emily. "What happened?" She blinked.

"The harpy put us under its spell," Emily explained.

With Kara's help, Emily quickly used the power of the rainbow jewel and their animal friends to break the spell. One by one, each shook off the lingering wisps of hypnotic music.

"Where's Lorelei?" Adriane asked, looking at the spinning portal still hanging open in the air before them.

"The harpy took her," Emily told her, frantically. "We have to go after her!"

Adriane shook her head. "Are you crazy?"

"It's starting to close," Ozzie called out.

The portal was spinning in on itself, shrinking.

"Emily," Adriane said, "we can't just jump through! What if we end up in the shadowlands of Aldenmor — or worse?"

Emily tried to explain how important this was. "The whole magic web is at stake," she told them, her voice thick with tension and fear. "Lorelei is supposed to protect the web. If she can't repair it quickly, it will continue to disintegrate!"

"But going into the portal — it's too dangerous," Ozzie said.

"I'm going through!" Emily said defiantly.

"How will we find Lorelei even if we do go through?" Kara asked.

Emily didn't have an answer to that one.

"I know how." Ghyll stepped forward. "I am a fairy creature, a magic tracker. If we go right now, I can find the unicorn on the web."

"I don't know," Ozzie said. "It sounds risky."

"I went through once before," Adriane reminded the others. "My wolf stone protected me."

"What will happen to the web, to Aldenmor and the Fairimentals, if we don't help Lorelei?" Emily asked. "We have to decide now!"

She looked to the portal. In a few moments it would be gone.

"One jumps, we all jump!" Adriane announced.

"Why I listen to you two is beyond me," Kara said.

"Storm, you and Lyra stay here and take care of the others," Adriane ordered.

"I will contact you if I do not hear from you," Storm told her.

"Hold onto me," Gyhll said.

The three girls grabbed hold of Ghyll as he took a mighty hop.

"Wait for me!" Ozzie yelled.

Emily reached out. Ozzie leaped and grabbed hold as they jumped through the misty veil and flew into the portal.

The flobbin drifted in space. Kara, Emily, Adriane, and Ozzie floated alongside. They seemed to be encased in a gold-and-blue bubble. The amber glow of the wolf stone and the blue-green glow of the rainbow jewel filled the bubble. Outside, streaks of light swept by as the bubble flew across an endless ribbon of stars.

Ghyll was concentrating on the rows of blazing lights that flew toward them. "To the left," he called.

Adriane and Emily shifted their stones to the left, and the bubble turned, careening into a connecting star path.

Emily's eyes were wide with astonishment. Long, wide swaths of stars, like roads in a highway system, spiraled and stretched, searing past them at enormous speed.

"Right!" Ghyll ordered.

The girls shifted their stones, banking the bubble right, where it soared onto another star path, flying out over the vast web.

"This is amazing," Emily exclaimed.

"I remember actually riding on the strands of the web," Kara said, referring to her wild unicorn ride. "But this is intense!"

"Are we there yet?" Ozzie covered his eyes as the bubble dipped, then dropped down a vertical well of stars, spinning upside down and jumping forward once again. "*GarG!*" The ferret was jolted into the air. "Doesn't this thing come with seat belts?"

"Hurry, Ghyll," Emily cried.

"I can only track the unicorn," said the flobbin. "You can increase the speed with your magic."

"Hold on!" Kara touched her fingers to each of

the jewels, and the bubble shot forward like a rocket.

"*Ahh!*" Ozzie cried out.

The bubble sped across the web like a shooting star, arcing toward an intersection of pathways.

"There!" Ghyll called out.

"Where? Which one?" Adriane asked.

"The starway just to the right." He pointed.

Emily and Adriane moved their jewels, and the bubble slid into the approaching pathway. Bouncing slightly, they came to a halt. The bubble flared and disappeared.

Splashes of light danced behind Emily's eyes, inside her head. Music filled the air — bright, brilliant, enormous, and pure, as if the universe itself were singing.

Emily opened her eyes, awestruck. They stood on a wide, circular platform, looking out upon the web itself. The magic web! An endless array of gleaming, starry strands stretched out in every direction, woven into impossibly complex patterns. At every intersection, tiny glittering stars twinkled with pure white energy. When she looked down, Emily realized the platform was made of thousands of tightly woven strands. The platform formed the base of a giant circle, surrounded by walls of intricate patterns of web. Smoke plumed from various places upon the walls. Upon closer inspection, she could see that sections of the web had been burned away. Loose strands unraveled as sparking embers of green glow spread from the edges — Black Fire. Through the gaping holes she could see where sections of starways crumbled and burned, falling away into the black of nothingness. Even the flobbin seemed stunned by the devastation of the ruined web.

"Where are we?" Adriane asked.

"A nexus," Ghyll said quietly.

"A what?"

"There are sections of the web where many paths converge in one place," Ghyll explained. "This is a nexus."

"Like a train station," Emily said.

"If you follow the right path, you can jump to different places, worlds."

"Is it safe here?" Kara asked.

"I've never seen the web destroyed before. It's terrible. And dangerously unstable," Ghyll explained.

"Where is Lorelei?" Emily asked, looking through the smoke that swirled from the base of the wide circle.

Ghyll pointed to a wall, woven thick with strands of web. Clouds of smoke parted to reveal the unicorn standing beside the harpy. Ribbons of glowing light streamed from Lorelei's crystal horn. Like a magnet, the pale green horn in the harpy's hand pulled the flowing magic toward it, warping the ribbons and sending them streaming toward the wall of web. A dreadful, whining music blared from the green horn. As the magic hit the wall, the silvery strands withered, sending up plumes of ugly, greenish smoke. Sections of web shifted, raveled, and unraveled, reconfiguring into a different pattern. The harpy laughed, buzzing with its evil song.

"What are they doing?" Kara asked.

"It looks like the harpy is using Lorelei's magic to reweave the web, to make a new pathway from the connecting portals here," Ghyll said.

Lorelei stood entranced, magic and music flowing from her horn in rich, deep, sad notes.

"Lorelei!" she called sharply.

The harpy swung to face them. The horn in its hand blazed a sickly green. "You are too late. The unicorn is under my spell. I will soon have the right pathway open."

The harpy began crooning soft music, beautiful, beguiling music.

"You know what the Sorceress wants, don't you, Ghyll?" it said to the flobbin.

"What are you talking about?" Adriane asked, feeling the enchantment of the harpy closing in.

"That fairy creature is not what it seems," the harpy hissed. "Who do you think turned him into a flobbin?"

"No!" Ghyll hopped forward. The bubble they were encased in dissolved. "You don't have to tell them!"

"Why not?" the harpy crooned. "It is time for secrets to be revealed. Ghyll is after the unicorn for himself, aren't you?"

Ghyll remained silent, looking at the others.

"I knew it!" yelled Ozzie, stomping over and kicking the flobbin. "Cousin Brommy doesn't have the sirens of Waterknell. It's in the hall of elders! Everyone knows that!"

"So you tricked us, too," Emily said to the flobbin.

"I can explain —" Ghyll started.

"You wanted to send the unicorn to the Dark Sorceress!" Adriane yelled.

"It's not like —" Ghyll tried again.

"Of course it is," the harpy sang.

Emily felt the hypnotic magic reaching for them, trying to trap them under its spell. "Start yelling, singing — anything to break the spell!" she cried out.

Taking a deep breath, Emily opened her mouth and began to sing. At first, her voice was shaky and uncertain. As her confidence grew, the rainbow jewel flared with brilliant blue light. Colorful star-bursts appeared all around her as Emily felt her own music strengthening Lorelei.

The horn in the harpy's hand sparked wildly as the connection with the unicorn faltered. The harpy narrowed its eyes and raised its voice.

Hopelessness gripped Emily in an icy grasp. Was she strong enough to save Lorelei?

Then Ozzie's reedy voice piped up, thin but clear. A moment later, Ghyll started croaking along in a deep bass.

Adriane stepped forward and raised her wolf stone. She tilted her head back and howled, the wolf song ringing out, strong and sure. The harpy's magic wavered, the green horn dimmed. Kara looked at her friends, then stepped forward and opened her mouth, letting out a screech that made everyone cover their ears.

The harpy faltered, almost dropping the horn in fright. It cringed as Kara's voice hit it with a sudden, strong, magic force.

"Keep singing, Kara!" Emily yelled over her shoulder as she ran to Lorelei.

"La, *laaaa!*" Kara sang out.

"Go, girl!" Adriane called.

"La, la, *LAAAAAA!*"

The harpy turned away, trying to shield itself from the awful music bombarding it.

Emily. Doleful, forlorn music filled Emily's head. She could feel that Lorelei was deeply traumatized by having her own horn turned on her. How could Emily hope to help the unicorn through this?

If the spirit does not desire healing, Gran's voice said in her head, *no true healing can take place. If you want to help, you have to be willing to give the kind of help that's needed.*

Emily hugged the unicorn close. "I know how you feel," she said. "I lost my family — the life I was so sure of. My parents split up, and I thought that was the end of everything good and safe."

"Laa, *LAAAAAA*!!!!" Kara was advancing on the harpy, forcing the monster to cower in pain.

Emily focused on the unicorn. She had to make her understand, make her realize she wasn't alone.

"But just when I was ready to give up, I found Ravenswood, met Adriane and Kara and Ozzie," she went on. "And I realized I had magic inside of me. Strong magic that couldn't be taken away no matter what happened."

"My horn is everything."

"No, that's just it!" Emily remembered the confusion she had felt in Lorelei before her horn had come back — and also the power, the beautiful, strong, harmonious power lying just beneath the surface chaos.

"Your horn may focus your magic, like our jewels." She held up her wrist and stared at the rainbow stone, which was glowing softly with pastel colors. "But the real magic is inside of you. Right here." Emily touched her hand to Lorelei's chest, covering the unicorn's beating heart.

The music in Emily's head was uncertain.

Emily held the rainbow jewel out toward the unicorn's chest. Lorelei hesitated, then stepped forward to meet her touch. As soon as the jewel on Emily's wrist made contact, there was an explosion of chords, strong, magical bursts of sound that filled her and surrounded her, echoing across the nexus.

Aaaaaaaaarrrrrrrrrrrrrrrhhhhhh!

The harpy's cry rolled toward them in a powerful, deadly wave of sound and energy as it flung its song like a weapon. Emily braced herself just in time as the wave barreled over her, but out of the corner of her eye she saw a section of platform flare with green fire and dissolve. Kara wobbled and slipped, her left leg disappearing into the nothingness!

"Kara!" Emily screamed, watching in horror as Kara lost her grip and slipped farther.

Emily and Adriane lunged toward their friend. With a snort, the unicorn's eyes flew open, and she spun around and raced in their direction as well.

But Ghyll got there first. Locking his blue flippers around a strand of web, he flicked out his long purple tongue, wrapped it around Kara's arm, and hauled her up.

"I'm okay," she said shakily once she was back atop the web. She glanced down quickly and gulped. "No problem."

Lorelei's hooves flashed with golden fire as she danced across the hole in the web. Everywhere she touched, the broken strands healed, coming back together and vibrating with life.

The harpy waved the green horn and let out a burst of angry sound, sending another strong wave of magic slamming into the group.

Another hole ripped open right next to them. Adriane and Ozzie scattered to avoid falling into emptiness.

"Stop!" Lorelei's voice rang in all their heads.

The harpy turned to her, eyes burning with greed and hate.

"Do not hurt them."

"Then give me what I want, unicorn."

"I will do as you ask."

"No, Lorelei, you can't," Emily cried.

"Do not interfere," the harpy commanded. "The unicorn will finish what we have started. Her horn was removed once. Do you want it removed again?"

Emily felt waves of fear coming from the unicorn at the mention of her horn.

She watched as Lorelei walked to the wall of tightly woven strands. The unicorn shook her head, waving her crystal horn at the web. A lovely melody drifted through the nexus. Sections of the wall shifted, coming apart, unraveling. Strands rewound themselves into a new pattern.

And a bluish-white whirlpool appeared — and opened.

"Yes, that's it!" the harpy cried gleefully.

"It looks like another portal," Ozzie said.

This portal was about half the size of the one at Ravenswood. Blue haze covered the opening as streams of smoke fell eerily upon the nexus floor.

The harpy turned in triumph, raising the green horn high. "It is done. The path has been revealed."

"Go. You have what you want," Lorelei said.

An evil grin spread across the harpy's face. "You first."

Lorelei stepped back. *"I cannot."*

"You didn't think I would trust you, did you? Just in case you didn't follow the fairy map exactly, you will come with me. Besides, you want to see your home again, don't you?"

The girls looked at each other.

"Please," Lorelei pleaded. *"I cannot return home in shame."*

"Where does the portal lead?" Emily called out.

The harpy's look of malice made the girls cringe. "Where? To where all dreams come true. The home of all magic: Avalon."

Whirling around, the harpy flew toward the unicorn, knocking them both into the portal in a flash of foul, greenish energy. In an instant they were gone.

Avalon?

"If the sorceress finds a way to get the magic of Avalon, all is lost," Ozzie cried, jumping up and down. "Everything the Fairimentals have worked for will have been for nothing!"

Kara, Emily, and Adriane stood side by side, looking at the misty opening that would lead them to the most mysterious and magical of all places.

"We must save the unicorn," Ghyll said firmly.

"We've come this far," Adriane said.

"Just one more," Emily added.

"One jumps, we all jump!" Kara said.

"Piece of pie," Ozzie concluded.

Emily reached out and clasped hands with Adriane and Kara. "Let's do it!" she exclaimed.

The five of them surged toward the portal. As they reached it, Emily took a deep breath, squeezed her eyes shut, and jumped.

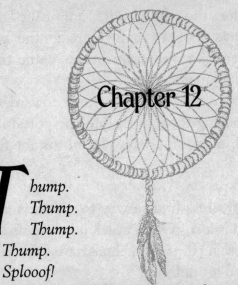

Chapter 12

*T*hump.
Thump.
Thump.
Thump.
Splooof!

Emily opened her eyes. Her friends were scattered around her — in a glistening, gleaming dreamworld. Enormous snowflakes, soft and pillowy white, drifted lazily up, down, and all around them. When one landed on her arm, instead of cold she felt a soft, soothing warmth that spread through her with a glorious sense of well-being.

"I . . . know this place," she whispered.

Adriane shook her head, staring out at the silvery-blue landscape. They were in a valley surrounded by rolling blue hills. Thick, billowy purple clouds floated around them, releasing the giant snowflakes. The valley floor was covered in soft, fine sand that sparkled like quartz. "It must be another world," she replied, her voice hushed with awe. "Like Earth, or Aldenmor."

"This can't be Avalon!" Kara said.

"I don't know," Emily whispered, looking for Lorelei. "I saw this place in a dream. I think I'm supposed to be here."

"Are you all right?" Ghyll asked Ozzie, who was scraping himself up from the sand.

"What's it to you?" Ozzie kicked the flobbin.

Ghyll looked flustered. "I'm sorry I lied to you."

"Yeah, sure. Save it for the Sorceress!" Ozzie brushed himself off.

Just then the sounds of music blared in the distance. Harsh, deep, piercing blasts, clashing like sounds of battle.

"Lorelei!" Emily exclaimed. "Come on!"

The five ran across the fine sand and rounded a bend in the silver hills. Suddenly a hideous scream ripped through the landscape. An overwhelming eruption of energy sent the snowflakes skidding away.

In front of them, Lorelei stood, facing the harpy. The monster was pointing the sickly green horn at the unicorn.

"You tricked me!" it screamed, enraged. "This is not Avalon!"

"No, it is not."

"Open the right portal. Now!" The harpy waved the green horn frantically. Sparks of fire jumped from the horn, but before they could reach Lorelei, they seemed to lose focus, splintering away in the misty breeze.

"Lorelei!" Emily called out.

The harpy watched the girls approach. It hissed, its ghoulish white face drawn taut and twisted with fury.

It turned the green horn at them, trying to build a wave of magic. Emily felt the wave start. She knew the feeling. She had felt this before, at the football field and in the woods. "Stand back," she warned the others.

Adriane shot her arm up, releasing a trail of golden fire from her jewel. She spun around, whipping the fire into a ring of blazing magic. Feet planted firmly, she threw the ring at the harpy. The ring arced through the air and slammed into the harpy with an explosion of golden light.

It staggered back, trying to deflect the force of the magic with the green horn. Instead, the horn absorbed the golden fire. The harpy pulled the horn down, sending the magic back at the group.

"Look out!" Ozzie yelled.

Everyone dove to the ground as the wave crashed over them with an eerie, wailing sound.

The harpy pulled the horn back, straining to lock onto more magic from the girls' stones.

Adriane jumped to her feet, arms raised for another attack.

Ghyll bounced back up. "Wait! The horn will draw magic from your jewels. You mustn't use them."

"You seem to know an awful lot about unicorns, frog face!" Ozzie yelled.

"I have studied them for years," Ghyll told the ferret.

"Well, study *this*!" Ozzie kicked the flobbin again.

"If one way doesn't work, try another," Emily called out.

Suddenly Lorelei raised her head and released clear, clean sounds of music. The notes echoed over the barren terrain.

The harpy held the green horn high. "I will control your magic!"

Lorelei's music spilled across the valley, strong and pure. Achingly beautiful, the song wove notes of pure feeling, echoing the joy, sorrow, and loss inside the unicorn.

Emily recognized the song instantly. It was the song she had heard in her dream. Her song.

She started to sing, adding her voice to the

melody, raising her hands for her friends to join in. Once again, one by one, her friends began to sing with her. Adriane grasped her hand and reached out for Kara. Emily felt the familiar surge of power swirling through the three of them. Sparks flew off her rainbow jewel, and she saw the amber glow of Adriane's wolf stone. Kara's fingers touched the jewels on her friends' wrists and the magic exploded into a blaze of power. The music swirled and eddied around them, gathering energy as it grew. Huge snowflakes skipped in place, moving with the rhythm of the song, glowing with soft colors. Lorelei added layers of exquisitely sweet harmony in jewel-like chords.

The harpy kept the green horn raised in front of it, trying to draw in the magic. "Yes, send me your magic and I will use it!"

The song built, riding the crest of intense rhythmic waves. Energy thrummed all around them.

And Emily danced, twirling and spinning, feeling the music sweep her away. Her heart felt it would break as she opened herself fully to the unicorn's feelings. She felt the pain and frustration, the sadness and shame, and the pure wonder and joy of the dance. The music skyrocketed into fireworks of power as she felt the strongest emotions ever from Lorelei. It wasn't a song of anger or hatred, it wasn't even a song of love that Lorelei sung. It was stronger, pushing the magic faster and farther than Emily could have believed possible. Emily spun faster, flashing on her own life — her father, sad and desperately searching for fulfillment; her mother, worried and afraid for her daughter — and suddenly she knew what she was feeling from the unicorn's music. It was a song of forgiveness.

Emily let the song ring out in a rush of feeling. The magic swirled, becoming a lightning bolt of power, and slammed into the harpy, shattering the green horn into a thousand fragments.

The harpy screamed and collapsed to the ground.

Squinting against the blast, Emily saw Lorelei standing over the dark, prone form of the harpy. With a swirl of the unicorn's head, magic erupted from the crystal horn, spinning into the air. The sparkles formed a circle, and a portal opened before them.

The harpy scrambled to its feet, clutching its hand and cowering in fear.

"Destroy me, now," it hissed. "The Sorceress will, if you don't."

"Without the power of my horn, you are no threat."

"Why couldn't I harness it? Tell me!" the harpy begged.

"Some things cannot be taken."

"I don't understand."

"*I know you don't. Be gone, harpy!*"

"Allow me!" Ghyll hopped over and bounded into the harpy, knocking it into the portal with his big blue belly. With a nod of her head, Lorelei swirled the portal closed, leaving only slight wisps of blue smoke hanging in the air.

"Now, *that's* teamwork, frog boy!" Ozzie jumped up, slapping his paw against the flobbin's flipper.

Before she could catch her breath, Emily saw the unicorn walking toward her, white flakes drifting in her wake.

"*The dark creature will not hurt you anymore.*" The unicorn's musical voice was strong but anxious. "*But its evil work remains. I must repair what was destroyed.*"

Suddenly Emily understood. "*You* didn't fail!" she told Lorelei. "The harpy destroyed the web, not you."

"*You were right. Without my horn, I could not focus my magic.*"

"It's not your fault," Emily said. "The harpy used you. It tried to steal your magic." She knew that the harpy had used her, too. But Lorelei had forgiven her, even when the unicorn had almost given up on herself.

"*You showed me that,*" Lorelei told her, gazing deeply into her eyes. "*And now I must do what I was meant to — repair the damaged web.*"

Emily nodded. "Tell us how we can help."

"You cannot stay on the web. It is not safe for you. Your place is at Ravenswood, Emily, with your friends."

"Can you get another unicorn to help you, to repair the damage before it's too late?"

Lorelei shook her head sadly. *"The web is too vast. Any of the others would need to leave their own areas unprotected."*

Emily bit her lip. Things sounded worse than she and her friends had imagined. They had all known that the Dark Sorceress was ruthless — that she would do anything to gain control of all the magic. She was so fixated on her goal that she didn't care who or what she destroyed along the way — even the web itself!

"So the harpy tried to use your horn to force you to find Avalon," Adriane said.

"The Sorceress took my horn, but she could not harness its power. She gave it to the harpy to use, because like unicorns, harpies use musical magic. But my magic could not work for the harpy, and its attempts to use it damaged the web."

"What would happen if the web wasn't repaired?" Kara asked.

"The web connects everything. If it were to fail, the very fabric of life would be in jeopardy."

Lorelei's expression was somber but determined. Sparks danced from her horn, lighting up nearby snowflakes with bursts of color. With a wave of her head, she spun open another portal. Light from the swirling mist spilled over the pillowy bluish-white ground.

"Is this Avalon?" Emily asked, looking around at the stark landscape.

"No, this is my special place."

"I've seen it before, in my dreams."

"In friendship we are bound."

"I'll always be around," Emily finished, smiling.

"Do you know where Avalon is?" Kara asked. Everyone looked at her.

"What?" she said sheepishly. She shrugged. "Maybe she knows."

"My home is Avalon, but you cannot get there through portals."

"But you go there," Kara pressed.

"I can run on the web itself."

"And —?"

"Have patience, young mages." Lorelei's eyes sparkled.

"I understand you must go," Emily said to the unicorn. "I'm only glad that you are better."

"You must go now, as well." Lorelei nodded to the portal.

"Um, I hate to intrude," Ozzie said. "But that thing goes to Ravenswood, right?"

Lorelei shook her head. *"It leads to another nexus."*

"Then how are we gonna get home?" the ferret asked anxiously.

Lorelei looked uncertain. *"Only a unicorn can navigate the web . . . or . . ."* She trailed off, her song fading.

Emily leaned in closer. "Lorelei, what?"

The unicorn bowed her head. Her horn stretched toward Emily. *". . . or you must use the magic of a unicorn."*

For a second Emily wasn't sure what Lorelei meant. "Your horn?" she cried.

"The horn of a unicorn gives the one who possesses it magic of any type she desires."

"But didn't it work for the Dark Sorceress?" Emily said, confused.

"The Sorceress took the horn from me. It was never truly hers. The magic of a unicorn can only be used when it is freely given. That is our secret."

Emily looked to her friends

"It's up to you, Emily," Kara said. "I couldn't keep my unicorn jewel, because it was never given to me."

Emily looked at Adriane.

"I've seen the Black Fire and what it's doing to Aldenmor," the black-haired girl said. "We have to get back to Ravenswood to help."

Still Emily hesitated, images flooding her mind. Lorelei broken and scared in the forest. The deadly, gleaming blade of the Dark Sorceress flashing ruthlessly down. The sickening, charred remains of the web where the harpy's evil music had destroyed its magic.

Then a different image flashed into her mind. Lorelei dancing across the web, repairing and strengthening it — doing what she was created to do, horn or no horn, filled with the magic that was inside of her.

Taking a deep breath, Emily reached out and grasped the horn. A dizzying, jangling feeling overwhelmed all of her senses, and she felt herself falling.

She opened her eyes and saw that she was holding the horn in her hand. It sparkled in the white light filtering through the snowflakes.

"I am always here." Lorelei nudged Emily's chest with her nose, pressing against the beating of her heart.

She stepped back, reared, and spun around, then raced away. With a mighty leap, she vanished.

"Good-bye," Emily whispered, her heart twisting with loss.

"Come on," Adriane said. "Let's go."

She led the way toward the portal. Emily lifted Ozzie onto her shoulder and briefly patted Ghyll's warty neck. Making sure everyone was right beside her, she took a breath and stepped through — into darkness.

Emily stood in the blackness. The darkness felt almost solid, as if it were literally pressing against her skin. It was as if they had been transported to a place where light did not exist. Never had she experienced such total darkness. Her only solace was the horn she clutched tightly in her hand.

"I can't make my wolf stone glow," Adriane said, concerned.

"Me, either," Emily said, straining her eyes in the dark for even a glimpse of the rainbow jewel at her wrist.

It seemed the darkness had sucked the light even from their magic jewels.

"Stay close, everyone," she said into the void.

"That'll be easy," Ozzie said, clutching her neck.

Emily thought about what Lorelei had told her. The magic of the horn had been given to her. It would bring what she desired most. "Lead us home," she whispered, raising the horn high. "Keep us safe."

The horn flashed in the darkness, and as her eyes adjusted, she saw that it was illuminating a path along the wide strands of the web. She hurried forward, the others following behind, small specks on an infinite highway of stars. Ahead, twinkling lights beckoned, but which one led back home?

Emily called to Lorelei for help. She felt a hint of the unicorn's presence and heard a brief echo of music. Light sparkled from the horn, pulling her, guiding her.

"This way," she whispered. She led them along the web toward the growing stars.

"Ahh! Watch it, ferret! You tickled me!" Kara called out.

"That wasn't me!"

"Wasn't me," Ghyll said.

"Hey, that tickles!" Ozzie yelled.

"I felt something, too," Adriane said.

"Look, it's the horn," Emily said in wonder.

Long snaky strands flew off the horn. Emily tried to shake them loose. But as she waved the horn, more and more strands began to collect on it, like sparkling gold cotton candy.

The horn began to grow heavy under the weight.

"It's drawing strands of the web," Emily exclaimed.

"Well, hurry, it's falling all over us!" Kara cried, wiping wispy, sparkling strands from her blond hair.

Emily picked up the pace, carefully following

the ghostly path before her. "This way. Everyone stay together!"

At last they came to another nexus. Three portals floated there.

"Which one?" Kara asked uncertainly.

Emily stood and stared, searching for the right answer. "I . . . don't know," she admitted.

"Well, if we end up in China, I'm going to be grounded for a year!" Kara said.

Emily closed her eyes and held the horn up high. She felt Lorelei's magic race through her. The newfound strength of her friend filled her with joy, love, and hope.

"This one." She pointed to the portal in the center.

Grasping hands, paws, and flippers, the friends stepped forward and leaped through the portal together.

Chapter 13

"Ooof!" Ozzie spluttered, landing on Emily's stomach with a thump. "Sorry about that."

"No problem." Emily set the ferret down on the grass. Glancing around, she saw that Kara, Adriane, and Ghyll had tumbled safely through the portal as well.

"You're back!" Stormbringer raced toward them, almost bowling Adriane over as she licked her face.

Adriane giggled and hugged the big wolf tightly.

Lyra ran to Kara and allowed herself to be caught in a big hug.

"Good thing I'm back," Kara said, inspecting the large cat. "You need a shampoo."

"I let myself get extra dirty for you."

"Aww, how sweet!"

"Hey!" Ozzie called out. "It was no picnic for me, either, you know."

Storm and Lyra walked to the ferret, each licking a side of Ozzie's face. Ozzie was lifted into the air by two giant tongues.

"*AKK!* Watch it, furballs!"

Loud cheers, squeaks, roars, and peeps rose over the field as the animals barreled in, crowding around the girls.

"They made it!" a brimbee yelled.

Emily, Adriane, and Kara took a bow.

"Your humble junior mages have returned," Kara announced. "And the harpy is gone!"

Louder cheers erupted from the group.

"Hey, what's that?" Ronif pointed to the portal.

The girls turned and gasped. Long, glowing strands spilled out of the swirling hole, piling up on the ground in a tremendous heap.

"It's strands of the web!" Adriane said.

"They must have come loose from the horn when we jumped through." Emily gazed down at the sparkling, clean horn in her hand. It was her last connection to Lorelei, and she felt a pang of deep sadness when she realized how much she would miss her new friend.

Pop! Pop! Pop! Pop! Pop!

The air exploded in colorful bubbles as five overexcited dragonflies dove into the girls. They made a beeline right for Kara's blond head.

"Oh, no!" Kara clamped her hands on her hair as the dragonflies zipped around her.

Kee-kee! Goldie ecstatically cried out.

"Yeah, hello," Kara said grumpily.

OOoooOOO!!!!

Fred, Barney, Fiona, and Blaze swept past her and fell into the pile of glowing web strands. In a minute, strands went flying everywhere as the little dragons careened about, holding pieces in their tiny beaks.

Emily watched them with wonder. She looked at the horn. *Keep us safe.* She had wished for that with the magic of the horn. "That's it!" she cried out.

"What?" Adriane asked, ducking as Fred flew over, dangling a pile of strands.

"The strands! What better magic is there than the web itself to build a dreamcatcher?"

"You're right!" Adriane exclaimed. "Kara, do your thing!"

"You know," Kara answered snottily, "I'm perfectly capable of doing other *things* besides playing with dragonflies."

"Right," Adriane agreed. "Just do us a favor."

"Yes?"

"Don't sing!"

Emily couldn't help giggling as she watched Kara stomp over to the pile of strands.

"Hey! D-flies! Front and center!" Kara called out.

"*OOOooo, kee-kee.*" Goldie landed on her shoulder, nuzzling into her hair.

"Nuh-uh! No cuddles! Get to work and start spinning!"

"*Oookee-dookee!*" Goldie sprang into the air and started squeaking. The others buzzed with excitement, flocking over the pile of magic strands. Soon the dragonflies were busy weaving a new dream-catcher.

"All righty then," Kara said, wiping her hands together. "Anything else?"

"Gee, let me think." Adriane scratched her chin thoughtfully.

"Um, guys."

The girls looked down at Ozzie. The ferret nodded over to the side of the field where Ghyll sat, hunched over and looking very sad.

Adriane and Emliy looked to Kara.

"What?" Kara stared back, then rolled her eyes. "Okay, let's get this over with."

Ozzie and the girls walked over to the depressed flobbin.

"Hey, big guy," Adriane said.

Ghyll looked up. "Oh, hi."

Look," Kara began. "You helped us save Lorelei, and you did save me from falling into a bottomless void. So . . ." She puckered up. "I'll lay one on ya."

Ghyll looked down again.

"What's wrong, Ghyll?" Emily asked.

"I lied to you all, and I know it wasn't right."

"So why did you do it?" Emily asked.

"The Dark Sorceress turned me into a flobbin, and I thought she would turn me back if I helped her get the unicorn."

"What a chump!" Ozzie said.

"Ozzie!" Emily scolded.

"Sorry," the ferret mumbled.

"So I tried to get you to send it back. I know now that I was wrong. The Sorceress was using me just as she uses everyone and everything. When I saw *her*" — he gestured at Kara — "I figured with her magic, she might be able to change me back without having to get the unicorn involved."

"And Cousin Brommy!" Ozzie said.

"I thought that if you liked me, you might help me and be my friend." The flobbin blinked his big eyes at Ozzie.

"Ghyll, you made a mistake," Emily said. "We all do. But then you helped us. That's what counts. That's what makes friends." She smiled.

"I don't have any friends," the flobbin said sadly. "Who would like a flobbin?"

"Hey! I'm all puckered here!" Kara called out. "Last chance for a magical kiss!"

Ghyll turned sad eyes down to his big flippers.

"I made that up, too. There's no such thing as a magic kiss," he said dolefully.

"Oh, really?" Kara said, eyes narrowed. "You have no idea what you're dealing with, flubber. Girls? Shall we?"

Kara daintily held out her hands. Emily and Adriane stepped closer, allowing Kara to touch their jewels. The wolf stone and the rainbow jewel flared to life, glowing with magical energy.

Bending over, Kara planted a kiss right on Ghyll's lumpy blue forehead. The flobbin's eyes went wide.

Sprllllannnnnnng!

A brilliant white burst of magic exploded into the air around them, hiding Ghyll from sight.

"Yaaaak!" Ozzie cried. "What a kiss!"

Popping and sparking, the magic cloud swirled around Ghyll for a moment, then faded away . . .

. . . revealing a glowing purple figure the size of Ozzie. Dressed in a long, belted jacket and pointed shoes, the new Ghyll sported a humanlike face, shiny skin, and a long tail. He looked like a cross between an elf and a purple lizard.

Kara put her hands on her knees and bent down for a better look. "Little short for a prince."

"Well, I've been told I bear a striking resemblance to — whoa!" Ghyll cried as he looked down at himself. "I'm back!"

"Hey!" Ozzie exclaimed. "How come you never told us you're really a spriggle?"

"I'm a spriggle!" Ghyll yelped. "You did it!"

Kara shrugged. "Okay, cool. You're not a flobbin anymore. Case closed." She wiped her hands and stepped away.

"You *are* a princess of magic!" Ghyll jumped up and down, stamping his small, pointed feet.

"And don't you forget it!" Kara said.

"How can I ever thank you?" Ghyll's purple ears quivered in joy.

"You can thank us just by doing the right thing," Emily told him.

"I will. I'll go back to Aldenmor and work with the mistwolves." He looked quickly up at Storm. "You don't eat spriggles, do you?"

"Not lately," the mistwolf replied.

Emily looked to the portal. The dragonflies were buzzing like busy bees, stretching the golden dreamcatcher tight over the opening of the portal. "If you want to go, you'd better do it now," she told him. "Before it closes."

"With the web all messed up, how will I be sure I get to Aldenmor?" Ghyll asked.

Emily held up the unicorn horn. "Lorelei did say that I could have magic of any type I desire."

She pointed the horn at the portal and made a wish. "I wish for our friend to get to Aldenmor safely." The horn glowed, briefly followed by an answering flare from inside the portal.

Ghyll walked proudly to the portal.

"Hey, Ghyll!" Ozzie called out.

The spriggle turned to Ozzie. "Yes?"

"If you see Brommy . . ."

Ghyll looked at the ground, embarrassed.

"Give him my regards," Ozzie finished, and smiled.

Ghyll smiled back. "Will do." With that he jumped through the dreamcatcher and vanished into the mists.

"Well, this princess of magic is going home to take a six-hour bath," Kara announced.

"What are we going to do with the horn?" Adriane asked.

Kara stopped, turning to eye the horn in Emily's hands.

"No, you can't wear it," Adriane said.

"I think it'd be best if we hide it in the library," Emily suggested. "Until we figure out what to do with it."

"Agreed," Adriane said. "That's the best solution."

Kara pouted. "Okay," she said at last. "But I still want a jewel!"

"Say, about this magic kiss business." Ozzie ran over to Kara. "You got another wet one in there?"

Kara swooped up the astonished ferret and spun around, planting kisses all over his furry head.

"*Gahh!* Watch the fur! Put me down!"

Adriane fell to the ground, laughing, her arms tight around Storm's neck.

Emily watched her friends and smiled. They had learned a lot about magic in such a stunningly short time, learned its potential for destruction and renewal, its wildness and control. But most of all they had learned of its responsibility. Inside, Emily felt a new hope, a strength not born of pride and conceit but of lessons taught in fire. The Fairimentals would be proud. In just a few short months they had learned more of what it meant to be a mage than if they had apprenticed for years, not in the knowledge of spells and jewels but something more essential, the truth in their hearts.

Chapter 14

Emily opened the door to the Pet Palace and slipped quietly inside. She hadn't seen Ozzie all day. Her mind flashed back to the disastrous scene with the dog food the other day, and she sighed, scurrying to track him down. If he made another mess, her mother would probably ship her off to military school and have the ferret stuffed. Besides, it was past time to do the afternoon feeding.

Emily heard humming. She hesitated, tempted to sneak back out.

But Carolyn looked up and saw her. "Em!" she exclaimed with a smile. "Come here, sweetie. Did you know your ferret could do tricks?"

"Huh?" Emily blinked, noticing for the first time that Ozzie was standing on a wooden box, juggling liver snaps. He tossed them into the air, then one by one caught them in his open mouth.

She narrowed her eyes at him. He merely grinned in response, then did a backflip.

Carolyn laughed with delight. "You know, this is the smartest ferret I have ever seen. I just love him!" She grabbed Ozzie and gave him a hug. "You were lucky to rescue him, Emily."

"I know." Emily stared at the grinning ferret, thinking back to the day she and Adriane had discovered him caught in a trap in Ravenswood forest. That day had changed her life forever. And it never would have happened if her mother hadn't forced her to move to Stonehill. No matter how hard it had been to start a whole new life, she would never regret any of it. Ever.

She suddenly realized that Carolyn was watching her. With a flash of guilt, Emily remembered their argument again. How could she have said such terrible, hurtful things to her mother?

"Mom," she said softly, "I — I —"

"Yes?" Carolyn turned away from Ozzie, facing her daughter.

Emily took a deep breath. This was harder than she would have believed possible. Still, she knew she had to do it. She had to take responsibility for her own actions.

"I'm sorry," she said simply. "I acted like a total brat. I didn't mean to hurt you with those stupid things I said."

Carolyn sighed and looked down at her hands.

Then she took a step toward Emily. "I know," she said softly. "This move hasn't been easy for either of us. And I'm sorry, too — I had no idea how much you were hurting. You seemed so happy with your new friends."

"Oh, I am!" Emily put in quickly. "I really am. I guess I just wasn't as over it all as I thought, you know?"

Carolyn nodded. "You know you can always talk to me, no matter what's on your mind. And I'll do the same, okay?"

"Yes." Emily smiled and stepped forward into her mother's embrace. They hugged for a long, safe, comfortable moment.

"I love you, sweetie."

"I love you, too, Mom."

Rrrrrrip!

"Ozzie!" Emily cried. Over Carolyn's shoulder, she spotted the ferret tearing open a fresh bag of liver snaps.

Carolyn turned and laughed. "Naughty, naughty!" she exclaimed, hurrying over to pull the bag out of Ozzie's grasp. "Come along, now. If you're a good boy, maybe I'll let you taste my special vegetarian lasagna." She cradled Ozzie in her arms, then glanced at Emily. "Dinner will be ready in an hour or so, okay, hon?"

"Uh, okay, Mom." Emily watched in surprise as her mother headed to the door with Ozzie. The ferret waved as he passed her.

Emily shook her head in confusion. Who would ever have guessed that Carolyn would bond with Ozzie like that?

Oh, well, Emily thought. It's nice that Mom has a new friend, even if it is a wacky magical elf disguised as a ferret. Of course, that leaves me with nobody at all. She thought about Lorelei. They had become so important to each other in such a short time. They had healed each other, become friends. Why couldn't they stay together? After all, Adriane had Storm. Kara had Lyra. Who did Emily have?

Seeing that her mother had already filled the dogs' food dishes and taken care of the rest of her chores, Emily sighed and headed for the door. Outside, the reddish glare of the setting sun made her squint. As her vision adjusted, she saw two figures walking toward her across the lawn.

"Hey!" Kara called cheerily. "There you are. We were just thinking about walking into town for some ice cream. What do you say?"

"Yeah." Adriane added. "I need you to buffer-zone Miss Goddess of Magic. Her radiance is blinding me."

A feeling of warmth flooded through Emily.

They understood. Her friends understood. They would be there for her, no matter what.

"Sure," she said.

They walked slowly back across the lawn. "So I'm still totally psyched about the benefit concert," Kara said. "You'll never guess who's going to be a musical act."

Adriane shook her head. "No, but I'm sure you'll tell us."

"Well, what do you think about Be*Tween?"

"Yeah, sure," Adriane scoffed.

"Huh? Huh? How cool is that?"

"I've heard them — they're really good," Emily said.

"They totally rock!" Kara exclaimed.

"And they're coming to Stonehill?" Adriane asked incredulously.

"Right into your backyard, baby."

"Wow, Kara. That's cool," Emily smiled.

"What are we going to do about Mrs. Windor?" Adriane asked.

"Oh, I'll take care of that. I'll send her free tickets."

"No way!"

As her friends continued to chat, Emily felt a flash of sadness mixed with pride. As much as she wished Lorelei could have stayed on Earth with her, she knew her friend had important work to do on the web. Yes, it was hard to accept that they couldn't be together — almost as hard as accepting her parents' divorce. It was going to hurt for a long time. But she still wouldn't change a thing, even if she could.

Before encountering the unicorn, Emily herself hadn't even realized how deeply wounded she was. She had done such a good job of hiding her pain and sadness from everyone else that she'd hidden it from herself, too. She had been chasing an elusive ending to a song that needed to be sung. Now they both had to move forward, take what they had learned, and do their best to make things better.

Emily took a deep breath of the crisp autumn air, lagging a bit behind her friends. The sun had just dipped below the horizon, and the clear evening sky was growing darker with every passing moment. As Emily looked up, she saw that stars were starting to wink into sight here and there. Out of the corner of her eye, she spotted a flash of light diving toward the horizon — a shooting star.

Emily smiled up at it, still thinking about Lorelei. Their friendship was like that star — all too brief, but bright and unforgettable.

Thank you, she thought, hoping that somehow, some way, Lorelei would hear her and understand. *Thank you for everything.*

In return, she heard a faint, melodic whisper of

a reply, like the distant echo of a shooting star's celestial song. And it was perfect.

Listen to the sound
I'll always be around
Hear my words
Feel the magic in them
In friendship we are bound
I'll always be around

Spellsinger

Chapter 1

I'm in my moon phase, my pink days
When everything is okay
I am beautiful, invincible
Perfectly impossible

The music blasted through Kara's stereo, filling her bedroom with the rockin' sounds of Be*Tween. She slid across the polished wood floor, wildly shaking her head of golden hair. Stomping her pink-socked feet to the beat, she spun into a carefully choreographed move and leaped into her closet.

And nothing in this world can shake me
Trip me up or complicate me
Love is all that motivates me 'cause
I'm on a supernatural high

Clothes went flying, piling up everywhere. Kara hopped out, pulling on a pair of jeans and slipping into a blue sweater at the same time. Lyra's spotted head popped out from a mound of clothes as Kara spun past the bed, pulling the cat up by her front paws, sweeping the big animal back and forth.

Kara bent low, feeling the rhythm launch into a wave of guitars and synths. Lyra fell back into a pile of stuffed animals as Kara bounded high into the air, flinging her arms wide. Spinning around, she grabbed her hair dryer and sang into it:

> I'm a free bird, the magic word
> The sweetest sound you've ever heard
> I've got a sure thing, a gold ring
> I'm wakin' up my wildest dreams

Against the windowsill, Lyra lay on her back in the middle of Kara's stuffed audience. Kara dove into the fluffy mountain and tickled the cat's belly, causing Lyra to yelp as they both sang along with their favorite new band:

> And nothing in this world can change it
> Turn me around or rearrange me
> Love is all that matters lately 'cause
> I'm on a supernatural high

Kara was multitasking — dressing, dancing, singing, and celebrating all at the same time. She was so cool — life was so cool. Since she had received word that Be*Tween would play at the Ravenswood Wildlife Preserve benefit concert, Kara had been pumped, playing the CD nonstop. No one believed she could really pull this off. But she had stayed focused and determined, stationing herself at Town Hall every day for the past two weeks. A barrage of E-mails and a phone call from her dad, Mayor Davies, had convinced Be*Tween's manager that the popular girl band could make a stop in Kara's town, Stonehill.

She danced over to her desk, stuffed a stack of papers into her new briefcase, and snapped it closed. When she put her mind to something, there wasn't anything she couldn't do. And for the first time since Kara had convinced her dad to let her, Adriane, and Emily become tour guides for the preserve, the council actually seemed excited. All except Mrs. Beasley Windor, who had made it her personal task to keep an eye on the girls. Mrs. Windor had wanted the old manor house torn down and the land redeveloped into a country club and golf course. But thanks to Kara, this was going to be the event of the year and it would be Ravenswood — 1, Windor — 0.

Outside, a horn honked. Kara turned to Lyra. "It's show time!"

"Already?" Lyra peeked out from behind the bed where she had toppled onto a comfortable pillow.

Kara heard the cat's voice in her mind. At first, it had felt odd, but now it was like second nature, as if she and the magical cat had been best friends forever.

She opened the big window over her desk. "I'll see you at Ravenswood."

Lyra leaped to the windowsill, brushing her face against Kara's. *"Later."*

"Love you." Kara gave the cat a quick kiss and ran for the door.

She took the stairs two at a time. "Mom! I'm going! Dad's taking me over to Ravenswood."

"Okay," Mrs. Davies called from her study. She sounded preoccupied; she was probably working on another big divorce case or looking up case studies.

Kara shot out the front door, bolting into a crisp October morning.

"Are you okay?" Lyra peeked out from behind a hedge.

"Of course. Go before my dad sees you," Kara called out as the big cat slunk into the woods bordering the Davies' property. A golden glow ran up and down the cat's spotted back as two large wings unfolded.

"And don't let anyone see you flying!"

"Cats don't fly." In a moment, Lyra was soaring

over the Chitakaway River and into the dense woodlands beyond.

Kara ran across the front lawn to the dark green Lexus waiting in the driveway. She hopped into the passenger seat, popping down the sun visor to check her hair in the mirror. "Hi, Daddy."

"All ready, princess?" The handsome mayor of Stonehill smiled, running fingers through his graying but thick hair.

"I have all the papers right here." She smiled, showing off her new leather case, a gift from the mayor's staff. They'd been very impressed with the diligence of Ravenswood's young president. At least *some* people appreciated her efforts.

"You still have to get final approval from Mrs. Windor and the rest of the Ravenswood committee for the construction of your stage," Mayor Davies reminded her, pulling the car out of the driveway.

"No prob, Mayor Davies. Everything's under control."

❧   ❧   ❧

Mrs. Beasley Windor tapped her foot impatiently, beady eyes darting back and forth. She raised the large lion's head door knocker and pounded away at the front door to Ravenswood Manor. A few members of the council were with her, including Sid Stewart, Lionel Waxxer, and

Mary Rollins. While they waited, they looked out over the front lawn toward the sculpture gardens.

"We haven't seen anything unusual so far, Beasley," Sid remarked.

"Just keep your eyes open," Mrs. Windor said, scanning the thick woods that bordered the property. "Something strange is going on out here, and I'm going to find out what."

"Hoo doo yoo doo."

Startled, Mrs. Windor spun around. Emily walked across the gravel driveway toward the group. A great snow owl was perched on the girl's shoulder. The owl's flared wing tips sparkled with flecks of turquoise and lavender. Mrs. Windor eyed the owl suspiciously. She could have sworn the owl just spoke. No one else seemed to have heard anything unusual. But the girl, Emily . . . did she just give that bird a warning look?

"Hi, everyone," Emily said, quickly stroking the owl's wings closed. "Er . . . Kara's on her way, and Adriane must be in the library at the computer."

"Hello, Emily. We hear your Ravenswood Website has gotten quite a few hits," Sid Stewart said.

Emily smiled. "It's getting really busy! We've linked to the kids' division of the National Humane Society called NAHEE. It's all about helping animals."

"Very interesting," Mary Rollins said, clearly impressed.

"Yes, and our teacher is giving us extra credit for sharing it with the school." Emily looked at Mrs. Windor. "I'd be happy to show you —"

"I want to see everything!" Mrs. Windor snapped. "And I want a list of every animal here on the preserve. Every since that *peculiar* incident at Miller's Industrial Park, animals have shown up at the mall and even at the school. Your disruption at the football game with that — *horse* thing was too much!"

Emily winced, thinking about the unicorn, Lorelei. Emily had felt such a strong bond with her, and although the unicorn had been gone for only a few weeks, Emily missed her greatly. "We thought the Stonehill Sparks could use a mascot. It would tie into the whole theme of Ravenswood Preserve being such an important place for animals."

"You're saying a *unicorn* represents the theme of Ravenswood?" Mrs. Windor snarled.

"No . . . it's just . . ."

"Oh c'mon, Beasley," Sid chuckled. "It was just a make-believe unicorn. Very imaginative, too."

"And the kids loved it," added Lionel.

Mrs. Windor glared at Emily. "Just what kind of

animals are you hiding here?" she asked accusingly.

From the corner of her eye, Emily caught Lyra dropping from the skies behind the manor.

"Just the ones that live here . . . I mean —" she sputtered nervously.

"We do have a deal with the Town Council, if you remember, to protect *all* the animals that live here," said a new voice.

Everyone turned as Nakoda Chardáy, Adriane's grandmother and the official caretaker of Ravenswood, emerged from the front door of the manor house. "In the absence of the owner, Mr. Gardener, the girls have done a wonderful job managing Ravenswood."

"Our *deal* is to see if the preserve makes economic sense for the town," Mrs. Windor countered.

"And we're willing to open the preserve for the benefit concert," Gran reminded her. "With a percentage of the profits going to the Stonehill Council."

"Assuming there *are* profits," Mrs. Windor said. "You're asking us to pay for some rock-and-roll concert when this land could be put to a real benefit for everyone."

"Tourism dollars are the backbone of many small communities," Lionel mused.

"You'll see," Emily said. "It's going to be great."

"It's not going to *be* anything at all, young lady," Mrs. Windor reminded her. "Not until *we* say it is."

The mayor's Lexus pulled into the wide circular driveway and came to a stop. Kara bounded out. "Hey, kids!"

"Ah, Mayor Davies," Lionel said as he walked to the mayor to shake his hand. Sid was right behind him.

"Greetings, Sid, Lionel, Mary. A beautiful day, isn't it, Beasley?"

"Mayor Davies," Mrs. Windor said gruffly, wagging her finger. "I expect a complete break-down of this proposed event."

"Right! I have all the specs right here." Kara flipped her hair back and opened her briefcase.

"Good day to you, Mrs. Chardáy." The mayor bowed to Gran and turned to face Mrs. Windor. "Kara has it all worked up, Beasley," he said.

Kara smiled and glanced down at the papers and gasped. They were all out of order!

Emily slid in with a save. "Come on, we'll show you where the event will take place out on the great lawn."

Shuffling papers, Kara followed Emily as she herded the group along the path that led to the magnificent back lawn bordered by wondrous gardens. The surrounding trees were ablaze with the colors of autumn.

A sudden rustling made Mrs. Windor look around furtively. Something with soft blue-and-pink fur danced past the trees.

"The stage will go there," Kara pointed out quickly, managing to draw Mrs. Windor's attention away from the magical animals that should have been safely hidden. *That is supposed to be Adriane's responsibility,* Kara thought, annoyed.

"The stage is really just a raised platform," Mayor Davies added. "The show goes on from four till six, Saturday afternoon."

Kara finished sorting out the papers. She held them out to Mrs. Windor. "It's all right here."

Mrs. Windor glared at Kara as she took the papers.

"With the newest, hottest band coming, it's sure to be a hit!" Kara exclaimed.

"Not exactly."

The group whirled around. Adriane walked toward them, a paper fluttering in her hand. "Be*Tween isn't coming."

"What?" Kara ran over to her.

"Look for yourself." Adriane held up a printout.

Kara snatched the E-mail.

Dear Miss Davies,
Unfortunately, Be*Tween will not be able
to make an appearance at your benefit

concert. Their entire tour has been canceled due to unforeseen events. We hope this does not interfere with your plans and we regret the inconvenience.

Joseph Blackpool, CEO

Cigam Management

"Be*Tween isn't coming?" Kara repeated glumly, all the energy draining out of her.

"Well, there goes your little show," Mrs. Windor said with a smirk.

"No way!" Kara said, trying to think fast. "They *have* to show up!"

"They're missing," Adriane said.

"Huh?"

"Word on the Net says Be*Tween vanished. Just disappeared."

"Disappeared? How does a group like Be*Tween just disappear?" It was probably all part of some bogus publicity stunt, to get people talking. And who cares about some little benefit concert, right? Kara kicked a small stone. "That's just great!"

"However . . ." Adriane said with a sly edge to her voice.

"What?" Kara was almost afraid to ask.

"There's a second E-mail." Adriane's dark eyes twinkled as she held up a second printout.

"What? What?!" Kara grabbed for it.

"Let's see here . . ." Adriane teased her, moving the paper out of Kara's clasping fingers.

"Hurry up! Oh, give me that!" Kara grabbed the E-mail.

Miss Davies,
Further to our last E-mail, we received notice that one of our premier musical performers has volunteered to personally replace Be*Tween at your benefit event: Johnny Conrad.

Kara's eyes went wide.

"Johnny Conrad . . ." Kara wobbled and sank to the ground. "Johnny Conrad . . . coming here!" she screamed.

"Johnny Conrad? Even I've heard of him!" Mary Rollins exclaimed.

"Wow! He's one of the biggest stars in the world!" Emily said, amazed.

Kara jumped to her feet. "Johnny Conrad is coming here!" She swooned and promptly sat down again.

"Can you believe it?" Adriane grinned. "This town is going to rock!"

"*Ahhh!*" Kara screamed.

Emily and Adriane screamed.

The three girls were hugging and jumping up and down together.

"Well, I would say this is an event sure to generate some publicity for Ravenswood," Mayor Davies smiled. "Good work, girls."

"Johnny Conrad!" Kara squealed, stomping her pink sneakers into the grass.

Sid pulled Mrs. Windor aside. "Do you know what kind of crowd a star name like that will attract?" he whispered. "Thousands of people are going to show up!"

"Yes . . ." Mrs. Windor smiled. "Think of it, thousands of kids, press, and tourists all coming here to the Ravenswood Preserve."

"This will surely put Ravenswood on the map," Sid said proudly.

"If there's anything left of it after it's over," Mrs. Windor whispered, grinning.

Chapter 2

beachbunny: have you heard the l8est?

irishrose: 4sure, Be*Tween's the greatest

swandiver: they've got every new band beat

beachbunny: no one can compete

Sunlight poured through the large round windows of Ravenswood Manor's library, gently caressing Kara's face as she watched the messages flying in the Ravenswood chat room. With the buzz of Be*Tween coming to town, the number of visitors had risen considerably. Drawing a deep breath, she let her fingers dance over the keyboard.

kstar: got some news today — Be*Tween can't come and play

chinadoll: :-! what happened?

swandiver: :-(what's wrong?

irishrose: I just heard their latest song

beachbunny: they didn't break up, did they?

irishrose: =^..^= tell me that's not what u'r gonna say

For an instant, Kara considered admitting the band's disappearance, but the truth was, Kara had no idea what was *really* going on with Be*Tween. She'd learned to be careful about believing a lot of stuff people posted on the Net.

kstar: fear nottest, we got the hottest

irishrose: who could be so cool?

beachbunny: we must tell everyone at school

kstar: Johnny Conrad!

swandiver: Johnny Conrad? I'm screamin! :-O O-:

irishrose: that's incredible!

chinadoll: he's so hot!

beachbunny: Johnny Conrad! i must be dreamin!

A sudden tap on the shoulder made Kara jump half out of her skin. "Hey, Britney!"

"What?" Kara snapped. She whirled around to see Adriane standing behind her with a grave expression.

"We got a problem," Adriane said. "It's Mrs. Windor. She came in with the construction teams."

"So? Let her boss them around for a bit. Give her something to do."

"She's snuck off into the woods. She's out there right now and she's got a camera."

Kara's stomach tightened. "Did you get the feeling that she caved too easily on this concert?"

"Yeah, it had crossed my mind," Adriane said.

"Let's go!" Kara exclaimed.

Logging off, Kara and Adriane raced from the library, down the rear stairs and out the back of the mansion. About ten men were hauling huge planks of wood across the great lawn. Another group rolled cable and equipment. Others stood looking at a set of plans.

"Where is she now?" Kara asked Adriane.

"Storm, what's happening?" Adriane called into empty air. Instantly, she heard the silver mistwolf's answer in her mind. *She's headed for the Rocking Stone.*

Kara heard, too. "Oh, great! What if she finds the glade?" Kara hissed. "What's Storm going to do? Wrestle Mrs. W. to the ground and take her camera? That would look really good!"

"That's why you're here," Adriane smirked. "We need some presidential action."

They flew past the hedge maze toward the woods. Only a small barrier of trees separated the giant Rocking Stone boulder from the magical glade where so many of the homeless animals from the magic world of Aldenmor lived.

Mrs. Windor was determined to shut down Ravenswood through any means necessary, and if she could show the Town Council pictures of strange creatures — or even what looked like bizarre animals — running loose in the preserve, she'd almost certainly get her way. And that would only be the start of the trouble they'd all face. If scientists or some other government agency examined any of the magical animals at Ravenswood, the truth would be discovered and they would remain in cages, possibly the subject of experiments — or worse — for the rest of their lives.

They could not let that happen to their friends. Frowning, Kara and Adriane ran into the woods.

❧   ❧   ❧

Beasley Windor nearly tripped a half dozen times on roots she could have sworn were trying to snag her. She had whacked her head twice on low-lying branches that she was certain swept in at her out of nowhere — it simply couldn't have been that she was looking one way and walking another. This was a dangerous place.

It had to go.

Giggling and whispers floated through the woods.

Who was that?

More giggles followed, then a flutter of leaves

made Mrs. Windor turn to a large outcropping of willow trees. She carefully tiptoed off the trail.

Slightly hunched over, she peered into the small square of the digital camera she had borrowed from her niece.

Strange creatures were here, and they were playing games with her. They were certain they had nothing to fear — and that belief would be their undoing.

"I've got you now," she whispered.

🌀 🌀 🌀

"She's moving away from the glade," Kara whispered. She couldn't believe their luck —

Adriane gasped, pointing. "Right into trouble."

Kara and Adriane hid behind a tree, watching as Mrs. Windor walked directly toward a space between two bushy willow trees where a pack of quiffles waited. The strange, ducklike creatures were holding a large tree branch pulled back tight, ready to let it fly at their unsuspecting visitor. Their big, webbed feet tapped silently with anticipation and they kept looking up to steal glances at the woman moving in their direction.

"We've got to do something!" Adriane said urgently.

"We can tell her they're migrating visitors from Canada," Kara suggested.

"Uh-huh, and what about that?" Adriane pointed behind the quiffles. "A visitor from Atlantis?"

Kara's eyes widened. Standing a dozen feet beyond the quiffles, in a pool of warm golden light, stood a pony with green-and-purple wings — a pegasus. All Mrs. Windor had to do was turn to the right with her camera and she would get the video of the year.

"Do something!" Adriane pushed Kara.

"All right, all right. You create a diversion with your jewel." Kara pointed to the golden wolf stone locked in the black band around Adriane's right wrist. "I'll take care of Mrs. Windor."

Boldly, Kara stepped out from behind the tree. Behind her she heard a faint crackling and felt magical power building. Turning sharply, she saw Adriane snap into a fighting stance, whirling her arm in a circle. The wolf stone glowed brightly with sparkling energy.

"On second thought —" Kara said, reaching out to Adriane, but she was too late. A searing bolt of golden light ripped from the stone, smashing into a cluster of dead branches over Mrs. Windor with a terrible explosion.

Whammm-crrrackkkk!

Three quiffles went flying as the branch shot forward. Mrs. Windor shrieked and all but flung the

camera away. She whirled toward the opening —
where a collection of seared branches crackled down,
quickly piling up to obscure her view of the pegasus.

Kara gave Adriane a stern look.

"You said create a diversion," Adriane said innocently.

"I didn't say to knock down the whole forest!"

A small blur of gold-and-brown fur dashed behind the new barrier, kicking the magical animals
away, herding them deeper into the wilds of
Ravenswood. Kara breathed a sigh of relief as she
saw Ozzie, the magical ferret, give her a thumbs-
up — well, actually a paws-up.

Mrs. Windor was frantically whirling in every
direction, rocking on her heels as if she had just
made herself dizzy.

"Who's out there?" Mrs. Windor hollered.

Kara and Adriane ducked back behind the
cover of the wide tree trunk.

Something rustled through the trees again.

Mrs. Windor began shouting. "Come out of
there, right now!"

Kara and Adriane poked their heads out from
either side of the tree just in time to see Mrs. Windor about to trip over Rommel the wommel!

"Get out there and get rid of her!" Adriane said
as she pressed her back against the tree trunk.

"Okay, okay. And no more magic!"

"Right."

"Hey, watch where you're —!" Rommel started, but his warning came too late.

Mrs. Windor, still holding onto the camera with pale, trembling fingers, looked into the face of the small, talking koalalike bear. She leaped back, cried out, and tripped, landing in a patch of mud and muck.

By the time she raised her camera and wiped the lens clean, Rommel had rushed off.

"I've got you!" Mrs. Windor shouted, spitting out muddy goop.

"Oh, no," Kara said. What were they supposed to do now?

A sudden gust of wind blew around the woman, a spiral of force that kicked up mud and earth and stone, quickly forming what looked like a mini-twister!

"Adriane!" Kara hissed. "Stop it!"

The dark-haired girl looked at her wolf stone. The jewel was pulsing with strong amber light. "I'm not doing that!"

Then the ground beneath Mrs. Windor trembled. The circling winds drew closer to the struggling woman.

Suddenly, Mrs. Windor's camera was ripped from her hands by the winds. It flew into the air, smashing into pieces as it hit a hard, flat stone.

"What are you *doing*?" Kara yelled.

Adriane threw up her hands. "It's not me, it's not me!"

Next to Mrs. Windor, the whirlwind picked up earth and stone, grass and vine, twigs, branches, leaves, and more dirt, magically forming into a round, tumbleweed shape.

The wind settled, but within its "body," the elements continued to ebb and flow. Sticks, dirt, and leaves swirled.

"It's an earth Fairimental!" Adriane gasped.

Fairimentals were extremely magical beings, the keepers and protectors of good magic on Aldenmor.

"What's it doing here?" Kara asked.

"Warrriorrr," the tumbleweed rumbled, bits of leaves and dirt flying as it wobbled about.

"What the —?" Mrs. Windor looked closely at the twirling mass.

With a sudden shudder, the Fairimental exploded, sending fragments of debris everywhere.

Mrs. Windor whirled around and raced back through the woods, howling.

Adriane and Kara ran to the various pieces of the Fairimental. Two tiny whirlpools of dirt and leaves spun from the ground, desperately trying to regain shape.

"Warrior," one said. Rattling crazily, the whirlpool flew apart.

"We need help," the other small pile managed to say. It, too, was starting to break up.

"What's happened?" Adriane asked urgently.

"— protect Avalon — blazing star must — careful —" words rushed forward, broken like pieces of earth flying from the creature's magical form.

"Spellsing as three — whatever — will be —"

Then whatever force was holding the Fairimental together abruptly vanished, and its elements crumbled to the ground.

Adriane looked at Kara.

The girls knew that the Dark Sorceress of Aldenmor would stop at nothing to find magic. Avalon was the legendary source of *all* magic. Her most recent attempts had damaged the magic web itself, the strands of magical energy that connected worlds everywhere, and supposedly reached all the way to Avalon. As far as the girls knew, the portals to the fairy glen on Aldenmor — where the Fairimentals lived — were still missing. No one had seen or heard from the Fairimentals since those portals had disappeared . . . until now.

"We have to tell Emily about this. The Fairimentals need our help," Adriane called to her.

Kara shot her a withering gaze. "Well, that's

your department, isn't it? Saving the day? I just have my stupid little concert to take care of, thank you very much!"

She walked off, head held high.

"Wait!" Adriane ran after her. "It said you had to be careful."

"It's a twig!" Kara yelled. "It was hard to understand anything it said."

"We have to get a message to Zach," Adriane insisted, referring to the human boy she'd met on Aldenmor who'd been raised by mistwolves.

Now Kara tossed her hands in the air. She spun back to face Adriane. "And how do you propose we do that?" she yelled. "We've got Mrs. Windor running around and Johnny Conrad is arriving in two days! We can't have Fairimentals and who knows what else popping up! And now you want a long-distance dragonfly phone call to Aldenmor. That's the *last* thing I need right now!"

Adriane had to agree with Kara on that one. "Maybe we should just postpone the benefit," she suggested quietly.

"No *way!*" Kara insisted. "This show is going on! The Fairy Glen and Avalon are just going to have to wait."

Chapter 3

Emily raced up the steps of Stonehill's Town Hall. It was a little after four on Thursday, and hundreds of people were gathered on the sidewalk facing the old redbrick building. Main Street had been cleared of parked cars and blocked off, and the park across the street from the Town Hall was filled with even more spectators. Photographers and people with video cameras — including professional TV news crews — had descended upon the normally quiet town square.

At the top of the steps, near the front entrance, stood a small podium with a microphone stand. A WELCOME JOHNNY CONRAD banner fluttered.

A pudgy security guard with curly red hair and freckles stood beside the main doors. "Hello, Emily. Got quite a crowd today."

"Hey, George!" Emily said breathlessly as she slipped past him. She flew down the dark wood-paneled corridor, passing dozens of photographs detailing Stonehill's history. She whipped past an open door where she smelled food and heard laughter. Inside, Mayor Davies and the Town Council gathered in the small room, chatting.

The real activity was centered in the main meeting room. Emily burst through the doors and was nearly run over by Kara's brother, Kyle, and his friend Marcus, who were rushing by with stacks of folding chairs in their arms. The meeting room had been transformed into a reception hall, complete with streamers strung across the walls, balloons bouncing above wide, neatly decorated tables, and a budget-busting buffet piled with enough food to satisfy the entire population of Stonehill — twice!

"Over to the left . . . a bit higher," Kara commanded, standing in the midst of her "troops," more than two dozen volunteers from school. Her buddies Heather, Tiffany, and Molly were doing their best to center a big poster of Johnny Conrad on the rear wall.

"It looks great, Kara!" Heather yelled.

"My arm is getting sore!" Molly muttered.

"No pain, no party!" Kara hollered. She looked down and brushed the front of her new blue sweater, one eyebrow raised defensively at the possibility of a stray crumb.

Emily approached slowly and cautiously. "Hi. My name is Emily. Can Kara come out to play?"

Kara slumped against the door. "I'm acting like a witch, aren't I?"

"Are you a good witch, or a bad witch?"

"Very funny." Kara sighed. "There's just so much going on. . . ."

"You're doing a great job," Emily reassured her. "And so is everyone else. It would be nice if they heard that now and then."

"Yeah." Kara looked away. "Um . . . is Adriane coming?"

"Are you kidding?" Emily exclaimed. "This is Johnny Conrad!"

"What do you think we should do about the Fairimental's message?"

"We should contact Zach after the press conference, when everything calms down — whenever you're ready," Emily answered.

"The last thing we need are those dragonflies popping up! I'll never get rid of them."

Something *squawked* in Kara's bag. She hauled out a small walkie-talkie.

"Ground control," she said.

"Drone One to Queen Bee," a voice hissed.

"Go ahead, Drone One."

"Target spotted. Headed right toward Main Street. You are not going to believe it!"

"Stay calm, Drone One . . ." Kara urged.

"It's Johnny *Conrad*! *Ahhhh!*" The walkie-talkie crackled and cut off.

"We've lost Drone One," Kara said. She quickly checked her watch. "T-minus five and counting. How do I look?" She fluffed her blond hair.

"Perfect."

Kara grinned. "Let's move out!"

They ran into the room where her father and the other council members were still chatting away.

"People! People!" Kara hollered. "Let's go. Our guest of honor has arrived!"

"Ooo, how exciting," Mary Rollins exclaimed.

"Let's keep this orderly now," Mayor Davies stated. "Just another visitor to our humble town."

"Look! It's Johnny Conrad!" Heather was jumping up and down, pointing out the front window.

"*Ahhhh!*" Tiffany screamed.

Everyone in the room rushed for the door at once, squashing the mayor to get past him. Soon the vast crowd outside started screaming.

This was it. Kara was about to become a star.

❧ ❧ ❧

Outside the Town Hall, Kara stood beside her dad. She heard the rumble of engines and the blare of car horns.

And in the distance . . . music?

Kara's eyes widened as she and everyone else in the enormous crowd turned toward the street, where a jet-black convertible T-Bird with the top down drifted their way. A young, dark-haired guy stood on the front hood, a microphone in his hand. A tour bus crept along at a respectful distance behind the singer. Two huge speakers hung on either side of the T-Bird, and a guy with black sunglasses sat with a mixer board in the back while another one drove, their heads bobbing to the beat of the thundering, pulsating, blisteringly happening song that was currently topping the charts.

Let me tell you, if I sing it true, get up and start the dance,
A rock-and-roll rap with some zap, come on now and take a chance,
No matter what you do, it's your life, you're you,
So come on and take a chance and dance!

Johnny Conrad's thick, tousled black hair glistened in the golden afternoon sunlight and the deep, model-perfect cheekbones filled with dusky shadows as he rapped. His soulful deep blue eyes were cast heavenward, and his lanky muscular body swayed with the music, his pale shirt clinging, his black leather boots and pants shining as his long leather jacket curled behind him. The booming music seemed to ensnare his listeners as everyone moved to the beat. Molly, Heather, and

Tiffany were bopping like crazy, dancing around the black car as it rolled up to the curb.

DANCE! DANCE! DANCE! TAKE A CHANCE AND DANCE!

The entire crowd was caught in the rhythm, the enveloping sounds, and the enchantment that was Johnny Conrad. Dancing, moving, shaking, and screaming, adults, teens, and children all rocked out to the sounds of the latest teen sensation.

Johnny leaped from the hood, his wireless microphone catching every note as he sang his heart out. Security held the crowds back as Johnny climbed the wide steps of the Town Hall, heading right for the podium, while constantly turning, reaching out, his soulful eyes connecting with as many people in the crowd as he could.

The song ended and Johnny took a bow, prompting another round of searing screams from his audience. Smiling, he waved and tossed the microphone to his driver.

Mayor Davies stared in slack-jawed wonder at Johnny, who patiently nodded and waved to his fans — and the press. Cameras flashed, bursting bright lights against the singer's brilliant blue eyes.

"Hello, Stonehill!" Johnny called out.

The crowd erupted in frantic, ear-piercing screams. "Johnny! Johnny!"

Kara was practically beside herself as the superstar approached. But she had a job to do, so she nudged her dad's arm, snapping him to attention. She noticed Adriane next to Emily, jumping and cheering.

Mayor Davies cleared his throat four times, right into the podium's microphone, but nothing happened until Johnny put a single finger to his lips and winked at the adoring crowd — which suddenly fell completely silent.

"They're all yours," Johnny whispered, nodding to the mayor.

Kara watched Johnny, transfixed.

Whoa. This guy was *hot*.

"Johnny Conrad, thank you for taking time out of your busy schedule to help Ravenswood Wildlife Preserve — your act of generosity has moved us all," Mayor Davies read from the script Kara had written. She nodded, smiling ear to ear. "The Town Council would like to offer you and your band our best suites at the Stonehill Inn. And as mayor of Stonehill, I'd like to present you with the key to our city!"

Covering the microphone, Mayor Davies nodded toward Kara, "I think you've already won the key to my daughter's heart."

"Dad!" Kara wailed.

Johnny smiled at Kara — and she managed not to faint. Then he turned to the crowd and shot them a dazzling smile, holding the big golden key high over his head.

"Thank you very much. We're proud to play for the wonderful cause of the Ravenswood Preservation Society." He winked at Kara.

Kara practically leaped into the air, but instead hopped around and screamed like a starstruck little girl.

"And we've got something really special planned," Johnny said. "As part of a promotion for my new CD, *Under Your Spell* —"

Screams broke the speech, but quieted down as Johnny raised his arms.

"I'm hereby inviting one fan to sing onstage with me during the concert Saturday. The performance will be simulcast via the Internet all over the world!"

"Ahhh!" Kara screamed.

"Ahhhhh!" dozens of girls screamed with her.

"Ahhhhhhhh!" the crowd screamed and screamed and screamed some more.

Sid Stewart put his hands over his ears, screaming in pain.

"That's right, I'm offering a place for one special person to sing with me . . . if I can only find him . . . or her." Johnny eyed Adriane, who blushed but smiled back. Then he looked at Emily. And then, suddenly, Johnny zoomed in on Kara and seemed to see . . . something. "Maybe I already have."

Kara's heart skipped a beat.

He means me, she thought. *Yes! He's talking about me!*

Kara struggled to control herself. She took a step toward the microphone and was about to speak when Adriane stepped on Kara's foot and took the mike. "I'd like to invite you and the band to stay at Ravenswood Manor," she quickly said, holding the mike away from Kara's grabbing fingers. "What better way to get exposure for Ravenswood than for Johnny Conrad himself to stay there?" She smiled.

"Whoa, Ravenswood Manor." Johnny beamed. "*Now* you're talking!"

Adriane smiled at Kara, then stuck her tongue out.

Kara felt unsteady. *What did Adriane think she was doing?* She gestured to Emily. "Do something," she mouthed. Emily shook her head. What could she do? Tell Johnny no?

Kara saw flashes of light and heard the photographers snapping away — and felt the white-hot fire of fury rise within her.

"Outstanding!" Johnny said. "I'd be honored to

make Ravenswood Manor my home away from home." He turned to his entourage. "How do you guys like that for hospitality?"

The members of Johnny's band all nodded enthusiastically.

The crowd cheered.

Adriane strutted past Kara, whispering, "And you thought I wasn't taking any interest in the concert."

It was all Kara could do to keep from screaming at the tall girl.

"I can't wait to practice with Johnny," Adriane said snidely.

"Listen up! I'm going to win that contest," Kara hissed. "It'll be *me* onstage singing with Johnny."

"I guess we'll see about that." Adriane strutted off.

Kara looked around nervously, putting her best smile on display for the crowd as she and her dad prepared to take the activities inside, where the Town Council members and their friends and families would get a chance to meet and greet the great Johnny Conrad.

Ooooh! That Adriane! *I will win,* Kara thought.

There was just one slight glitch: Kara couldn't sing a note in tune if her life depended on it. And everyone knew it.

Chapter 4

Streaks of lavender stretched across the horizon as stars winked into existence. Kara and Emily raced down the gravel driveway to Ravenswood Manor. The girls had about an *hour* before Johnny and his entourage showed up at the manor.

"How could she *do* that?" Kara was steaming at Adriane's totally irritating behavior. "She's trying to outdo me, steal my thunder."

"You're not in this alone, Kara," Emily reminded her.

"Then how are *we* going to get the entire Ravenswood Manor ready?"

"It'll be fine," Emily assured her. "We just have to keep everyone out of the library."

She stopped at the head of the circular driveway. "And we have to keep the magical animals out of sight!"

"About time!" Ozzie called out.

A small gathering of animals milled around in

front of the manor's doors led by Ozzie, Lyra, the pegasus called Balthazar, and Ronif, leader of the ducklike quiffles — all key members of the girls' inner circle of trusted magical animal friends.

"What's kept you?" Ozzie asked, crossing his furry, ferret arms and tapping a rear paw. *"Everyone's waiting for Fairimental updates."*

"Adriane returned a short time ago, acting very strangely," Lyra said softly.

"Strange like how?" Kara asked.

"There have been bursts of her magic all through the manor house."

Kara and Emily exchanged worried glances.

"Looks like we're going to have some guests for a few days," Emily announced to the animals.

"Who?" Balthazar asked.

"Johnny Conrad," Kara said excitedly.

The animals looked at one another, bewildered. Ronif shrugged.

"A musical band," Emily explained.

"I see . . ." Balthazar said worriedly.

"Believe me, I won't forget what Lorelei taught us," Emily said.

The unicorn had shown the girls just how powerful music could be — it created magic, good and bad.

"Gather everyone together back at the glade," Emily ordered. "I want a complete head count."

Ozzie led the animals off toward the lawn behind the manor and the woods beyond.

Kara added, "And make sure everyone stays there!"

"I'm going to assign Storm, Lyra, Balthazar, and Ronif perimeter watch," Emily said. "You find Adriane and see what's going on. And play nice."

"I *can* sing, you know." Kara sniffed.

"Adriane is really talented, too," Emily said. "It's not about who's the best."

"Yeah, it's about being onstage in front of a zillion people with Johnny Conrad!" Kara exclaimed, then added under her breath, "Besides, she started it."

"It doesn't matter who started it. What's important is that the two of you work this out."

Kara frowned. "Okay. But hurry and get back and help me get this place ready. There's probably a million things to do."

Emily dashed off toward the woods following after the animals, while Kara hauled the front door open and bolted into the shadowed foyer of the manor.

"This place is always so dusty and —"

She hit the hall light switch and stopped dead in her tracks.

The manor had been transformed. WELCOME JOHNNY banners and band posters were everywhere, and the manor itself sparkled. Little signs with arrows and notes like THIS WAY TO THE KITCHEN, THIS WAY TO JOHNNY'S ROOM, THIS WAY TO BAND QUARTERS, THIS WAY TO REHEARSAL AREA, and many more were all over the place.

"*Adriane!*" Kara screamed, stomping into the wide lobby.

A loud power chord ripped through the empty halls and echoed throughout the manor. With the volume turned up a notch, a succession of new chords barreled over Kara, bouncing around the entryway in a catchy rhythm.

Adriane was practicing her guitar already? How had she gotten the manor ready so fast? Putting all of this together must have taken days! Unless, of course, she had a little magical help. And Adriane was certainly the most adept at using her magic to make things happen.

Ignoring her relief that everything seemed ready for Johnny, Kara stomped up the wide main staircase to the second floor.

Funky chords shuffled down the hallway as Kara checked through the place. Every room she looked in had been thoroughly cleaned and dusted, sparkling and ready for guests.

Squealing guitar feedback echoed away into silence as Kara walked along the brightly lit corridor to the library. Then she heard something else and froze. Footsteps. From one of the rooms just ahead of her. Someone moving things around.

The lights suddenly went out, closing the hall in darkness. Pale moonlight streamed through a small window at the end of the corridor as Kara's eyes took a moment to adjust. Suddenly, a figure sprang from the library and raced toward the window, cutting a hard left and disappearing down another corridor before Kara could get a decent glimpse of whoever it was.

"Hey, Miss Rock Star!" Kara called out.

She ran toward the window, nearly tripping on a section of rug that had been bunched up. By the time she reached the corridor's intersection, the long hallway leading down to other rooms was empty.

"Adriane, come on!" Kara yelled. She didn't have time for this. Then she noticed a weird, golden glow at her feet, making her shadow stretch far and wide before her. Turning, she saw a flickering light reaching out from the open door to the library.

"Adriane?" she called out, peering inside the library cautiously.

No one was there. The library felt oppressively silent.

Kara walked into the large circular room. Row upon row of books lined the walls. The panel concealing the giant computer screen was closed and untouched. Everything seemed okay.

A shadow moved near Kara's feet. She looked up and stared at the giant mobile that hung from the center of the library's domed ceiling. It was made of a series of celestial pieces, a sun, planets with moons, comets, and stars all designed to swing in synchronous movement. It swayed lightly in the air. Had someone just hurried by it?

Moving under the mobile, she bumped into the large reading table. Rich leather-bound books with gold trim were piled high. Had Adriane been reading all these volumes?

Kara stopped. One of the old musty books lay open. A tall candle cast a wavering light upon its pages. A low, whistling breeze taunted the flame as it flowed into the room from an open window a dozen feet away.

Someone had been in here, reading this book. She looked at the ancient gold lettering along the book's spine, *The Art of Spellsinging*. What kind of research was Adriane doing?

A shuffling noise from out in the hall made Kara spin around again. She didn't like this game Adriane seemed to be playing one bit.

But *was* it Adriane?

She thought about calling Lyra, but Johnny and his people would be there any minute. She examined the book. She was about to close it when the wind kicked up, making the candlelight shine brightly upon one particular passage.

> *The strongest of magic is the gift of song*
> *In the heart of the spellsinger is where it belongs*
> *Song of truth, words of age*
> *Spread in song what you read on this page*
> *Music will awaken the true power of the*
>   *lightbringer*
> *For stars to shine, call upon the spellsinger*

Kara stared at the passage for several long moments, the rest of the world, all her responsibilities, even her fight with Adriane, suddenly swept away and forgotten.

The power of the lightbringer? It almost sounded like the book was talking about *her*. She was the blazing star, after all. That's what the Fairimentals said, even if none of the girls had figured out exactly what that meant. The three had been chosen to become mages, magic masters. Emily was to become a healing mage, using the power of her rainbow jewel to help animals. Adriane was a warrior, using the magic of her wolf stone to defend the magic. But Kara hadn't yet found her power. . . . What's a spellsinger? Isn't that what the Fairimental said? Could this be her path?

"What's that you're reading?" a familiar voice said over her shoulder.

Kara jumped and stumbled away from the table, knocking over the candle in the process. She reached for it — but Adriane was closer, and quicker, and snatched the candle before it could fall and harm the book. The dark-eyed girl set it back upright, its flame never going out.

She didn't even look at Kara. She swung her cherry-red electric guitar across her back on its black leather strap and stared at the open pages, her lips forming the words Kara had just read. "Spellsinging. That's cool. . . ."

"Yeah, well, it's better than loud obnoxious power chords! That's like so last century!"

Kara stared daggers at Adriane, but Adriane was oblivious.

"Didn't the Fairimental say something about spellsinging? Where did you find this book?"

Kara crossed her arms. "Oh, like you weren't so reading it before I got here!"

Adriane looked up. "I've never seen it before."

"Tell me another one." Kara paced back and forth under the mobile. "I can't believe you are so jealous that I'm going to sing with Johnny."

"No one said it's going to be you, Miss Center of the Universe," Adriane retorted. "Besides, I wouldn't exactly call what you do singing."

Kara flushed. A loud *squawk* buzzed from her backpack. She fished out the walkie-talkie.

"What!" she snapped.

"Drone One to Queen —"

"Yeah, yeah, what is it?"

"Target on route to Ravenswood —"

Kara's eyes went wide as she shut off the walkie-talkie. "He's coming!" She surveyed the room frantically. There were several strange-looking objects strewn across the tables. "We have to put away anything that looks magical!"

"We can hide everything behind the computer screen," Adriane said, gathering up the books from the table and walking to the secret wall panel. "Since only our jewels can open it, everything should be safe there."

Kara tapped her foot and crossed her arms.

"Oh." Adriane smiled wryly. "I forgot. You don't have a jewel."

"Yet." Kara stepped aside as Adriane lifted her wrist, exposing the amber wolf stone. She held it in front of the secret panel and concentrated. The stone pulsed with golden light outlining the wall with bright lines. The panel silently slid back, revealing the computer screen of the Ravenswood library.

Frustrated, Kara stormed across the room and started gathering items. A snow globe that was anything but what it looked like, several talismans of protection given by the wondrous creatures who had taken refuge in Ravenswood, and a small woven dreamcatcher.

"What's the deal with all these candles?" Adriane asked. "Why didn't you just turn on a light?"

"I thought that was *your* touch. You have been, like, so busy around here," Kara retorted.

"Yeah," Adriane chuckled. "I was cleaning up the manor with Storm, but we weren't in the library —" She looked at Kara, then pointed to the books. "If you didn't find these books and I didn't —"

Kara felt a chill that had nothing to do with the cool air filtering in through the open window. Someone else *had* been here. The person she had glimpsed in the hall hadn't been Adriane. Was that person still here, in the manor?

She regarded the open window. "Someone else has been here," Kara said stiffly.

"No way," Adriane disagreed, picking up the book about spellsinging again. "Storm would have warned me if someone had snuck into the manor."

Kara dumped the items she had gathered behind the secret panel.

"I think I'll hold on to this," Adriane said, opening the book again. "I understand music better than you, anyway. If there's something important here about musical magic, I should know about it." She gave Kara a quick glance. "And this could be very useful for my singing debut with Johnny."

Kara's entire body tensed. She was about to start screaming when something sparkled from the hiding place. Kara's eyes opened wide. It was the horn of the unicorn Lorelei, given to Emily to lead the girls across the magic web and back home to Ravenswood. The power of the horn was supposed to grant the user *any* magic he or she desired. Kara cut a quick glimpse back at Adriane and saw that the raven-haired girl was riffling through the pages.

With one quick, furtive motion, Kara snatched the crystalline unicorn horn and slipped it in her backpack.

Emily was right, Kara decided. It didn't matter who started this business between her and Adriane — only who finished it.

In other words, whoever stood onstage with Johnny Conrad, singing in front of the world, the envy of everyone, was the winner!

The unicorn horn sparkled with magical energy as she closed her backpack.

Chapter 5

Kara heard the knock at the manor's front door and only barely beat Adriane to it. She smiled brightly as Johnny and his manager, a dude called Inky Toon, stepped inside.

Johnny was, as always, totally laid-back and cool.

"Hello, paradise!" Johnny whistled as he looked around the spacious foyer. "This place is awesome!"

"Cool crib, girl," Inky said. "You know what I say, life is always a par-tay, and this is a place where we can work it."

Kara smiled. "Welcome to Ravenswood Manor. I'll be happy to show you guys the digs."

Looking vexed that Kara was getting credit for welcoming Johnny and his people to the manor, Adriane cleared her throat. Inky nodded toward the raven-haired girl and handed her his leather jacket. "Yo, guitar girl — hang that up for me? We got a few things out in the car, too. Thanks!"

Adriane took the jacket, adjusting the guitar still hung over her back, and walked off with it. "Yeah, sure, you're welcome. . . ."

"A few more are arriving shortly," Inky said.

"A few more?" Kara stopped in mid-grin.

"Yeah, you know what I'm sayin — we got our crew to take care of."

"Sure . . . okay, I guess."

Soon, the entire mansion was buzzing. Johnny's band and all his technical people had arrived, along with Emily and Gran. Adriane's grandmother looked concerned about the way the manor was being taken over. Gran even took Adriane outside for what looked like a stern talking-to.

Good, Kara thought.

The band's equipment took over the immense dining room, which would be used for rehearsal space. The parlor, kitchen, and adjoining sitting rooms were overflowing with the newcomers. Kara found Emily and led her to the main living room to "mix it up!" as Kara had put it.

Someone slipped a disk in a boom box and the room filled with a hip-hop blaster that was tearing up the charts. Johnny spun around the room demonstrating some of the hot dance moves that had catapulted him to stardom. Everyone cheered and got into the groove.

Kara leaned next to Emily against the wall beside the fireplace. Johnny had a way of making her feel so relaxed. He was just *so* cool.

"What do you think of Johnny?" she asked.

Emily fluttered her hand over her heart and rolled her eyes. "He is so cute!"

"Back at ya!"

"Everything okay with you and Adriane?" Emily asked.

Kara tensed, suddenly thinking of the unicorn horn she had swiped. Guilt overwhelmed her at the thought of Emily finding out what she had done. "Don't ask."

"That bad?"

"Worse." Kara remembered the book she'd found in the library — and the mysterious visitor who must have been looking it over. She told Emily about it and they quietly slipped upstairs to investigate further, away from their company. They unlocked the library and went inside. Emily popped on the light. She started — and pointed at the rug. "Look!"

Kara focused on the large woven area rug by the door. The red, blue, and gold weave was splotched with brown.

"Someone tracked mud in here," Emily said. Those weren't splotches — they were footprints. Looking closer, she determined the prints were wide, with three toes. "Only these prints are not human. Some kind of animal."

Kara and Emily exchanged worried glances. "It can't be bad," Kara remarked, remembering what Adriane had told her. "Storm would have warned us."

"That Fairimental told you to be careful," Emily reminded her.

Was this what the Fairimental had meant? Maybe this "spellsinging" stuff had something to do with helping them.

"Is that the book?" Emily asked.

"That's it." Kara had seen Adriane put the book into her backpack, then rush out without it when the doorbell rang. Smugly, she had retrieved it.

For an instant, Kara thought she heard someone humming or singing in the hall. Then the sound faded.

Deciding it was just music from downstairs, Emily and Kara read a passage from the book:

Spellsing as one
And see your work done
Spellsing as three
And whatever you picture will be

"It sounds like it's talking about us," Emily said. "The power of three."

"But what's spellsinging?"

"Some kind of spell-casting using music?" Emily suggested.

"You think whatever was in here was looking for this magic?"

"Knock, knock," a deep voice called.

"Ahhh!" the girls cried together.

Kara and Emily spun to see Johnny standing in the open doorway, leaning against the frame with his confident grin. Kara thought she had closed and locked the door behind them. Apparently, she'd been too distracted.

"What an incredible room!" Johnny eased into the library, looking around and admiring all the shelves of books and the odd little curios, all fashioned in an animal motif. "So this is the famous Ravenswood Manor library!"

Kara slapped the book closed and passed it to Emily, who slid it behind her back.

"Look at all these books!" he continued, walking around the circular room. "And these paintings are awesome! An original Parrish, a Bates, and this . . . whoa! The Munro Orrery." He gazed up at the intricate mobile.

"Awesome," Kara agreed, totally in awe of her guest.

"How do you know so much about Ravenswood?" Emily asked.

"I'm a history-head." Johnny smiled. "Especially when it comes to haunted houses."

"Haunted houses?" Emily glanced at Kara.

"Yeah, I live for this stuff. Ravenswood and the woods around the preserve are famous, full of ghosts, witches, and monsters!" He laughed.

"The woods aren't haunted," Emily said. "That's just kids' stories."

"No? I'm sure there are some extra-special things going on here." Johnny's deep blue eyes sparkled as he smiled.

Kara nudged Emily's arm. "Maybe you should take our *homework* to Adriane."

"Yeah, good idea," Emily said, bumping into bookshelves as she edged out the door.

"Soooo," Kara said, smiling and sidling to the reading table, away from the secret computer panel. "You're a Ravenswood buff. That's cool, Johnny." Her smile faltered and her heart started racing and suddenly she felt like a complete buffoon. "Johnny. I called you Johnny. . . . *Can* I call you Johnny? Or should it be Mr. Conrad, or Mr. C, or —"

Johnny laughed, and it was such a friendly laugh, an almost musical sound, that it instantly calmed Kara's sudden case of the jitters.

"Johnny's my name, don't wear it out." The rock star smiled, turning his baby blues to the rows of books. "I love to read." He ran long fingers over the rich leather-bound volumes.

"You do?"

He laughed again and a warm, comforting breeze seemed to caress her.

"Of course," Johnny said softly as he intently scanned the titles on the shelves. "I'm on the road all the time. I've got to do something to make it less boring."

"Boring?" Kara asked incredulously. "Your life, boring? I don't believe it."

He glanced her way. "Well, there are some pretty exciting moments. Like meeting new people and seeing new places. . . ."

His sigh even sounded like music, and it made Kara's heart beat like thunder.

"And getting up onstage," Johnny said quickly, "performing for my fans, singing my music. It's like . . . magic." He turned to face Kara, and for a split second, she caught a flash of fire in his eyes.

Kara took a step back. She felt feverish. This was unreal. *She* was spending time alone with Johnny Conrad!

Just wait until she told Heather and Molly about this. . . .

"So you're a singer, too," Johnny said brightly.

Kara was startled. "Huh?"

"Your dad told me you were dying to win the

contest. You and your pal with the guitar. Though I hope for her sake that she's got one top-notch voice, 'cause you've got her way beat where it counts."

Kara nearly choked. "I do? R — r — really?"

"I know about these things," he said, low, musical tones seeming to echo beneath each of his words . . . words that filled her with that same confidence that radiated from the singer. "You've got something special. I can feel it. You know what that is?"

Kara thought of the unicorn horn. . . . No, that was crazy. Johnny didn't have anything to do with magic. He was talking about something inside her, a special quality.

"Star power," he answered for her. "And I'm never wrong."

Before Kara could even think of what to say in reply, Inky and two others were in the doorway.

"Wow. What a spread!" Inky commented, taking in the vast library. "This place rocks!"

"Come on, Johnny, press is here," one of the others said, nodding her gold-and-pink-haired head into the room. "We promised you'd do some interviews."

"Okay," Johnny said, walking to the door. He turned back and gave Kara a wink. "Star power," he repeated.

Johnny left Kara and went into the hallway. As she heard them hurry off, she felt her head start to clear and realized she'd have to be more careful in the future. This library had to remain off-limits to visitors. And there was the computer, which held secret knowledge about subjects practically beyond imagining, like other worlds.

She locked the door on her way out.

Star power! Kara beamed. "Finally, someone notices!"

❧   ❧   ❧

Late that night, an exhausted Emily dropped onto her bed without even bothering to change into pajamas. She wanted to read more of the book she had taken from the mansion. . . . What little she had read about spellsinging had completely captured her imagination. Magic spellcasting with music — awesome!

What a day this had been — and things were only going to get more exciting. It would all be wonderful, absolutely perfect — if only Kara and Adriane could work out their differences.

Then again, there was that warning from the Fairimental. Was something going on? Had the Dark Sorceress set another of her plots in motion to take advantage of how busy and distracted the girls were now that Johnny was at Ravenswood? Emily decided tomorrow they would have to get

Kara to call the dragonflies. They would contact Zach, on Aldenmor, and find out what was happening there. Whatever the Dark Sorceress was up to, it was not good.

Clank!

Slam!

Cheep-cheep!

Emily bolted upright in bed, still fully dressed. Those sounds had come from outside. She ran to the window and looked out at the converted barn behind their house.

"Eeep-eep-ooooook!"

"Krrrrang!"

Someone was in the Pet Palace.

Emily burst from her bedroom, zoomed downstairs, and headed toward the back door.

"Emily?" her mom called out. Carolyn had been downstairs in her office with a reporter, a journalist who wanted an animal specialist's viewpoint on the Ravenswood Preserve.

"Just checking on Dr. Ehrlich's monkeys," Emily called out as she whizzed by.

She ran across the small expanse of yard and entered the Pet Palace. Bizarre! Some old woman was prying open the cages that held the former circus monkeys and letting them go free!

"Hey!" Emily hollered.

The old woman turned and Emily froze. Fear

ripped up her spine, tickling the hairs on her neck. Mrs. Windor's eyes glowed with red fire. She was hunched over, slobbering like a wild animal. A long tongue wagged from her mouth as saliva dripped to the wooden floor. A sudden burst of white light filled the space. For a moment, Emily didn't know what had happened — then she saw her mother appear outside the nearby open window and saw the reporter with a flash camera.

Dr. Carolyn Fletcher's jaw dropped. "What's going on in here? What are you —"

The photographer snapped another shot, his flash blinding mother and daughter.

"Yiiieeeee-eeek-eeek-eeek!"

The monkeys howled and hollered, the sudden flash making them leap from the top of one cage to another.

"Sorry," the photographer said. Screaming madly, Mrs. Windor flung herself past the astonished group and out the door, running across the backyard, toward the woods. The monkeys followed, one flying through the window and knocking the photographer flat on his back before bounding off into the darkness, another racing around and leading Emily and her mother in circles before running off and escaping through the open back door.

In the distance, Mrs. Windor cackled like a wild beast.

Emily and her mother went outside, just in time to see the photographer drive off in his car.

"What was *that* all about?" Emily's mom asked, startled.

Emily knew Mrs. Windor wanted to disrupt the concert any way she could and prove to everyone the animals here weren't safe. But this was crazy! And the way Mrs. Windor had looked. Almost as if she weren't human. A cold chill lodged in her spine.

Shaking her head, Emily said, "I guess Mrs. Windor finally went over the edge."

They went back inside to grab flashlights so they could hunt for the missing monkeys.

Had they remained outside, they might have seen Mrs. Windor peeking out from behind the tallest tree at the edge of the grove, watching their house carefully . . . and they might have heard the strange little song she hummed.

The monkeys came to her then, their heads lolling, their eyes glazed, looking completely entranced by the sounds she made.

Then, suddenly, Mrs. Windor bent low and hissed at the animals, her features melting and changing, her skin turning green and scaly, her eyes turning to smoldering yellow slits in the night, her teeth sharpening to nasty little points.

The monkeys shrieked and ran off in terror as the creature who used to be Beasley Windor straightened to its full seven-foot form, its long arms swaying, its claws clicking and clacking in the near dark. It leaned back its massive head and roared.

Across the expanse of woods, deep in the heart of Ravenswood, cries of fear erupted in the magic glade. Magical animals that had been sleeping soundly suddenly awoke, horrified by the presence they sensed, a monstrous apparition: a creature dank and foul, from the darkest depths of their worst nightmares. And it was here.

Chapter 6

The morning sun cast deep, long shadows behind Kara as she trudged along the high, grassy bank of the Chitakaway River, head down, feet dragging. She swung her backpack by its straps, letting it graze the dewy grass and earth, not even caring if it collected stains. Sparkling water danced and crashed over wide, flat stones jutting from the river, the roaring and rushing creating its own special music.

She had suffered the most restless night's sleep she could possibly have imagined, one minute flying high in amazing dreams of success, basking in the glow of superstardom, the envy of all her friends — and the next, tossed into throes of anxiety, running scared in the blackest nightmares of failure, feeling utter humiliation as everyone laughed at her, their hoots and snickers echoing in her mind.

"Okay, okay, just breathe," Kara said aloud, painfully aware of her own shortcomings as a singer — and the event looming over her this evening: The preliminary karaoke-style audition for the big contest would be held at seven in the main auditorium. Inky Toon would pick five lucky winners who'd be allowed to sing during the preshow on Saturday. Johnny would judge that round of competition personally.

Kara would have to sing in front of dozens of people tonight — maybe even hundreds . . . including Adriane.

She clutched her backpack tighter, tormented by indecision. She could feel the unicorn horn inside, radiating with power, calling to her. Yet she also felt a nagging twinge of guilt for taking it in the first place, and for what she planned on doing with it. She knew the effect she had upon Emily's and Adriane's jewels, amplifying their power, allowing them to do amazing things with their magic. Why should she, Kara Davies, have to play the role of helper, powering their magic as they honed and fine-tuned *their* skills? What if she had no special magic of her own or worse, was destined to *never* have a stone?

No! She had felt the call of the magic before. A shiver passed through her. She was chosen, too, you know. With trembling fingers, Kara opened the backpack and touched the unicorn horn. It felt cool and solid in her hand.

She remembered the wild magic of the unicorn

jewel she had found a month ago. In her hands, that jewel was awesome in its power. Although she had given it back to the unicorn's maidens, the magic of the unicorn jewel had awakened in her feelings that would never again lie dormant. Feelings that would not, could not, be denied. A part of her needed to unleash the magic. It lay pent up inside, dark, cold, and vicious, like a coiled snake, ready to strike.

A fluttering in the breeze behind her made her turn just in time to see Lyra descend. Kara marveled at the cat's powerful magic wings. Unlike the feathery butterfly-shaped wings of a pegasus, Lyra's were sleek, hawklike, built for speed and fast maneuvering. The tapered, golden wings folded to the cat's sides, flashed, and disappeared.

"No ride this morning?" Lyra asked, brushing up against Kara's hip.

Kara scratched the great cat behind the ears and shrugged. "I decided to walk."

"Storm and I checked the entire preserve. We've found no sign of any intruder that scared the animals last night."

"Maybe it was just a nightmare," Kara said.

"Then they all had the same nightmare."

"Even if something bad had managed to slip through the dreamcatcher, you or Storm would have sensed anything dangerous."

"Just the same, with all these fans starting to arrive in Ravenswood, we're on high alert."

"Okay." Kara looked down, shuffling her feet.

"Are you still concerned about this singing contest?"

"No! Yes. Maybe . . ."

"You sounded great the other morning."

"Yeah, it's easy when you have a band like Be*Tween to sing along with. Tonight I have to sing all by myself!"

"You're making too much out of this." Lyra whammed her flank playfully against Kara, hard enough to make the girl wobble for a second before regaining her footing.

"Quit it! I am not! The entire school is going to be there!"

As they neared the Saddleback Bridge that would take Kara over the river and onto the main road to the middle school, Lyra stopped and sat back on her haunches.

"Okay, let's hear," Lyra said.

"What, now?" Kara stopped, irritated.

"Give it your best shot," the cat said patiently.

Kara looked around. A few blackbirds sat in an ancient oak. Other than the birds, the area was empty.

She took a breath. "Okay, you asked for it." She put down her backpack and struck her best singing-star pose.

She hummed a bit and started her choreographed steps, adding a few new ones she picked up watching Johnny and his crew.

Lyra bobbed her head along. *"Good moves, but can you sing a little louder?*

Kara went for it.

I've got it made
I know someone really loves me
Someone who won't turn me away
I'm not afraid
With the strength of us together
Nothing's going to stand in our way

The blackbirds screamed in protest of the obnoxious, screeching voice that had interrupted their day. They flew away, squawking back a few insults.

Lyra listened patiently. Kara couldn't tell if the cat was smiling or about to hurl a furball.

I know with time
We'll get closer every minute
Know each other's secrets so well
We'll touch the sky and we'll find a new tomorrow
We'll discover dreams in ourselves
After all we've been through
I know I've found a friend in you

Kara swung around and faced Lyra. "Well?"

Lyra sat for a second then stretched her back and stood. *"Well . . ."*

"I knew it." Kara swept up her backpack and stomped off. "I stink!"

Lyra caught up to her. *"I wouldn't say that."*

"Well, what would you say?"

"You just need a little help."

"Exactly what I was thinking!" Kara looked relieved as she held up her backpack.

"A few lessons with a singing coach and maybe choir practice."

"Oh — yeah . . ." Kara lowered the backpack.

Lyra cocked her head. *"What were you thinking?"*

"Uh . . . yeah, I should practice with the choir," she said, embarrassed now to admit what she was *really* thinking about.

They headed across the pedestrian bridge. Beyond it lay the road leading to the school. Kara knew that Lyra would have to turn back once they got there, or else risk drawing attention. That meant if Kara wanted to tell Lyra what was on her mind, she'd have to do it quickly. Yet she was torn.

As much as Kara deeply needed to unburden herself to her friend, there were so many things she was trying to come to grips with. She wasn't exactly proud of what she had done, and though she knew she could trust Lyra, Kara still worried about how the cat would react once she knew the truth — not only had she taken the unicorn horn after the girls had made a promise to one another to always keep it hidden away, but she was planning to use the magic for her own selfish gain.

"Lyra, have you ever done something you know you really shouldn't have? Something a part of you wishes you could take back, while another part of you is saying, hey, I'd do it again."

The cat's eyes twinkled. *"Why are you asking?"*

Kara looked away. If she told the cat about the unicorn horn, she'd never be able to keep it; she'd feel too guilty about making Lyra an accomplice after the fact.

"This thing you're talking about," Lyra said, *"it can't be undone?"*

The thought finally occurred to Kara that she could go to the manor *right now* and put the unicorn horn where it belonged. Provided she wasn't caught, no one would ever know she'd taken it in the first place.

But . . . she needed it. How could she hope to compete in the contest *without* using magic? Magic that was given to the girls. Well, to Emily actually. But it had been given to help all three of them.

"She's your friend, she will understand," Lyra said. *"I think you should just talk to her."*

"Huh?" Kara asked, startled.

"Adriane's just stubborn, unlike someone else I know," the cat said, rubbing playfully against Kara's side.

"Yeah," Kara said, quickly recovering from her surprise. "She should be apologizing to me!"

Lyra sighed.

"I've got to get to school!" Kara rushed ahead, anxious to get away from Lyra before she was forced to look her friend in the eye — she knew she couldn't do that — and tell a lie, even a little white lie like pretending she'd meant Adriane all along.

❧   ❧   ❧

Kara lasted exactly three class periods before the urge to do something she had never done before became overpowering. She couldn't concentrate on classwork. She only barely heard Emily as the girl went on about the craziness with Mrs. Windor the night before, which, thanks to the picture-snapping reporter, was even more fully reported in the morning edition of the *Stonehill Gazette*.

Kara barely paid attention even as Heather, Molly, and Tiffany crowded around her, wanting to know all the details of what Johnny Conrad was really like. She was the "center of the universe," as Adriane had put it, just like she wanted to be . . . but for how long?

Just before fourth period, she did something she'd never done before — Kara cut class.

Soon she was outside the building, standing behind a large maple tree. Peering around the tree, she saw the open doors that led from the music room to the track behind the school. The ground was worn in spots from the treads of large tires. Vans and trucks were often parked here so that big pieces of musical equipment could be moved in and out for sporting events or performances around town.

She listened to the uplifting voices of the school's choir practicing in the spacious music room. They sounded so rich and beautiful. A soloist took the lead and Kara sang along, desperately attempting to match the girl's incredible voice. But every note Kara sang was either flat or sharp, early or late, always somehow just plain wrong. Even when she tried to take the easier route of singing along with the rest of the choir, she was never in tune with them.

Kara tried to belt it out like she did when singing along to Be*Tween. A few stray dogs ran around the tree, barking. She quickly shut her mouth, looking around. The last thing she needed was to get caught and end up in detention. As it was, she kept an eye on the time. She had a route figured out that would get her back inside and to the nurse's station way before the period was over. She even had her lines scripted in advance: *Oh, Nurse Sherman, I felt so faint. I have so much going on with the benefit concert and everything. . . .*

And the nurse would say Kara was pushing herself too hard — which was true — and write her an excuse to give to her fourth-period teacher so she wouldn't get in trouble for cutting.

She had it all worked out — the only problem was that this little practice session wasn't helping. For a moment, she thought about just giving up. Then she thought of Adriane's defiant, triumphant smile, the one she'd give her when Kara wimped out.

No, she *had* to sing at the contest tonight. She had to make it to the final round and prove to Adriane that she was . . . that she was *someone. The best!*

Johnny thought she was. He said she had something special: star power.

And he should know.

Okay, Kara knew that in this arena, she was no match for Adriane. Not without a lot of practice — or a little magical help. Adriane had used magic to get Ravenswood all ready for Johnny. Why shouldn't Kara use magic now?

She opened her backpack and took out the unicorn horn. The crystalline horn shone in the noon sun, rainbow sparkles running up and down its intricately spiraled curves.

"I want to sing like a star!" Kara said.

She held it tight and tried a chorus of "Supernatural High."

It wasn't working — she sounded just the same. Kara felt close to panicking. This was her last hope. What's she doing wrong? Maybe the horn worked just for Emily.

I need to focus, like Emily and Adriane do when they use their stones, she thought.

Think musical magic. Magic to make music. Music to make magic. She thought of the book she had found in the library. The strange words of spellsinging drifted in her mind.

Spellsing as one
And see your work done

"Okay . . ." Kara whispered. Spellsinging. What did that have to do with seeing her "work done"?
A good spell could help focus energy.

I want to sing like a bird
The best in the world
Make my voice ring
I'm super-stylin'

Cute, she thought. Not too bad for her first magic spell.

She tried saying the words again, but nothing happened. Then she tried singing them in a rapping rhythm, the unicorn horn clutched tightly in her hand. Suddenly, she felt the wind kick up around her, lifting her long blond hair.

Whoa!

It stopped the moment she fell silent.

Kara tried the spell again, singing the words a little more loudly now, with more confidence and control — and somehow, even though she wasn't singing what the choir was singing, she was in tune with them, her rhythms in sync, her notes flowing perfectly with theirs.

An ember of brilliant blue light suddenly flared from the horn. Kara leaped back, scared. She watched in amazement as the light spread between her fingers. Kara felt dizzy as power grew in her hands, a massive force building. The air felt heavy as it swirled around her. Her heart thundered in a chorus of power.

This was wrong! She knew it and fought against its call. But another part of her sang with the harmonies of her magic. *Her magic!* The power was exhilarating. The wind screamed in her ears, whipping around her in a mad cyclone of magically charged air.

Her hands blazed with blue fire as the magic crackled across her skin. The power seemed so much larger than her small frame. How could it stay contained? And once released, how could she control it?

Taking a deep breath, she cleared her mind of anything but the flows and ebbs of the magic. In a few heartbeats, the glow grew back to an intense blaze. She could do this!

Kara squeezed her eyes closed and centered her breathing. With a certainty that rocked her world, she locked the magic to her will.

Kara started to sing. A perfect "A" note rang from her mouth. She moved to a C, an F-sharp, then began running up the scale, notes perfectly in tune, each rising in perfect pitch. Her control was incredible. Her voice became a lilting, wondrous sound, cascading like sweet summer rain as it moved up and down the scale.

The horn blazed with power. The magic inside of her sang for release.

And Kara was ready.

She raced up a three-octave scale and, with perfect breath control, she hit a triple high C.

Magic exploded from the horn, a cold fire raging out into the world.

The tree trunk burst with an explosive *crack!*

Waves of invisible force rippled out from her

body, her mind, her soul — as a window shattered in the school!

She heard the choir screaming in surprise.

A flicker of a smile fluttered around her mouth before Kara forced her lips to a stern line — but somewhere deep inside, somewhere she feared to look too closely, a part of her crackled with wicked delight. The magic was hers.

❧   ❧   ❧

"You can go now, Mrs. Windor," the desk sergeant said as he opened the cell door.

"It's about time!" Mrs. Windor clutched a copy of the *Stonehill Gazette,* revealing the photograph of her at the Pet Palace, a monkey on her back. "I was nowhere near that house!"

The sergeant looked at her wearily. He was a big man with salt-and-pepper hair. "Uh-huh. Besides the pictures, there were three eyewitness accounts. The photographer, Dr. Fletcher, her daughter . . ."

"All of them at Ravenswood are in on this together. I bet it was that Mrs. Chardáy who dressed up as me for these clearly *staged* photographs!"

"Ah," the officer said. "And why would she do that?"

"To discredit me, of course."

The desk sergeant said, "I'm just stating the facts, ma'am. Now why don't you go home, cool off, and have a nice long rest? You might even consider seeing a . . . doctor."

"That was not me last night!" Mrs. Windor shrieked as she nervously backed out of the building.

The desk sergeant was no longer listening. Instead, he was watching out of the corner of his eye to see if the door might be kind enough to hit Mrs. Windor in the rear end on her way out.

"Whaaaah!" she yelped.

He chuckled as it did.

Chapter 7

The chaos caused by Kara's accidental magical window shattering turned to an advantage when she reached the nurse's office. No one had been hurt by the shattered glass. But a lot of students had been badly shaken by the sudden "windstorm." She was checked out and got a note to excuse her for missing fourth period.

The worst of it was that Kara *knew* she should feel terrible about what she had done — but she didn't. She carefully tested her new vocal proficiency as she walked down the hallway. Humming a tune under her breath, she heard a light musical ringing and felt a tingling throughout her body. After what happened outside, she couldn't risk anything louder. She was dying to find out what the effects of the spell involved were, and if they were lasting. As soon as she could get free, she had to find a secluded area to do further tests. She just had to force herself to make it through the rest of the school day.

Her greatest frustration was that she didn't

have the spellsinging book. If she had been more on top of things, she would have gotten it back from Emily the night before. But the time spent with Johnny had cast kind of a spell on her, making her feel light-headed with joy, not able to think as clearly as she usually did. And today, whenever she was with her pals Heather, Molly, and Tiffany, she could hardly concentrate. All she could think about was spellsinging. And Johnny.

Finally, the three o'clock bell sounded, and Kara rushed to her locker. All around her, kids were buzzing with excitement over the karaoke contest to take place this evening. Kara ignored them all, collecting her backpack and her books as fast as she could.

"Hey!"

She looked up to see Adriane standing there, glaring at her.

"Hey is for horses."

"You haven't said one word to me or Emily today, and now you're rushing off again!" Adriane said angrily. The wolf stone on Adriane's wrist suddenly pulsed with hot light as Kara lifted her backpack from her locker. Adriane quickly covered her wrist with the sleeve of her jacket.

Adriane leaned in close and hissed, "Aren't you even the least bit concerned about what happened to the animals last night?"

"No. Should I be?"

"They think some kind of monster might have gotten through the dreamcatcher," Adriane whispered, glancing around to make sure no one else was listening.

"A monster *can't* get through. That's the whole point, duh!"

"We need you to make a dragonfly call to Zach."

Kara bit her lip. This was so not the time for those pests!

"And just where were you when that 'windstorm' hit?" Adriane asked suspiciously, rubbing her gemstone as if it irritated her.

"Uh . . . getting stuff done . . ." Kara held the backpack behind her, as far away from Adriane's wrist as she could.

"You have to get this concert back under control. Gran is getting really annoyed."

"You were the one who put Johnny and his people at Ravenswood. Don't come crying to me!" Kara pointed out.

"This is *your* show, superstar! You need to get over to Ravenswood right now and finalize a million details."

"I can't. . . . I . . . I'm busy."

Adriane's eyebrow raised. "With what?"

"I'm going to . . ." Guilt flashed through her.

There might be something dangerous at the pre-serve. The girls had no idea what was going on in Aldenmor. They needed to talk to Zach. And there *were* a million details to deal with on the concert.

Kara sighed. All she really wanted to do was lose herself in the dream that was Johnny and her sharing the spotlight, singing before a crowd, basking in their love —

Shouts and screams broke her thoughts. Hundreds of kids were suddenly pouring out the front door of the school.

What now? Kara thought as she followed and bolted from the building.

Suddenly, everyone turned to look at her. Silence fell as the crowd parted like a sea to reveal a long black limo parked by the curb. Johnny stood to the side, leaning on the car's trunk, grinning as the horde of fans flocked around him.

Laughing, he signed notebooks, articles of clothing, even one kid's arm. Then he turned and looked right at Kara.

"Good luck with the contest, everyone. We'll be seeing you all at the show tomorrow." He raised a fist into the air. "Ravenswood!" he shouted.

"Johnny!" the crowd yelled back. "Johnny!"

"Let's hear it for the other star of this concert. The one responsible for the entire show," Johnny said, holding out his hand in Kara's direction. Kara walked through the crowd in a daze. Johnny opened the rear door for Kara to climb in. Then he hopped into the other side, and in seconds, they were off.

Kara was startled at the cheers and cries from behind them, and shocked when she looked back at the expressions on the faces of so many kids; they were calling Kara's name just as often as Johnny's, and many looked at her with the same awe they had reserved for the singer.

From the corner of her eye, she glanced at Adriane yelling something. Ooo, she must be so jealous! Smiling to herself, Kara turned and settled back in her seat, as the limo left the school far behind.

"You know, anyone who tells you it isn't fun being a star is either lying or crazy." Johnny smiled as they drove on, heading toward a scenic road that skirted the woods and fields surrounding Stonehill.

Kara nodded. For a moment, *she* had been the one so many people were looking at with adoration. . . .

"But I'm not a star, I mean like you are," she said self-consciously.

"Don't be so modest," he said. "You put this whole show together. Everyone in this town knows you're special."

That pretty much was true, Kara thought. Not to brag, but the facts spoke for themselves. She'd been the most popular girl in school even before all this stuff with the concert started up.

"The way I figure it, sometimes that light's already there, inside a person," Johnny mused.

"What light?" Kara asked.

"The light that makes someone shine like a star. The only difference between the people who make it and those who don't is whether or not those people are willing to do whatever it takes to make the whole world see that light."

Kara raised her chin and tossed back her golden hair. "I want to make the whole world see what I'm about."

"There you go," Johnny said, his voice once again sounding like music, a perfect, enchanting song that made her feel better about everything, more confident than she had in days. She had done the right thing using the unicorn horn. She knew that now.

Johnny continued, "Everyone does whatever they have to do to get what they want. It's a game. The only thing that matters is if you play to win. There's the easy way and the hard way of handling things. Why take the long road around and have to wait for something you want when someone's pointing out a shortcut?"

Thinking about the karaoke contest, Kara couldn't have agreed more.

Cool as it was listening to him, being with him, Kara had something more urgent to do. She had to practice for the audition! She asked to be dropped off near the orchard fields. She could walk home from there.

Johnny signaled to the driver and the limo stopped by the side of the road.

Kara smiled as she hopped out of the car. "Thanks for the ride."

"Anytime," Johnny said rummaging in a bag. "Wait . . . Here, take this."

Kara took the small locket on a slim gold chain he handed her.

"I was given this before my first big show. It brought me luck." He shrugged. "Now you can use it to bring *you* luck."

Kara nodded eagerly. "Wow. Thanks." She clutched the locket in her hand.

"I thought you might like to have it with you for the first round tonight. Not that I think you'll need it — I know you're gonna knock everyone out." Johnny winked.

You've never even heard me sing, Kara thought, suddenly horrified. Then she relaxed. After all, she had the unicorn horn, plus she was learning about spellsinging, her secret weapon.

Her sudden confidence must have shown on her face, because Johnny winked at her. Then the limo headed off down the country road.

Kara looked at the locket in her hand. She would wear it during the preliminary judging tonight.

She took a deep breath, put the locket in her backpack, and looked around. She was alone. She crossed the field to the pedestrian bridge that arched over the Chitakaway River. The oaks and maples were so thick on both sides, she knew no one would see or hear her practicing. The beautiful suspension bridge arched like a web over the flowing waters that ran in the ravine far below. She set off across, feeling the bridge gently sway under her feet. About halfway across, she stopped and took a breath.

There's magic in the air
Love is everywhere
All our friends are gathered round
To celebrate the fair

Kara was shocked. Her voice screeched across the ravine. Whatever happened before *wasn't* happening now. Her voice hadn't improved! She tried three more times, but her singing didn't get any better. What was she going to do? How would

Johnny react when he heard her voice for the first time and it wasn't as wonderful as he thought it would be?

Johnny wasn't like everyone else. He really listened to her. He respected her point of view, and he was willing to talk to her in ways no one ever had before.

She had no choice now. Opening her backpack, she took out the horn. This time she would be more careful. She felt the energy already sparking in her hands as she held the horn out in front of her. The words of spellsinging raced through her mind

Spellsing as one
And see your work done

The magic of the unicorn was just what she needed to jump-start her spell!

Sing a spell make it come true
Let my voice ring loud and clear
Change how I sing, and what they hear
I'll be as perfect as can be,
Make each note a part of me.

Blue fire flashed in the horn. She was a little nervous as she felt the winds kick up, the bridge tremble lightly as it swayed, then pulse like a back-

beat. Soon, her fear melted away into pure anticipation and excitement. Power surged forth from
the horn, but this time she was ready, holding it
fast with her will.

She opened her mouth and tried again.

The sun goes round the moon
The flowers are in bloom
You got to follow every dream
'Cause your time is coming soon
Feel the magic Can you feel it
Feel the magic Can you feel it

This time, her voice carried true, ringing out
across the river in waves of sonic bliss. She sang
perfectly in tune, every word as perfect as she had
heard it on the Be*Tween CD. Tapping her feet to
the rhythm, Kara started to dance on the bridge.
Arms moving in a tight routine, she felt light as air,
dancing in the orange glow of the afternoon sun.

A dark shadow passed overhead. Kara spun,
and the bridge swayed. Still in step, she looked up
at wide, fluffy white clouds, rolling under a blue-
domed sky. She continued her singing. No one
had a chance against her style. She was super-
stylin'!

BUMP!

The bridge lunged sideways, throwing Kara off

balance. Something had knocked into it from underneath. Underneath? She was at least ten stories in the air. She held the rope railing as the bridge settled, and peered out. The river ran fast, cascading over the rocks below and sending sprays of water high into the air.

Kara began to get an uneasy feeling in the pit of her stomach as she slipped the unicorn horn into her backpack. She was about to start for the far side of the bridge when the dark shadow passed over her feet. She whipped her head up and squinted against the sun. Something big was flying right toward her. Then she saw the familiar golden wings and spotted fur. She let out her breath.

"Geez, Lyra, you scared me half to death!"

The cat angled down over the far side of the bridge and swooped straight at her, coming in fast.

"What's with you?" Kara slipped her arms into her backpack. She looked up just as Lyra collided into her, sending Kara flying back. The girl was driven to the floor of the bridge, the wind knocked out of her.

"*Lyra!*" she sputtered, shaken to the core. "What are you doing?"

Kara tried to get back on her feet but Lyra was too swift and strong. The cat smashed into her back, and Kara slammed face-first against the railing. She found herself staring straight down at the rushing river below.

Kara was too astonished to even think. Cold fear rushed up her body as she scrambled back onto the bridge. Clutching the rope, she turned — just as the cat roared and lunged for her again. Sharp claws raked down her side, tearing out patches of denim and silk.

"*Lyra!*" Kara screamed, beating her arms to keep the razor claws from slicing at her neck and face. "Stop it!"

The cat brutally swiped at the girl, sending Kara hurtling toward the other side of the bridge. The rope caught her stomach, almost flipping her completely over. She crumbled to the bridge, her sweater ripped, one long gash down her left leg.

"Please! Lyra, don't hurt me!" she cried out. Sweeping sweat-streaked hair from her face, she tried to scramble across the bridge. Her left leg gave out and she stumbled. Her eyes caught glimpses of the riverbank only a few dozen yards away, and the path to her house that lay beyond it.

Lyra landed on the bridge, blocking Kara's way. The cat crouched, the fur on her flanks upright, her eyes dark with cold fire. Baring razor teeth, snarling low and vicious, the cat advanced.

Tears streaming down her face, Kara searched

her friend's eyes, looking for an answer. "I didn't mean to lie to you."

Lyra stared at Kara as if the girl were a hated enemy — one to be torn from this world.

"I took the horn . . . I'm sorry," she cried. Kara pushed to her knees. She felt numb, as if a hole had opened in her chest where her heart had once been. She saw Lyra's growling face as the great cat pounced!

The girl instinctively threw her backpack in front of her. Sharp teeth sank into the pack like a vise and blue fire exploded around the cat's head. Lyra wailed, shaking her head in pain. The pack tumbled to the ground.

Kara staggered to her feet. The unicorn horn was in her hand. It blazed with power.

Feral eyes turned to the girl, flaring bright with hatred.

"Don't make me do this!" Kara shrieked. Blue fire ran up and down her arms, encircling her.

The cat opened her great wings and rose into the air, razor claws fully extended. With a terrifying roar, she attacked.

"No!" Kara screamed, sending every ounce of will into the horn. The fire leaped free and crashed into the cat. For a second, Lyra was held frozen in the air, seared by intense, burning magic.

Something seemed to rip open inside Kara, a deep, bitter pain, screaming for release. And she couldn't stop it. She strained, trying to pull back the power, but it streamed out of her, slamming into the cat.

Lyra was thrown over the rope. For a breathless heartbeat, Kara waited. The wet thud as the cat's body hit sent spasms of sickness racking through her. She couldn't breathe. She wished she would faint. She wanted cool blackness to envelop her, to take her away from the nightmare.

Her heart thundered in her ears as she stumbled to her feet and raced for the trees beyond the riverbank. Kara strained her muscles until they burned and felt like they might rip apart inside her body, but then she was ducking branches, making sharp turns, and diving between narrow clusters of trees.

Kara burst out of the grove, her heart racing, her breath coming in ragged gasps.

Lyra! What had happened? How could she have been so viciously attacked by the one creature on the planet she thought she could trust more than any other?

And now Lyra was dead — killed by her best friend! At last, she fell into her empty house, her eyes burning, and raced upstairs to her room. All she wanted was to hide away forever from the blackness that welled inside, threatening to devour her.

She flung open the door to her bedroom — and froze.

Lyra lay on her bed, amid a pile of stuffed animals and the mad mess of papers and pamphlets for the concert. Her eyes were closed. The cat was *snoring*!

Kara backed away in fear as Lyra's head lazily rose from the pillow. The cat yawned. *"I feel so strange. It's not like me to take a catnap."*

Kara's back hit the door — and she gasped as she accidentally knocked it shut. "Keep away from me!"

Lyra struggled up from the bed, her limbs seemingly heavy with sleep. She looked at Kara with wide, confused eyes. *"Kara, what's happened to you? You're hurt!"*

"Just go!" Kara yelled. "Go!"

Lyra bounded from the bed, her back turned to Kara. *"I don't understand. Did I do something —"*

Kara's chest rose and fell with terror as she slumped to the rug, hands covering her face. "Get out! I don't ever want to see you again!"

Lyra sailed past her, giving one last look of worry and hurt before she leaped out the window. Kara slammed the window shut — and locked it.

Then she collapsed on her bed, reaching into her torn backpack and retrieving the locket that had miraculously not been lost at the bridge.

She cried for a very long time.

❧ ❧ ❧

By the rushing waters of the river, a second winged cat carefully pulled its broken body onto the damp earth. It shook its head and cried out in pain. Then, in a single fluid movement, the creature changed. Animal limbs extended, bones reshaped and straightened becoming long, human legs. Gashes healed as claws turned into fingers. Fur retreated into flesh.

The Skultum stood, carefully examining itself for any other injuries. The girl wielded the power of a unicorn horn! Considering the forces he had seen Kara unleash on the bridge, there could be little doubt now about the girl's ability to do what was required. The blazing star must not be allowed to learn any more than what she already knew. The magic had been meant for Kara alone, but there were two others who knew of the book.

Perhaps he could use this to his advantage.

After all, evil wore many faces and the Skultum could wear any he desired.

Chapter 8

Evening had fallen and Kara had pulled herself together as best she could. She had been lucky. None of the wounds were deep. She bandaged her leg and cleaned the scratches on her arms and sides. She had to tell Emily and Adriane, but she didn't know what to say. It still made no sense. She hid her feelings from Heather, Tiffany, and Molly, who had dropped by with a triple-cheese pizza, to help with the concert preparations. They had no clue that Kara secretly felt her world was coming apart at the seams.

Trying to pretend everything was normal, Kara went into overdrive, making a grand show of flaunting the locket Johnny had given her — which now hung from her neck — regaling her friends with stories of Johnny and his infinite wonder. She was the fearless leader, and she pushed away all the confusion and chaos she felt inside by talking non-stop about the details for Saturday's show, all the time trying her hardest to pretend that her closest friend hadn't tried to rip her to shreds. . . . While Kara sorted through a pile of papers, talking about ticket takers, additional parking, concession stands, placement of banners, and a hundred other things, Heather drifted over to the window and ran through a few simple voice exercises.

Kara kept talking until Tiff and Molly shushed her into silence. When Heather was done, they stared at her in shock.

"That's *amazing*," Tiffany exclaimed.

"You've been holding out on us, girl!" Molly roared.

They're right, Kara thought. She had never realized how beautiful Heather's voice was.

"How long have you been singing?" Kara asked, looking away and trying to sound like it was no big deal.

"It's no big thing," Heather said modestly, pulling her long red hair back into a ponytail. "You know my mom used to sing, and it gives us something to do together at church."

"Well, tomorrow you're singing at the church of JC," Tiffany quipped. "Johnny Conrad!"

Heather blushed. "You think I really have a chance?"

Tiffany swiveled her hips and shimmied into a

dance step. *"Let me tell you, if I sing it true, get up and start the dance,"* she sang, imitating Johnny.

Molly jumped to her friend's side and sang the next verse. *"A rock-and-roll rap with some zap, come on now and take a chance."*

The three girls sang the third verse together. *"No matter what you do, it's your life, you're you."*

They circled Kara and pushed her between them. *"So come on and take a chance and dance!"*

"DANCE! DANCE DANCE! TAKE A CHANCE AND DANCE!" they screamed, hopping and dancing around the room.

"Cut it out!" Kara said, annoyed. She couldn't help thinking of the way she and Lyra had played together in the same way just the other morning.

Molly, Tiffany, and Heather collapsed on the bed in a giggle fit, sending flying pizza remains everywhere.

Only Kara wasn't laughing.

Watching them, Kara felt a sudden flash of jealousy. Heather had natural talent. She could really sing . . . while Kara had to resort to magic. She had borrowed, no — let's get real — *stolen* the unicorn horn.

It was wrong! Or was it . . . ?

Inside, Kara knew she was somehow linked to

the magic. She could be so much more — she had star power!

I don't care if Heather is better than me, Kara thought. *She doesn't want it as much as I do. She doesn't deserve it like I do. . . .*

"C'mon, Heather," Molly squealed, "sing 'Supernatural High,' Be*Tween's song."

Come on, Heather, Kara mimicked Molly in her mind, *let up already, will you?*

Heather started singing.

I'm in my moon phase, my pink days
When everything is okay
I am beautiful, invincible
Perfectly impossible

Kara wished the girl would stop. That was *her* special song. The one she sang with Lyra!

Tiff and Molly barely seemed to notice Kara's distress.

Kara cleared her throat. "*I'm* going over to see Johnny rehearse tomorrow, and then we're doing a radio interview, then Johnny and I, we're gonna —"

Kara had to stop talking as Heather nailed another perfect note.

I can't take anymore, Kara thought. Turning, her

hands over her ears, she shouted, "Heather, will you please stop that noise? It's making me sick!"

Heather stared at Kara in shock. Tiffany and Molly also fell silent.

"Noise?" Heather asked, clearly upset.

Kara stared at Molly and Tiffany. She moved her lips but no words came out.

"Sick?" Tiffany said, springing to her feet and facing Kara. "I'll tell you what's sickening! Hearing you go on and on about how tight you are with Johnny!"

"*Noise* is all the hot air that's been coming out of you ever since this whole concert thing started up!" Molly added.

"This concert thing," Kara repeated, rolling her eyes. "It's *only* to save Ravenswood! Geez. You're all involved in that."

"For you," Molly said in a low, soft voice, shaking her head of short dark hair.

"Yeah," Tiffany said. "My dad says it's no big deal if those animals get shipped off to a zoo or a *professionally* run preserve. It might even be better for them."

"And sometimes it can be a little scary, giving tours with that wolf and that big cat wandering around," Heather noted.

Kara stiffened. "Fine!" she yelled, scattering

the entire pile of papers against the wall with a wide swing of her hand. She couldn't bear to think about the way Lyra had attacked her today. She could still smell the sweet scent of the cat in the room — and she burst into tears.

"Kara, are you all right?" Molly asked.

Kara gave a sharp nod, quickly wiping her eyes. "If you three have better things to do, then don't let me stop you."

Heather picked up the papers and gently handed them back to Kara. "Here. We'd better go."

Kara grabbed the papers and turned away. "Like I said, there's the door, it's not hard to figure out how it works."

Heather pinned Kara with her intense gaze. "Ever since you got involved with Ravenswood, you've changed, Kara! I wish we never heard of Ravenswood!"

Kara felt like she was watching through someone else's eyes as her friends filed out of the room. They were all turning their backs on her! Or was she sending them away?

She slammed the door shut. "Fine. I can do this without you. I don't need anyone!"

A moment later, a knock came at the door.

Ha, Kara thought. *That didn't take long.*

She was certain that when she opened the

door, she would find Heather and the girls looking all upset, and ready to apologize for their selfishness. Instead, she was confronted by Emily.

For an instant, she felt a twinge of guilt — and worry. Had Emily or Adriane realized she'd taken the unicorn horn?

No, that didn't appear to be it. Emily didn't look like she was angry, just a little distracted.

Kara bent to collect what was left of the mass of papers she'd strewn about a few minutes ago. "Emily! Good! I — we have a lot of work to do."

"I can't do any concert stuff tonight," Emily said. "That's not why I'm here."

Kara slumped on the bed, tears threatening to spill once again. She wanted so much to tell Emily about the craziness with Lyra . . . but instinct told her to keep silent. She didn't understand it, but the moment she opened her mouth to speak about the incident, it was as if her throat started closing with panic, her chest seizing up.

Emily sat beside her. "What's wrong, Kara?"

"Nothing. Just a weird day."

"Listen, I've been reading this book we found and —"

Kara was stunned. Did Emily know what she had been up to?

"We have to be really careful with this stuff."

Emily dug into her bag. "Look, I photocopied part of the spellsinging book for you. I'll give Adriane another part and look through the rest myself." She handed some pages to Kara. "If this is what the Fairimental was talking about, then it's important," she added. "We need to read it and then combine our notes, figure out what to do with it."

"Why did they choose us?" Kara asked quietly.

"What do you mean?"

"Why did the Fairimentals have to choose us? They've ruined my life!" Kara wailed. "Everything was fine before I got involved with Ravenswood and this magic stuff!"

"Kara, I don't know why it's us. . . . It just is," Emily said softly. "Now it's up to us to decide what we're going to do about it."

"Like how? How far is this going to go?"

"I don't know," Emily said truthfully. "I think about that a lot, too. Kara, I believe we're each being tested. You remember what Adriane told us about the Prophecy of Three?"

"Yes." Kara did. The Fairimentals had told Adriane about the Prophecy in the Fairy Glen on Aldenmor.

One will follow her heart
One will see in darkness
One will change completely and utterly

287

"Adriane followed her heart when she went after Storm on Aldenmor. I saw in darkness when I led us across the magic web and back home to Ravenswood. . . ."

"So . . . the third one is mine," Kara said, eyes opening wide. "One will change completely. . . . But I don't want to change!"

Emily took Kara's hand. "Your magic is different than the rest of ours. It's special. We all know that. And we'll stick by you no matter what happens." Emily smiled.

Kara gave her a quick smile in return. "I'd better not change into a flobbin!"

The two friends laughed.

"I have to go," Emily said. "But look over the spells and we'll meet tomorrow at the glade to talk about what we do next. Okay?"

"Okay."

Emily gave Kara a quick hug, then left.

Kara knew she should come clean about the unicorn horn, but she still needed it. She couldn't part with it yet. She looked over the pages Emily had copied for her. There were pages of spells and lessons on how to use singing to control magic. *Here's an interesting one: Spell of Silence — I'd like to use that on Adriane,* Kara mused.

Then she thought about the power she had unleashed behind the school. If her one little rhyme had held such power, especially when combined with the unicorn horn, maybe these real spells could help her make the finals.

She wished she could get her hands on the book itself. But this would have to do.

It looked like everything was going to turn out all right after all.

Chapter 9

The preliminary auditions were held at the school auditorium. After running through a half-dozen outfits, Kara settled on a long beige cardigan over a dark mini, black tights, and her new Valero boots; one moment she thought the outfit looked stylish beyond compare — the next, she was convinced it was hideous. But Kara hadn't been truly satisfied with anything she'd tried on: Nothing would be good enough, Kara was beginning to think . . . especially herself.

Even more frustrating, she had gone through every page that Emily had copied for her of the spellsinging book and hadn't been able to find a single rhyme that was specifically designed to make her magically enhanced singing voice last. The rhymes . . . the *spells* . . . all seemed to have been created for some other purpose. She had tried to sing as soon as she had gotten up, but had found that her voice was back to normal — horrible! She would have to take the unicorn horn with her again.

Lurking around the backstage wings now, Kara stole quick peeks at the audience. Inky Toon, who was presiding over this round of the competition, was chitchatting with reporters. Johnny was talking with folks in the front row, mostly members of the Town Council and their families, along with teachers and a few representatives of the school board. TV cameramen and Web cam operators had set up their equipment to capture the entire event.

When Johnny suddenly turned and looked right at Kara, a half dozen photographers automatically swung around with him and aimed their cameras toward the darkened stage. A barrage of flashes pinned Kara against the curtain, blinding her for a moment. They weren't bright enough to prevent her from making eye contact with Johnny. The instant their gazes met, her fear melted away, replaced by her excitement at all the possibilities he'd offered. She produced her perfect Kara smile for the crowd.

It was as if she was under Johnny's spell every time he looked her way. Touching the locket he had given her, she felt more determined than ever to be a winner and make him proud. Every one of the girls she had talked with backstage had recognized the good-luck charm she wore as Johnny's. A picture of it had appeared in his authorized biography and had been on many of his fan Web sites and in a slew of music magazines.

Some of the girls who recognized it were just excited, and wanted to touch it, or try it on — not that Kara would let them. Several others really were jealous, and shot daggers at her for wearing the locket at all.

Good, Kara thought. Maybe some of them would get psyched out, and that would make it easier for her.

Closing her eyes and leaning against a back wall, Kara smiled. The din created by techies racing around making last-minute checks on the microphone and karaoke equipment simply didn't phase her. Nor did the collective roar of all the nervous contestants who chatted away among themselves.

Touching Johnny's locket, Kara actually felt like she had a chance against her competitors!

A light knocking made Kara open her eyes. She was startled to see Adriane standing before her wearing a black leather jacket and skirt, a black tube top, and black leather boots. Her hair, glistening with subtle red highlights, looked amazing.

"Hey," Adriane said.

Kara nodded. "You look . . . good."

"Thanks, I just, um . . ." Adriane frowned. "We need to talk."

Kara hesitated, a sudden pang of guilt jabbing her . . . then she shrugged. "Now? Can't this wait till later?" she asked impatiently, looking past Adriane to where the contestants were starting to line up.

Kara had drawn her lot when she first arrived. She was number twenty-three. Thank goodness she didn't have to go first!

"No, we can't," Adriane grimaced. "Listen, Kara, I know you've been really . . . busy lately."

"So?"

"*So,* we all need to work together if we're going to figure out how to help the Fairimentals," Adriane insisted.

Kara restrained her urge to agree with Adriane. She wanted to trust her friend . . . but some instinct told her not to let her guard down.

"The thing is," Adriane said, "maybe I've pushed too far, making you go through with this. I don't want to compete with you . . . I mean, let's just call a truce before —"

Kara stared at Adriane cautiously. "Before what?"

"Well . . . before something else happens," Adriane whispered, adding, "I've heard you sing, you know."

Anger flared within Kara. "And you're worried I'm gonna embarrass myself?"

Adriane threw her hands up. "This contest . . . it was *never* supposed to be about the *two of us*. This is for Ravenswood. You're the president, our leader. If you go out there and —"

"That's it," Kara said, her cheeks flushing crimson. She pushed past Adriane to join the others.

"I didn't mean it like that!" Adriane called.

Kara stopped listening. She took her place in line and saw both Adriane and Heather take their places close to the front. Good. She didn't want to deal with either of them right now. She was nervous enough as it was — and Adriane trying to psych her out. . . . That was really too much to deal with.

As the music started and the curtain went up, Kara noticed two of the other girls casting worried looks at her locket. Suddenly feeling like a prize creep, Kara slipped the locket under her blouse, hiding it from view. *A minute ago, I thought it was cool showing it off. What's happening to me?*

Then the show kicked off!

The waiting — and the watching — turned out to be a lot harder than Kara had expected. One by one, boys and girls took the stage, and some were *really* good. Much better than Kara . . . and Kara knew it.

Adriane performed a cover of a classic rock-and-roll song, and she was extraordinary! Kara twiddled with the locket again. Then Inky was onstage again, introducing "lucky" number seven — Heather Wilson. Heather started to sing and the entire auditorium fell silent. Everyone backstage was buzzing — even Adriane — saying Heather not only had it in the bag to be one of the finalists, but that she would be the one to beat on Saturday during the preshow! Kara noticed several of the girls who were scheduled to go on after Heather walk away from the line and bow out. Others were asking to have their numbers reassigned. It seemed no one wanted to face the humiliation of following Heather's amazing performance. Kara saw Inky nodding and laughing, hanging on to her every note. Even Johnny was enthusiastically caught up in the performance!

Kara knew she should support her friend but she just couldn't bring herself to care. Instead, she drew comfort from the warmth of Johnny's locket.

"Ms. Davies! You're up next!" One of the teachers rushed over to her.

Kara allowed the teacher to lead her to her place in front of the handful of remaining girls. She nervously rubbed the locket around her neck. Several of the other girls looked at her locket once again — and she thought about putting it away.

Then she saw Johnny sitting in the first row, front and center, staring right at her with his bright, winning smile. His eyes flashed with blue fire.

No, she thought. *Why should I hide it? This is my lucky charm!*

Kara was ushered onto the stage, sweaty and shaking. The bright lights seared her eyes as she heard the music start up. It was one of Johnny's hits, a song she knew by heart. And so far tonight, she had been the only one to pick this song.

Two points for me, she thought, terrified. She looked out into the audience and felt her head go light, her knees threaten to turn to water. Just about everyone she knew was watching her, waiting for her to mess up. . . .

Well, to heck with that! Kara thought. Raising her head defiantly, she took the microphone, praying there wouldn't be some embarrassing feedback squawk, or that her voice would keep from breaking as she opened her mouth and prepared to sing her first line. She looked at Johnny, and saw his lips moving, as if he were singing the first verse himself.

And then —

The world stopped. There was a sudden heat at her throat, a fire where the amulet hung. For just a moment Kara experienced a sudden silence, a vacuum that drew all light and sound and sensation from her. She thought she was passing out.

No, this can't be happening!

Then . . . everyone was clapping. Kara shuddered, feeling disoriented and confused. She wondered why the music had stopped, and why she was being showered with applause.

She was still on her feet. She hadn't passed out, clearly. But . . . looking around, Kara saw everyone cheering, and Inky coming out to take the microphone from her.

"But . . ." she whispered, confused and yet feeling — all right, somehow. Like everything was fine.

"You rocked, girl! Totally cool," Inky said.

She'd had some kind of blackout, it seemed. She'd sung the song, and apparently did an okay job — she just couldn't remember doing it.

Weird!

"Kara Davies, everyone!" Inky said. "Everyone, give it up for contestant number twenty-three, Kara Davies!"

The applause rose and Kara bowed, grinning as she felt the adoration of the crowd seep into her like a physical thing, a comforting warmth. She could certainly get used to this part.

Just before she left the stage, she saw Johnny wink at her.

Backstage, Adriane glared at her suspiciously, but Kara didn't care. She had a really good feeling about how things had gone . . . even if she could not exactly remember the event.

The next hour passed in a blur. The other girls did their numbers, with Inky off in the corner, making notes about them. Then he took the stage and announced the finalists.

Heather had made the cut, *duh* there. But so had two girls Kara barely knew, along with Adriane, and —

"Our fifth finalist, Kara Davies!" Inky roared.

Kara raced out onto the stage, thrilled to be part of the winner's circle. She posed with the others for photographs, and Inky said he hoped to see everyone tomorrow — with a healthy donation for the preserve, of course!

Kara was ecstatic — for all of about five seconds.

Before she could say a word, Adriane grabbed her arm and yanked her aside.

"Okay," the tall, slender girl said. "I don't know how you did it, and I don't care."

"Did . . . did what?" Kara asked.

"You went out there and you didn't stink," Adriane said bluntly. "That's great."

"Yeah, thanks," Kara said. "I had so much encouragement from my *friends*." She delivered that last word like an icy dagger.

"And some help, too, no doubt!"

"What do you mean?" Kara asked innocently.

"I mean — this!" Adriane held up her wrist. The wolf stone was pulsing with strong amber light. "I know you used some kind of magic! Don't deny it!"

"No way."

"You cheated!" Adriane hissed. "You took unfair advantage from the start and you shouldn't have been allowed to enter the contest!"

"My singing was just as good as yours," Kara countered.

"In your dreams. You're bowing out of the finals!"

Kara stared at Adriane in absolute fury. "You've gotta be kidding!"

One look into Adriane's eyes — and Kara knew she was deadly serious.

"Wait!" she exclaimed. "I have to be in the finals!"

"Kara, this is about Ravenswood!" Adriane said. "The spotlight needs to be on the preserve, the animals, what we're trying to do for them . . . not about you."

"So why aren't you backing out?" Kara asked. "You cheated, too! You used magic to get the home-court advantage. You've got Johnny practically living right next door. You think people aren't going to talk about that if you win?"

"I haven't been getting Johnny's attention every single minute. You have. I mean . . . look at what you're wearing!"

Shaking with rage, Kara moved to slip the locket out of sight once more . . . then changed her mind.

"Fine! But if I can't sing in the contest, neither can you!" Kara said to Adriane's face. "Or I'll tell everyone how you practiced with Johnny at Ravenswood!"

Adriane looked furious.

"Do we have a deal?" Kara asked.

"Fine! I don't want to be in this stupid contest anymore!" And she stormed off.

Kara turned her back on Adriane and went to talk with Inky. He wasn't exactly happy to hear that she was withdrawing, but there were backup choices for the contest, and so long as this is what Kara really wanted . . . well, then he'd be fine with it.

So maybe she wouldn't sing with Johnny as the contest winner, Kara thought.

There were plenty of other ways to get even for what Adriane had pulled. She looked in her backpack at the photocopies.

Plenty of other spells, too.

Chapter 10

Kara didn't sleep at all that night. Now it was morning — *the* morning, the concert was *today* — but she couldn't get out of bed. She lay buried under blankets and pillows.

It was just so weird . . . why couldn't she remember singing that song?

Maybe it was like one of those things she'd read about. . . . People getting so nervous about a thing that they blank it out of their minds. Except — the song had gone so well. Kara could recall exactly how it felt to stand in front of all those people, to be under the glaring lights, to hear their applause — but that was it. Her mind had taken a shortcut, leaping right over the part that was really difficult, headed right to the instant reward she had craved.

Which . . . wasn't bad, right? Somehow, she really had delivered on that song, and if things had gone the way they should have, the way they were meant to, she would have netted that spot singing with Johnny. Only — Adriane had discovered her secret, part of it, anyway. That Kara had used magic to cheat her way to winning.

Kara was furious with Adriane, but at the same time, she also felt relieved. She hated lying and she hated being a cheater! What had possessed her to even consider such a stupid thing? What would her parents and friends think of her if they knew? She chewed her lip. And the way she had treated Heather . . . that was so cruel. To top it off, she had skipped classes, even destroyed school property! No wonder she hadn't slept much.

Well, it's all over! Am I a girl or a mouse? She tossed the pillows, kicked away the blankets, and sprang out of bed. She would meet Adriane and Emily at the portal field as they had agreed, use the dragonfly phone, and contact Zach. Then she would spill it all and beg her friends to forgive her. She would return the horn immediately before something really dangerous happened. She would forget singing onstage with Johnny and get back to what was really important: getting the word out to the world about Ravenswood!

Someone knocked at her door. "Hey, sleeping beauty!" her father called. "You've got a visitor!"

"I'm not here!" Kara replied. A visitor. Probably Molly or Tiffany . . .

"Not here?" came another voice, light and musical, from downstairs. "Not even for me?"

It was Johnny!

Flying into a pile of clothes, she threw on a pair of jeans and a T-shirt. She yanked open the door, barreled past her startled father, bolted down the steps, then stopped short. Johnny was standing in her living room. Wavy black hair brushed his forehead — his gorgeous blue eyes twinkled.

He grinned. "Ready for the big day?"

Kara nervously ran her hand through her hair, which she knew was a total mess. "Um, uh . . . sure," she said, accompanied by a self-conscious little laugh.

"I have a feeling this is going to be a day people will talk about for years to come." His melodic tones filled her with confidence.

Kara smiled back. Cool.

"So, what's up?" she asked.

"Inky tells me you've decided to back out of the competition."

"Uh, yeah . . ." How was she going to explain this one?

"That's just like you, you know," Johnny said, moving past her to examine the family photos on the fireplace mantle. "Always thinking of your friends first. I have something for you," he added.

Kara waited. The locket Johnny had given her suddenly became warm. Her skin tingled and she tried to stay cool — but suddenly, it was hard to think straight.

"I wrote a song for you," Johnny said.

Kara practically stopped breathing. "You what?"

Johnny took a thin sheet of paper from his pocket. "I wrote it originally for Be*Tween. You know, Inky manages them, too. We're pretty sure it's going to be a number one hit. The problem is — Be*Tween's missing. The way I heard it, they wanted a little time off."

Kara's heart thundered as she scanned the lyrics. He had to be kidding . . . but the look in his eyes was icy calm, deadly serious. This wasn't a gag.

"It's called 'Open the Door,'" Johnny explained. "It's about tearing down walls and letting friends know who you really are inside."

"Why me?" Kara asked.

"First of all, you were great last night," Johnny said. "And second, it's the least I can do for all the work you've done organizing and putting together the concert. And like I said before, you've got something . . . special."

Kara thought of the unicorn horn. Then she felt the heat of Johnny's locket. . . . She felt light-headed and the thought went out of her head.

"And I want you to sing the song tonight, for the first time, during the concert," Johnny said.

"Wow!" A brand-new Johnny Conrad song, and Kara was going to debut it tonight! "But what about the contest?"

"Don't worry about that," Johnny answered her. "We'll get that over with early on. You're going to be the showstopper!"

Kara just couldn't believe it.

"You know what being a star is?"

"What?" Kara whispered.

"When you shine brighter than anyone else in the world."

Kara smiled, eyes wide.

"Brief, bright . . . and then it's over."

"Not for you, Johnny," Kara said, holding her breath.

"Oh, yes, even for me. I'm just this month's musical flavor. A year from now, no one will have ever heard of Johnny Conrad. I'll be yesterday's news."

"No *way!*"

He smiled sadly. "There will be someone newer, cooler. It's just the way it is. But while we *are* stars, we do our best to shine, shooting across the heavens in a blaze of glory! You get all you can, any way you can! And tonight your star will blaze brighter than anyone else's!"

Kara was speechless. She was a blazing star. Is

that what it meant? To flame brighter than anyone else — only to burn out in a blaze of glory? She shuddered.

❧ ❧ ❧

"Blaze!"
"Barney!"
"Fiona!"
"Fred!"
"Goldie!"

Adriane, Emily, Balthazar, Ozzie, Storm, and Ronif moved through the large empty field calling the names of Kara's favorite dragonflies. Although usually complete pests, the magical, flying mini-dragons were useful at times. They had woven the dreamcatcher that protected the portal to Aldenmor from strands of the magic web. They could also open a small window to Aldenmor. The girls called it a dragonfly phone.

But without Kara the dragonflies were not showing up.

"One thing I can say about her," Adriane grumbled. "She's consistent."

The early morning mist had evaporated from the tall grass, revealing the deep woods of the preserve that lay beyond the field.

Emily looked at her watch again. Nine o'clock. Kara was an hour late.

"All right," she said. "We need another plan."

306

"It's useless," Ozzie complained. "*Those dragon-flies will only come to Kara!*"

Adriane turned to Storm. "Storm, do you think you can reach out and call to Moonshadow?"

"*The wolfsong is strong, but not strong enough on its own to cross between worlds.*"

Emily's face brightened. "Maybe we can use the dreamcatcher."

"*The wolves did contact me through the portal once before,*" Storm said.

"*But how do we open the portal?*" Balthazar asked.

"The magic of Lorelei's horn can open it," Emily said.

"I don't think we want to do that," commented Ozzie.

"Maybe the portal doesn't even need to be opened!" Adriane exclaimed, eyes shining. This dreamcatcher is made of the magic web itself." She turned to Storm. "The web might amplify your call."

"*Then how do we call upon the dreamcatcher with-out opening the portal?*" Ronif asked.

"With this," Emily said, looking through the pages from the spellsinging book she had taken from her backpack. She handed pages to Adriane and some to Ozzie.

"I saw 'Summoning Spells' in here the other

night," she said. "Try and find them. Maybe we can use one to summon the dreamcatcher."

"All right," Adriane said, looking through the pages. "Beats standing around waiting for Goldilocks." Considering the way Kara had been acting lately, the last thing Adriane wanted to admit was that they actually needed her.

"Here's one," Ozzie exclaimed. *"Say it loud but reverse the words, you'll speak in tongues from a mirror's curve."*

"That's a backward spell, Ozzie," Emily said. "Makes everything you say come out backward."

"Oops. I have enough trouble just being a ferret!"

"Float like a cloud, so high, so light," Adriane read. *"Hear these words and fly like a kite."*

"Lightness of Being Spell," Emily said. "Makes you lighter than air."

"Can't wait to try *that* one out on Rapunzel," Adriane giggled.

Emily gave her a stern look.

"You're right," Adriane commented. "She'd just put designer cement in her boots."

"Here." Emily found the page she had been looking for and scanned the text. *"Come to us, so strong and clear. We use this song to bring you near. We summon you before us, the image we see inside. We need your power, by this spell, abide."*

"Sound okay to you?" Adriane asked, looking to the others.

"If we all focus on the dreamcatcher, it might work," Balthazar said.

"Just one last thing," Emily said. "These spell-songs can only be used *once*. After we use it, we'll forget how it goes, and the words will disappear from the book, and probably from these pages, too. I read that in the introduction."

"Okay, so we get one shot. Let's add some rainbow and wolf power to the mix," Adriane said, holding up her wrist and exposing her wolf stone.

"Okay." Emily held her rainbow jewel next to Adriane's jewel. A spark of magic jumped between the stones, connecting them.

"You take it, Adriane." Emily handed the page to her friend.

"Okay." Adriane started humming a small phrase from a familiar song and then added the lyrics of the spell.

"Come to us, so strong and clear. We use this song to bring you near. We summon you before us, the image we see inside. We need your power, by this spell abide."

At first, nothing happened. The wind stirred a little, then died down. Adriane had reached the end of the song, but the words were still fresh in her mind, the characters still printed on the pages.

"Once more," Emily said to Adriane. She

turned to the others. "Picture the dreamcatcher in your minds. Focus."

Adriane nodded and sang again, and this time — the air began to swirl faster. Winds blew across the grass. Adriane looked down — the words were vanishing from the page. They had done it right!

The air filled with twinkling lights as a giant shape took form in front of them. And a dreamcatcher sparkled, hanging in the sky! The intricate weavings of threads caught the light of the rising sun and sparkled like a thousand diamonds. A circle opened in the center.

"We did it!" Ronif yelled.

"Hurry, Storm," Emily said. "I don't know how long the spell will last."

The silver wolf stood in front of the dreamcatcher and raised her silver-maned head majestically. She howled into the morning sky. In response, the dreamcatcher gently fluttered.

Then Adriane threw back her head and howled with her friend.

Mist filled the circle in the center of the dreamcatcher.

"Again!" Adriane called out. Storm howled her wolf song filled with the spirit of thousands of years of wolf memories.

Suddenly, another howl cut through the morning air, echoing across the field.

"Moonshadow!" Storm called out. *"Hear me!"*

The group gathered and peered into the dreamcatcher's center.

The mist began to clear and they saw darkness. It seemed to be nighttime. Dimly, they saw tree-covered hills spreading into the distance. Dark shapes moved.

"Moonshadow," Storm called out again.

A giant black wolf head slid into the misty picture, bright green eyes aglow. *"Stormbringer! My heart fills with happiness!"*

"As does mine, my wolf brother," Storm answered.

"There is so — arrg!" A blond head of hair shoved the big wolf aside. Zach's face filled the window.

"Adriane! Are you there, too?" Zach called out.

"Zach! It's me!" Adriane's heart flew with joy at the sight of her friend. "Are you all right?"

"Yes. We're at the Packhome*gahh* —" Zach was shoved out of the window by the huge black wolf.

"There is much to say and not much time," Moonshadow warned.

"Tell us," Emily called.

"The Black Fire has stopped raining from the skies."

"That's good news!" Adriane exclaimed.

Zach shoved in next to his wolf brother, angling for position. "We thought so, at first. We've been camped on the foothills near the Shadowlands, sending in scouting teams."

He looks tired, Adriane thought. She wished she could sit beside him, comfort him, talk and laugh with him like she had done on Aldenmor. She tried to ignore the sadness welling in her chest. "What is the Dark Sorceress up to now?" she asked.

"She's planning something big!" Zach told them. "She has completed building four giant crystals. We think they have been designed to hold magic, lots of it."

"Aldenmor grows barren of magic. We fear for the Fairimentals!" Moonshadow howled sadly. The howls of his pack mates echoed behind him.

"If there is so little magic left on Aldenmor, then why has she built these crystals?" Balthazar asked.

"She means to draw magic from somewhere else," Zach said worriedly.

No one had to ask where that might be. There was only one place that held the kind of magic the Sorceress desired. The home of all magic: Avalon.

"We know the Sorceress damaged sections of the web trying to do something to the portals," Emily said. "She even tried to use the magic of a unicorn horn, but it wouldn't work for her."

"Yeah, so how is she going to succeed this time?" Adriane asked.

Zach was silent for a few seconds. "She has the

fairy map to show the sequence of portals that lead to Avalon."

"I, too, carry a fairy map, of Aldenmor, given to me by my human wolf sister!" Moonshadow managed to stick his nose in.

Adriane smiled. "It was a gift from the Fairimentals. I just brought it to you from them."

"Wait!" Emily said. "We know that you can only use fairy magic if it's given to you. The Sorceress stole that fairy map. She can't use it."

"But there is one person it was *meant for,"* Ozzie said, almost to himself. *"Who* can *use it."*

Emily and Adriane knew. "Kara," they said at the same time.

"The dreamcatcher is fading," Ronif yelled.

"Be careful," Zach said, talking faster. "The Sorceress may have sent someone to your world to get Kara to use it for her."

"Someone new *did* show up at Ravenswood recently . . ." Emily began.

"Yeah, someone who *volunteered* to come," Adriane continued.

"Someone who Kara is spending an awful lot of time with . . ." Emily added.

"Johnny!" Adriane finished.

"Adriane, whatever happens here," Zach called out, "you cannot allow Kara to use that fairy map!"

"Yes," Adriane said. "Stay strong, Zach. I promise we will see you and the wolves again. Soon! And you'd better be right at the portal when I get there!" She had to fight back her tears.

Zach smiled, his green eyes warm and full of light as he faded away.

The dreamcatcher was vanishing, sparkling lights twinkling back into mist.

Suddenly, a mighty howl rose from the entire wolf pack, reaching across the worlds. Adriane and Storm howled back, cementing their bond with the promise of hope.

❧　　❧　　❧

Later, Emily headed for Kara's house, in case Kara was still at home but not answering her phone, getting ready for the concert.

Adriane went straight back to the manor.

"Adriane!" Gran was standing in the open doorway of their cottage, waving. "Come here a moment!"

"Can it wait?" Adriane asked, pausing on the cobblestone pathway. "I'm kind of in a hurry."

"This will just take a minute. I need to show you something."

Shrugging, Adriane turned and followed her grandmother into the house.

"What's up?" she asked as they entered the living room.

"I don't feel so good," Gran told her, pointing at the couch.

Adriane spun around — and was shocked to see . . . her *grandmother* lying on it? She heard the front door lock behind her.

"Huh?" Adriane whirled around to face the "other" grandmother, who was smiling sweetly. There were *two* Grans. But that was impossible!

"This is where you're supposed to say: 'My, what sharp teeth you have, Grandmother.'" The imposter leaned toward her with a little snicker.

Before Adriane could react, the old woman sprang at her with a strength and speed that Adriane would have thought impossible — if she'd had the chance to think at all. She was too busy screaming as her grandmother's face changed. For a brief moment, Adriane thought she was looking at Johnny, and then, the creature's skin turned green and scaly, fingernails turned to talons, teeth grew sharp and long, and the eyes blazed with a terrible inhuman fire.

"Time for a little nap, dear," the Skultum said, its huge hands covering Adriane's face.

Adriane felt tingling magic sink deep into her as she caught a sudden, terrifying glimpse of the creature's form changing once more, becoming a perfect duplicate of Adriane herself. Then all was black.

Chapter 11

Rows of people stretched all the way down the driveway leading into Ravenswood Preserve, in line for the concert. Behind the manor, those already there wandered in the crisp afternoon sun. Families strolled with children, kids and teens hung out, music filled the air, blasting from the stage set on the great lawn. The entire town had shown up. Kara had heard upward of three thousand people were in attendance, not huge by stadium standards, but a smashing success for Stonehill and for Ravenswood. Concession stands were doing brisk business selling popcorn, hot dogs, and soda. Everyone wore Ravenswood T-shirts, sweatshirts, hats, and bandannas. There were even small, stuffed toys of favorite Ravenswood animals, Ariel, Storm, Ozzie, and Lyra.

A huge banner hung behind the stage. The words SAVE RAVENSWOOD! were stenciled over an image of a giant dreamcatcher. That had been

Adriane's idea. Kara wished she had thought of it first.

Kara wandered, waving to the crowds spread out across the great lawn. *This is going unbelievably well,* she thought. Sporting a Ravenswood hat and shiny dreamcatcher lapel pin, she looked great in her new cords, boots, and brand-new brown suede jacket worn over her Ravenswood T-shirt. So why did she feel like a total loser? She knew exactly why. Although she had learned Johnny's new song, she was torn between using the magical help of the unicorn horn and just being herself, no matter what she sounded like. The pressure of debuting a Johnny Conrad original was unbearable! She had never felt so nervous, so out of sorts. How could she *not* use the magic!

"Kara!"

It was her dad. Mayor Davies was standing with the Town Council. A group of reporters were interviewing them near the side of the stage. The mayor was waving to her. "Kara, honey! Over here!"

Kara trudged over as a woman reporter moved to intercept her.

"Ms. Davies," the reporter beamed. She stuck the mike in Kara's face.

"What's your message to the world about Ravenswood?"

Kara thought hard. All those long months of planning, all the worry, the problems, the dreams had all come down to these few moments. Images of her friends flashed through her mind. Emily, Adriane, Molly, Heather, Tiffany . . . the animals, Ozzie, Storm, and once upon a time, Lyra.

"Ravenswood is more than just a wildlife preserve," she said at last. "It's . . . it represents our whole planet. We share our world with animal friends who count on us, and we count on them. And with help from all our friends, we can make our world a better place for everyone."

"Well said." The reporter was clearly impressed. "I'm putting this on the national feed," she told an elated council.

"The whole world will soon see what a fine example you have set for young people everywhere," the reporter said, shaking Kara's hand.

Kara stiffened. What if the whole world saw that she was a cheater? "Um, thank you," she said uncomfortably. She had to get out of here — and take care of this once and for all. "Dad, I have to go . . . check on some final details."

"Okay, honey." The mayor didn't miss a beat, continuing to smile and talk proudly about Stonehill's future, as Kara slipped away.

"A fine example for young people everywhere . . ." What a crock! She *had* to fix this. Clutching her backpack tight against her chest, she hurried through the laughing crowds and snuck in through the back door of the manor house.

She scurried up the stairs to the library. She would do what she had come here to do. She would do what was right — put the magical unicorn horn back. And whatever happened onstage later when she sang would happen. At least she would do it on her own. She was through with the cheating, the lying. In the end, she knew, she had only deceived herself.

She reached the library door and was surprised to find it unlocked and open a crack. Then she heard sounds from within. *Click-clack. Tap-tap-tap.*

Someone was using the computer!

Kara grabbed the knob and swung the door open, ready to ask Emily or Adriane why they were in there with the door unlocked when so many strangers had free run of the mansion.

But it wasn't Emily or Adriane at the computer. It was Johnny.

Johnny Conrad sat at the keyboard to their secret computer, weird images flickering on the screen before him. He looked over at Kara and grinned. "Hey, what's up?"

"I — I —" she stammered. Trying to mask her surprise, she ran her hands through her mane of blond hair. "What are *you* doing in here?"

The computer was way off-limits to anyone but the girls. The information locked away held all kinds of files about . . . magic.

Johnny looked confused. "I was just checking my E-mail. Adriane told me it would be okay. What, did I do something wrong?"

Worried that someone else might walk in, Kara swung the door closed behind her. Johnny seemed relaxed and confident as ever, not at all like someone who was about to perform in front of thousands of people . . . in about ten minutes! "Aren't you supposed to be, like, in your dressing room, getting ready?"

"I don't have a dressing room. This isn't exactly the Staples Center, you know," he joked. "Hey. Check this out. I found the Ravenswood Website. There's a live Web feed of the whole event."

Kara walked over and stared at the screen. A window was opened. It displayed a live camera view of the stage and great lawns. Had Johnny seen her walking to the manor?

"Adriane also showed me all these cool files you've set up for your Website." Johnny swung back around and hit some keys. Pictures of the animals appeared in windows. "It's really great."

Kara drew a sharp breath. Crossing her arms over her chest, Kara cautiously came closer and got a better look at the screen. *Had Adriane completely lost her mind? The girls had made a solemn pact to keep the computer secret!*

"So, you all set for your number?" Johnny got up and stretched like a sleek jungle cat. He moved to one of the large windows overlooking the event out back. The window was open, and the sounds of laughter drifted up to the library.

"I guess." Kara frowned as she joined him. They looked out at the vast crowd. Onstage, techies were finishing the last of the sound and light checks. "So . . . Adriane let you in here?" she asked.

"Well, *yeah*." Johnny smiled. Then his gaze narrowed. "What — did you think I picked the lock or something? If I wanted to be sneaky I would have snuck in at, like, three in the morning."

Good point, Kara realized. Yet . . .

"I just don't get why Adriane would do that," Kara said suspiciously. "Some of the things we keep in here are . . . private."

For the first time, Johnny looked uncomfortable. "You and Adriane *are* friends, right?"

"Of course. Why do you ask that?"

Johnny pointed out the open window. Chants and cheers began to rise from the happy crowd. "Johnny! Johnny!"

"Remember what we talked about, about what being a star means?" Johnny asked her.

"Yes." Kara suddenly felt the locket she was wearing grow warmer against her skin.

"Stars have to make sacrifices. Look at the crowd out there. When you're onstage, it's all for them. Giving everything you have."

Kara felt the excitement of performing starting to build.

"They expect the best you can be," Johnny reminded her, "and you have to deliver, no matter what it takes. Not everyone can be a star. Being special, one in a million, means standing alone. It changes everything. People you thought were friends can turn on you, betray you."

The words snaked into Kara's mind. *Adriane has always been jealous of me.*

Johnny looked at her with his deep, dark, soulful blue eyes. "How well do you really know Adriane?"

Kara was taken aback. Had he read her mind? "I've only known her for a few months. . . . Why?"

"When you're a star, friends can do things, act weird. Has anything happened recently? Anything that, I dunno, might have *changed* her?"

Again the locket felt warm against her skin — and suddenly, Kara thought about the time Adriane had spent on Aldenmor . . . and in the Dark Sorceress's dungeon. Was it possible that Adriane had come back *changed,* somehow? That maybe the Dark Sorceress had gotten to her, had made her evil? It would explain why Adriane had been acting like such a little *witch* lately.

"Adriane . . . went away for a little while," Kara said. "She met some not-so-nice people."

"I've seen it before." Johnny rubbed his temples. "Listen, I hate to be the one to tell you this, but it's for your own good."

"What? Tell me," Kara demanded.

"Your friend Adriane has been asking me and Inky, right from the beginning, how she can get a record contract. She wants to sing her own song, which Inky thinks could be a single, onstage at the concert."

Kara flinched. The locket was even warmer now — but nowhere near as fiery as her anger. "What else?"

"She said . . . *she* should be the *Blazing Star.* Not you."

Kara was speechless.

"I . . . I don't believe that," Kara stammered.

Johnny's eyes filled with sympathy. "Well, she's in the ballroom right now rehearsing."

Her brow furrowed in confusion and anger.

She spun around and started pacing. "I cannot believe that girl!" Kara yelled. "She told me she wasn't going to sing onstage. We had a deal!"

Johnny watched her. "I'm sorry. But like I said, when you're a star, friends can turn on you."

The locket flared — Kara was enraged. How could Adriane do this to her?

Spellsinging under his breath so softly she wouldn't hear it, wouldn't detect his lips moving at all, he exerted just enough influence. He had to be careful, even the slightest magic could alert the magic of the horn.

"Why did you come to the library, Kara?"

"Huh? I was going to return something. . . ."

"Remember what I said. You need to use whatever you can to make sure you deliver. You have to shine and show the world that *you* are the blazing star. That's the only way you can beat Adriane." A slight smile played across Johnny's lips.

"Oh, don't worry about that! I am going to blaze so bright the entire audience will need sunglasses." She didn't give another thought to returning the unicorn horn or leaving Johnny alone in the library. Kara stormed out of the room.

The *only* thing she cared about right now was dealing with Adriane once and for all!

Behind her, Johnny Conrad watched her go. A cruel smile appeared on his perfect face.

He sang a little tune and spread his fingers. A twinkling ball of stars winked into existence, floating in midair. He grinned as he stared at the sparkling fairy map, at the bright silver glow in its center . . . so much like a *blazing star*.

"Poor, confused little Kara," Johnny sneered, raising his hand and touching the floating orb. "You have no idea of the power that's inside you."

The little fool. He knew her weaknesses, her vulnerabilities, her needs. . . . She was so pathetically easy to read — and to manipulate. Hardly a challenge at all. The unicorn horn had been a surprise, but that had proved a blessing in disguise. He chuckled at his selection of words.

He had practically *smelled* its power on her. But he could do nothing with it directly. The unicorn horn had been freely given to the Three, and as a result, only Kara, or one of her friends, could unleash its power.

He was, of course, much more powerful than Kara as a spellsinger. But magic was more than spellsinging . . . much more.

And, as he had told her quite honestly, she had something others simply didn't possess. Star power. She would go out like a blazing star, a burst of magical energy as bright as the sun. If anyone's life was going to be sacrificed in this endeavor, it wasn't going to be his. And if by some miracle she survived tonight's events, his instructions were to turn her over to the Dark Sorceress. She would disappear. Just as Be*Tween had disappeared. He pictured the famous girl band. They would never find a way to defeat him or any dark magic again.

With her power — strengthened by her use of the unicorn horn — his song could not fail. "Open the Door" was his greatest creation. Kara would spellsing the words that would unlock the fairy map. With that much power, the portals between this world, Aldenmor, and Avalon itself would open in just the right order, laying the path for the Sorceress to do as she pleased.

He had to make *very sure* that Kara sang her song tonight. The locket could help to sway her, influence her, but it could not control her completely.

There was one final thing left to do, to lock Kara to his will and make her use her magic with enough force to open the portal and trigger the map. Her spirit must be broken.

He smiled, his voice musical, chiming and tremulous. Before him, the fairy map returned to its invisible hiding place. "Places to go, people to be . . ."

Closing his eyes, he stood by the open window. He concentrated, reaching out with his other-worldly senses.

"Show time. Guess I better fly," Johnny said. Throwing his arms open wide, he allowed his form to shimmer and change, to melt as his arms transformed to wings and his body shrank to the size of a large dark bat.

With a flutter of bat wings, the Skultum flew out the window.

Chapter 12

Throwing open the double doors, Kara stomped into the large ballroom. The clip-clop of her boots against the hardwood floor echoed in the empty space. All of the band's equipment had been moved out. The formal dining table, which had been moved to the side, was covered with bottles of water, fresh fruit in large bowls, and platters with meat and cheese, cakes, brownies, and other leftover sweet treats. Drapes covered the immense windows leaving the room dark.

Kara stopped and stared in utter amazement as she saw what hung on the walls. The heavy wood-framed pictures of wilderness scenes were gone. In their place were posters, each featuring Adriane singing, dancing, and playing guitar. They read: #1 WITH A BULLET, HOT HOT HOTTIE, THE NEW MUSIC SENSATION, OOPS, I WIN AGAIN!

Kara was stunned.

Suddenly, a spotlight splashed onto the wood

floor at one end of the room. From the dark shadows, Adriane stepped into the center of it. She was decked out in shiny silver pants, black crop top with the words ROCK'N'ROLL WARRIOR emblazoned on it, silver boots, and sunglasses. Her hair was layered in streaks of red, gold, and pink. She had a sparkling purple metal-flake guitar strapped across her back. With a swift martial arts move, she swung the guitar in position and strummed a loud chord.

The chord filled the room, resonating with power. Kara stood in total shock as Adriane began to sing.

> *One, Two — take a look at you*
> *You're standin' there, you think I care*
> *but don't you know,*
> *Anything you can do,*
> *I can do better.*
> *Three Four — you're such a bore*
> *It's all about me, can't you see*
> *that in the end,*
> *Anything you can do,*
> *I can do better.*

The spotlight followed Adriane as she moved around the room, singing and dancing like a superstar.

"That's enough!" Kara yelled in fury.

Adriane strummed the guitar one more time, then swung it back over her shoulder. "And that's just my warm-up number," she said coolly.

"You look totally. . . . *stupid*!" Kara announced.

Adriane laughed. "You're funny."

Kara crossed her arms. "We had a deal! You said you weren't going to sing in the show," she yelled.

"I said I wasn't going to sing in the contest! You're the one sneaking around getting your own spot! Why shouldn't I get my own spot? I'm so much better than you'll ever be!" Adriane taunted her.

"Are not!" Kara yelled.

"Am too!" Adriane retorted.

"Not!"

"Too!"

"You think all this magic is going to make you a star?" Kara waved her arm around the room.

"Hey, you started it," Adriane said, cruel glimmers of dark delight dancing in her eyes. "You're the one who cheated. You stole the horn."

Kara's face flushed. How had Adriane discovered that?

"So don't lecture me about magic! Cheater!" Adriane snickered.

Kara shook her head. "This can't be happening."

"But it is," Adriane said, walking to the table and taking a swig from a water bottle. She chucked the plastic bottle against the wall and swung her guitar into position. "You know what you are? You're a blazing *dud*! I'm the one who's going to shine tonight!"

"That's my spot and no one is going to take it from me!" Kara said angrily.

Adriane spun around and played a fast series of notes, fingers running up the guitar neck, sending out sounds so loud Kara thought they'd make her head explode — Adriane played faster and jumped, doing a split in the air. She landed, stomping her boots on the floor. A fiery crimson streak of energy ripped from the instrument and slammed into the wall, just missing Kara by inches.

"Hey! This is real suede, you know!"

Adriane strolled to the table and ate a piece of cake while Kara struggled to her feet.

"I don't know what's gotten into you," Kara said quickly, "but there's only one spot open in the show. And that spot is for me!"

Adriane giggled. She gripped her guitar again. "Really? You think you're gonna be up for that, Miss Clueless, or should I say, Miss Jewel-less?"

Kara saw Adriane's lips begin to move, and a soft song rose into the air. Was Adriane *spellsinging*? Then, whirling, Adriane jammed on her guitar, letting loose another volley of crimson bolts at Kara.

But this time, Kara was ready for her. She leaped out of the way, holding up the unicorn horn like a lightsaber.

Desperately, she tried to remember the spellsongs she had seen. The Spell of Silence came to her — but the words were all scrambled. For some reason, she just couldn't remember it right. Other spellsongs flashed in her mind. All she needed was a chance, a few seconds to deliver one of the songs —

"Look at you!" Adriane sneered. "You're magically impaired!"

Kara gripped the horn tight. "Be . . . *quiet!*"

Power rippled through Kara, and Adriane darted back, her fingers moving over the frets in a blur. A crackling red shield of energy appeared around her. The shield buckled in a half-dozen places as the magic from the unicorn horn crashed into it — but it didn't yield.

"What's the problem, Kara?" Adriane asked, her guitar wailing again, crimson sparkles of energy surrounding her. "Can't take the heat? You gonna wimp out onstage, too?"

"Stop it!" Kara commanded. The table rattled with energy. A chocolate layer cake lifted and smashed into Adriane's face, making her gasp in surprise.

Kara laughed.

Wiping off the chocolate, Adriane walked to the table and eyed the bowl of fruit. "Messy, huh?"

Kara's eyes went wide. "Oh no! Don't even think about it!"

Adriane strummed the guitar again. Kara dove into the corner, waving the horn about to defend her clothes from flying fruit, cookies, pretzels, and chips.

Kara stood up triumphant. Then she looked down. There was a big stain right on the front pocket of her new suede jacket! "That's it!" she screamed.

Holding up the horn, Kara sent a blazing arc of blue fire hurtling across the room, smashing into the table, sending food, dishes, and Adriane flying. Adriane landed with a graceless *oomf!* as her crimson shield faded away.

"The truth is, you don't have what it takes," Adriane shot back, rising on wobbly legs. "*I'm* the one Johnny really wants to sing with."

"You are, like, so deluded!" Kara said, raising the horn again. "I'm glad I took the horn!" She tingled with delight — and felt a matching warmth against her heart where Johnny's locket lay — as Adriane's face went pale.

"So I can teach you a lesson," Kara said, advancing on the other girl. "Lesson one: You have no . . . taste!"

Kara waved the horn in a circle like a magic wand, releasing sparkles of magic. The posters glowed with light, and suddenly the pictures of Adriane were all replaced by images of Kara. She was dressed in the coolest outfit, singing and dancing like a star. A blazing star!

Kara smiled in satisfaction.

❧   ❧   ❧

Carolyn Fletcher drove the green Suburban through the gates of Ravenswood. Emily sat in the passenger seat, nervously looking out the window. Cars were parked along the driveway past the gate and all the way down Tioga Road. Crowds of people were walking toward the back of the preserve, some carrying picnic baskets.

"Look at all these cars," Carolyn commented. "This is really incredible, Em. And all the people! I can't wait to see Mrs. Windor's face when she —"

"Healer!"

Emily jumped against the shoulder strap. "Storm?"

"It's a beautiful day, hon," Carolyn said to her. "No chance of a storm."

"Come quickly!"

"What is it?" Emily frantically scanned the grounds.

"It's just a bit of traffic. Emily, are you all right?"

"Adriane has been hurt! We're at the cottage."

"Mom! Stop the car!"

"What?"

"Let me out! I have to . . . fix something!"

Carolyn pulled the car to the side as Emily bolted out the door. "I'll catch up to you later!" she yelled as she ran across the front lawn to the far side of the manor.

Storm practically bowled her over as she rounded the cobblestone path that ran to the Chardáy cottage. The mistwolf's fur bristled with distress.

"Something's happened to her," Stormbringer said.

Emily burst through the front door. Adriane was on the floor. Gran was on the couch. Emily ran to Adriane and checked her pulse. Then she moved to check Gran.

"Ahhhh!"

Emily swung around at the scream. Ozzie stood in the door, mouth open. He was flanked by Lyra, Ronif, and a few other quiffles. Four pegasii stood behind him along with some brimbees and wommels, all peering into the cottage.

Ozzie ran over and looked into Adriane's face. "She's dead!"

"No, Ozzie," Emily said calmly. "She's sleeping. So is Gran."

Ozzie flopped to the floor. "Thank goodness."

"Adriane. Adriane, wake up!" Emily called. "Storm, what happened?"

"I felt her distress, her fear . . . then nothing."

"Come on, Adriane, rise and shine!" Ozzie murmured, patting the side of Adriane's face.

But, no matter how hard they tried, they couldn't bring Adriane around. Gran was in the exact same state.

"Something is not right here," Emily said. She turned to all the animals that had gathered outside of the cottage.

"Everyone! Inside! Quickly!" Emily commanded. "You're supposed to all be in the glade!"

The animals barreled into the cottage. Although it wasn't a small house, it was soon overstuffed with fur, beaks, flippers, and wings.

"Gather around me," Emily said.

"Gah! That shouldn't be hard!" Ozzie's muffled voice said.

Emily looked around for Ozzie and found him stuck between a wommel and a hard place.

Pulling him free, she settled next to Adriane

and held out her wrist. The rainbow jewel pulsed with blue-green light. Emily concentrated and sent out her healing magic to her sleeping friend. She sensed no physical injury, just a deep blackness. Adriane stirred but did not awaken.

"*She's in some kind of deep trance,*" Ozzie realized.

"*A spell,*" Ronif said.

"Yes . . ." Emily mused, "a spell."

"Everyone concentrate with me," Emily commanded. "Send healing strength to help Adriane."

She focused her jewel and reached out again.

The wolf stone on Adriane's wrist flashed with light. Emily quickly placed her gem next to the wolf stone, willing the healing magic to flow into Adriane. Both gems flared with magic and Adriane's eyes fluttered opened. "Hey," she said groggily. "Is that a ferret in my face?"

❧   ❧   ❧

The Skultum had no idea what was happening. Not at first. He was wearing Adriane's form and had Kara fighting to give it all up onstage, just as he had planned.

Then, he'd suddenly started to feel weak. His entire body trembled, his flesh crawled, and it was hard to keep posing as Adriane.

He was beginning to change. That meant his

victim had awakened, which should have been impossible! The only way that spell could be broken was with . . . magic.

The other young mages would know what was going on — and so would the real Adriane!

Hissing, the Skultum threw down the guitar and stumbled back, his stolen "Adriane" form losing its shape as he looked around for a way out.

Kara gasped. Adriane's face was *changing* . . . no, not just her face, it was the girl's entire form! For a shocking, mind-splintering instant, Kara saw — or *thought* she saw — Adriane morph into Johnny and *become* the singer. His hands danced, fingers moving in complex patterns as a strange song left his lips. Then, in a heartbeat, the figure before her shimmered and transformed into a monstrous creature covered in green scales. Slivered reptile eyes shone from its hideous face. Then it was gone.

"What . . . what just happened?" Kara began, attempting to wrap her thoughts around the horrific thing she had just seen . . . or *thought* she had just seen. . . .

"Ahhouch!" Johnny's locket flared red hot against her skin. She flinched and looked away. Her thoughts grew hazy, her head throbbed. Then the locket cooled and Kara felt a deep sense of triumph and exhilaration. So what if Adriane had gotten away? Kara had proved to Adriane that she was the blazing star, and now she would prove it to the world! Nothing would stand in the way of her singing the big number with Johnny! She *was* a star, baby! A blazing star!

Suddenly, something flew by Kara, flapping down the corridor into which Adriane had somehow disappeared. *Ewww!* A bat! A few seconds later, she heard footsteps behind her and turned to see Johnny entering the ballroom from the entrance across the room.

The singer quickly covered the distance separating them. Concern tinged his words. "Kara, what happened? Are you all right?"

"You were right, Johnny," she told him. "Adriane wanted to sing in the spotlight. She wanted to take my place!"

"Well, don't worry. No one can take your place! I'll make sure Adriane doesn't get anywhere near you during the show."

"Thanks," Kara said, still feeling a little shaky.

Johnny smiled as he led Kara to the back door of the manor and onto the great lawn. The crowd was chanting for Johnny. His band had taken their places onstage, ready to rock.

"It's show time." Johnny straightened his leather jacket as he led Kara to the side of the stage. People covered the entire field.

"Johnny! Johnny!"

"Are you ready?" he asked Kara.

"Kara! Kara!" Did she hear the crowd shouting her name also?

"Yeah!" Kara wiped the dried stain from her jacket. "I'm ready to shine!"

"All right! Let's kick it!"

❧   ❧   ❧

Adriane paced back and forth as Emily entered the living room. "Gran's fine now. Just resting," she reported.

"We were right," Adriane said, her hands balled into fists, wolf stone pulsing. "It's Johnny! Only it's worse than we thought. . . . Whatever he is, he's not human."

"*A shape-shifter*," Balthazar said.

"*That's what we sensed the other night,*" Ronif added.

"*That's bad,*" Ozzie said

"How bad?" Adriane asked, pacing.

"*Worse than a werebeast.*" Ozzie paced with her. "This one is real cunning. I'd say demon level."

"*Kara is in terrible danger!*" Lyra was wildly pacing now. "*We have to help her!*"

"You have to get back to the glade!" Emily said, then turned to the rest of the group. "All of you!"

From outside, they heard the sounds of rockin' drums, a thumping bass, and a wild electric guitar.

"The show's started!" Ozzie yelled.

Then the most powerful spellsinging voice in the world rang out. Johnny Conrad had taken the stage.

Chapter 13

"**D**ANCE! DANCE! DANCE! TAKE A CHANCE AND DANCE!"

Buzzing with excitement, Kara watched from the wings, as Johnny launched into his opening number. The audience loved it, moving, clapping, dancing to the music. Johnny had them in the palm of his hand.

Kara thought back to how she had first pictured the event, months ago. And now it was really happening! Here she was with Johnny Conrad, about to become a star!

She would use the magic. She had no choice. Her song with Johnny had to go perfectly.

"Kara! Kara!"

Was the crowd calling out her name already? She scanned the rows of faces. They were all intently watching Johnny, center stage.

"Over here!"

Just outside the roped-off area beside the stage, Emily and Adriane were jumping and waving. Adriane was in her black skirt, sweater, and dark green jacket. *When did she have time to change?* Kara wondered.

They were yelling something but she couldn't make it out above the music.

She turned back to the stage as Johnny finished his first song.

"Hello, Stonehill!" the pop star shouted. "It's a great night for Ravenswood!" The audience exploded in applause. Then, the band blazed into their second number. Johnny rocked out, doing the moves that had made him famous.

Kara danced along in the wings, jumping and — *ow!* Something had just bitten her! She spun around but nothing was there. Another spark stung her leg. What was that? Then she caught a telltale flash of amber light. *Zing!* She'd been bitten again! Adriane! Angry, she whirled around and saw the black-haired girl standing, arm raised, golden light flaring from her jewel. Kara narrowed her eyes and stuck her tongue out. She was just starting to turn away when she saw Adriane pointing. Kara followed Adriane's finger. Emily was holding up a sign. IT WASN'T LYRA!

Kara stopped moving. It wasn't Lyra? She loved Lyra more than anyone, but she'd been avoiding the cat. She hadn't even really thought of her since . . . it wasn't Lyra!

Something twisted in her stomach. She looked back at Emily again, who now had a second sign raised: IT WASN'T ADRIANE!

What did Emily mean? Lyra and Adriane had been *horrible* to her. Of course it was them! She'd seen them! A tingle of fear crept up Kara's back, tickling its way to her neck. She took a tentative step toward her friends.

Suddenly, the locket around her neck burned with intense heat. Her mind became hazy. Johnny was finishing his second number, but he was looking directly at her, anger flaring across his face. Kara shook her head — she must be crazy! She turned back to the stage and was relieved to see Johnny's look soften before he faced the crowd and bowed.

"Before we continue," he announced, "I know you're all excited about the contest. And I have picked the winner!"

What? Kara's face mirrored the surprise on the contestants' — no one had performed yet!

Johnny continued, "Let's hear it for the person who made this whole day possible, Ravenswood's very own Kara Davies!"

Applause thundered as Johnny beckoned Kara. In a daze, she stepped out onstage.

"And we have a surprise for you — we're going to perform a brand-new song dedicated to the

Ravenswood Preserve!" Johnny smiled at Kara. "Give it all you got!"

He nodded to the band, and the music started. Kara felt light-headed. Would she even remember her performance this time?

The audience sat waiting as the band reached her cue. Kara opened her mouth and sang.

In a world that spins so fast
Can't keep your feet on the floor
Where the future has no past
Open the door, open the door, open the door . . .

Kara scanned the crowd and felt her cheeks flush. Wincing, she spied Heather flanked by Molly and Tiffany, all snickering. This was awful. Kara's voice hadn't changed a bit

"Sing it!" Johnny hissed. "You're the star! Make it happen! Use your star power."

The locket around her neck flared with heat and Kara thought, *When they see what kind of star I am, they'll come back to me.*

She *deserved* to be the blazing star. That was her destiny, and Johnny could make it happen.

Reaching into her jacket, she felt the comforting coolness of the unicorn horn. Gripping it tightly, she called upon its magic . . . and sang.

Opportunity is just a window
So no matter what's in store
Open it up and let it flow
Open the door, open the door . . .

Kara's voice suddenly soared into the air, hitting perfect notes. She sang louder, moving her feet to the backbeat.

Johnny leaped into the air and danced. "That's it!"

The audience cheered.

Open the door, let it flow

As Kara sang the chorus, she could feel the mystical energies flowing from the unicorn horn. Lights behind the stage flashed in time to the beat as a wave of blue light pulsed around her.

Johnny was ecstatic. "Beautiful! More! Give it more! Open the door!"

And she did.

❧   ❧   ❧

In the distance, away from the surging crowd, Storm and Lyra ran into the open field. The portal to Ravenswood opened wide, ripping the air with shrieking winds against the darkening horizon. The sparkling dreamcatcher that kept Ravenswood safe stretched across it, strong and ready to amplify any magic sent into it.

Emily and Adriane were pushed to the side of the great lawn as people surged forward to get closer to the stage. *"Warrior! Healer!"* The girls heard the mistwolf's urgent voice.

"What is it, Storm?" Adriane asked.

"There is strong magic in the air. The portal has opened!"

The girls looked back up at Kara and saw the blue glow around her. That wasn't special effects! That was magic!

They pushed and shoved their way to the stage.

"Kara, stop!" Emily called. "You're opening the portal!"

Kara heard them and faltered. But before she could react, there was a blast of heat from the locket — and suddenly, she was singing louder than ever, releasing more and more of the horn's magic.

"Johnny!" Adriane shouted, nodding toward the wildly grinning singer. "He's making her do it!"

And though Kara was singing like an angel, there was pain and fear in her eyes.

The bass thrummed a thumping rhythm, and the band began its instrumental break. Johnny pumped his fist in the air as he swaggered across the stage, drawing the crowd to their feet.

His fingers reached into the sky and he began to spin. A blistering lead solo kept the fevered pace. Suddenly the music stopped — and so did Johnny. In his hands he cradled a ball of light.

He grinned at the audience as the orb grew brighter, revealing inside twinkling stars. The crowd cheered louder.

With a graceful toss, he sent the ball floating gently over his head. It sparkled as it caught the stage lights, glistening like a mirror ball, sailing through the air right toward Kara.

Kara recognized it instantly, the twinkling ball of stars with the bright silver glow in its center. She was looking at the fairy map. The gift from the Fairimentals to her. The one stolen last summer by the monstrous manticore.

Kara gazed at Johnny in fear. Then she felt the heat of the locket on her skin, and her thoughts began to get hazy again. In a burst of sudden panic, she tightened her grip on the unicorn horn.

But Johnny was no longer looking at her. His gaze was firmly fixed on the fairy map.

"Do what you have been destined for." His musical voice sounded like a chant. "You are the blazing star."

The fairy map began to settle around her, covering her in stars.

"Sing, Kara!" Johnny cried. "Make it happen."

The audience was on its feet breathlessly waiting to see what would follow this special effects extravaganza.

Kara struggled to fight Johnny's spell, to stop the song before it was too late. But she didn't have the strength. The unicorn horn could not protect her. She was just *another* falling star who had chosen the quick and easy path to achieving her dreams.

No! She *had* to fight this. "Lyra," she called out.

"*I'm here,*" the cat answered.

Kara started the next verse — but reaching out to her friend for strength she changed the words.

A web of lies spun so fast
I won't listen anymore
I can see through you at last,
Close the door, close the door, close the —

Suddenly, a chill wind kicked up and surrounded Johnny. In fury, he swung around and glared at Kara. What was that girl doing?

Kara tried to sing again, but she could barely catch her breath.

The crowd gasped. Her voice sounded horrible. She couldn't hit any of the notes.

"What's she doing?" Emily asked nervously.

"She's trying to change the words," Adriane said, surprised.

Kara's locket, the one Johnny had given her, was glowing white-hot, like a flame, making Kara cringe.

So *that* was what Johnny was using to control Kara!

Without a second thought, Adriane launched herself onstage. She ran to Kara and knocked the fairy map away from her. The ball floated gently over the crowd.

People in the audience started to bat it around, like a translucent beach ball.

Rage flared on Johnny's face, but only for a second. Dancing to the edge of the stage, he motioned for the crowd to send the ball back to him.

Adriane surged toward Kara, her hand reaching for the locket — but she was yanked back. A burly guard carried the struggling girl back to the wings.

A sudden, instinctive awareness flooded into Kara. The fairy map was always meant for her. Only she could sing the spell — to open it — and find Avalon.

She heard Johnny. "Kara, you are the blazing star — now *finish* the spell!"

Wide-eyed with horror, Kara realized the horrible mistake she'd made — all the wrong decisions and all the wrong ways she had used to justify them.

She felt herself spinning out of control, spiraling and turning inside out from the dark magic Johnny had worked on her.

She had to sing.

It was her dream.

Her *nightmare*.

There was a loud commotion backstage. Kara heard growls, scuffling, and people running. And then Adriane was before her, reaching for the locket. Kara had a flash that this was a mistake, the most terrible mistake anyone could make.

Or maybe that was just what Johnny wanted her to think.

Adriane's hand closed over the locket —

And for a single instant, Kara's and Adriane's minds were linked. In that instant, Kara understood that Adriane hadn't grabbed the locket for the sake of Ravenswood, or for Avalon, or even to protect herself; her only thought was to help her friend. Kara had been so wrong.

The chain securing the locket snapped — and Adriane threw it down, crushing it with her boot. Kara looked at Adriane, her eyes brimming with tears.

Adriane just nodded.

Howling with rage, Johnny ran around the stage, gesturing, and singing wildly.

The fairy map floated above the audience as they gently tapped it to and fro. Bright stars moved inside it in complex patterns.

If anyone had been out in the open field, they might have seen a much larger light show. Paths of stars swirled in the portal, creating a chain reaction of other portals opening, one by one, a frantic tumbling of cosmic dominoes.

Johnny sang and a swirling cloud of intense energy formed several feet above his head. Deep shades of red and blue blended together as bolts of lightning shot out from its center, reaching for the fairy map. Suddenly, something else bobbed up into the air above the audience. It swatted the fairy map away then fell back into the crowd.

"What was that?" Emily asked.

Some sort of furry animal was being tossed into the air above the heads of the crowd.

"Ozzie!" Emily cried.

"Whoo-hoo!" the ferret chortled as the crowd tossed him around. Each time Ozzie flew into the air, he swiped at the fairy map, knocking it further away from Johnny's grasp.

But all eyes were fixed on Kara, who was shining in a midnight-blue light that bathed the stage and the crowd.

She felt the blue fire of the horn engulfing her, burning away the very fabric of her being. Her star was going out in a blaze of glory.

Suddenly, a loud guitar chord barreled over the crowd. An enormous cheer rose up.

Adriane was standing beside Kara, guitar in hand. "Let's rock and roll!"

Together they sang, their voices mixing in magical harmony.

Together we stand
Able to do much more
Between us the power is ours,
Close the door, close the door, CLOSE THE DOOR!

Whirling around to signal his band, Johnny switched to another tune, his voice thundering out over the stage. Tossing his head back, he delivered a spellsong that released a blazing phoenix of red fire from the cloud above the stage. Adriane could feel its heat as it crackled and looked down at them, opening its maw as if to bake the girls where they stood.

Kara held the unicorn horn tight, and magic leaped forth. A blue-white unicorn made of clouds attacked the phoenix, impaling the fire creature with its horn. Cool silver sparkles rained down on the amazed audience as the images vanished.

Johnny turned to his band and launched into a smoldering version of the title song from his new CD.

I put a spell on you,
One look in my eyes, you know it's true
One note of my voice tells you what to do
Don't you know, I put a spell on you

Adriane's guitar squealed in feedback as sparks flew from it. The girls' voices faded as they began to sway under the spell of the song.

Suddenly, the sound of a flute sent a wondrous melody arcing over the crowd. It was Emily. She stood next to Kara and Adriane. Playing her flute, she sent out the song of Lorelei, the song of friendship she shared with the unicorn.

Johnny stopped singing. Was he weakening?

"Come on, girls," Kara yelled, "one for Be*Tween."

Kara, Adriane, and Emily sang together.

One chance for us all to stand together
One hope it's going to last forever
We've got the spirit
We're going to make it
I know we can
I know the magic's on our side

Kara's voice sounded like . . . Kara's voice, but to her friends it was the voice of an angel. Adriane and Emily joined in with perfect harmony.

"Everybody help us! Join in!" Kara called out.

The entire audience sang the chorus with the girls.

> *Don't wait for the sign*
> *It's one magic moment in time*
> *And you'll see through the haze*
> *One thousand lights will show you the way*
> *We've got the spirit*
> *We're going to make it*
> *I know the magic's on our side*
> *We've got the power in the darkest hour*
> *So don't give up the Spirit of Avalon*

Johnny was quivering, shimmering in lights. Be*Tween's song carried powerful magic. He ran behind the amplifiers as he began to lose his human form.

Kara saw a dark shadow and caught sight of a bat flying away from the stage. She stood between Adriane and Emily and held out her arms. Adriane and Emily held their wrists out and Kara touched each of their jewels. A bolt of magic flew from the gems, arcing out into the evening sky.

Fireworks lit up the night, as the Skultum was

ensnared in the magical blast. It was swept into the dreamcatcher and pulled into the swirling vortex. The portal closed.

For several long moments, there was nothing but silence on the great lawn of Ravenswood. Then someone in the audience started clapping and others joined in. The audience surged to its feet, crying out for more!

Kara embraced her friends as they took a bow to a thundering round of applause. The band was looking around uncertainly for Johnny.

Holding the mike, Kara announced, "Johnny had to fly. But before we go, I'd like to invite all the contest finalists to sing with us. Tonight, we're all stars!"

The excited girls and guys rushed onstage, surrounding Kara, Emily, and Adriane.

"I'd like our special animal friends to join us, too. They are the spirit of Ravenswood. Let's have a big hand for Stormbringer!"

The crowd cheered as the silver wolf loped onstage and stood next to Adriane.

"My best friend ever, Lyra!"

Lyra padded over to Kara. Kara knelt and hugged the cat so tightly, Lyra thought she would burst.

"Arial!" Emily shouted out.

The snow owl swooped over the astonished crowd and landed on Emily's arm.

Adriane took the mike. "And the one and only rock-and-roll ferret, Ozzie!"

The crowd went crazy cheering as Ozzie scampered onstage and took a bow.

Kara turned to Heather and smiled. "You start."

Heather smiled back and sang.

Nothing in this world can shake me
Trip me up or complicate me
Love is all that motivates me 'cause
I'm on a supernatural high

Everyone sang together. Their voices joined as one, sending the sweetest, truest, most powerful magic there was ringing out across the preserve, across their world, and across the magic web to what lay beyond. They sang from their hearts.

Chapter 14

Whtat were you thinking, Kara?" Adriane paced the floor of the library, throwing her arms in the air. "You and magic! It's like throwing gasoline on fire!"

Emily was there, too, next to Storm, Lyra, Ronif, and Balthazar. It had taken most of Sunday to get the great lawn cleaned up. It would still take some weeks before everything was back to normal. If that would ever be possible.

Kara nodded in agreement, eyes downcast, acting properly chagrined. She thought about how much she'd wanted to believe Johnny's lies, remembering the way she had almost given the Dark Sorceress the key to draw upon the power of Avalon itself. She had really messed up big time. Evil was easy, it provided shortcuts, instant rewards. Why was doing good so hard? But she already knew the answer. It sometimes involved sacrifice and wasn't always appreciated. And in the end, it was its own reward. Destruction was easy, building things that last was hard, like the friendships she had almost so carelessly thrown away. She leaned into Lyra, hugging her friend quietly.

The unicorn horn lay on the table where Kara had put it. Next to the crystal horn sat the glowing orb of stars, the tiny points of light inside configured in some still unknown pattern.

"We have retrieved the fairy map," Balthazar said. *"This is a major victory."*

"We haven't finished the 'I told you so's' yet," Adriane said, turning to the old pegasus.

"I've never seen so many messages," Ozzie called out. The ferret was at the computer, reading through hundreds of E-mails that had been pouring in from all over the world.

Best special effects we ever saw.

Congrats on a great show.

Are you available to appear in Springfield?

Ravenswood rules!

"Ha! Check this out," the ferret said. *"Teen singer Johnny Conrad rejoined his band in Memphis. When*

asked about the successful benefit performance at Ravenswood, he seemed in a daze and couldn't remember the show!"

Emily looked over the ferret's head. "Well, at least he's okay."

"Great!" Kara was on her feet. "The *real* Johnny Conrad won't remember anything!" she exclaimed sadly. Kara's star had come and gone.

"Here's one from the Town Council," Ozzie said.

Congratulations on a terrific event. Stone-hill has been on the news all day. The Parks Commission wants representatives to go to Washington. How about it, girls?

"Look out," Emily said. "Kara goes to Washington."

Kara hopped to her feet. "Tell them to send Mrs. Windor," she said, walking to the window.

The others stared at her.

"Let *her* take the credit. I've had my time in the spotlight," she said, staring wistfully out the window.

Emily glanced at Adriane and nudged her.

"Okay, okay," Adriane said. She reached into her backpack and lifted out a small box. "Face it, Barbie. You're a star, whether you like it or not." Kara stared at the dark-haired girl, then looked at the gift, a small smile appearing on her lips. "What's that?"

"We all wanted to get you something," Emily said. "So you would remember the concert and know that we will never forget what you have done."

"Thanks . . . but I wish I could forget what I did. You shouldn't have."

"Yeah, but we did anyway," Adriane said.

"I acted like such an idiot." Kara opened the box and removed a silver and gold band. And in the center was a small clasp ready to hold a stone — or jewel. "Wow. This is really nice!" Kara admitted truthfully.

"Read the inscription," Emily said, smiling.

To Kara,
Your star will always shine in our hearts.
Love, your friends at Ravenswood

"It's beautiful," Kara sniffled. She hugged Emily then turned to Adriane. "C'mon, you're next."

Adriane was about to protest but was caught in a hug.

"I know what the Fairimentals were trying to say to us," Kara said, turning to the group.

"What's that?" Adriane asked.

"They said, 'Spellsing as three.' Not one, but three. And that's what we did." Kara looked at all her friends. "We beat that monster by singing together, as three."

"We don't know what happened to the portals, whether they opened or not," Balthazar said, staring at the fairy map.

"Yes, but whatever the Sorceress tries next, she's got the *three* of us to deal with! Right, girls?" Kara held out her hand. Emily and Adriane stood strong and ready, jewels sparkling, hinting at concealed power.

"Right!" Emily put her hand on top of Kara's.

"Right!" Adriane put her hand on her friends' hands.

Sounds of music drifted from the computer monitor.

"Here's one!" Ozzie called out. The girls looked over the ferret's head at a bright icon arcing across the browser. It looked like a tiny shooting star.

"What kind of icon is that?" Adriane asked.

Ozzie clicked on the star. It was a file folder containing two messages. He opened the first.

Your concert was wonderful. We're sorry we could not be there. We hope that until we return, you will continue to spread good magic with music. There is much to

be done. Music to heal, music to fire our passions, and music to blaze forever as inspirations of goodness. *Don't give up on the Spirit of Avalon.*
Your friends,
Be*Tween

"Be*Tween!" Kara said, amazed. "They know about the magic?"

Ozzie then opened the second message.

Your path has been opened, young mages. Now you must go forward, together as three, and alone as a healer, a warrior, and a blazing star. It is time to walk your path . . . and come home. The magic is with you, now and forever.
Henry Gardener

Trial by Fire

Chapter 1

Dark clouds slid over twin moons, covering the night like a blanket. Behind the swirling veil, stars fell like tears as earth, mountain, and sky faded away.

A lone howl pierced the blackness.

Sweet smells of fresh grass, cool springs, and new life filled the air. Above, colors rippled across the heavens as if strewn by some painter's wild brush. Fiery reds, ocean blues, brilliant yellow-greens, purplish red-oranges, deep forest greens curled and danced, a pulsating patchwork that flowed across the sky.

Faint howls, a chorus of spirits echoed from the past, rising into one song, the collective song of ages, the wolfsong.

Run with us!

The ground trembled as hooves pounded the earth. Mistwolves, hundreds, then thousands strong, thundered across the sky.

Swept into the song of the mistwolves, the

power of the mystical vision grew. Towering canyons, fertile plains, immense forests rich and full of life swept past as the pack came upon the land's edge, where sand and sea met, where worlds joined. Thousands of mistwolves stood upon the beachhead. Before them great crystalline towers rose, catching glints of sun and spray. Giant interlocking rocks set in an immense jigsaw puzzle led the way to the crystal city at the edge of forever. Creatures of untold power and magic inhabited the city, sharing its wonders with the world of humans. Families of griffins and dragons circled the skies. Unicorns big and small ran free through the resplendent gardens playing with human students of magic. Sea dragons and merfolk crested the waves, gesturing and smiling as the pack stood.

My spirit sings to be with you! the lone mistwolf cried out.

Take from the past and lead us into the future, Moonshadow.

Lightning flashed, splitting the past from future. The images faded like tracks in the dust.

Moonshadow, leader of the mistwolves, sat alone on the peak of Mount Hope. Tilting his head toward Aldenmor's twin moons, the mighty pack leader tried to draw as much strength from his ancestors as he could. But the vision had ended. Once tens of thousands strong, the pack now numbered only a hundred. Since the erosion of magic from Aldenmor, the wolves had been hunted, feared as enemies, and slaughtered by creatures that had risen in the shadows of darkness. With his ears pressed back, Moonshadow felt what his ancestors had once felt. He knew what they had known. The mistwolves were strong, proud protectors. Then, as now, they were the guardians of Aldenmor.

At last, the mistwolf opened his golden eyes. Moonshadow's heart ached. The once glorious realm of Aldenmor lay before him in ruins — ravaged by black fire, devoid of trees and grass, burned and scarred from the dark magic.

Moonshadow howled into the wind, crying for what was lost. For a moment, his cry lingered, echoing across the Shadowlands. Then, all was silent.

Moonshadow knew then what his spirit vision meant. The pack's images spoke of hope, of humans and magical creatures working together as in ancient times. Moonshadow held the sliver of renewed hope to his chest as he shook the morning dew from his coat. He felt the cool object dangling around his neck. The fairy map, a magical talisman given to him by the fairimentals and Adriane, his human wolf sister. He'd been using the fairy map to guide the pack through the portals on Aldenmor in an attempt to defend the land from the Dark Sorceress. She was rapidly destroying the planet, draining magic, and storing it in giant crystals deep underground in the dark circle of the Shadowlands. The crystal constructions were dangerous and difficult to complete — each successive attempt to twist the magic had caused massive black fire fallout — but as Moonshadow had seen in his vision, not impossible. Even with the help of the map, the battle to protect Aldenmor was being slowly lost. Time and magic were running out.

The facets of the talisman flashed and twinkled in the rays of the morning sun. Moonshadow thought again of his vision and suddenly wondered if the map had been given to him for a different purpose altogether.

If only he could contact the fairimentals. They would know what he was supposed to do, but the Fairy Glen had been cut off. No one had been able to reach it or the fairimentals for weeks.

Suddenly, the fur on the back of Moonshadow's neck stood up. He sniffed at the air. Something smelled foul. Perhaps wafts of further decay from the Shadowlands — the howl cut through his thoughts as a gray mistwolf broke through the brush.

"Come quickly," the wolf called, *"the mistwolves are under attack."* Moonshadow leaped to his feet

and turned toward his approaching wolf brother. *"Who dares to attack the mistwolves?"* the leader asked.

"I do," the mistwolf replied, fiercely baring long, sharp teeth.

Moonshadow tensed. But before he could move, searing pain lanced across his shoulder. He fell to his knees as pain washed over him in waves of agony. Snarling and short of breath, he saw the riders appear, as if out of thin air. Thick bodies sat heavily on their mounts, eyes gleaming menacing green through the ports of steel helmets. Sharp serrated teeth grinned wildly from stout heads with pointed ears. They wore leather armor and spiked boots and held long whips that dripped venomous green poison. Goblins. And they were riding nightmares. The fiendish giant mounts snorted bursts of fire as their eyes glowed demon red. Jet black imps dangled glowing nets between them.

Ropes could not hold a mistwolf — even this traitor should know that. Moonshadow concentrated on releasing his physical body free of its corporal trappings. He closed his eyes and summoned his magic, waiting for the feeling of lightness that came when he turned to mist. But he couldn't. He felt locked in place, as if something was controlling his magic.

The enchanted net flew over the giant wolf. He

felt fire digging into his sides, tightening around his neck. He desperately tried to turn to mist, but every struggle increased the nets' hold over him.

His haunches were caught and pulled tight, slamming the wolf to the ground.

"White Fang! Dream Runner!" Moonshadow howled in fury.

"Don't bother," the gray wolf snarled, as he watched the struggling pack leader. *"We've already taken care of the others. You're the last."*

The riders shouted in oblique, rough tongues as their nightmares snorted, encircling the wolf. The pack leader made no further move to escape, knowing that his struggles would only suffocate him. Instead, he slowed his panting and moved his mind away from the pain. Growling low, he tried to see past the nightmares' long legs. He needed to identify the traitor.

Moonshadow locked eyes with the wolf that had dared to betray the pack. The net was yanked tight as the goblin riders pulled the wolf leader down hard. But Moonshadow no longer felt the pain. He kept his eyes on the traitor wolf.

The goblin riders jeered before kicking their mounts, dragging Moonshadow quickly behind them.

Alone on the peak, the traitor watched the riders disappear into the valley of dark shadows below. Golden eyes flickered fiery red as smooth fur shimmered, dissolving into scales. The wolf's body flowed and twisted as it rose up on its two hind legs. A lizard-shaped head twisted free with a mouthful of pointed teeth. Long scaly legs with splayed feet stood tall, and webbed claws sharpened into nails as the Skultum resumed his true form.

Chapter 2

Kara Davies watched the fire dance behind the ornate wrought-iron screen. The fireplace tools stood to the right in a metal basket tipped with animal claws. The sides of the hearth were trimmed with stone wings. Just about everything in Ravenswood Manor had been inspired or influenced by animals. Some were easily recognizable like the famous wildlife paintings of lions hunting the Serengeti Plain, Siberian tigers from India, massive grizzlies from the Canadian northwest, wild horses running across the open Dakota plains. Other objects hinted at more unusual creatures — a unicorn engraving in the wood paneling, a dragonhead of ebony set on chair arms. If you didn't know better, these were merely decorative touches inspired by fanciful myths and legends.

But Kara Davies, Emily Fletcher, and Adriane Charday knew that fantastic creatures like these still existed in a magical world called Aldenmor. At one time, these amazing creatures were plentiful. But like so many great species of Earth caught forever frozen in paintings and pieces of ornamental art, there were very few, if any, real ones left.

Perhaps that was why the guardians of the magical world, known as fairimentals, had sent for the girls, enfolding them in a mystery as profound as the magic itself. Three among millions had been chosen, gifted with the magic. Their lives were now bound forever with animals and creatures they used to think only lived in fairy tales.

Shadows coiled across the rows of stacked books as Kara took in warmth and comfort from the Ravenswood Manor library. She gazed out the large windows that looked upon the great lawn behind the manor house. Many creatures had come to Ravenswood for refuge. The animals out there weren't paintings, they were real. So many. Endangered and lost. How could she, Emily, and Adriane protect them when they were just learning about the magic themselves? How could she help them when she couldn't even help herself?

Lyra, the big orange spotted cat, arched her back and stretched her long front legs. *"You're thinking again,"* she purred.

"I do have a brain, you know," the blond-haired girl quipped. "Contrary to popular opinion."

"I didn't say anything."

Kara regarded the computer station on one of

the shelves of the library wall. When the girls were not using the library as their clubhouse, the computer remained hidden behind a sliding bookcase.

Ozzie had been one of the first magical animals to arrive here. In Aldenmor, he'd been an elf. Now, he was stuck in a ferret's body. A very smart ferret! Now Ozzie quickly turned back to the data he was reviewing. The list of animals scrolling down the screen had grown since the girls had first met the magical ferret back at the end of August. Some fifty creatures, big and small, now resided here along with deer, peacocks, monkeys, and birds. There were a lot of animals to watch over. Winter was coming. Normally at this time of year, Kara was all about Thanksgiving with friends and family, Christmas trees, parties and presents, ice-skating, and hot chocolate. Now all she thought about was how they were going to feed so many hungry and cold creatures. Depressing thoughts. This was her responsibility. She had convinced her father, the mayor of Stonehill, to let the girls take care of Ravenswood. So many were counting on her, and so far, she had failed miserably.

Lyra sat up and looked at Kara. *"So many sad thoughts."*

"Oh." Kara's expression softened. Though the room was toasty warm, Kara shivered at the memory of what had happened at the Ravenswood Benefit Concert last weekend. She had dabbled in a form of magic called spellsinging, and it had backfired big-time. She had fallen under the spell of an evil shape-shifter who had used her to open the Ravenswood portal — the magical door that connected Earth to the magic web and to Aldenmor.

Her friends had saved her. By spellsinging together, Emily and Adriane had broken the spell and helped Kara banish the shape-shifter and close the Ravenswood portal after it. But there were other portals, and Kara had no idea what had happened to them. Were they open still? And where did they lead? She couldn't help but feel the path was manipulated by the Dark Sorceress herself, the evil witch who'd caused the destruction of Aldenmor and the poisoning of its inhabitants. A path that could only lead to one place: Avalon, the home of all magic.

Since then, Kara had fallen into despair, questioning her ability to do anything right and her role as a blazing star. And underneath it all was the fear that she was changing, careening away from her life as it had been before magic, plunging headlong into some other weird place.

"I just finished unloading three truckloads of supplies!" Adriane's voice cut through Kara's thoughts as the dark-haired girl bounded into the library followed by Stormbringer, the mistwolf. "Where were you?"

"I was doing some homework." Kara casually gestured to her pile of closed schoolbooks neatly stacked on the oak reading table.

Adriane opened her mouth to comment, but Storm stopped her with a gentle nudge. Adriane shrugged and flopped onto one of the large velvet pillows on the sofa, pulling Storm into a big hug. The great silver mistwolf sprawled over the girl.

"That was a good run." Though the wolf didn't speak out loud, Adriane heard Storm clearly in her head. Lyra could communicate in the same way.

"Gran's had us running all over the place," Adriane said. "Salt strips had to be set up for the deer, and I had to prepare food blends to include turkey, pheasants, quail . . . and quiffles."

Kara wasn't listening. She just stared into the crackling fire.

Adriane frowned. She had never seen Kara like this before. And she didn't like it. They had come a long way together in a few months. When she'd first met Kara, she thought her shallow as a rain puddle. Now she knew that underneath that perfectly coordinated exterior was a real brain, a real heart, and some incredible magical power. Kara was truly a blazing star.

Emily was a natural healer. In the beginning, she helped Kara and Adriane see eye-to-eye, which hadn't been easy. Adriane's warrior temper wasn't easy to keep in check. But in the end, what mattered was that they had taken care of one another and against all odds, forged an unspoken bond of friendship.

Everyone was concerned about Kara's unusual depression, aware of how deeply the spell had affected her. Even her friends at school had noticed Kara's obvious retreat from the normal boisterous, self-assured, perfect being of total cool.

Suddenly, the door burst open. "Mail call!" Emily Fletcher announced as she hurried inside. "Get yer latest copy of the *Stonehill Gazette*."

A small herd of creatures followed the bundled redheaded girl, including Ronif, Balthazar, and Rasha, trusted magical friends. While the pegasi, quiffles, and wommels warmed themselves in front of the fire, Emily dropped her backpack to rub her hands together. Her cheeks were pink with cold. "How's it going, Ozzie?" She looked over the ferret's head as he pounded away on the keys.

"I put all the new E-mails in your "to be answered" file. Ozzie, the fuzzy former elf, had become quite a pro on the computer. He loved dealing with all the E-mail from the fans of Ravenswood. Ozzie had also found a very useful place for himself reviewing and cataloging the mass of information Mr. Gardener, the owner of Ravenswood, had left behind before vanishing.

"Take a break. Look what I brought." Emily pulled four boxes of graham crackers, a dozen chocolate bars, and a bag of marshmallows out of her backpack, dangling the goodies in front of Ozzie's face.

The ferret's eyes practically bugged out of his furry head. "Oooo! What's that?"

"Come on, I'll show you," Emily giggled, walking over to the fireplace.

Ozzie followed her, *and* the tantalizing bag of white marshmallows.

Kara was still staring out the window.

Emily glanced from Kara to Adriane as she pulled out a bunch of long wooden sticks from her pack, handing them to each of the animals.

"The feed supplies arrived," Adriane said, taking a stick and nestling herself between Rommel and Rasha. She deftly stuck a marshmallow onto the end of the stick as the others watched, fascinated.

Ozzie stuffed two marshmallows into his mouth. "YUM!"

"Wait, Ozzie," Emily instructed. "You have to toast the marshmallow and make a sandwich on the crackers."

Adriane, Emily, Ozzie, and the others gathered around the fireplace armed with wooden sticks. "With the new landmark status, the town council has allocated funds for food, but a lot of our animals are just not eating," Adriane said to Ronif.

"They are restless and homesick," Storm said.

"And not everyone is used to cold weather," Ronif the quiffle added. "Most come from warmer climates."

"Ahh!" Ozzie pulled a flaming stick out of the fire, waving it around his head.

"Careful, Ozzie!" Adriane exclaimed, covering her hair.

Ronif and Rasha weren't faring much better, each losing their marshmallows to the hungry flames.

"You're doing it wrong," Kara said softly.

"What?"

"Here. Give me that." Kara took the wooden stick from Ozzie's paw and speared a marshmallow. "You have to lightly brown the marshmallow without letting it burn. See?"

Kara held it over the flame, twirling it lightly until it was golden brown.

"Ooo. That's very good."

"Then," Kara continued. "you place it between *two* layers of chocolate. This way the chocolate covers both graham crackers."

"She's a genius!" Ronif exclaimed.

Emily and Adriane suppressed smiles.

The others, except for Storm and Lyra, followed suit. Soon Ozzie was happily covered in melted marshmallow fluff, chocolate, and crumbs.

Adriane picked up the paper Emily had brought in. The front page displayed a picture of Mrs. Beasley Windor and the town council. Windor was holding a landmark status certificate for Ravenswood. The headline read, RAVENSWOOD A ROARING SUCCESS, PUTS STONEHILL ON THE MAP.

Adriane snorted, "Look at this. Windor hated the idea of Ravenswood from the start, and now she is totally taking credit for our success!"

"That's politics," Emily said. "All things considered, we should be grateful. Why do you think we were able to get the funds for the winter supplies so fast? Windor personally approved the invoices!"

"Yeah, but I still don't have to like it." Adriane threw the paper down.

"Even with the supplies, what if we get more refugees from Aldenmor?" Balthazar, the older pegasi, asked. "We can't turn them away."

Ronif waddled over, testing a marshmallow sandwich in his rubbery beak. "Even with the tours closed for the cold season, someone is bound to discover us."

Emily knew that Ronif was right. Even on a

preserve as big as Ravenswood, they could not hide all of the refugees forever. Although it seemed Mrs. Windor was on their side now, they all knew how quickly things could change.

Kara picked up the newspaper and regarded the picture. Yes, the girls had pulled off the concert and fooled the whole crowd into thinking that the magical battle they saw was all part of the show. But the evil shape-shifting monster pretending to be pop star Johnny Conrad had put Kara under its spell. That was no illusion.

"Kawaaa," Ozzie jumped onto the table, his mouth exploding with marshmallows. "Makemeemee sommmorre!"

"The fairimentals should have made you a pig instead of a ferret," Kara commented.

POP. The fire surged upward in the hearth with a huge crackle, startling the group.

"I've been thinking about the E-mails," Adriane finally said. "I mean, after all this time, why would Gardener and Be*Tween suddenly contact us, and through the computer no less?"

"Maybe they couldn't before," Rasha offered.

"Yes, maybe they were trapped somewhere," Ronif added.

"That's what I was thinking," Adriane said. "Suppose when Kara opened the portals, she freed them. Or at least allowed them to contact us briefly."

That caught Kara's interest. "You're saying it's a good thing that I opened the portals?"

"Well, you do have a knack for using magic in unusually lucky ways." Adriane smiled warmly.

"That's a big suppose," Kara snorted, but nonetheless, a sparkle appeared in her eyes. "I still believed in Johnny and got burned big-time."

"But that wasn't your fault," Emily said. "Any one of us would have fallen victim to such strong magic."

"Still, Gardener and Be*Tween didn't give us much information," Ozzie continued, munching another s'more.

"Maybe they couldn't," Rasha said excitedly. "Afraid they might get caught."

"Remember when the fairimentals first came to us at the glade?" Adriane stood and asked.

"Yes," Emily remembered all too well. "They told us to find Avalon."

"And that's what Kara was doing," Adriane continued as she paced in front of the fire.

"Maybe that's what she did!" Ozzie finished.

Kara's eyes flew open wide. "So maybe . . . I did good."

"Kara," Adriane stopped in front of the blond girl. "Whatever you did, we know you *meant* to do good and that's what counts."

"That's right!" Ozzie leaned over the table to

hug the blond girl. "We're always with you no matter what!"

Kara flushed but smiled, holding the gooey ferret away from her sweater. "Thanks." She placed Ozzie back on the rug to toast some more marshmallows.

"The Dark Sorceress means to take the magic from wherever she can get it. It's just a matter of time before Aldenmor is completely destroyed!" Adriane pounded her fist. A quick glance at her friends told Adriane that they were all thinking the same thing. The three had been chosen by the fairimentals to save Aldenmor. Each had magical power and each had a job to do — find Avalon.

"Hey. Watch the fur," Storm rumbled, licking a dollop of melted marshmallow off her shimmering coat.

"Sorry," Ozzie said, holding the stick of marshmallows behind him as he faced the group.

Sparks of fire leaped from the crackling logs, licking at the melting six marshmallows Ozzie had crammed onto a stick.

"Be careful, Ozzie," Ronif complained. "That's hot!"

"And it smells awful." The ferret scrunched his marshmallow mustache, sniffing the air around him. "Smells like —"

"Ozzie!" Emily yelled.

"Your tail's on fire!" Balthazar observed.

"Huh?" Ozzie looked over his shoulder. "Ahhhh!"

The ferret tossed his marshmallows as he ran across the room, a plume of smoke trailing him. Everyone jumped out of the way, grabbing rugs, towels, and anything they could find to throw over the smoking ferret.

"ARG! Gah!"

Kara grabbed a vase from an end table, threw away the flowers, and emptied the water over Ozzie.

"Glub!"

Smoke hissed from the soaked ferret.

"Are you okay, Ozzie?" Emily asked, grabbing and hoisting him upside down to examine his tail.

"Watch it! Watch it!"

"Hold still." Emily's rainbow jewel pulsed with blue healing light. It bathed the ferret in a cool glow. "How's that?"

"Put me down!"

The soft lights in the library flickered and went dark.

The girls looked around. Smoke was slowly encircling the room.

"We blow a fuse?" Adriane asked.

The fireplace blazed, flames leaping high, sending sparks into the air as shadows skittered and crawled across the walls.

Suddenly, the fire hissed and with a loud *POP!*, flames leaped out, licking at the mantel.

The s'more eaters scrambled back.

"The fire's too big!" Adriane yelled.

With a shudder, the flames erupted out of the stone hearth, pushing aside the screen to roll across the rug in a fiery wave.

Hssssssssssss.

Like snakes, tendrils of flame reached up and coiled around itself.

"Get the extinguisher!" Emily yelled.

"Wait," Lyra told the three girls all at once. The big cat was on her feet, fur standing along the scruff of her neck.

"It's not burning anything," Ronif observed.

The fire was now completely outside the fireplace, on the carpet in the center of the room. Strangely, nothing burned. The flames left no mark on what they touched as if the fire were merely a ghost.

Swirling yellow, red, and blue flames reached to the domed ceiling of the library. They formed a figure, shimmering and glowing before the group.

A fairimental!

"Thank goodness, we thought you were lost," Ozzie said to the fire figure, holding on to Emily's neck.

The fire wavered. *"Fairy glennn iss dyinng,"* the flaming figure hissed.

"It's a *firemental!*" Balthazar said, astonished. Everyone looked to the Pegasus. "The most powerful and dangerous of the fairimentals."

"Usssssse mappp," the firemental hissed, reaching out with flaming arms.

A tendril snapped like a whip, flicking at Kara. The blond girl squealed and stepped back. But the flames found her, wrapping around and encasing her in a web of fire. The fire separated into strands, then wove into a ball of flame.

"Stand still, Kara!"

Kara stood motionless as the fire swirled around her.

"It's telling Kara to use the fairy map!" Ozzie yelled.

Kara felt desperate waves of magic flowing, forcing the fire figure to hold together. She barely heard the small voice hissing in her ear.

"Uu mussst findd Avvalonnn," the fire hissed, spattered and flickered out.

"Wait!" Adriane gasped. "Come back."

"Is everyone all right?" Emily scanned the room making sure no one was burned.

"I've never seen anything like that before," Balthazar said.

"No one has," Lyra checked her coat for burn

marks. *"If they risked sending a firemental, things must be bad."*

There was concern in Storm's golden eyes. *"The situation on Aldenmor must be worsening."*

Emily said, "What do we do now?"

"Should we contact Zach?" Adriane asked. Zach lived on Aldenmor and would know how bad things had gotten. Adriane was worried about him and the mistwolves.

"What good would that do?" Kara said, suddenly aware of how much she hated feeling helpless and scared.

"If we're going to save Aldenmor, we've got to stop talking about it and *do* it!" She tossed her golden hair over a shoulder, forging ahead before she could stop to think about what she was saying. "The firemental came for us!" Kara said sternly.

The room was silent. They all knew Kara was right. The time had come for the girls to put all they had learned to the test. To act now. Or it would be too late.

"There *is* only one way to find out what Kara did to the portals," Adriane said.

"We have to use the unicorn horn and open the portal here on Ravenswood," Kara said. "Just like I did before."

"And go through it wherever it leads," Emily added.

"The fairimentals sent me to find you," Ozzie said sadly. "It's time to bring you back."

"Time to save our friends," Storm said.

Lyra pushed her large head into Kara's side. *"We stand together."*

"We'll bring the unicorn horn and the fairy map," Kara said, racing ahead before she could change her mind. "The magic of the horn should keep us safe."

"I'll tell Gran we're going on a school trip," Adriane said.

"I'll get the Pet Palace shut down," Emily said.

"I'll go pack," Kara concluded firmly.

Everyone looked at Kara.

"What?" the blond-haired girl said demurely. "I'm not going without a change of clothes!"

"Good to have you back, Kara," Emily smiled.

Kara grinned and glanced at Adriane.

The dark-haired girl raised her fist and touched Kara's fist. "Okay, we'll meet at the portal field in half an hour."

"What should we tell the others?" asked Ronif.

"Tell them to get ready!" Kara said. "We're going to bring them home."

Chapter 3

The noon sun broke through patchwork clouds as animals filled the large, open field in the north quadrant of the wildlife preserve. It was here they had first appeared in Ravenswood — wommels, brimbees, pegasi, jeeran, and all the others, desperately rushing through the hidden doorway from their world to be healed.

The surrounding forest was already thinning as maples and oaks offered their final gift of colors. Soon they would submit to their cold slumber. Only the never-changing green of the pines would tough it out until spring.

Emily, Adriane, Kara, Lyra, Storm, and Ozzie made their way through the throng of adoring, cheering creatures. Rasha, Ronif, and Balthazar followed, setting off another round of hoots, hollers, neighs, and chirps. Word had spread fast that the girls had been called by the firemental. The ancient prophecy was about to be fulfilled.

Three young mages and their magical animal friends were going to save their world.

Ozzie spoke first.

"When I first met the fairimentals," he began, "they told me I would play a part in fighting dark magic and saving our world. I'm a ferr — an elf! I didn't believe it possible. Now, I'm here to tell you I believe!" The ferret raised his furry arms dramatically as the crowd reacted with more cheers.

"I believe in our friends and I believe in the magic." Ozzie began shuffling back and forth, calling out to the crowd. "And with a little luck, you'll all see home again." Dramatically, he fell to one knee, arms outstretched. "You just have to believe!"

More cheers met Ozzie's impassioned speech. They all needed to hear those words. Uncertainties lay ahead. The girls knew it. Their journey together had been as unpredictable as it had been rewarding. Yet each knew one thing for sure — something the fairimentals had told them: *There is no going back.*

Did they really believe they could do what they were chosen for?

Emily thought about how far she'd come, only to now stand at the crossroads between science and faith. Her first magical friend, Phel, had taught her healing was more than knowledge of medicine and technique, it was rooted deep in compassion and empathy. What would she believe when her faith was put to the test?

Adriane looked at her amber wolfstone set in the onyx and turquoise band on her wrist. The silver mistwolf beside her matched the reflective stripes down the sides of Adriane's black track pants.

Her grandmother called Adriane "Little Bird," an homage to their Indian heritage. Headstrong, Adriane had always fought with an iron will, barreling forward in a straight line, determined to find her own name, her own place. Thanks to Stormbringer, she knew she was not just a fighter, but a warrior with courage to soar free like a . . . bird. She smiled. No, to run free like a wolf. She was bonded forever with the mistwolves and Stormbringer.

"Little Wolf," Storm said, looking at her with deep golden eyes.

With Storm at her side, Adriane could do anything.

"All right, Ronif, Rasha, Balthazar, you're in charge now," Emily said. "Just try to keep everyone's spirits up."

"We will do our best," Balthazar said.

"As soon as the portal opens, call to Moonshadow and Silver Eyes," Adriane told Storm. "See if you can get a reading on what's going on over there."

"*I will try.*" Storm remained ever calm, ever strong.

"I think I have everything," Kara said, brushing her long blond hair back while rummaging in her backpack. Lyra stood beside her friend, grooming her own lustrous spotted fur. Kara was wearing designer hiking boots, dark denim jeans, and a faux fur-trimmed safari coat. Slung over her shoulder was a bright red backpack.

Kara was beginning to understand that her journey was tied to the magic more than anyone had thought possible. She was the conductor. Without her, magic had little focus, no direction. With her, magic shone in endless circles, spreading like the golden radiance of her smile. It had a profound effect on everyone — human and animal — she came into contact with. But just as still waters ran deep, she felt something more, a darkness just below the surface, waiting to drag her down.

"Kara, you have the fairy map?" Emily asked.

"Fairy map, check." She lifted the glowing ball from her pack. Tiny star patterns sparkled inside, a mysterious key to the pathways of the web.

Everyone looked with awe upon the gift given to Kara by the fairimentals. With this map, Kara had opened pathways of portals to parts unknown on the magic web.

"Unicorn horn?" Adriane asked.

"Right here," Kara held up the horn. Sunlight split the crystal, and a thousand sparkles raced up and down the swirled horn.

"Kara, what else is in there?" Emily asked, curiously eyeing her bulging backpack.

"Just some essentials," Kara replied. "Granola bars, a toothbrush, hairspray, Breath Blast, hair clips, a change of socks, some lip balms, chips. . . ."

"Where do you think we're going? Paris?" Adriane asked.

"Well, we don't really know, do we?" Kara shot back.

"Let's find out," Emily said.

Kara held the unicorn horn up high.

The crowd fanned out to a wide circle giving the young mages room.

The three girls stood close together, Ozzie before them, Lyra and Storm on either side.

Slowly, Adriane reached out and grasped Kara's hand, wrapping her fingers around it and the unicorn horn. Adriane's wolf stone glinted, then glowed bright gold.

Then Emily reached out, adding her hand to the others. Her rainbow jewel began to glow, pulsing blue-green light.

The crowd fell silent as spirals of amber and blue-green magic raced from the jewels swirling around the girls' arms. They could feel the animals in the field adding their own individual strength of will, helping to focus the magic.

"Okay, here we go." Kara pushed fear from her mind as she felt the magic surging though her. She recognized it and opened herself as it built, rising into waves of power, using her as a vehicle for its release. She focused and bent the power to her will.

"Concentrate on the dreamcatcher," Emily said, closing her eyes. "Picture it opening!"

A hidden, magical dreamcatcher protected the portal. It was constructed from strands of the magic web itself. One thing the girls had learned was that magic attracts magic. Power surged from Adriane's and Emily's jewels and flowed through Kara, around her body, up her arms, and right into the horn of the unicorn. A stream of magic fire burst from the horn, skyrocketing into the sky.

"Hold it steady!" Adriane yelled.

Kara whirled the beam of crystal starlight in a giant circle slicing the air with twinkles. The dreamcatcher appeared before them, hanging in the air just above the ground. Its circular center widened, revealing a curtain of mist. It was through this opening they'd have to go.

Lightning sparked even though there was no sign of a storm. The meadow below them suddenly lurched as the air seemed to twist. Thunder rolled and the sky cracked, splitting open the dark void. Winking stars that seemed to sit on glowing lines stretched behind the dreamcatcher. Although the girls had seen it before, looking into the yawning void was breathtaking. The magic web was incredible, at once beautiful and awesome, and, as they well knew, incredibly dangerous.

Emily drew in a breath. "Here we go," she murmured.

"Stay close together. Concentrate on forming a single protective bubble so we don't get separated," Emily instructed. Ozzie scampered up her leg to sit upon her shoulder.

"Okay." Adriane stood strong, holding onto Storm's neck.

The magic swirled, dancing faster around them. Gold, blue, and silver lit the field with dazzling brightness.

The center of the dreamcatcher opened wider before them.

"One jumps —" Adriane said.

"We all jump!" Kara finished.

And with that, Emily, Adriane, Kara, Ozzie, Lyra, and Storm leaped through the dreamcatcher into the portal beyond.

"Emily!" Ozzie cried, grasping Emily's neck.

"I've got you," Emily shouted back.

Triggered by the immense power of the web,

magic flew from Emily's rainbow jewel, Adriane's wolf stone, and the unicorn horn held by Kara. At once, an amber bubble covered in crackling blue light encircled them.

The bubble floated above the strands of stars like a giant balloon.

Emily quickly took count to make sure they were all still together. "It's okay, Ozzie. You can open your eyes."

The ferret open one eye and gazed through the translucent bubble at the endless spirals of web. *"Gah!"*

The bubble quickly picked up speed as it slid between stands of golden lines. They were traveling toward a sequence of portals, winking in the distance.

"We're on the web," Adriane said.

"It's awesome!" Ozzie exclaimed.

The orb dropped onto another tier of golden strands. The web spread out before them like a galaxy. Pinpoints sparkled, but it was impossible to tell how far away the stars were — or how close.

"Are you getting anything, Storm?" Emily asked.

"When I jumped through before, it took me right to Aldenmor," Storm answered.

"Same here," Adriane added.

"And that's how all the animals came through," Emily reminded them.

"So why aren't we going to Aldenmor?" Kara asked.

"Because Kara's spellsinging changed the pathway," Ozzie realized.

"There's something else," Storm said. *"Something has happened to Moonshadow."*

"What?" Adriane asked worriedly.

"I can't get a clear picture. The mistwolves wait for us at Mount Hope."

"So where are we going?" Kara asked.

"What I wouldn't give for a flobbin right now!" Ozzie commented, remembering the magic tracking creature.

"I thought the unicorns were fixing the web," Kara pointed out as the bubble sped past sections of web — broken, hanging, and tangled.

"Stay away from the broken strands," Emily called out.

Adriane raised her wolf stone, guiding the bubble along the path.

Emily pointed to the unicorn horn in Kara's hand. The crystal pulsed with brilliant light. "Lorelei's horn," Emily said. "Remember what she told us. We can use the magic of the unicorn. It was given to us."

Emily thought of her magical friend. Unicorns ran along the strands of the web itself, repairing it so magic could flow where it was supposed to go.

But here strands were horribly distorted, broken, and sparking like downed electrical cables. How could the unicorns hope to repair such immense damage?

The girls once again held hands as Kara raised the horn.

"Lorelei! Take us to where we're supposed to go!" Emily called out.

Instantly, the bubble took a sharp dip, spiraling into a sweeping curve, right toward a knot of broken, tangled strands. The knot sparked dangerously ahead.

"Not that way!" Ozzie yelled, trying to push the bubble in the opposite direction.

"Hang on!" Adriane shouted.

"To what?"

FLASH.

Dead silence.

For a split second, everyone was silhouetted in a blaze of white — then the web appeared, hurtling around them as they shot from the open portal.

Stars became streaks as the orb careened down layers of strands.

Adriane held onto the fur of Storm's neck as the bubble twisted, picking up more speed. Its thin walls were beginning to stretch, sizzling with power.

"Keep focused!" Kara shouted. "Hold it together!"

The bubble spun violently, dropped like a runaway roller coaster and — *FLASH* — rocketed though another portal like a meteor.

Emily lost her grip and was thrown against the thin walls of the bubble. Electricity sparked from her jewel, sending fire racing around the orb. She reached out and snatched Ozzie's leg before he bounced away.

Kara and Lyra were flattened against the other side. Electrical energy flashed and crackled along the bubble.

Kara felt her hand push right through the wall! Their protective shell was not going to hold together much longer.

"It's breaking up," Kara yelled. Wind whipped around them, sounding like a tornado. "We've got to stay together!"

Emily and Adriane strained forward, reaching to grasp hands, but the forces holding them apart were too strong.

"Something's coming up and fast!" Ozzie screamed, falling over Emily's head.

Ahead of them, a tight cluster of shimmering stars was getting bigger by the second.

"It's a nexus!" Emily called out.

The nexus hung like a thickly woven platform of light. Surrounding it were high walls that held dozens of portals. Here, strands of the web interconnected, each portal leading to a different destination.

"Try to stay together!" Adriane commanded.

"As long as we stay together, we'll be okay," Emily called, hand outstretched, trying to inch her way toward Adriane.

"We're coming in too fast!" Ozzie screamed.

"We're going to hit," Emily yelled.

The bubble careened toward the nexus floor and spun out of control.

"Ahhh!"

Adriane clung to Storm. Ozzie buried his head into Emily's neck. Lyra's magical wings flared open to protect Kara.

The bubble hit hard, bouncing into the air, coming down again, skidding and rolling. With a sudden blast of twinkling lights, the protective orb exploded apart and vanished.

They were all thrown in different directions.

"Emily!"

"Adriane!"

Instantly, a blue-green bubble formed around Emily and Ozzie.

An amber bubble formed around Adriane and Storm.

Silver diamond power blazed from the horn in Kara's hand, wrapping her and Lyra in a crystal cocoon.

The bubbles smashed into the walls of the nexus and vanished, swallowed into three different portals.

Chapter 4

Wind whipped waves of white, wrapping Adriane in cold. She covered her face, trying to see through the blizzard, thankful she had worn a down vest and heavy sweater.

"Storm?" She called out, suddenly afraid her friend had landed some place far from her.

"I am here," the wolf called out.

Adriane turned at the sound of the voice in her head. She instantly felt better. That connection, no matter how far away, was always a part of her.

She pulled her wool hat tight over her ears and trudged, head low, through the heavy snow. Within seconds, she found Storm. Dropping to her knees, she hugged the wolf close. "Thank goodness you're okay. I can't see a thing!"

"We have to get out of the storm."

"Can you sense the others?" Adriane asked hopefully.

"No."

"What about the portal we fell through?"

"There's nothing here now. We have to move. I sense danger."

Adriane quickly turned, trying to see through the blinding storm. "Which way?"

"We must move toward the mountains."

"Okay. Let's go." She got to her feet, and pulled the cuff of her sweater up to expose the wolf stone on her wrist. She concentrated. Instantly, the stone flared to light, casting a golden glow against the haze of ice and snow. The pair moved as fast as they could through the wall of white.

"Are we on Aldenmor?" Adriane tried to ignore the sharp cold hammering down.

"Yes."

"Okay, well at least we're here . . . wherever that is."

"Somewhere in the northern coastal region."

"How do you know that?"

"I can smell brine of the ocean mixed in the wind. The storm is passing over."

Her mistwolf senses were sharp. Sure enough, it wasn't long before the blizzard began to trail away. The fog separated, and the vista in front of them was breathtaking. Towering glacier-covered mountains rose from the rolling tundra, bordered by huge brown cliffs.

Sounds seeped through the wind. Soaring gulls skimmed the dunes that ran not fifty yards from where they stood.

Adriane turned in a slow circle hoping to catch a glimpse of Emily, Kara, Lyra, or even Ozzie. She scanned the wide plateau they had crossed, but all she saw was stark white landscape whipped by cold winds.

"Are we still in danger?"

"Yes. Something is hunting."

Adriane bit her lower lip. She'd been hunted once before on Aldenmor. Creatures had used her magic jewel like a LoJack to track her. Quickly, she covered the bracelet with her sleeve.

"Can you reach the mistwolves?" she asked Storm.

The mistwolf looked out beyond the giant ice mountains and closed her eyes. Adriane strained to hear a response from the wolfpack, but only the wind echoed in her ears.

"Help!"

Adriane whipped her head around.

Storm's ears pricked up. *"The hunters have found prey."*

"Where?"

Storm nodded toward the dunes.

Adriane focused.

"Help us!"

The call came again, this time more frantic. And then another sound. The unmistakable cry of an animal in pain.

Adriane and Storm took off toward the cry. The icy ground was slippery, but they were swift and sure. They covered the open snowy ground quickly, carefully picking their way up the rock-strewn dunes. Adriane crouched and eased herself toward the crest — she looked over.

She caught a quick glimpse of rocky beach and ice-covered water before *the thing* was on her!

It leaped from the far side, a wave of fur and teeth, roaring like a hurricane. Startled, Adriane fell back, tripping over loose shale and coral. It was the fall that saved her as a razor-clawed paw swept the air where she had been a second before. Big as a bear with piercing eyes black as coal, the snow creature stood on massive hind legs, its matted white fur thick with congealed mud and dirt. Adriane rolled into a fighting stance. Suddenly, the creature vanished, toppled over the dune by a roaring rush of silver-furred fury.

Adriane jumped over the dune and skidded to the bottom. The snow creature rolled across the stone-covered beach, attempting to remove the mistwolf from its back.

"Storm!"

Three other snow monsters turned at once,

looking up from the shallow waters of the wide bay. They were using their sharp, long claws to drag a large sea creature out of the waves and onto the frozen shore. Hazy sun reflected off emerald scales as the huge animal thrashed in the shallow water. It was the size of a whale but much sleeker, with tremendous flippers that it used to slap at its attackers. Gills along its sinewy neck opened and closed, fanning desperately for air. A long slash just below its dorsal leaked fluid into the crystal-blue waters, white with froth and red with blood.

Confident their prey was sufficiently wounded, the snow monsters abandoned the scaled sea beast and moved toward the dunes.

Adriane chanced a quick look up the beach and saw the first attacker lying motionless. Storm was nowhere to be seen. With a roar, the monsters raced toward Adriane.

"I think I got their attention," she whispered, sweeping her right arm into the air. Her damp sweater fell away exposing the wolf stone wild with bright amber light.

The creatures slowed at the sight, then fanned out to box in the intruder.

Locking into a fighting stance, Adriane felt the fire building along her arm, waiting to be let loose.

She eyed the bear creatures, choosing the biggest and most dangerous. She settled on the one in the middle, a huge mass of fur and teeth. She'd take him out first.

Magic fire flew from her jewel and whipped out in a golden ring. Instantly, the ring circled the giant bear. The creature leaped back in fright, trying to rip away the fire. The others skidded to a stop, unsure how to deal with this new situation.

Adriane stepped forward, whipping concentric rings of fire into the air, trying her best to make a fearsome display. Before the creatures could decide what to do, a terrifying growl erupted behind them — a silver mistwolf. Lips pulled back to reveal fierce teeth, ears flat, Storm was ready to spring.

The bear creatures decided to abandon their prey for the moment, slinking down the beach, then moving behind the dunes.

Adriane turned to the sea creature they'd attacked. During the fight, it must have managed to work itself into the surf. With a final painful cry and what looked like a wave of its flipper, it dove beneath the waves.

Adriane and Storm stood together on the windswept shore. Before them was a vast ocean strewn with ice. It stretched as far as the eye could see. Waves tipped with froth churned against the large ice flows.

"We surprised them, but they'll be back," Storm said, catching the worry in Adriane's dark eyes.

"What do we do?"

"We have to get to Mount Hope," Storm answered.

"Suggestions?"

"It's a long trek."

Suddenly, geysers of water erupted offshore. With gruff snorts, four sea creatures broke the surface. Giant green dragonlike heads with large slitted golden eyes stared at the girl and wolf. But Adriane's gaze was drawn to what sat upon their backs. Green-skinned with long flowing kelplike hair, they stared at Adriane and Storm.

"You there!" A young man called out from the back of his sea dragon. He looked to be sixteen or seventeen, but it was hard to tell.

"Who are you? What are you doing here?" Adriane asked, astonished.

"Waiting," he answered.

"For what?"

"You."

❧   ❧   ❧

"Here, try this." Ozzie emerged from the thick bushes, and handed Emily a paw full of red berries. "Bubbleberries. Should settle your tummy."

"How do you know they're safe to eat?" Uncertainly, Emily looked at the small berries in her hands.

"Spoof!" Ozzie spit out a slew of berries. "Quick! Is my tongue green?" He stuck out a red tongue.

"No."

"Good. Then they're okay." He went back to stuffing his mouth. "I used to pick these all the time when I was younger. They grow all over the Moorgroves."

Broken sunlight dappled through boughs of tall treetops. Emily and Ozzie walked along a wide road they'd discovered soon after arriving in the forest lands. Ozzie was sure they were in the Moorgroves, a dense forest region covering an immense area of Aldenmor. Even though the sun shone overhead, they could see twin moons, Della and Orpheus, rising just above the horizon.

"If we stay on the road, we'll end up somewhere," Ozzie said, munching away. "Arahoo Wells, Dumble Downs, Billicontwee. I was going to visit my cousins, Crusp and Tonin, in Dumble Downs that night I ran into the fairimentals."

"Is the Fairy Glen somewhere in the Moorgroves?" Emily asked.

"Could be. There's a portal somewhere near Dream Lake, I remember that."

No one had heard from the fairimentals for weeks until that firemental had come for the girls.

"As long as we don't wander into the Misty Marshes, we should be okay," Ozzie said, looking worriedly up at Emily. "How are you feeling?"

"Better," Emily answered bravely, rubbing at

her wrist. As soon as they had arrived in the thick forests, she knew something wasn't right. Dancing shadows moved across the road, making her feel dizzy and feverish. Her clothes clung, heavy with sweat, her mind seemed thick and foggy. And her stomach churned, threatening to empty her breakfast upon the trail.

Trying to keep focused, she asked, "So you really grew up near here?"

"The Moorgroves border Elf country. My village of Farthingdale is on the eastern Grassy Plains in the most beautiful rolling hills full of wildflowers. Wait till you see!"

"But we haven't seen anyone since we started on this road," Emily said, observing patches of open hills through the forests as they walked.

Shadows skimmed the ground fading into the woods.

"We're sure to spot someone, and they can tell us how to find someone who knows someone who knows how to get to Mount Hope —"

Ozzie looked behind him. Emily had stopped, rubbing at her wrist.

"What?" Ozzie asked, suddenly aware he'd been talking to himself.

"I don't know. Something doesn't feel right."

Ozzie ran back. "Let's have a look."

Emily pulled up the sleeve of her cardigan

sweater. Deep red and purple light burst from the rainbow jewel, erratically pulsing like a dull heartbeat.

Ozzie's eyes widened. "That doesn't look right at all."

"It's hurting me, Ozzie!" Emily said, rubbing the jewel harder, willing the itching burn to stop.

But the jewel only pulsed darker, deep purples swirling to green and black.

Emily felt the darkness infecting her jewel. She tried to focus. Think. When had she felt these strange, sickening feelings before? Suddenly, she remembered —

"Emily!"

Ozzie's scream broke her concentration. She saw the ferret yanking at her jeans, trying to pull her from the open road.

A dark shadow passed overhead. Emily raised her jewel to cover her eyes as she looked up. Something huge blotted the brightness. It looked like a giant bat, glistening black wings swept behind a sleek head. It had a short hooked beak and red flashing eyes. On its back, a gruesome figure rode, apelike and covered in rough armor of leather and steel. It held a crooked staff of polished metal tipped with a red crystal. A wedge of sharp teeth formed a grin as it bore down on the flying beast.

"Run!"

Emily saw the ferret hopping up and down, gesturing wildly.

She willed her legs to move off the road and into the cool darkness of shadows. Dust and dirt flew in her face from the sharp beating of wings.

"Run, Emily!" Ozzie screamed again.

The dark rider skimmed above Emily's head, almost knocking her to the ground. The crystal upon its staff flared like a demon sun. Ground, grass, and rock exploded, sending Emily flying past a tree. Coughing and choking, she propped herself on her elbows, trying to find Ozzie.

"Over here!" the ferret whispered as loud as he could.

Emily quickly crawled over a grassy mound and fell behind a wide, narrow knoll, thick with moss.

Shadows circled overhead, dark shapes breaking above the open treetops.

"What are they, Ozzie?" Emily was breathing hard, pulling twigs from her curly red hair as she hunkered half buried in deep ferns.

"Goblin riders. This is bad. What are they doing in the Moorgroves — *oh, no!*"

Emily capped her hand over the ferret's mouth. "Shhhh!"

"*Garg* — don't you understand?" the ferret asked, pushing her hand away. "The fairimentals have protected this part of Aldenmor for years. Now that they're gone — everyone here is in danger!"

"Where should we go?"

"We can't stay here. We have to find the elves!"

Emily's jewel had cooled to a dim glow but still swirled with maroon and black.

She was a healer. But could she heal herself?

She closed her eyes, willing herself to cleanse the jewel. To feel something clean, pure, and good — but all she felt was the familiar sickening poison, seeping with darkness.

"Ozzie, I feel something."

"What?"

"It's . . . I think . . . maybe . . . it's —"

"What, what?!"

"Black Fire," she said finally.

"*Gah!* Where?"

"Not far. Over that way." Emily pointed toward a thicket of forest.

Ozzie was on his feet pulling at her arm. "Can you make it?"

"I think so."

"Let's go!"

They scampered through the undergrowth, carefully picking their way over logs, fallen trees, rocks, and brush.

With an eye to the skies for any sign of the goblin riders, they quickly made their way to a hillside that sloped into a valley of green beyond.

"How close are we to your home?" Emily asked, worriedly.

"That's the Grassy Plains. Not far."

They didn't have to say what they really feared. If Black Fire had spread beyond the dark circle of the Shadowlands, Aldenmor was in terrible danger.

Distracted by her thoughts, Emily didn't see the edge where most of the forest floor had eroded.

"Look out!" Ozzie shouted as Emily set her foot down.

Emily tried to grab onto a thin sapling — but her foot slipped. Chunks of wet dirt fell away as her body hit the ground. She rolled and tumbled down the incline before coming to stop at the bottom of a wide gully. Arms out, splayed flat, Emily steadied herself and gingerly pushed to her knees.

She sensed them before she saw them. About a dozen small creatures surrounding her, each standing about four feet tall, wearing boots of tanned leather, woolen pants and leather shirts and vests. Each carried a long, sharp spear, pointed directly at her. She looked to see their faces and gasped. Their heads were contorted and gruesome, snarling, and heavily adorned with war paint.

Pink.

That's pretty, Kara thought, walking upon golden grass soft as rabbit fur through swirling mists of pinks, yellows, greens, and purples. She didn't feel scared. In fact, she felt strangely happy, almost giddy.

"Where do you think we are, Lyra?" she asked the large cat close by her side.

"I don't know," Lyra replied. *"But we're sure not on Aldenmor."*

> *There's magic in the air*
> *Love is everywhere*
> *All our friends are gathered 'round*
> *To celebrate the fair*

Singing! Someone's singing.

"Over that way," Lyra said, sensing Kara's thoughts.

An expanse of forest wild with oak and ivy became visible as the pinks and yellows thinned. Excited voices became clear, cheering, whooping and giggling.

"Sounds like someone's having a party!" Kara said, looking at multicolored lights flashing in the distance.

Come and join the fun
Dancing under the sun
Let's wave our hands
To all our fans
The party's just begun

"Can you feel it, feel the magic." Kara was humming along to the catchy song, skipping light as air as she danced through the mist and into the full-blown fairy rave!

Feel the magic
Can you feel it
Feel the magic
Everyone can't help but sing along

The music pounded, loud and strong, sending infectious sounds soaring over the enchanted gardens.

"Whoa!" Kara raised her arms, swaying to the beat.

Even the magic glade at Ravenswood couldn't hold a candle to this place — wherever she was. Explosions of color seemed to burst from everywhere. Fragrant, buttery yellow flowers, each painted with bright red stars hung like trees over the main party area. Long spears of heather, turquoise and golden, swayed to the rhythms. Violet primrose and garlands of silver birch glittered over rings of toadstools.

The music blasted from a stage set upon a circle of tumbled stones at the far end of the immense garden where three performers played.

The air bristled as rainbow sparkles cascaded gently, making everyone twinkle and glitter. And the place was jammed, teeming with all kinds of magical creatures Kara had never seen before.

"Fairy rave," Lyra said with disgust. *"Don't get too close. The magic is intoxicating. They'll lure you —* Kara?" Lyra looked around for her missing blond friend.

Kara danced by shimmying big-footed kobolds. She shook and hopped past cute little brownies and hooting hobgoblins. She bopped and boogied with five raucous long-bearded gnomes. Somewhere in the back of her mind a nagging thought told her she didn't have time for this. She should be looking for someone, Kara thought. Some friends. They were supposed to be doing something important, only she couldn't remember exactly what it was. And at the moment, it didn't seem all that urgent. All she wanted to do was rock out to the music.

> *I looked up to the skies*
> *And much to my surprise*
> *Things are changing right before my eyes*

You got to follow every dream
'Cause your time is coming soon

"Kara!" Lyra called, slinking through the silky, hypnotic rhythm of the music, paws firmly on the ground.

Pint-sized purple pixies perched on purled fronds. Fat big-eyed bogles tossed toadstools and drank from thimble-sized cups on the huge lawn. Spriggles and sproggins huddled under tables gobbling strange-looking foods. Leprechauns wandered around knocking into one another belly first and hooting hysterically. And darting over all of them, perching on blooms and dancing in circles were vibrant, luminous beings, beautiful gossamer-winged fairies!

Feel the magic
Can you feel it
Feel the magic
Everyone can't help but sing along

Kara was in the center of the party, all kinds of creatures were dancing around her.

Then she saw three performers onstage. They were totally kickin' it. The band was human-sized, like her. The lead singer's long raven hair flowed as she moved and twirled, scarves billowing around her like silk clouds.

With hair of neon pink and flaming red, the drummer leaped and jumped, pounding out the rhythm on anything she could find — including the heads of two overzealous bridge trolls!

Golden-skinned with dark blue hair, the guitar player hammered a strange-looking instrument of burnished wood that flared and glowed under her amazingly talented fingers.

"Woooo!! They totally rock!" Kara yelled, waving her arms, moving to the beat. The music was glorious, filling the garden with the most incredible magic. It was as if nothing else mattered, nothing else felt this good.

Kara danced with a pointy-toed, top-hatted, purple spriggle. The fairy creature raised his feet and arms, dancing up a storm.

"I'm Kara, what's your name?" Kara giggled, giving the pint-sized fairy her best smile.

"Me name?!" the fairy creature said, abruptly coming to a stop. "Why, I'll wark ye muckle tarrie!"

"Okaaaay." Kara danced away and into a cloud of sparkling wings.

"Ya poof git!" the angry fairy yelled, waving his small fist at her.

Beautiful silver- and blue-winged fairies converged about her, lifting her hair, tickling her arms and legs. A few beady-eyed hobgoblins dropped into the fray struggling with Kara's backpack. Snickering and hooting, they opened the zipper, diving in and rifling through the treasures.

One pulled out a granola bar. "Ye moog haggle!"

"Gimme, ya booty bogger!" Another cried.

They struggled over the power bar, falling to the ground as another pulled out an orange sock, which he promptly put over his head. "Farf doodle!"

Kara was surrounded by fairy creatures, converging all over her.

"Git, yer pookin muckle!"

There was a loud commotion behind her.

The fairy map — it floated out of the backpack! Sparkling stars winked and blinked inside the orb. A dozen spriggles had piled up on top of one another, trying to grab it, but the orb floated out of their reach. It rose into the air and hovered above the excited crowd.

"Hey, that's mine!" Kara said, easily grabbing the blue orb back into her arms.

The music came to an abrupt halt.

Everyone stopped dancing, frozen, staring at Kara with wide eyes and dropped jaws.

"The magic is with you."

She spun around to the stage. The band was staring at Kara.

"What?" Kara checked her clothes. "Did I get any on me?"

The flaming-haired drummer leaped from the stage, landing gracefully at Kara's feet in a deep bow. "We've awaited your return, Princess."

The entire crowd fell to the ground, bowing profusely and groveling at Kara's feet.

"What gives? Who are you?" Kara asked the pointy-eared fairy musicians.

"We are spellsingers," the silky siren singer said.

The drummer jumped to her feet, tapping a fast rhythm with her boots, "Maybe you've heard of us. We're Be*Tween."

Chapter 5

Icy blue waters rolled past the sleek sea dragon as it sped along the surface, leaving a wake of froth in its trail. Powerful fins and a long tail skimming like a rudder kept the riders on its back steady and sure. Adriane and Storm sat in front of the sleek dorsal fin. They watched the green-skinned boy from the sea talk to his mount as he sat astride its wide neck, gently stroking tapered fins behind the beast's wide, scaled head. It made Adriane think of Zachariah and the way he had been with Windy, his brave Griffin friend.

The merboy's clothes were sea-green and blue, like a diver's wetsuit. Around his neck hung an opalescent star-shaped jewel. His long green hair was pulled back and tied with several cords draped with shells. Pointy ears peeked from his kelplike hair.

"How did you know we would be here?" Adriane asked the boy, whose name was Jaaran. "We were told you would come," Jaaran explained.

Adriane noticed the boy's eyes had two sets of lids. She guessed one was for protection underwater. He had wide webbing between his fingers, and his bare feet formed natural fins of webbed toes.

"Told by whom?" Adriane asked.

"The mistwolves."

Before she could react, the sea erupted. Geysers of water spiraled high into the air around them. Adriane and Storm watched, astonished, as several sea dragons leaped, arcing high into the air and gracefully diving nose-first back into the water. They were amazing creatures. And atop each rode a merboy or mergirl! One sea dragon cut through the rolling ocean currents, swimming alongside Adriane and Storm. It snorted and opened translucent lids revealing large golden eyes.

On its back sat a girl, long green hair flowing in the wind. Like the merboy, she had webbed fingers and toes. A sea-green shell sparkled around her neck. "Meerka sends her thanks to you. As do I, Mage," she said. Her webbed fingers formed a fist and tapped it to her chest.

Adriane noticed the ragged wounds along the creature's side. This was the one they had saved from the snow monsters.

"I am Kee-Lyn," the mergirl said, pulling Meerka close alongside. "The beasts caught us off guard and attacked." Her voice lilted like waves lapping on the shore. "They are not from this realm of Aldenmor. They appeared out of nowhere."

"I know the feeling," Adriane said. She added, "I'm Adriane and this is Storm."

Jaaran nodded. "The magic of Aldenmor runs wild."

"Is Meerka all right?" Adriane asked.

Kee-Lyn hunched forward, hugging her sea dragon's thick scaled neck. "If not for you, Meerka would have been killed. The sea heals her now."

"When did the mistwolves call to you?" Storm asked.

"When did you hear from them last?" Adriane added anxiously.

"Two days ago. The pack leader told us you would come to bring the rain of lights."

"Rain of lights?" Adriane asked Storm.

"The lights may be a reaction to the portals Kara opened with her spellsinging," Storm mused.

"How magnificent to bond with a mistwolf," the mergirl said with reverence and awe.

Adriane nodded. "Stormbringer and I are from Earth. We both run with the pack."

"The sea dragons and mistwolves run the same path." Jaaran told them.

"How so?" Storm asked.

"Once long ago, there were thousands of sea dragons as there were mistwolves. Not anymore."

"The Dark Sorceress hunts them for their magic," Kee-lyn explained, her ocean-blue eyes full of grief.

Adriane understood. "I have been in the witch's lair. I know she covets the magic of such great creatures."

The riders looked at one another, astonished.

"You escaped the dark circle?" Jaaran asked.

"With the help of the pack and a boy named Zach," Adriane explained. "I thought there were no other humans on Aldenmor . . . until I met Zach."

"We are descended from humans thousands of years ago," Jaaran said, "but our home now is in the great oceans with the sea dragons."

It was Adriane's turn to look astonished.

Human? How could this be possible?

"But the magic of Aldenmor grows weaker each day. And with it so does the race of merfolk," Jaaran added.

"You also wear jewels. They must hold magic," Adriane observed.

"These are the Jewels of the Sea, designated to the chosen riders. We are the select few chosen to ride with the dragons to protect our world."

"And one day we, too, shall be mages, friend!" Kee-lyn added.

"I am honored to be called friend by you, but I am not a mage." Adriane told them.

Meerka snorted, turning deep, golden eyes on Adriane. *"You fight well. The magic is with you."*

Adriane stared into the deep eyes.

"She is a warrior," Storm said.

Satisfied, Meerka turned back to the sea. *"When the lights appear, magic will rain."*

Magic rain?

"Will it be dark or light rain that falls?" Kee-Lyn asked.

"The time is at hand, and we stand ready to fight or die with our world," Jaaran said.

"How do you know all this?" Adriane was awed.

"It was the last message from the fairimentals before they vanished," Jaaran said.

The fairimentals! "Do you know what's happened to them?"

Kee-Lyn's face fell. "We fear for them," she said sadly. "We fear the Dark Sorceress has broken their magic. Soon the seas will suffer the same fate."

"You said you know a portal that can take us to Mount Hope. Is that portal still safe?" Adriane asked, hugging herself to keep warm.

Jaaran said, "The pack leader wore a fairy map. He told us the portal remains true."

Adriane smiled inwardly. She had given the fairy map to Moonshadow as a gift from the fairimentals. "Where is this portal?" she asked.

The sea dragon came to a stop, gently bobbing on the open sea.

"Here," Jaaran spoke.

Adriane looked around, confused. All she saw was open water. Large ice flows drifted in the distance, and beyond a stark coastline, spotted with browns and greens.

With a snort, Leeka pointed his great head into the waters.

"The coral forest, below," Jaaran explained.

Leaning slightly to the side, Adriane rested her head on Storm's soft silver fur and drew strength from the mistwolf. Squeezing Storm's flank lightly, Adriane straightened, stood, and took a deep breath. Whatever grand scheme was unfolding, she and her friends had a destiny to fulfill.

Ready or not, they would fight for this world.

She raised her jewel and concentrated. The wolf stone blazed to life with an amber glow. There *was* strong magic here.

"You will lead us there?" Adriane asked.

"Yes," Kee-Lyn answered.

Adriane rolled back her sleeve and focused on her wolf stone. The amber stone grew warm and began to shimmer. When the shimmer became a broad arc of light, Adriane waved her arm, forming a circle of light. Storm pressed close to her, and the circle slowly surrounded them, sealing itself closed.

"We're ready," Adriane said.

Kee-Lyn looked into Adriane's eyes and nodded. "The magic is with you."

Meerka rolled her body forward in a smooth motion, and suddenly Adriane was watching the surface light fall away like a hazy dream.

Adriane focused hard on her stone, keeping the bubble protectively closed.

They sank fast, watching a thousand bubbles circle around them.

Below, the immense forest of coral revealed itself, like a jungle across the sea floor.

They dove below towering reefs of vivid colors, oranges, reds, purples, and blues. And the sea teemed with a cornucopia of colorful fish, plants, and sea creatures unlike Adriane had ever seen — or imagined. Schools of large sea horses swam through swaying kelp curiously watching the dragons and the strange creatures inside the magical globe.

"*Kelpies,*" Storm observed, her golden eyes focused intently on the bubble wall. "*Sea horses.*"

"It's incredible," Adriane was overwhelmed by the magnificent beauty. Would there be enough time to save it all from disappearing?

At the base of the reef, the sea dragons banked under a coral bridge and arrived at a giant underwater cave.

"This is it," Kee-Lyn said. "The portal is just on the other side of the mouth of the cave."

"Thank you," Adriane said. "I hope we will meet again."

"*As do we, Warrior Mage Adriane,*" Meerka said.

"We pledge ourselves to your service, Mage," Kee-Lyn said.

Adriane lowered her arm, and the bubble moved forward, lightly floating from the dragon's back. With a final glance toward her new friends, she and Storm moved into the cave and were swallowed by a blaze of light.

Chapter 6

Who are you?" The figure poked Emily with a sharp-pointed spear. Its face was particularly hideous, a viper's open mouth baring long fangs below deadly glowing eyes. A dozen others stood around her, each face more monstrous than the other. Their spears were front and ready.

"My name is Emily. I mean you no harm." She struggled to remain calm.

One of the creatures pointed to her wrist. Her jewel pulsed with reds and blacks. "What is that dark power?" it asked.

"A witch!" came a shout.

"No, I . . ." Emily began.

"Hey, you! Leave her alon-*agggrrrrhhh!*" Ozzie's voice came tumbling down the ravine as the ferret rolled into a heap at Emily's side. *"Doof!"*

He sprang to his feet, boldly pushing the spear away from Emily.

"What is this sorcery?" the creature asked, clearly taken aback by the talking ferret.

"A woodland spirit!" someone shouted.

"*Gah!* I am not a spirit." Ozzie faced the creatures. "Take off that war mask, Crusp. You look like a tree wart!" Ozzie turned to Emily. "Are you all right?"

"I think so," she replied. Emily then noticed that all the short creatures wore wooden masks! Which accounted for the scary faces.

The one Ozzie spoke to stepped back, clearly shaken. "How do you know my name, Spirit?"

"Talk!" Another poked a spear at Ozzie's rump.

"Yeee! Watch it, Tonin! Or I'll tell Aunti Melba to whack your elfish bottom!"

The figures were clearly flabbergasted, talking and muttering to one another.

"And your tag is still stuck on the back!" Ozzie pointed to Crusp's head.

Crusp slipped off his wooden mask. A frightened face with big eyes, bushy eyebrows, and a small nose and mouth greeted them. Masses of curly brown hair flopped over his head. He turned the mask to see his name etched on the back.

The other elves removed their masks as well. They stood about four feet tall, handsome and strong with thickets of long curly hair. Some were clean-shaven, some had neatly trimmed beards and mustaches.

"You know my name. Who are you, Woodland Spirit?" Crusp asked.

"Don't you even recognize your cousin Ozymandius?" Ozzie demanded.

The elves gasped.

"Ozymandius?" another elf stepped forward. "That elf was whisked away by dark forces. He's gone!"

"Well, now I'm back!" Ozzie stomped toward the shaken elves. "And this is my friend Emily. A great mage."

"A mage?!"

"That's right, knothead!" Ozzie said.

"This is nonsense!" Tonin stepped forward. "You . . . you're a . . ."

"Don't say it! The fairimentals transformed me so I could find Emily and her friends."

"Ridiculous! You're all fuzzy!" Crusp exclaimed.

"Ozzie . . ." Emily moaned softly, rubbing at her wrist.

"Have you all gone looney? Elven war masks are for decorating your house. No one *wears* these."

"Goblin riders have come to the Moorgroves. We stand ready to protect our homes!" Tonin declared.

"Ozzie . . ." Emily said again, louder.

"What!" He turned around. "Oo! What is it?" he asked, running to Emily's side.

"That way," she pointed, her wrist ablaze. The pain was worse, which meant someone nearby was also in pain.

The elves looked to the section of woods where she pointed.

"No way!" Crusp stated. "No one goes there. There is darkness and poison."

"Who's sick?" Ozzie leaped to his feet, brazenly facing the elves.

"Brackie and his family," Tonin said, sadly. "They are in isolation."

"Elves are infected?!" Ozzie was jumping up and down. "You bimbots! She can help!"

"She can?" Whispers of suspicion ran through the group.

"Look, you elven wingdip!" Ozzie was out of patience. "Take us to those who are sick! Now!"

Crusp looked to Tonin and the others. "All right," the elf finally said. "But if you use dark magic against us, you will both die."

"Nice talk, Crusp!" Ozzie kicked the elf's leg as they started off down the wide gully. "Coming from an elf who cheated through every game of pushball."

"I did not. You always used a smaller ball — hey!" His eyes flew wide.

"Ohh!" Emily stood but nearly keeled over in pain.

Ozzie was at her side in an instant. "Can you make it?"

Emily's face was covered in sweat. Clearly, she had a fever.

"I'm dizzy . . . feel so weak . . ." she mumbled.

"Hey!" Ozzie called to the elves. "We need some help here!"

The elves gathered around Emily, supporting her. Ozzie had never seen her so weak. "Ready?" he asked, keeping the worry from his voice.

"Yes . . . let's go," she said breathlessly.

"She is very sick for a mage," Tonin commented. "How is she supposed —"

"She'll be okay, just get there — and fast," Ozzie said.

The elves whisked through the thick forests, keeping the drooping girl upright and moving. At the edge of a clearing, they spotted farmland with acres of vegetables and cornlike husks growing in neat rows. The farmhouse lay nestled in a rolling hill beyond. It was a small structure made of wood and stone.

As they crossed, Ozzie saw why the farmland was in isolation. Deep grooves cut through the tall corn, ragged and ugly. Within the grooves, familiar sickly green glowed and pulsed. Black Fire.

Ozzie was heartsick. How could this have happened here?

"The fairimentals have vanished. We are no longer protected," Tonin said, as if reading his mind.

"Ozzie," Emily pointed. Dozens of animals lay in the grass near the side of the house, covered in green glowing wounds.

The group hurried across the field. Opening the wooden front door, Emily found two elves lying listlessly on beds of reed mattresses. Their breathing was shallow, and their skin glowed sickly green.

Emily immediately checked each one. A little elf girl was in her crib. Emily would have to act quickly. "The little one first," she said.

"Stand back! Give her some room!" Ozzie pushed the worried elves back.

Emily pushed her curly hair behind her ears, then raised her wrist. The jewel pulsed erratically, shifting from deep red, to blacks and sparking blues. There was no time to think, no time to worry, only to act.

"Shhh, it's okay little one," she whispered, stroking the baby elf's long hair. Big eyes looked up at her. "What's your name?"

"Vela," the little elf squeaked.

"Don't be afraid, Vela. Just hold my hand."

The small elf hand slipped into Emily's.

The healer closed her eyes — and fell into darkness. Swirling blackness thick as darkest night blanketed her. She fought to stay conscious. The Black Fire had never felt this strong before. It was like a vise locking her in its grip. She had always fought the fire on Earth. Here on Aldenmor, its power was so much stronger, overwheleming.

Emily screamed, making the elves jump.

Ozzie ran to her, leapt, and threw his arm around Emily's neck, as if to hold her in place to keep her from falling. "Hang on, Emily," he whispered.

Emily's jewel pulsed with a surge of rainbow light, slowly at first and then more quickly.

"You can do it," Ozzie hugged her close.

"The ferret is a healer, too?" an elf asked.

"Yes, he helps me." Emily focused harder. Ozzie's words echoed in her clouded vision. She reached for the power as it warped and twisted, like a live snake in her grasp.

Then Emily felt pressure in her hand. The little elf had closed her eyes squeezing Emily's hand as tight as she could.

Emily pushed her will into her jewel. If she faltered now, she would be lost.

Suddenly, the darkness turned lighter. A soft purple haze filtered into her mind, taking form.

The giant fairy creature stood, reaching out great paws, touching Emily with powerful magic.

"Phel!" Emily gasped.

She grabbed for the magic, a lifeline to pull her back from despair.

The rainbow jewel exploded with light, bathing the entire room in cascading pure blue of healing.

Emily grabbed the power, bent it to her will, until she felt little Vela's heartbeat sure and strong. Emily pushed harder. She could feel the fever leaving her body, her vision becoming sharp and clear, focused and strong.

The light faded along with her vision of Phelonius, but Emily no longer felt drained. She was strong, whole again.

She opened her eyes to see Vela sitting up and smiling, no longer covered in sickly green.

Ozzie leaped in front of Vela. "How do you feel?"

"Ooo, a mookrat!" she squealed, squashing the ferret into a big hug. "Can I keep it?"

"*Gah!*"

A cheer went up from the elves as they surrounded Emily.

"Okay, everyone," Emily smiled, then gently pushed the elves aside to tend to the parents. "Bring the animals to the front of the house, one by one. I'll get to them as soon as I take care of Vela's parents."

The elves made a mad rush to the door, trying to squish through all at once.

"She is a great mage," they rumbled.

"I told you!" Ozzie called out.

"What did you do to Ozzie?" the elves chorused in return.

"Oh, geez," Ozzie slumped forward.

Emily wasted no time. Phel had come to her. Once again, the fairy creature had helped her and in the process, she had discovered something vital. *In healing others, she had healed herself.* Her true path lay in helping — and that was the only true path to herself.

Emily attacked the Black Fire with a vengeance, strengthened with the joy that Phel was alive somewhere on Aldenmor. Finally, all of the sick had been made well.

"We are so grateful," Tonin told Emily when she'd finished her work, "We would be honored if you'd share supper with us."

"We cannot stay. We have to join our friends at Mount Hope," Emily explained.

"We'll take it to go," Ozzie called out, still in the grasp of little Vela's strong hug.

Suddenly, three elves ran through the front door. "Goblin riders!" they exclaimed, breathlessly. "They come!"

"My jewel," Emily said, watching soft rainbow

swirls in the gem. "It's attracted them. We must leave! Can you lead us to Mount Hope?"

"We can take you to the portal at Dream Lake. If it still works, you should arrive nearby." Crusp turned to the elves. "Tonin and I will take them. You take the others to the Far Falls to distract the riders."

"Right!" The elf ran out to tell the others.

"Ozymandius, you have changed," Crusp said, facing the ferret.

"Tell me about it."

"No, I don't mean physically. I mean you have changed. You are . . . a hero."

"Coming from you, Crusp, that's fine praise. Tell her to put some more grain cakes in there, will you, Cousin?"

"Sweetheart, Ozzie has to go now," Emily gently pried the ferret loose from Vela's arms.

"Mooki!" the little elf cried.

"Hush now, darling," her mother said. She handed Emily a bag of goodies. "Come back to us, Healer."

"I'll be back, too." Ozzie gave Vela a kiss. "And next time without fleas!"

Chapter 7

Welcome to the fairy rave."

Kara was awestruck. She couldn't think of a single thing to say! "You're B*Tween!" she finally blurted.

The lead singer stepped forward. Flowing silk scarves swirled around her. She had sparkling azure eyes and cute pointy ears. Dazzling jewels hung from chains around her arms and neck. "I am Sylina, a siren." Her voice was light as air, soft as a cloud.

"I'm Crimson." The red-and-pink-haired percussionist twirled, lightly tapping a rhythm on tiny bells that magically surrounded her like twinkling bubbles. "I'm from the pixie nation." She wore a bright jumpsuit and had bracelets around her ankles and arms. "And I believe this belongs to you," she said finishing the beat on the fairy map before handing it to Kara.

With a spin and bow, the blue-haired instrumentalist introduced herself. "I am Andiluna. A sprightly sprite to my friends. You can call me Andi." She swung her arm striking a thunderous chord from her glowing instrument.

"And you are Kara, the blazing star," the dark-haired siren singer said.

"I love your CD!" was all Kara, completely baffled, could think of to say.

Lyra stood protectively by Kara's side.

"There is no reason to fear us, Lyra." Sylina smiled at the big cat. "Kara is perfectly safe here."

"Fairy raves contain dangerous magic," Lyra spoke.

Crimson's laugh tinkled in the air. "Only some fairies are tricksters, Lyra."

A few nosy hobgoblins landed on Lyra's head, hanging over the cat's face. *"Shooo!"* Lyra shook the pesky creatures away.

"Where are we?" Kara asked, looking around.

"The twilight realm between worlds," Andi told her.

"Huh?"

"Come, walk with us," Sylina led Kara and Lyra away from the curious throngs of fairy creatures. "You are here for answers."

"Everyone, back to the party!" Crimson jumped, sending a row of toadstools spinning around the garden. The crowd began dancing wildly around the thumping drum shapes.

Kara walked among wiggling and dancing

fairies. A little purple spriggle stood, arms crossed, mumbling and scowling at her.

"What's with him?" Kara asked. "I only asked his name."

"It is very rude to ask a fairy his or her name," Sylina said.

"Fairy names are secret. They are only given as a powerful gift," Crimson continued.

"If you trick it into telling you, you capture its magic," Andi explained.

"I'm not up on my fairy etiquette," Kara said. "Sorry, little purple guy."

The spriggle smiled and threw himself onto a crowd of dancing boggles.

Kara had a million questions for Be*Tween. "What are you doing here? Aren't you on tour? What is this place? And how come you're, like, all fairied out?"

Crimson skipped a beat and laughed. "Slow down. First of all, we *are* fairies."

Kara shook her head. "Okay. Go back to where we are."

"You have run the web of magic," Sylina began.

"I did?"

"The web is a bridge between many worlds," the siren singer went on. "But there are different planes of existence known as the astral planes."

"You are in such a place, a twilight realm," Crimson said.

"Fairies spread magic through nature," Sylina explained. "It is elemental, flowing through earth, sky, water, and fire."

"You mean like fairimentals?" Kara asked.

"Fairimentals are guardians of special places of beauty and magic like Aldenmor," Sylina said. "They are the highest power of fairies, existing as pure, flowing energy."

"They are only visible when cloaked in shapes of nature," Andi added.

"Where are they?" Kara asked.

"They have closed themselves off, like a seed, waiting for the rain," Sylina explained.

"So what kind of fairies are you? I mean you're, like, big!" Kara exclaimed.

"We are Be*Tween. We are muses," Sylina continued, "Muses inspire creativity and imagination, powerful forces of magic that connect humans and the fairy realm."

"But you're all over the radio," Kara noted. "And what about your tour?"

"We were called back by a human wizard to protect the fairies of Aldenmor," Crimson said. "You may know of him, Henry Gardener."

"Mr. Gardener? A wizard?" Kara's eyes widened.

"Descended from the great wizards of long ago," Crimson explained.

"Many years ago, humans and magical creatures worked together," Sylina continued slowly. "When the portals between worlds closed, some of the magic remained locked on Earth. Many animals of Earth descend from magical ancestors."

"The same is true for humans as well," Crimson said. "Some humans still carry its seeds. Every few generations the magic becomes strong in them." The trio stared at Kara pointedly.

"But I . . ." Kara's eyes went wide with realization. "You're telling me someone in my, like, great, great, great, past was a magic fairy?" she looked aghast at the spriggles and sproggins dancing around the gardens.

"Not just any fairy, Kara. A fairy queen. Fairy Queen Lucinda, the greatest and most powerful of fairy queens."

Kara rolled her eyes at Lyra. "Fairy Queen, uh-huh."

Everyone knows you're a princess, Lyra quipped.

"Others draw magic from their past, as well," Sylina said seriously, "One has been transformed and now uses magic for evil."

"The Dark Sorceress," Lyra said.

"Yes."

Kara's head was spinning. "This is crazy!"

"The sorceress has released a powerful fairy from the otherworlds. This creature has aligned with the sorceress — in return for the promise of becoming King of the Fairies and ruler of all their magic."

"Powerful fairies can appear in many different guises, flowing from one element to another — shapeshifters," Crimson explained. "This one has potent powers, and it is very dangerous."

Kara's face grew pale. "A shape-shifter. He . . . it came to me," Kara was suddenly frightened of what was being revealed.

Andi told her, "It is called the Skultum. And it is a spellsinging master as well as a powerful fairy."

"You and your friends did well, but the Skultum is not defeated," the raven-haired siren said.

"But I opened those portals!" Kara confessed.

"You did what had to be done," Sylina reassured her, "The fairy map was given to you to open the pathways, to bring magic to Aldenmor."

"There is a darkness spreading across the web, coming from Aldenmor. We called the fairies to this place with our music," Crimson said, "a place of protection, until the web is once again healed. Only the purest of magic can make that happen."

"From only one source," Andi added.

"Avalon," Kara said.

"You must defeat the fairy king and return him to the fairy realms, Kara," Sylina explained, "otherwise he'll spread dark magic through nature."

"How do I do that?" Kara wailed.

"You must get the creature to tell you its true name," Andi said.

"How come you don't you know what its name is?" Kara asked.

"Once we did, but when the Dark Sorceress released the creature from the otherworlds, it took on a new name," Crimson told her.

"Kara, if you get the fairy creature to reveal its true name, you will be granted all of its powers. They will be your own, and the dark fairy will be left powerless."

Kara was beginning to feel this was way over her head.

The band members looked to one another.

"Fairy magic is not always what it appears to be. Sometimes dance, music, riddles, tricks — the most absurd thing can make a fairy forget a secret."

"What, I'm supposed to stand on my head?"

"Very good." Andi clapped. "You're learning."

"But I fell under its power so easily," Kara moaned.

"Kara, no demon can possess you if you maintain the ability to turn and laugh at it," Sylina told her.

"Easy for you to say!"

"Not all meanings are meant to be clear at once," Sylina said, "Good luck, Mage, you must join your friends now."

They had arrived back at the raised stone stage. Andiluna picked up a sparkling silver fiddle and began weaving an infectious song. The rave jumped back into full swing as the fairy creatures began leaping and dancing about, hooting and laughing in glorious havoc.

Kara watched Be*Tween rock out. She turned to Lyra.

You have an interesting past, Lyra commented.

"To paraphrase a certain ferret — *Gah!*" Kara said. "Let's go find the others."

Kara opened her backpack and took out the unicorn horn. One hand wrapped around the horn, the other on Lyra's back, she called out, "Take us to our friends at Mount Hope!"

Rainbow beams flowed from the horn's tip, glowing brighter and brighter, bathing them in incandescent light. Then the light began to swirl, faster and faster . . . until a portal yawned open before them.

"Don't give up the spirit of Avalon." She heard Be*Tween call as she and Lyra stepped into the portal and vanished.

Chapter 8

Bright sun broke over the crest of Mount Hope as Kara and Lyra made their way along the dusty trail and up sprawling hillocks at the base of the mountain range. Valleys spread below, and in the far distance the broken landscape of the Shadowlands loomed — a blight upon the land. But here it was relatively green. Tall trees led back to the forests on the western regions. The air was chilly.

"Anything?" Kara asked.

"Over there," Lyra nodded her head toward an outcropping of rocks that covered the openings to a series of caves.

Lyra had picked up a mistwolf call but, it was weak and — tiny. *"It's a mistwolf and it's very angry . . . and scared."*

"Where are the other mistwolves? The pack?"

"I don't know, but there's something else here. I can't make it out."

"We didn't see anything," Kara said.

Suddenly, a growl echoed across the small path. More of a bark, actually.

Lyra nodded toward the rocks.

They advanced slowly. Kara reached inside the backpack for the unicorn jewel. Brandishing it like a weapon, she eyed the surrounding bushes suspiciously. "What is it?" she asked.

"*Mistwolf,*" Lyra replied, cocking her head to listen. She turned and positioned herself in front of Kara.

"Hellooo," Kara called out. "Who's there?"

The growl got louder. One of the bushes began to shake.

"*Odd behavior for a mistwolf,*" Lyra said. "*As if it's protecting the caves.*"

Lyra and Kara slowly approached the scary sounds.

Suddenly, a small dog-sized creature leaped from the bush. It was a furry black wolf puppy with white paws and chest.

"Grrrr-uf!" It barked, hackles raised, teeth bared. It lowered its body and leaped forward, trying to attack and with a *yelp* — promptly fell on its nose, stumbling over its too large paws. The pup sprang back to its feet and barked louder.

Lyra regarded the scruffy little pup.

"Kinda small for a mistwolf," Kara said as she watched the fuzzy creature.

"It's a pup," Lyra explained.

"Duh . . . hey little fellow, where's your mommy?" Kara stepped forward.

The pup backed away, snarling.

"I'm going to check out the caves. You keep it occupied."

"How do I —" the little pup lunged and bit Kara's pant leg, shaking his head back and forth.

"Hey, those are Calvins," she complained as she shook him off. She bent down and opened her pack. "How about biting into something you can actually eat?"

She pulled out a granola bar.

The pup carefully sniffed it.

Kara watched Lyra circle around back and enter the caves. "It's okay, see . . . yummmmy," Kara took a small bite. The pup tentatively stepped closer as Kara held out the food. Snapping it away from her fingers, it hungrily began to chew, keeping a wary eye on Kara. It quickly backed away as she tried to pet it.

All at once, Kara felt a sharp pain in her head and deep sadness seep through her. "Lyra, are you all right?" she asked, worried about her friend.

"Yes," came the cat's reply.

Kara saw Lyra emerge from the cave. The pup eyed the cat suspiciously, edging back to give the big animal room.

"*Mistwolves,*" Lyra said

"You found them?"

"*Some.*"

Kara looked into her friend's deep green eyes and knew what Lyra had found in the caves.

"Oh." She looked at the pup sadly, tears welling up in her eyes.

Lyra sharply raised her nose, sniffing the air.

"What is it?"

"*Stormbringer!*"

"And Adriane?"

"*They come.*"

"Thank goodness. What about Emily and Ozzie?"

"*Not yet.*"

Ghostly mist snaked between the trees, and suddenly the great silver mistwolf appeared, hackles raised.

The pup jumped to its feet, stumbling back on its paws.

"Storm!" Kara called out.

The mistwolf stared at Lyra for a second then leaped up the rocky incline and vanished into the caves.

"Hey, Barbie! That you?"

Kara whirled to see Adriane walking around the bend along the rocky path.

"Xena!" Kara cried, running to the dark-haired

girl and catching her friend in a big hug. The girls hugged tightly for a moment, then abruptly stepped back, embarrassed.

"You okay?" Adriane asked.

"Yeah, you?"

Adriane nodded and saw Storm outside the caves. The mistwolf's hackles lay flat, her ears laid back against her head. Then she tilted her head back and let out a mournful howl.

Adriane started to run to her friend, but Kara held her back.

"Oh, no," Adriane cried.

"The mistwolves have been attacked," Storm said.

Twelve had been lost to the enemy.

Adriane squeezed Kara's hand hard, blinking back tears, then walked to look over the bluff at the forests beyond. There were no other mistwolves in sight — the caves and rocky outcroppings appeared to be deserted.

"No sign of the other mistwolves," Lyra said, confirming Adriane's thoughts.

Storm looked down to find the cub standing between her feet.

"Over here!" Adriane was shouting and waving down the ravine.

"I told you we were heading in the right direction!" It was Ozzie.

A moment later Emily's curly hair became visible as she and Ozzie appeared on the path.

"We're here!" Ozzie exclaimed. "Come and hug me!"

"Emily!" Adriane and Kara cried.

Emily raced to embrace her friends.

"I was so worried," Emily said.

"Storm and I were in the Ice Peaks, way up north," Adriane said. "We were helped by friends I met, real merfolk, and they had sea dragons!" Adriane explained breathlessly.

"Wow, that's so cool," Emily laughed.

"Well, I danced with a fairy and met Be*Tween!" Kara said.

"Be*Tween?" Ozzie exclaimed.

"Yeah, cool, huh?"

Emily and Adriane were astounded.

"You found them here — ?" Emily asked, flabbergasted.

"Not exactly here," Kara replied. "They're in an in-between world. Be*Tween are fairy creatures, spellsingers. They're protecting the fairies of Aldenmor."

"Ozzie and I were in the Moorgroves," Emily told her friends. "I'm afraid the Black Fire has spread to other parts of Aldenmor."

Emily heard barking and growling. "Who's

Storm's friend?" she asked. The little wolf was on its back, batting away Storm's playful paws.

"His name is Dreamer," Storm started. *"His parents run with the spirit pack now."*

Emily's face fell. "Hello there, little one." Dreamer let Emily scratch him behind the ears and rub his tummy. "Where are the others, Storm?"

"I don't know. I sense something . . ."

"Well, at least we're all together," Kara said. "I got all kinds of news from Be*Tween."

"They're not shape-shifters are they?" Adriane asked sarcastically.

"No, but they are fairies, real magical stuff."

Adriane eyed the wolf pup, then turned to the others. "Maybe we should get the D'flies to phone Zach. Something's wrong. He should have been here."

"I *am* here!" a familiar voice came from the crest of a hill.

The group turned at the voice. On a high ridge nearby stood a cute boy in a white shirt, beige pants, and sandals.

Adriane gasped. "Zach! Have you been here the whole time?"

"Over here, come quickly!" he called out and disappeared behind the ridge.

"Come on," Adriane took off in a run.

The others followed.

"*Something is not right,*" Storm said.

"*There is strong magic somewhere,*" Lyra said to Storm.

"*Yes, mistwolf magic!*"

"Hurry!" Adriane called to make sure her friends were right behind her as she ascended the rise.

At the top, she peered down at the boy. He stood in an open field, waving for her to join him. "Here! I have something to show you!" he yelled.

"Zach, what's up?" Adriane asked, worriedly. Heat bit at her wrist. She looked at her stone. The wolf stone pulsed with danger.

The others crested the hill and started down the rise.

Adriane ran toward Zach, but skidded to a stop about ten yards away. Fear tingled up her spine. Her stone was blazing. She looked closely at the strange shimmer cascading around the boy.

Adriane whipped around. "No!" she screamed at her friends. "Go back!"

"*Adriane,*" Storm called, leaping down the hill, teeth bared.

The hair along Lyra's back rose, and a low growl rumbled in her throat.

Dark clouds of mist seemed to fill the valley as if out of thin air.

The mist fell away, and the valley was completely full. Huge, horrid nightmares snorted fire, training red eyes on the trapped group. Upon their backs sat armored goblins, fierce and deadly. And behind them stood short, black as ink, faceless imps, at least one hundred strong.

Adriane watched in horror as Zach walked right up to the goblin leader atop the biggest and most frightening of the nightmares. The boy's eyes narrowed to evil yellow slits, then glowed blood red. His body seemed to melt as it changed to a shadowy lizard form. It continued past the riders, vanishing behind the attackers.

"Zach, no," Adriane said, feeling her tears threaten to fall.

"How is that possible?" Ozzie asked. "They appeared out of nowhere — like the mistwolves."

"They are using the magic of the mistwolves," Storm told them. *"The mistwolves are lost."*

"Form a circle!" Adriane screamed.

Trying to stop shaking, Emily, Adriane, and Kara stood back to back, to face the impossible enemy.

Storm, Lyra, and Ozzie surrounded the trio, ready to sacrifice themselves to protect their friends. Dreamer stood between Storm's front feet, growling and barking.

"Kara, stand between us," Adriane ordered, moving Kara. "Focus, Kara! We hit the lead riders first!"

The imps stood their ground as the goblin riders approached.

"There's too many!" Kara screamed.

"Kara, the horn!" Emily reminded her, urgently.

"Ooo!" Kara reached into her pack and removed the unicorn horn. It sparkled like a diamond in the sun.

The lead goblin raised a clawed fist and pulled his fierce steed to a halt. "You will come with us either way," it hissed.

"Leave us alone!" Adriane shouted out. "Or you'll regret it!"

The goblin's apelike head grinned. Its pointed teeth made it look like a deranged Halloween pumpkin.

"*The imps!*" Storm shouted.

Electrical sparks danced in the air as a swarm of imps came at the group from all sides. Flashing blue crackled along wide nets strung between them.

They were hopelessly outnumbered.

"Don't be afraid," Ozzie said to his friends.

"Emily," Kara said, terrified as she pushed the horn at the red-haired girl.

"Hold it up, Kara." Emily said.

Trembling, Kara held the unicorn horn as high as she could in the air.

"Lorelei!" The three girls called to the magic of the unicorn. "Protect us!"

The sky exploded with fire.

The girls shielded their faces from the intense heat as flames flew overhead.

But it was not the fire born of magic jewels.

It was the fire of a tremendous winged creature, a flying monster.

The huge beast swooped in, its massive wings cutting through the smoke and flames, making it hard to see exactly what it was.

"Oh, no!" Emily exclaimed.

"The manticore!" Kara screamed.

There was nowhere to go. The magic of the horn had failed them. They were completely surrounded.

Chapter 9

Pandemonium erupted in the field. Blue lightning flashed as plumes of smoke sent shadowy imps scurrying everywhere. Screams, yells, snorts, and roars added to the chaos.

"Stay together!" Adriane commanded, swinging her arm, tearing swatches of bright gold light through the smoke and haze.

The girls remained in position, jewels glowing and ready.

"Hey! They're running away!" Kara pointed.

The imps sparked with blue electricity as they moved away from the group, their nets disintegrated.

Ozzie jumped up and down shaking his fist, "And don't come back — uh-oh!"

But the imps had only retreated behind the leading edge of goblin riders. Nightmares reared, snorting flames, adding to the thick smoke flowing across the field. The riders held bright red staffs high, ready to release dark lightning as they bore down on the group, coming in fast.

Kara held up the unicorn horn as Emily and Adriane reached to touch Kara's hands. Gold and blue flew from the rainbow jewel and the wolf stone, swirling up Kara's arms and into the horn.

Adriane pulled the unicorn horn, pointing it to the ground in front of the incoming riders. Magic exploded forth. Four nightmares were blown to the sides, their riders flying as grass and dirt rained everywhere. Six more nightmares jumped the open fissure, firing lightning from their staffs.

Adriane and Storm leaped into the fire's path, spinning a shield of sparkling gold around themselves. Mistwolf and girl worked like a fine-tuned machine, whirling and turning to block every bolt, sending them exploding harmlessly into the air.

But the nightmares were strong and fast, barreling past Adriane straight toward Emily and Kara. Lyra pushed the girls behind her, teeth bared, wings unfurled, ready to absorb the crushing impact.

With a roar, a huge red tail swept through the haze, knocking the goblins off their mounts. The mutant horses ran, missing the group by yards. Emily and Kara felt fire breath heat as they passed.

The creature stood in front of the girls roaring defiantly at the goblins and imps. The attacking hoard was backing away over the far ridge, leaving the group, for now.

"That's not the manticore!" Ozzie exclaimed.

"What is it?" Emily asked, trembling.

The fierce creature turned a horselike head on its long sinewy neck. It was as big as a bus with a long tail covered in glimmering red scales. Large reptilian eyes narrowed dangerously as it snorted. With a rush, it stomped toward them on massive hind legs.

Something opened inside Adriane's mind. Something familiar, strong, and right — feelings of love rushed through her mind and body, it was like . . . coming home.

"That's a dragon!" Ozzie screamed.

Kara grabbed for Emily's and Adriane's hands.

"No, wait!" Adriane cried.

The dragon lumbered toward them, practically stumbling on its enormous feet. When it was only a few feet away, it stopped, folding its shimmering, iridescent wings. Smoke drifted from its nostrils as it leaned forward, opened its huge mouth —

"Momma!"

— and licked Adriane so hard, she was lifted several feet into the air.

"Drake?" Adriane said as she landed on the ground. "It *is* you!" She threw her arms around

Drake's neck, hugging the dragon as tight as she could. Then she stepped back to look him in the eye. "Wow. You've really grown!"

The dragon was happily shuffling back and forth from foot to foot, tongue lolling out. *"Momma! Momma!"*

THUD!

The ground shook as Drake rolled over onto his back, legs and arms akimbo, waiting for Adriane to scratch his belly.

"Tickle!"

Adriane giggled, reaching over to rub the great creature's amazingly soft belly. "I missed you so much!"

The group watched, mouths opened in stunned silence.

"Well, now I've seen everything!" Ozzie stomped over to inspect the dragon.

Emily smiled. "It's Adriane's baby dragon."

"Some baby," Kara muttered as she nervously scanned the skies. For all she knew, full-sized dragons traveled in packs like the pesky dragonflies. She could *not* handle another fan club — especially not one with members as big as Drake.

"Don't worry," Lyra told her, reading her mind. *"Dragons are one of a kind. The red dragons hatch only once every thousand years."* She eyed Adriane and Drake. *"He's imprinted on Adriane,"* she added.

"Everybody, this is Drake," Adriane said, introducing the dragon to her friends.

"Hello!" Drake snorted, sitting up. The dragon's lips parted, revealing rows and rows of razor-sharp teeth. Kara hoped it was a smile.

"Dragons grow very quickly," Storm explained.

"You can say that again," Kara replied.

Adriane first met Drake when he was still inside his egg. When she left Aldenmor, he'd barely hatched. She knew that dragon magic was incredibly powerful, but she never expected her friend to grow so fast.

"Such a sweet boy," Adriane cooed, playfully scratching Drake under his chin. The dragon laughed, shooting sparks out his nostrils. A small fireball shot out of his mouth.

Emily, Kara, and the others leaped back.

"Ahh!!" Ozzie shouted. "Try and keep it on low flame!"

"Sorry," Drake said, hanging his head over Adriane's.

"Drake, where's Zach?" Adriane suddenly realized Drake had flown in by himself. She tried to keep the worry out of her voice.

"He went after Moonshadow and the mistwolves," Drake replied. He sounded worried himself. *"Zach told me to stay outside so the witch would not capture me."*

"Wait, if that wasn't Zach, then who — oh."
Kara flashed on what Be*Tween had told her of
the dark fairy.

"That wasn't Zach, and I'll give you two guesses
who it really was," Adriane said grimly.

"That means Zach is captured, in a spell somewhere," Emily said.

"I have not heard from Zach at all," Drake admitted. *"Then I heard you in my mind and came
here."*

"The Dark Sorceress has the mistwolves," Storm
said. *"That is the only way she could be using their
magic."*

"But how is that possible, Storm?" Adriane
asked.

*"I do not know. It takes very strong magic to cap-
ture or kill a mistwolf,"* Storm said.

Drake nodded, shuffling on his huge feet again.
"Have not heard from Zach!"

"If she has Moonshadow," Adriane figured,
"then she has his fairy map. And she must be using
it to open the portals."

"The map was given to Moonshadow," Storm insisted. *"Fairy magic only works for those it is given. He
would guard that map with his life."*

"Perhaps he doesn't have the strength to prevent it,"
Lyra said quietly.

There was a long moment of silence as the

group considered this sobering thought — and another that nobody wanted to say aloud: Maybe Moonshadow *had* defended the map with his life.

"What else did Be*Tween tell you, Kara?" Emily asked.

"Um, long story," Kara said. "But they're in an in-between world. They told me the shape-shifter is really an evil fairy and it's going to spread magic when it comes."

"You mean like Phel spreading magic seeds?" Emily asked.

"That's what fairies do," Ozzie said. "They spread magic through nature."

"An evil fairy would use the magic to poison nature," Emily reasoned.

"Wait a minute," Adriane said. "The merfolk told me they were waiting for the magic rain."

"They didn't know whether it would be light or dark rain," Storm added. *"Good or bad magic."*

"Maybe the sorceress has opened portals, but there's no more magic," Emily suggested.

"No, no . . ." Ozzie was pacing back and forth, thinking.

"Or she hasn't found what she needs yet," Kara added.

"No, no . . ." Ozzie came to a stop. "The portals opened in a sequence. I think she opened the pipeline but can't start the magic flow."

"So she's found what she wants," Emily said, hoping she was wrong.

"Avalon," Ozzie said.

"It's possible."

Adriane sighed. "Anything is possible."

The three girls looked at one another but didn't speak. They didn't have to: They were all thinking the same thing. Anything was possible, but their task here on Aldenmor felt totally impossible. And they still didn't have any real answers. Just possibilities.

"One thing is for sure," Adriane finally said. "We have to go after Zach and the mistwolves."

"Well, we can't sit around here," Ozzie agreed. "Those goblins will be back any second. Probably with some orcs or worse!"

"We can't just waltz into the dark circle, either," Kara reminded them.

"She already knows we're here," Storm said.

"Then why didn't she attack us?" Emily asked. "We could have walked into a trap at the dark circle."

"Because."

They all looked at the ferret.

"She's afraid," Ozzie said.

"Of us?"

"Of course," Ozzie started shuffling back and forth. "Whatever she's doing, she doesn't want us anywhere near her place. She tried to take us out, all together, right here."

"So if we can get into the lair before those riders and imps regroup, maybe we have a chance!" Adriane hit her palm with a fist.

"Okay, but that's gotta be, like, miles from here," Kara looked toward the desolate plains beyond the open valleys. "How are we going to get there before the monsters attack us again?"

Adriane smiled and patted the dragon's neck. "Welcome to Air Drake."

"Oy, why did I think you were going to say that?" Ozzie replied.

Chapter 10

They slid off Drake's back as the dragon landed smoothly behind a large dune overlooking the Shadowlands. Lyra set down alongside, her magic wings folding and disappearing with a soft glow.

"This is it?" Kara asked incredulously.

It was hard to believe that this burned-out desert had once been lush, vibrant, and full of life. It was even harder to believe that the small band of travelers had any hope of restoring it.

Three girls, cat, mistwolves, ferret, and dragon peered over the gray ridge. Steam hissed across the barren landscape before them. Several rounded structures rose from the sandlike smokestacks. An open stone courtyard led to a pair of black doors leaning into the first tower.

"There's more," Lyra growled. *"Below."*

The Dark Sorceress's lair lay largely hidden underground. Adriane and Lyra were well aware of the vast caverns, catacombs, and labyrinth of mazes that wormed under the surface.

Adriane felt her stomach tighten, and a trickle of sweat trailed down her neck. She was back to a place out of her worst nightmares, a place she thought she'd never return to. And yet, here she was. The last time she had barely escaped, and that was with the help of the entire pack. Where was the pack now?

Storm sensed her friend's dread. *"Stay focused, warrior. Turn fear to strength. Use it."*

"What's that, Storm? Those weren't here before." Adriane pointed to several triangular crystals that pierced the ground in the center of the towers.

"Zach told us she was building those," Emily reminded them.

"That's where she's going to store the magic," Ozzie said.

The squirming wolf pup in Emily's arms sniffed the air and barked.

"Shhh. We have to be very quiet," Emily said, putting the pup on the ground.

"Good point, Dreamer," Kara said. "How do we get past those?" Kara's gaze was on the entrance to the lair.

Tall serpentine guards walked in groups out of

the doors, each holding long staffs that reflected sun in sparks of light. From around the base of the distant funnel, goblin riders rode patrol. Their nightmare beasts snorted, the goblins on their backs scowled into the distance.

"Won't be long before they sense us here," Lyra said.

Kara sucked in her breath. "Okay, so, what's the plan?"

"We go in under Mistwolf cover, then find Zach and the mistwolves," Adriane said.

"Right," Kara nodded. "So we don't have a plan."

"We stay on course, moving forward," Adriane responded.

"Cannot hear Zach!" Drake's voice echoed loudly in everyone's head.

Adriane looked into the dragon's deep crystalline eyes. They swirled in distressful shades of red and orange. "We need you to help us, Drake."

The dragon's eyes lit up with greens and blues. *"Yes, I help Zach!"*

"Yes. But you have to stay out here."

Drake's head drooped in disappointment, steam leaking from his nostrils. *"I help!"*

"You have a very important job," Adriane explained carefully. "When I say so, you have to create a diversion."

The dragon looked confused.

"Make lots of loud noise, swoop up and down, and keep the guards distracted."

"I can do that."

"Good dragon," Adriane said. "Wait for my call. And if any of the others that attacked us show up, let me know right away."

"Okay," Drake snorted.

Adriane reached up and hugged the dragon's neck, giving him a kiss on his wide nose. "We'll find Zach."

"What about Dreamer?" Kara asked.

The little mistwolf stood shyly next to Storm.

Adriane bent low to face the little guy. "You're a brave boy, aren't you, Dreamer?"

The mistwolf snarled and barked, showing Adriane his fiercest face.

Adriane smiled.

The dark-haired warrior stood and faced the others. "All right. We'll take him with us."

Adriane extended her arm. Emily put her hand on top of Adriane's. Kara's hand covered theirs. Ozzie, Storm, and Lyra stood close by.

The three girls looked into one another's eyes. There was only one thing to say.

"Let's do it!" Adriane said firmly.

Stormbringer shimmered under the hazy bright sun. A second later, her body disappeared — transforming into a thick white fog. Dreamer watched with interest as the silky mist thinned and slowly settled over the group.

From the desert floor, the dark riders and guards fanned out, carefully watching the skies. They didn't notice the swirling haze as it moved toward the double doors.

The tight group slipped quickly behind the doors, and instantly were swallowed in darkness.

"Which way, Storm?" Adriane whispered.

"Down."

❧ ❧ ❧

Cloudy images surfaced in the crystal-pure water. The Dark Sorceress bent over her seeing pool, stirring it with a single sharp claw. She waited for the pictures to clear.

A slow snarl curled the corner of her thin lips as she narrowed her animal eyes. A sparkling bubble burst in the pool. When it cleared, it revealed a room filled with three enormous crystals. The picture faded as another bubble rose to the surface and a new image floated before her — a small cloud drifting down a corridor toward the vast chamber of crystals.

"You see. It is like I told you!" She spoke to the tall, dark shape standing near her. Her claw retracted into a slender finger. "They have come."

The dark fairy glowered, as its body shimmered and flowed. It was called the Skultum, a being made of pure transcendence and energy. "These humans are incorrigible!" the thing hissed.

"You have no idea," the witch said in a velvety voice.

"The sequence of portals is opened, just as I said it would be," the Skultum groveled, trying to regain favor.

The Dark Sorceress swung at the hideous creature, her long robes whispering to the ground like a silent shroud. "You are a powerful fairy creature, are you not?"

"Yes, my mistress."

Waves of fear fouled the sorceress's sharp senses. She hated this mutant creature, but she had called it, releasing it from the forbidden otherworlds. At least it knew its place. And it still had a job to do. Complete and utter subservience was essential.

"Yet you could not unlock the map yourself. And worse, you let it fall back into the hands of these . . . these mages!"

"Mages!" The Skultum laughed, a hideous cackle. "They are merely girls!"

"You know nothing!" She snarled, spitting viciously, making the Skultum back up in alarm.

"These *girls* have power! These *girls* channel the fairimentals themselves!" The sorceress's voice rose in voracity. "These *GIRLS* channel magic through animals! The very lifeblood of Aldenmor channels through their jewels! So do not speak to me of what they can or cannot do!" The witch shuddered, then calmed.

The dark fairy stood silent, waiting.

"When the magic collects in the crystals, I trust you will do what you have agreed to."

The Skultum stepped into the light of the seeing pool. Reflections rippled over its distorted face, melting between flesh and bone. "I will drive the dark magic into the fabric of Aldenmor itself, through fairy magic, and it will be yours to command, my mistress."

"Then you shall have the fairy realms to do with as you wish."

The Skultum's mouth dissolved into a deathlike grin.

"But, my dear fairy king . . . you as yet do not possess both maps." The half-woman, half-animal smoothed back her silver blond hair to gaze at the fairy map floating above a pedestal just near the pool — the map she had taken from the fallen mistwolf. The map was fairy magic and such, only those it was intended for could use it. Combined with the other map, all secrets would unlock.

She needed the second map — *and* the blazing star to open them.

Both were already on their way.

The sorceress extended a claw from her fingertip and dipped her hand back into the pool, swirling the tainted liquid. The images faded as the Skultum began to weave its magic.

The creature shimmered and glowed, arms moving in hypnotic patterns, conjuring, casting. Then, arching its back, the Skultum began to chant a series of guttural, unintelligible words. They jumbled together, flowing, echoing in the chamber, a raw combination of animal grunts and melody. The power grew, palpable and electrical in the air. Then, with a wave of its serpentine claws, the Skultum unleashed the powerful spellsong of binding, sending it to the one it knew would have to answer.

🌀　🌀　🌀

The group silently made its way crisscrossing through dank, dark tunnels. Lights flashed in the distance. They neared a wide connecting corridor where the tunnel split into three adjoining passageways. At the end of one, red flames pulsed with heat, as shadow shapes scurried to and fro.

"The mistwolves are there," Storm's voice spoke through the mist.

"What about Zach?" Emily asked.

Adriane concentrated on her wolf stone, trying to keep her magic contained yet strong enough to get a reading from the dragon stone that Zach possessed. She got nothing.

"Let's find the mistwolves first, then," Ozzie suggested.

They silently moved up the right corridor, heading into the heat that poured through the tunnel.

They came to a wide doorway cut out of the rock itself. Beyond lay an immense cavern. Staying close to the shadowy walls, they snuck inside. Blinding light shone from three gigantic crystals towering in the center of the enormous chamber.

"Incredible!" Emily said in shock, craning her neck to see the tops of the crystals cut off by the ceiling. The rest of the crystals were on the surface.

"Oh, my!" Ozzie exclaimed, wide-eyed.

The girls had learned how powerful their jewels could be. But here, before them, these gigantic crystals dwarfed anything they could have possibly imagined. What power these giant jewels must have!

The magic these crystals could hold was beyond comprehension — as was the destruction they'd caused. Here was the *source* of the black fire, poisonous residue released from the sorceress's attempts to construct these monolithic giants.

Turn back, the voice of a mistwolf whispered in Adriane's head.

"Storm?" Adriane strained to see in the chamber, but the blanket that was Storm still covered the group.

Save yourselves, Little Wolf Daughter, the voice hissed. *Run!*

The voice was familiar — but it wasn't Storm.

"Silver Eyes!" Adriane cried.

The veil of mist swept from the group as Storm took shape, leaping into the chamber.

"What is that?" Ozzie asked.

With the veil removed, they could see the crystals were filled with a churning, roiling mist.

"Mistwolves," Storm snarled, making her way behind the first towering crystal. *"They're trapped inside."*

That would explain how the sorceress held them. Only cages of glass or crystal could contain mistwolves, prevent them escaping into mist.

"Storm, wait!" Adriane tried to stay calm. Shadows were moving toward them from the far side of the chamber.

"What's happening to them?" Ozzie asked, horrified.

"Their magic is being drained." Storm said from across the chamber. *"They cannot exist in mist form for much longer, or they will die."*

Dreamer barked and jumped to the shallow cavern floor, racing after Storm.

"How do we get them out?" Ozzie was frantically jumping up and down.

"Kara, hold up the horn!" Adriane pulled back her sleeve to release her wolf stone. The time for stealth was over. Things were getting out of control — and fast.

"Kara?" Emily asked, looking around, voice tight, like it was hard to breathe.

"She was right here a second ago!" Ozzie ran to look down the corridor. It was empty.

"Lyra, what happened?" Adriane asked.

Lyra paced, growling low in her throat. The fur on the back of her neck stood up. *I don't know. Something blocks my senses. I can't feel Kara!*

"Kara?" Adriane called, panic rising, threatening to topple her resolve.

"Kara!" Emily called for the third time. She was practically shouting, in spite of the danger.

There was no reply. Kara was gone.

The ground beneath their feet fell away, sending them sliding into darkness.

Chapter 11

Storm?" Adriane called out. "Can you hear me?"

Jewel light flashed erratically across the dark space.

"Are you . . . all right?" Storm's reply was broken, strained in static.

"Yeah, what's happening?"

"I am linked . . . mistwol — Holding them . . . from fading."

Adriane wanted desperately to be with her friend to help.

"Is everyone all right?" Emily used her light to search the room.

Lyra's magic wings unfurled as the big cat peered up through the open chute that had deposited them. She leaned back, ready to leap.

"No, Lyra. We have to stick together!" Adriane brushed the cat's raised hackles.

"Kara's up there, alone!" the cat hissed.

"Can you sense anything, Lyra?" Emily asked.

The cat closed her eyes, then shook her head. *"She is under a spell. I cannot reach her."*

Emily stroked Lyra's head and sent as much calm as she could into the cat's worried green eyes. "We'll find her. Okay?"

Gahfphooot!

"Ozzie? Where's Ozzie?" Emily beamed light across the barren room.

The ferret was stuck headfirst in a mound of dirt.

Adriane and Emily ran across the room and pulled him out by his feet.

"Spoof!"

"Are you all right?"

"How could I be so stupid!" Ozzie kicked the pile of dirt, sending dust flying. Particles hung in the air caught in beams of gold and blue.

"It's not your fault, Ozzie," Emily consoled him, arms around her chest. It was creepy, dank, and cold in there.

"We know she's susceptible to spellsinging!" Ozzie brushed dirt from his head and stomped around. "Now she's under another spell."

"You think the shape-shifter is here?" Emily whispered.

"I would bet on it! And we brought Kara right into its clutches." Ozzie looked around. "Where are we?"

"The dungeons," Adriane pushed away the dirt that had broken Ozzie's fall. "Help me here."

Emily and Lyra, working with Adriane, quickly swept away the dirt. A door was hidden behind it.

"I think you found the way out, Ozzie," Emily observed.

"Always had a nose for direction."

"Stand back!" Adriane shouted, raising her arm. The wolf stone pulsed with power. She swung once and a wave of golden power smashed into the door. With a loud *Poof!* the door flew open into a wide corridor.

The four made a run for it. Soft lights cast pale illumination from crystals imbedded in the walls. Long shadows seemed to slip and curl as if the tunnels were alive.

Emily noticed Lyra gazing up and down the darkened corridor, her green-gold eyes narrowed slightly. Not that long ago, the cat had been held prisoner here along with other magical animals. Lyra, horribly wounded, had escaped. Emily shuddered, thinking of how hard it must be for the cat to return to this terrible place.

"I sense something," Lyra said as she sniffed the air in the narrow hall. The fur on her neck was just beginning to relax. *"Someone's alive. Human."*

Adriane's eyes lit up. "Where?"

"This way," Lyra said, taking off down the darkened passageway.

The group followed, making their way into the catacombs that held the prison cells. The jagged hallway was lined with heavy doors, and the group split up to listen at each one.

Adriane took the doors at the very end. Each time she raised her wolf stone to sense beyond the cold metal and wood, she tried to push the apprehension and fear from her mind. The golden glow that emanated from her stone seemed tiny in the huge darkness of the catacombs. Somehow she knew that Storm was getting weaker.

Storm! Hang on, Adriane sent a message to her friend.

"Over here!" Emily called out, summoning everyone to the door she was standing at.

This time Adriane whipped a ring of gold and clasped the metal bars in the small window. She pulled hard. The others helped raise as much power from the wolf stone as they could. With a creak, the door opened into darkness.

They practically stumbled over the still figure on the floor.

"Zach!" Adriane cried, falling to her knees and searching the boy's ashen face for a sign of life. She saw the red dragon stone he wore on his wrist softly blink.

Emily was beside her in an instant, rainbow jewel pulsing strong. "He's in a trance, the Skultum's spell."

Lyra growled low nearby.

The healer wasted no time. She held out her jewel, sending out a beam of healing blue light.

There was no response. Emily gazed down at Zach's barely moving chest. The boy was in bad shape. He seemed too far away to be reached.

"He's been under awhile! Help me," Emily called out. Ozzie, Lyra, and Adriane pressed around her, concentrating on sending their own energy to break the spell. Emily, supported by her friends, focused her will. Her jewel flashed bright and fast and Emily felt a flutter of activity. The dragon stone flashed. Zach's heartbeat was strengthening, his breathing deepening.

Zach opened his eyes and blinked. "Adriane, you're in my dreams."

Adriane hugged the boy, her heart full of joy. "No dream, Zach."

They helped him sit up.

"What are you doing here?" he said, groggily.

"Rescuing you," Adriane said.

"Guess we're even," Zach smiled weakly.

"ZACH!"

"Agghh!" Zach covered his ears as the voice of Drake exploded in his head.

485

"Ooo, sorry, are you all right?"

"I *was* . . . yeah, okay."

"*Adriane told me to wait outside and make lots of noise when she tells me. I help!*"

"Okay, stay there," Zach instructed the dragon.

"How long have you been here?" Emily asked, rubbing Zach's arms to help circulation.

"I don't know," he said. "Last thing I remember, I had snuck into the lair, trying to contact the mistwolves — then I fell out."

"Zach, we found the crystals you told us about," Adriane told him.

"Where are the mistwolves?" Zach asked, his face growing grim.

"Trapped inside them," Emily finished.

"We have to get them out!" He pushed himself up — then slid back down, "Ow, my legs are numb."

"Easy, you have to stay still for a while," Emily said.

A sleek feline shape darted noiselessly through the door. "*I can't find a clear way out. I keep going in circles.*"

"I got out last time," Adriane said.

"The sorceress *let* you get out to try and lure in the mistwolves," Ozzie reminded her.

"Yeah, you're right," Adriane remembered.

Zach wiped matted blond hair from his forehead. "This time she got them."

"And Kara, too," Emily added.

"Kara?" Zach surveyed the rescue party realizing they were one member short.

"She's under a spellsinging spell," Ozzie informed him.

"That's fairy magic!" Zach exclaimed.

"The sorceress is working with a fairy creature," Adriane said. "A shape-shifter."

Zach sighed. "Fairy magic. That's what called the mistwolves and trapped them in the crystals."

"But why?" Emily asked.

"Mistwolf magic, of course," Ozzie said. "Magic attracts magic. She's using the mistwolves to draw magic into the crystals, where she can use it."

"That's why she's been hunting magical animals," Adriane said.

"No doubt she's gotten Moonshadow's fairy map," Zach said soberly. "Luckily, the fairimentals safeguarded the magic of the maps."

"What do you mean?" Emily asked.

"She may have opened portals," Zach explained. "But in order to find the source of the magic, she would need *two* fairy maps."

Everyone was startled — and concerned.

"What?" Zach asked.

"Kara has the second map," Adriane told him.

Zach struggled to get up again. "We have to get the mistwolves out. They can't survive in there."

"Storm is keeping them strong," Adriane said, her voice strained and cracking.

"She's only one wolf, she can't hold on to them for long!" Zach saw Adriane's face go white — he stopped talking.

The warrior got up and paced. She lifted her stone, sending a silent message to Storm. *"Storm, we found Zach,"* she told her pack mate. *"But Kara is missing. How are you doing?"*

"I am with you," came Storm's staticky reply.

"She's okay," Adriane could not hide the worry plainly visible on her face.

Lyra yowled, trying to reach Kara but to no avail.

"Some mages we turned out to be!" Adriane slumped next to Zach, head in her hands. What were they going to do? They had found Zach and he was okay. But the situation had gone from bad to horrible. Soon it would be hopeless.

🌀 🌀 🌀

The door to the throne room opened, and Kara stepped inside. Caught in the powerful spellsong, she felt like some sort of marionette, and she could not resist its pull.

"Come in, child." The Dark Sorceress was atop her high stone thrown. She was tall and striking. Long silver-blond hair slashed with white lightning streaks fell over her shoulders and down her back.

Her robe glided silently over the stone floor as the sorceress stood and came to Kara.

Then Kara saw the eyes. She had seen them before, the cold eyes of a beast. Vertical slits opened, pinning Kara in their icy stare.

Kara shivered, even though she didn't feel cold. She opened her mouth to speak, but nothing came out.

The witch moved long fingers.

"— me go!" Kara finished.

"Tsk, tsk. We have so much to catch up on, my dear," Her eyes bore into Kara's. "And you *must* tell me everything."

Kara watched, a prisoner inside her own head, her own body. "Yes."

"Perfection," the witch coldly inspected Kara. "With proper guidance, your power will be grand. You like using the magic, don't you?"

"Yes," Kara said honestly. She couldn't stop the words, as if they were being drawn out of her.

"I know you do. You're going to show me what you can do," the witch spoke firmly.

"Yes,"

"Good." The Dark Sorceress smiled, fangs gleaming.

Kara would have run screaming out of the room if she could've moved her feet.

"Well, come on, show me what you have brought," the witch commanded.

Kara struggled. A part of her knew she shouldn't — she couldn't resist. She reached into her backpack and felt cold fire. Power raced up and down her arm like a thousand pinpricks. With her eyes locked onto the sorceress, Kara pointed the unicorn horn at the witch. It blazed with light. But Kara could not release its magic.

The witch's animal eyes glowed with delight. The horn flew from Kara into her evil grasp. The light faded, cracks spiraled up and down. With a twist of her wrist, the horn splintered to dust, cascading to the floor like snow.

Kara watched helplessly.

"You know what I want!" she demanded.

"No!" Kara screamed silently. She willed her body to flee, then watched, horrified, as her sparkling fairy map floated gently into the air. At that moment, another map, almost identical, lifted from a pedestal nearby and drifted, drawn by its twin's magic.

"You realize only powerful fairy magic can use the maps," the witch said cooly.

"Yes, Be*Tween told me." What was she saying? But she couldn't help herself.

"Be*Tween? Ah, fairy spellsingers, of course."

The witch smiled, tapping her chin with a long claw. "Fairies are tricksters. They are users, like the fairimentals. They will use anything or anyone to get what they want."

Kara stood motionless as the Dark Sorceress circled her like a viper.

"They told you that you have fairy blood?"

"Yes, from Queen Lucinda," Kara answered.

"But they didn't tell you the rest." The witch stopped to watch Kara's confused expression.

She stared into Kara's eyes. "There is a reason you and I are alike, child. Lucinda was my sister."

Kara gasped. It can't be! But deep inside, she'd known the terrible truth, there was a bond between her and the sorceress. She'd felt it when they'd first met. The sorceress had even told her as much — but Kara refused to believe it.

"Open yourself to the truth." The witch's words bore into Kara like poison. "Embrace the magic that lies inside of you. And let it out!"

Music filled Kara's head, words so soothing and luxurious. For the first time, she noticed a tall, dark shape standing in the shadows, green scales running along sinewy arms raised in the dim lights.

Kara's arms waved in front of her in patterns she didn't recognize. She was confused at first, but it soon became clear that *she* was beckoning the fairy maps. They responded immediately. Floating side by side, pulsing and growing larger, they got closer.

Then, with a spark, the two maps converged and drifted over Kara. Star lines charged with electric energy surrounded her. Tiny points of light twinkled like diamonds.

Kara couldn't think. The maps were so incredibly beautiful.

"Use the fairy map," the firemental had told her. Is this what she was supposed to do?

"If you have fairy magic, why don't *you* use them?" Kara managed to get out.

The witch turned away, but not before Kara saw a hint of — sadness?

"I have traveled beyond what I once was," the Dark Sorceress said, then faced Kara again, eyes aflame. "Now, show me where the magic lies!"

Points of light began to flash in sequence, the strands of the web glowed.

Kara fought to clear her mind and regain control. But surrounded in the pathways of magic and under the spellsong, she could not stop what had begun. She felt helpless and for the first time . . . totally alone.

Chapter 12

T his place is nothing but a maze!" Zach complained, frustrated.

The group had struggled along, using all their senses and jewels combined to find the right way through the catacombs. Exhausted, they had arrived at another wide intersection with connecting tunnels.

"How are you doing?" Adriane asked Zach.

"Fine." He slumped against the wall. He was still weak from the spell.

"I have navigated these passageways before," Lyra shook her head. *"But the path lies hidden from me."*

There was a moment of depressed silence.

"Let's rest here for a few minutes," Emily suggested.

Adriane slid down next to Zach. Emily and Ozzie joined them, huddled close together. Nobody spoke. The only sound was the *pad, pad, pad* of Lyra's paws on the stone floor as she paced, examining each joining tunnel for the correct way back to the surface.

Adriane sighed. Hopelessness washed over her, making her feel even more tired than she was.

"You know, you're so lucky," Zach said to Adriane, then looked to the others. "All of you."

"Lucky?" Adriane echoed. "What do you mean?"

"I grew up alone. I never knew what it's like to have friends. Except for Windy, of course, and now Drake."

Everyone turned to Zach.

"Then I met you." He looked at Adriane, who blushed. "You have the best friends in the world."

"It wasn't always that way," Emily said, remembering.

"Yeah, when we first met Kara, we couldn't stand her," Adriane smiled.

"Really?"

"Oh, yeah, she was the self-appointed miss perfect Barbie princess of popularity," Adriane said.

"So what happened?" Zach asked, clearly interested.

Emily snorted. For a second, Adriane thought the redheaded girl was crying. But when Emily snorted again, it was clear that she was laughing.

"She's just so . . . so likable," Emily explained. "She's smart, funny, confident —"

"Pink," Adriane added, smiling.

"Remem —" Emily laughed again. "Remember when Kara had to talk to the whole school and the dragonflies stole her hat?"

Adriane nodded. Who could forget?

"That look on her face when her hat came off and her hair came tumbling out — rainbow-colored!" Tears were streaming down Emily's face. She could not stop cracking up.

Adriane laughed. "Yeah, she freaked."

"How'd that happen?" Zach asked.

Adriane recounted the story for Zach of Kara's magical bad-hair day. "Emily totally saved her," she explained. "She said that Kara had dyed her hair to symbolize the true meaning of Ravenswood, a tapestry of friends." Adriane was cracking up now, too.

"I think the best part of friends is having those memories you share, moments that make you feel so good inside." He smiled. "I'll never forget the feeling I got flying with Windy. Always makes me smile."

"I don't see my friends from Colorado anymore," Emily said. "But I still remember hot summer days and the old rope swing that dropped us right in this cool pond."

"I never used to think much of friends," Adriane slowly admitted. "I thought I didn't need

495

them. But that's 'cause I'd never met anyone like Emily, Storm, Ozzie, or Lyra before." She gave each a shy smile.

"And Kara," Ozzie added.

"Yeah, and Kara." She looked to her friends. "Now, I couldn't imagine a day without you crazy knuckleheads in my life."

"Having friends makes everything better," Ozzie chuckled.

"Like laughing till your face hurts," Emily giggled.

"Sharing banana milk shakes," Ozzie snuggled into Emily's arm.

"Birthday parties," Zach joined in, smiling at Adriane.

"Finding a true pack mate," Lyra sat next to Zach who scratched behind her ears.

"Watching a sun rise," Emily smiled, adding to the fun.

"Making chocolate chip cookies," Ozzie licked his lips.

"Dancing to favorite songs on the radio," Lyra said, remembering mornings with Kara.

"Getting a hug." Adriane spontaneously reached over and hugged Lyra. The cat licked Adriane's cheek. Ozzie, Emily, and Zach hugged the cat at the same time, making Lyra purr with pleasure.

The laughter was contagious. It filled the halls,

wafting like light summer rain, sending pure magic into the darkness of the catacombs.

❧   ❧   ❧

The glowing strands of the fairy maps surrounded Kara, spinning in a haze of twinkling light.

"You opened the correct combination of portals at your spellsinging debut," the Dark Sorceress said in her sickeningly smooth voice. Her long, flowing robes rustled as she circled Kara, raising her arms triumphantly. "Now, show me the final portal! Show me where the source of magic lies hidden!"

Kara was terrified. What was she doing? Her mind was spinning as she watched the maps. Yet with each star that blazed to life, she felt a connection, as if she were opening another key to unlock the final treasure. She was the center of the universe in a maelstrom of magic. And it was calling to her, building in ferocity, racing through her. The wonderful power, thrilling her senses. She controlled it all! Yes, I want it!

Had she screamed aloud? She couldn't tell. Time had seemed to stop. She felt no sense of herself, only of being carried away in the flow of an oncoming tidal wave of magic. Kara felt she would be crushed under its force, sweeping her away from everything she had known, everything that was real.

Suddenly, a strange image popped into Kara's head — Ozzie with a thick creamy mustache. A banana milk shake? That ferret will eat anything! For a moment, Kara's mind was jolted free from the spellsong.

Then it was viciously yanked back.

Kara was blinded. The maps were ablaze in lights. Somewhere a wild animal shrieked. It was the sorceress. Long horns sprouted from her head, fangs protruded from her open mouth. She was screaming — but Kara could hear nothing.

Another image popped in Kara's head. This time she saw Lyra dancing on her bed, covered in her clothes. Lyra, you silly!

Something was happening. Kara could feel her fingers moving. The spell was breaking. More pictures flashed through Kara's mind — sharing a cheeseburger with Emily and hogging all the fries — Adriane handing her a bracelet, a friendship bracelet.

She heard sounds — laughing? It was Emily, and Adriane and Ozzie and . . . Lyra! They were laughing!

Kara remembered what Be*Tween had told her, *"No demon can possess you if you maintain the ability to turn and laugh at it."*

Her friends had sent her magic and she reached for it, embracing it like . . . a friend.

The spell faded. Kara quickly hid the smile that broke across her face and looked at the figure. It had turned back into the Dark Sorceress. The animal/woman was staring at her through slitted, narrowed eyes.

Can she hear them, too? Kara wondered. Quickly, Kara started waving her arms again. Without moving her head, she looked around for a way out. Then she noticed that the fairy maps had stopped spinning. They now hung in the air above her like an umbrella, winking lights flashing against the darkened ceiling.

The sorceress seemed to have noticed, too. She was eyeing the illuminated stars.

Kara followed her gaze. At the far edge of the map, one tiny light moved. It was traveling on the strands, racing nearer and nearer to Kara.

"That's it!" the sorceress said. "That is the final portal. Open it!"

Kara swung her arms wildly, keeping one eye on the approaching light. It was moving fast, getting bigger. The light was suddenly running on — legs?! No, wait. It was taking the shape of a horse. No! A *unicorn*!

The realization hit Kara hard. The Dark Sorceress had tried to use Kara to lure the unicorn to her once before. Kara remembered how the sorceress had coveted the most magical of all animals.

Now, once again, the unicorn was traveling the web, coming for her!

"No!" Kara cried. This time the cry was out of her mouth before she could stop it.

The fairy maps exploded in light. Momentarily blinded, Kara fell.

She struggled to her feet, blinking. Long hair flicked across her shoulder, but it was not the Dark Sorceress's tresses — it was a long tail.

The unicorn stood in the room, as magnificent as Kara remembered. White hide smooth as a first snowfall, rippled over its muscled body. Its long mane and tail ruffled like silk. And upon its forehead, its crystalline horn flowed with rainbow light.

The Dark Sorceress saw the unicorn at the same moment Kara did. Her eyes flew wide with rage. "What is this trickery?!"

The mighty unicorn turned its deep golden eyes at Kara. Waves of emotion surged through the girl, sure, strong, and loving.

Then, in a voice as clear as rain and powerful as the breaking dawn, it spoke. *We must ride.*

Kara broke for the unicorn.

The sorceress was enraged. Somehow the girl had broken her binding spell! With the strength of an animal, the witch lunged at Kara.

Kara ducked. With a leap, she was on the unicorn's back, grabbing hold of his silken mane, bury-ing her face in his neck.

The creature gave a fierce snort, reared upon its hind legs, and leaped.

In a flash of light, unicorn and rider vanished.

Chapter 13

Lyra yowled, pacing like a trapped animal. *"Kara's gone!"*

"What do you mean?" Emily asked.

"She's not in the lair anymore. I'm sure of it!"

Adriane and Emily exchanged worried glances.

"Let's not jump to conclusions," Emily said as calmly as she could.

"C'mon, we have to get out of here." Zach stood on wobbly legs.

"Okay, we'll just have to choose a direction and go." Adriane helped brace the boy.

"And end up somewhere worse?" Ozzie cried. "Who knows what's lurking in this place!"

Lyra had stopped pacing. The cat stood stock still.

"What is it, Lyra?" Emily asked.

"Something comes," Lyra said softly.

Everyone stopped.

A high-pitched howl pierced the air, echoing through the tunnel like a ghost.

Lyra turned toward the sound. Adriane grasped the cat's shoulder. Down the dark hall, the strange cry echoed. It was coming closer.

Adriane raised her wolf stone, and golden fire sparked dangerously from her wrist. "Stay behind me," she ordered.

Another howl filled the corridor, short and mournful.

Adriane crept lightly down the hall, the others close behind. She put a finger to her lips and motioned for them to stay where they were.

The howl turned into a wailing cry as Adriane slowly approached. Whatever had come was just around the corner.

With a wave of her arm, Adriane spun into position. Sweeping her stone before her, she leaped into the darkness.

There was a scuffle and a loud *yelp!*

"Adriane!" Ozzie screamed, running to their friend.

"We're rescued!" Adriane said, calmly walking back into the corridor.

Behind her, a small fuzzy head peeked around the corner.

"Dreamer!" Emily cried, elated.

The group quickly surrounded the perplexed little mistwolf, hugging and scratching, rubbing, and hugging some more. Dreamer rolled about, happily barking and wagging his tail.

"I don't know who's happier to be found, us or Dreamer," Ozzie observed.

"How'd you find us?" Adriane knelt, staring into the pup's large green eyes. The mistwolf cocked his head. Adriane's mind flashed on quick images: long, dark, scary corridors, a small wet nose sniffing the air.

"You tracked our magic?" Adriane guessed, impressed.

Dreamer barked.

"Good boy," Adriane rubbed his scruffy neck. "Can you take us to Storm?"

The pup looked over its shoulder and growled. Then he barked.

"Okay, then," Adriane looked to her friends. "Looks like Dreamer here is a natural magic tracker. Don't be scared," she said to the mistwolf. "I'm here now. Take us to Storm."

❧   ❧   ❧

Kara leaned forward atop the unicorn's broad, smooth back. The path of light beneath his alabaster hooves glowed stronger as trails of sparkling magic streamed from his mane and tail. On his forehead, his horn shone brightly, illuminated from within.

Kara saw that they were racing on the web itself, following the pathways of magic. Beneath the unicorn's pounding hooves the endless strands shimmered with pure energy.

The unicorn did not pass *through* portals — instead he created them, matching the sequence of the star maps Kara had unlocked. Each portal opened a window of light in its wake, connecting the sequence along the web.

The unicorn raced faster and faster. Kara felt no fear. The unicorn drew strength from *her*, and she willed with all her heart for whatever magic she possessed to be given, freely and unconditionally. In that eternal moment, unicorn and rider became one, blazing forever across the infinite web of hope, dreams, and renewal.

One question remained.

Kara leaned forward. "Where are we going?"

Reflected from the glimmering web, glints of fire played across the unicorn's golden eyes. "*Home.*"

He lowered his head and shot forward. In a blinding flash, the web disappeared.

❦　❦　❦

The halls were so dark they could barely see, but Adriane did not want to use her wolf stone and tip off the sorceress of their approach. Lyra ran at her side. Her feline night vision helped them keep up with the determined Dreamer. At least they were going up.

"There's something ahead," Adriane felt her jewel spark with danger. She willed the wolf stone silent.

They were approaching an open series of large caverns.

"I remember this place," Adriane whispered. "There were forges of fire where imps worked building crystals!"

But the rooms ahead were silent, spilling a soft eerie green glow into the hall. Whatever activity had gone on in there before had long been abandoned. Zach felt his way around the wall, moving across the entrance. He quickly covered his dragon stone as it flashed. Lyra sniffed the air, growling low.

They peered into the chamber, jewels splashing light across shards of broken crystals. Spots glowed an ominous green. Black fire.

Dreamer scurried back, shaking his head as if stung.

Lyra hissed, the fur on her back raised in a long ridge.

"Oh, no!" Ozzie cried.

"Don't go in there!" Adriane ordered.

The structures were all cracked and broken, their sharp edges blackened and covered in green slime. Emily shuddered. Every jagged green edge reminded her of a horrible wound. They had to be the witch's failed experiments, and the cause of the Black Fire.

"Come on, let's go," Zach urged them. "Nothing we can do here."

They continued in the tunnel making their way to the last chamber, a vast opening in the earth.

"I can feel them!" Zach cried. The stones pulsed stronger.

Adriane tried to contain her wolf stone. Surely this close the sorceress would sense the magic of the jewels. But her caution fell by the wayside as they rounded the corner, entered the immense cavern — and saw the crystals.

They could all feel them — *mistwolves trapped inside.*

Adriane quickly scanned the room for Storm. The cavern was as big as a football field, the three crystals rising in the darkness pulsed with shifting, murky greens, blacks, and grays. Something was happening since they were last here. The air was filled with electricity.

Zach touched Adriane and pointed.

On the far side of the cavern, red-eyed creatures as black as night scurried everywhere, working to keep the crystals polished. Sparks of power jumped and raced, leaping from crystal to crystal.

Emily shivered, even though it was hot in the chamber. Something tickled at the back of her mind, pushing at her, and getting more intense.

"What is it, Emily?" Ozzie asked, looking at her drawn face.

"The magic is coming," Emily answered.

Dreamer looked to Adriane. The warrior nodded, and the small mistwolf jumped onto the shallow floor.

Adriane blocked Zach with her arm. "Not that way."

"Good idea."

They circled around the opposite way, staying in the shadows at the base of the crystals.

"Storm!" Adriane cried. The silver mistwolf stood in the center of the three crystals. Her body glowed, illuminated by waves of mist that wafted into the crystals.

Adriane ran to her friend, throwing her arms around the wolf's neck — and fell to the cold, stone floor. She had fallen right through Storm as if the wolf was a ghost. Adriane scrambled to her feet, confused and worried.

"Storm?"

"My heart soars to see you, Warrior."

"Storm! What's wrong?"

"Zachariah, my son" the voice of the mistwolf Silver Eyes called.

"I'm here!" Zach's face was pressed against the crystal. "Don't speak, save your energy!"

Emily carefully walked around the crystal, examining it, touching it lightly, sending her senses into its core, as she would a sick patient.

Wolf Sister! Moonshadow's voice filled Adriane's head. *Tell your packmate to release her hold on us!*

"Storm?" Adriane looked to her friend.

"Wolf Brother," the voice of Moonshadow called out. *"You must not break the crystal!"*

"What are you talking about?" Zach asked. "We are going to get you out of there!"

"No, you cannot!" Moonshadow insisted.

"Why not?"

"We are all infected with the poison," Moonshadow said. *"We cannot be released."*

Zach gasped and turned to Adriane and Emily.

"I have held them here until your return, Healer," Storm said to Emily.

Emily flinched. There must be one hundred mistwolves in there. How could she possibly save them all? She could feel the Black Fire swirling, ripping apart the fabric of the mistwolves' magic.

"Healer," Storm said. *"You must save them."*

A sudden commotion and flashes of blue turned their attention to the sides of the cavern. Dozens of imps had left the forges, aware of the strangers' intrusion into their chamber. Sparks of electricity jumped across them. With a wail, the imps pounced like a black wave.

Lyra roared as Adriane jumped, spinning in the air, landing and rolling across their path. She pulled up into a fighting stance, wolf stone raised and blazing. With a fierce swing, she launched a ring of golden fire. The imps in front exploded in inky blobs, splattering across the floor.

Shrieking, the others ran as fast as they could to the far side of the chamber and out the door.

Emily wanted to run with them but couldn't.

"If the sorceress hasn't noticed us yet, she sure has now," Zach said.

Adriane grabbed Emily's arms. "Can you do this? Can you save them . . . and Storm?"

Emily's mouth fluttered, her heart in her throat. "I . . . I don't know."

"Emily," Ozzie was at her side. "When that magic hits, they'll be killed for sure. You have to try."

Emily looked at her friends. She was a healer, she had to act. "I need time."

"I'll get it for you," Adriane said.

"What are you going to do?" Zach asked, stumbling to her side.

"I'm going to pay a visit to the sorceress."

"I'm going with you," Zach insisted.

"No. You stay here and help Emily. She needs the power of your dragon stone."

Zach was not convinced.

"Zach," she said carefully. "You're barely healed yourself. I need room to maneuver. I can't also be worried about you."

Zach nodded. "I've seen you in action. No one's better."

A twitch of a smile played across Adriane's lips.

"I'll go with her," Lyra snarled, lips drawn in a vicious snarl. *"It's payback time!"*

No one was going to argue with that cat.

"All right." Adriane said. "Let's go!" She took a step and faltered — and turned to Storm. She could not afford the emotion. Not now. She stared at her friend. The mistwolf was transparent — fading.

"I am always with you," Storm said.

Adriane turned away and closed her eyes, letting the feelings wash through her, twisting, honing, and fine-tuning them into a laser beam of purpose and will.

Without a backward glance, she purposely strode into the corridor. If she had looked back, she would have broken, knowing that was the last time she would ever see her pack mate alive.

Chapter 14

Kara stood on the beach, watching waves rolling lazily upon the warm sands. Before her, giant flat stones etched with an intricate mosaic pattern, stretched out across the waters itself.

A silken flower grazed her cheeks with a fragrance sweeter than freesia or jasmine blooms. She turned to see dozens of floating figures. Gossamer wings seemed to catch and hold the light, reflecting it onto their flawlessly smooth faces and flowing hair — fairy wraiths. Large emerald eyes watched her.

You have come back to us, blazing star, a wraith of unimaginable beauty spoke.

"Where am I?" Kara asked. But the moment the words left her tongue, she knew. She had been here before. Was it in a dream? "Is this the final portal?" she asked in amazement.

You cannot get to Avalon through a portal, the wraith replied.

Kara felt a chill run through her body.

Only a unicorn can bring you here, another wraith fluttered close by, its long silken body almost translucent as it sparkled in the air.

A warm wind whispered past Kara's face, tickling her neck and ears. Kara looked into the large exotic eyes of the wraiths. Warmth filled her body.

Close your eyes.

Wraith voices seemed to come from everywhere at once.

Now open them.

Kara gasped as she gazed out to the mystical island, the home of all magic.

The flat bridge led to three stone rings encircling the island off shore. She could make out no details, it was completely shrouded in mist.

What do you see?

"Everything's changed," Kara breathed. "Avalon really does exist!"

It does for you.

Kara turned toward the gentle voices. "I don't understand."

You choose to see it.

Kara slowly began to understand. If you believe hard enough, dreams can come true.

"Can you release the magic and save Aldenmor?" She asked the wraiths.

Once the magic begins to flow from this place, it

cannot be stopped, a wraith said. *It could be wonderful and it could be very dangerous. Do you understand, Mage?*

"Yes," Kara said. "I mean, no." She had so many questions she wasn't sure what to ask. How was she supposed to start the magic? Would it be enough? What about the danger? And where were her friends? Were they okay? She opened her mouth, "What is a blazing star?" she finally asked.

There are a few who not only choose their own destiny but also change the path of the future forever. Those few attract magic, they guide it, strengthen it. It is up to them to guide magic along the right path. The power is not in the magic. The power is being able to choose what to do with it.

Kara nodded. She still felt unsure and suddenly shy. "I don't feel special, I just want to help my friends."

The wraiths circled her.

May you always choose wisely.

They parted, and Kara saw something shimmering in the sand. It was a scalloped, teardrop-shaped jewel — the very one Kara had found in the pond at Ravenswood so long ago. She couldn't keep it, because it was not given to her.

Kara stared at the unicorn jewel, stunned. "But I returned it to you."

You have made it yours.

She knelt and reached for the jewel, grasped it in her hand. A spark of light flashed from the stone. A magic jewel! It was everything she had ever wanted — why didn't it seem so important now? All she wanted was to find her friends, to make sure they were okay. She wanted to help save the creatures of Aldenmor and Earth.

Kara turned the jewel over in her hands. It sparkled with magic. "Thank you," she said to the wraiths. Suddenly, there were no more questions. She knew what she must do and she chose to do it.

Kara held her unicorn jewel high and concentrated. The wraiths fell away, vanishing with the wind, leaving her with a whisper — *The magic is with you, now and forever.*

Kara pictured magic, pure and good, flowing to a world that desperately needed it.

The unicorn jewel blazed with diamond-bright light. The waters around the island between the stone rings began to swirl building into waves of energy. With a rush, the whirlpool lifted into the air and streamed across the sky. Ribbons of rippling lights cascaded onto the web. It had begun.

Kara smiled — and everything vanished as she was jerked backward, pulled into the forbidden Otherworld.

❧   ❧   ❧

The Dark Sorceress felt the wave like a jolt!

She watched the star map, hanging open like a twinkling dome. One by one, the portals flashed as magic flowed — she could feel it, coursing its way through the sequence of portals, right now heading for her crystals. She licked her lips with a pointed tongue. She would have liked once and for all to find out where the so-called "home" of magic was, but the girl had vanished before revealing the location. It didn't matter really. Magic was magic, and fairy magic happened to be quite powerful. The witch knew there were many different sources of magic. And yet, feelings of uneasiness prickled against her skin. A warning.

Another jolt!

Those fairimentals had tricked her! She had been wrong about the maps. There was no final portal. They had constructed a safety gap. The joining of the maps had called the unicorn. And that is what had found the magic.

Her blood boiled, bubbling like the tainted water in her seeing pool. The blazing star and the unicorn had been within her grasp — right here in the same room! And now they were gone.

Yet the magic *was* coming. She wasn't wrong about that. The blazing star must have released it.

Let the Skultum deal with her, she thought, robes whipping behind her as she dipped a claw into the pool. The crystals would be ready. With the mist-wolf magic slowly eaten away by the Black Fire, the flow would be drawn to their cries.

An image of a red-haired girl surfaced. Emanating from the magic stone on the girl's wrist was a strong, blue-green light. It pulsed, slowly at first and then rapidly. The light surrounded the huge crystals.

Another of those mages! How had they escaped the dungeons? For the first time in decades, the Dark Sorceress felt something worming its way through her, doubt . . . and fear.

She pounded her fist in the water, sending it flying across the floor — and over the boots of a tall dark-haired girl.

The witch stood with a start. How could this girl have gotten into her chamber past her senses? Then she noticed the large beast slinking from the shadows to stand next to the girl. The cat's eyes glowed with feral rage and its lips pulled back, revealing razor teeth.

Instantly suppressing her surprise, the sorceress carefully walked to the center of the room.

"Well, well, the warrior mage," A smile played across her thin lips. "I'll say one thing about you mages, you're stubborn."

"And you're dead meat!" Adriane's heart hammered in her chest.

"So eloquently put, but I wish you would learn some manners." The witch raised her hand, and the giant doors behind Adriane and Lyra slammed shut, locking them in the witch's chamber.

Adriane was suddenly aware of the stone wall at her back, and the fact that Stormbringer was not at her side. She didn't see any of the sorceress's serpent guards lurking about, but they could be hiding in the shadows.

The witch's eyes fixed on the wolf stone. "I know what you think you're doing, trying to by your friend some time to heal the mistwolves. But they're long gone." The sorceress's eyes sparked. "Just like your mistwolf."

Adriane faltered, stung.

"Oh, did I say something?" Her bloodred lips contorted into a wicked smile. "Your wolf is dying while we sit here and chat. And for what?"

For an instant, all Adriane wanted to do was turn and run back and fight alongside Storm. She fiercely pushed the feeling away.

"And what about you, great beast?" The sorceress swung to face Lyra. "Where's your friend, the blazing star, hmm?"

Adriane quickly scanned the room and spotted

Kara's backpack on the floor. But her friend was not there. "What have you done with her?" she demanded.

"Me? Why nothing. She has abandoned you. And as you can see," she swept her hand to the lights of the star map, "the blazing star has released magic for my crystals."

Lyra circled behind the sorceress, snarling, *You will pay for what you have done to my sisters.*

"Ah, yes," the witch extended long claws from her fingers. "I remember now. They were some of the first I tried in the crystals. I watched them carry the Black Fire for hours. And what did you do? You ran away because you couldn't help them."

Lyra roared in anger.

"Doesn't matter now. The magic comes, and it will be under my control. Do you really think you can stop me?" Her voice rose in anger. "Right now, my armies come! And with them my special warrior. You remember it, don't you?" She stared at Adriane. "It's called a manticore. Vicious creature, lethal."

Adriane signaled Lyra with her glance. The cat pounced, lunging straight for the sorceress. With a wave of the witch's hand, red fire shot across the room. Lyra's wings flew open, and she swooped into the air above the deadly magic. Purposely,

519

Lyra flew to the walls, as the witch followed, trying to hit the cat again. The distraction was long enough for Adriane to hide what she was doing.

"Drake!" Adriane called, raising her wolf stone in the air.

"*Adriane!*" the dragon's voice boomed in her head. "*There are many creatures here!*"

"Remember what I told you?"

"*Yes.*"

"Do it. Now!"

"*I help!*"

"Yes, Drake, help us!" Then Adriane leaped. She spun into a circle, weaving rings of golden fire from her stone. With every ounce of strength she could muster, she forged the rings into a fireball and hurled it at the sorceress.

The witch caught the movement and blocked the oncoming magic, sending it crashing into the walls. Adriane feinted to the left, sending another fireball straight at her enemy. This one smashed into the sorceress, covering her in blazing light.

Lyra landed at Adriane's side, forcing her own strength into the warrior's jewel. Adriane spun again, building the power, throwing a third ball of magic careening into the witch. Again and again, she pounded away, screaming in rage as fire consumed the sorceress, lighting the room in a rising inferno.

Adriane spun to a stop, breathing hard, exhausted. She had not meant to unleash such excessive force. Control yourself, she told herself. Save your strength! Don't let your emotions cloud your actions!

The tower of fire that was the sorceress blazed wildly. Then it began to move, gliding across the floor. In a sudden burst, the fire lifted from the witch — revealing her untouched.

She raised a clawed finger in a spiraling motion. Adriane suddenly felt dizzy and disoriented. The room seemed to shift as the witch sent the fire slamming back against Adriane and Lyra. They were thrown against the wall and crumbled to the ground.

Pinpricks of light burst in Adriane's head. Trying to stop the room from spinning, she saw Lyra slumped on the cold floor.

"That was very good. Very good. You know why I am not going to kill you, don't you?"

Adriane watched the sorceress brush herself off as if nothing had happened.

"I'm going to build a special crystal just for you and your friends. I think your magic is quite ready for harvesting." She casually sat on her throne and laughed.

Chapter 15

Kara didn't know where she was. Walls of flowing mists surrounded her even though she walked upon solid ground. The place was eerily quiet, but she knew she wasn't alone. She could sense him before she saw him, and he — the one she had to face — was the real danger.

He had deceived her. He'd made her believe she had talent, she could sing — and instead tricked her into spellsinging. That set off the chain reaction, one portal after another opened. Now the magic was flowing — who would control it?

"Kara Davies," she finally heard the deep, velvety voice she remembered so well.

Kara turned slowly, and defiantly stared into his eyes, dark as coal, mean as a bitter winter night. He looked exactly as he had at the Ravenswood benefit concert, morphed into the body of tall, dark-haired, magnetic Johnny Conrad.

"Congratulations," he clapped his hands and bowed. "A jewel. Just what you've always wanted. Pity it won't do you any good here."

Even now, she had to remind herself, this was *not* Johnny Conrad. This creature was not even flesh and blood. This was the dark fairy — the Skultum — Be*Tween had told her about. But it didn't matter what shape he took, or what he told her. Kara's fear turned to shimmering anger. No one made a fool of Kara Davies, not even him!

There was only one way to defeat him — make him reveal his real name, trick him into saying it out loud.

Now, dressed in Johnny's signature black leather slacks and open-neck silk shirt, he took a step closer. "The blazing star, going out in a blaze of glory," he taunted. "Maybe I'll even write a song about it."

"Where are we?" Kara asked.

"This is the Otherworlds, and only one of us will leave." He spun into a dance move. "It's only fitting that we meet here. You see this is where I was trapped until freed by the — oh, you know, it's all in the family."

Kara would not flinch. There was no way she would give him the satisfaction of frightening her. "By the way," she said, forcing herself to appear calm, "You're not Johnny Conrad. So what should I call you? Your zillions of inquiring fans want to know."

"It's — HA! Uh-uh," he wagged his finger, then singsonged, "I'll never te-ell."

Kara shrugged. "Have it your way. You tricked me once, but in the end, I sent you packing."

"That's the nice thing about life, isn't it?" he sneered. "You always get a second chance."

Kara held her defiant posture. And hoped he didn't see her swallow, didn't hear her heart thudding, her mind racing.

"This will be so much fun!" He clapped his hands.

"Don't underestimate me," Kara growled. He was so cocky, so sure of himself. There had to be a way she could trick him.

He began to circle her, taunting, "You have no friends here, no winged cats, mistwolves, or fast-talking ferrets — no one to save you. Let's see you spellsing your way out of this one!"

As he babbled, Kara pressed herself, Think! Think! What would Emily do? What would Adrianne do? What would the fairies do? "Oh, I know!" she said. "Why don't we play a game?"

That got his attention. Her mind raced — could she match him, use her wits to save herself, get him to blurt his own name?

He was wily though — and expecting her to try that. She looked to her jewel and concentrated. She never had a stone of her own before. What magic did she have? What magic had she ever been able to use that —

Pop! Pop! Pop! Pop!

Colored bubbles popped in the air. That sound, which usually annoyed her, was music to her ears.

"Kee-Kee!"

The Skultum scowled as five dragonflies flew and chirped happily around his head. "What are these fairy creatures?" He demanded.

The size of small birds, they were tiny flying dragons. Red Fiona, purple Barney, blue Fred, orange Blaze, and yellow Goldie. They were fairy creatures — the kind that didn't need portals to flit from one world to another. From the start, the dragonflies had been drawn to Kara and only Kara, and she'd learned to control them. It was the only magic she'd ever really had on her own.

While the Skultum was trying to swat them away, Kara's mind was on fast-forward. The d'flies, when she asked them, could form a magic circle and create portable portals, windows the girls had used to see and talk to one another, even from different worlds.

She could make them form a circle, what else could she . . . And then it hit her. If the dragonflies could form a circle, she reasoned, could they form . . . other things, like letters?

As if they read her mind, they answered her! Kara watched, amazed, as Barney flew in a K shape; Fiona twisted into an E, Fred formed another E, Goldie formed another K, Blaze zigzagged into more Es!

Her jaw dropped!! Kara got it. She whirled around to check, but the Skultum, still trying to bat the dragonflies away, had no clue what the miraculous little creatures were doing! Did they know the Skultum's new name?

All she needed to figure out now was how to make him say it. Kara looked up, as the dragonflies buzzed over her head. She took a deep breath, and went for it. "Hey, Skultum thing," she called, "My friends love playing, like all fairy creatures."

The Skultum was intrigued. She had hit on something.

"Look!" Kara prayed this would work. She cartwheeled — the dragonflies mimicked, fluttering around her, their jeweled eyes sparkling.

She ran in a figure eight, they followed, making the same patterns in the air.

Just as Kara had hoped, the Skultum couldn't help himself. He was hopping and clapping, running around repeating their figure eights. Games were his stock in trade.

"Watch this," Kara said, "I can get them to spellspeak."

"You cannot," he said.

"Yes, I can!" she responded.

"No, you can't," he insisted.

"Betcha! Just watch."

Kara drew her fingers in the air, and formed a T. As they'd done before, two dragonflies — Fred and Blaze — formed the letter. Kara grinned, encouraging them silently.

"You try it," she urged.

His eyes lit up. "Okay." Using the forefinger of his right hand, and a half-moon shape with his left, he made the letter D. Goldie, Barney, and Fiona gleefully did the same. "This is too easy."

"Oh, wait!" Kara cried, as if she'd just thought of it. "I have the best game of all. Dragonfly charades. I think of a word, they form the letters — you have to guess!"

He threw back his head and laughed. "You slay me, Kara, you really do."

Just wait, she thought. I'm not the blazing star for nothing! She said, "I'll start."

Kara started with an easy word. The d'flies' eyes swirled with excitement as they watched her form letters.

Then with a flurry of activity, the d'flies created the letters using their little bodies.

The Skultum guessed it: "Star."

Kara graciously bowed, extending her arm.

It was his turn. He signaled the motions, they flew into formation: Barney made a circle, Fiona, the squiggly line that finished the Q. "Queen," Kara guessed what it was before they were finished.

"You go," he directed. She asked for "Flobbin."

The Skultum's next word was another easy one for Kara, "Banshee."

She still wasn't close to what she needed. She needed to make him say the name — without realizing he was doing it. A silly joke she'd made to Be*Tween came back to her when they told her what she'd have to do. Kara had quipped, "What am I supposed to stand on my head?" It was worth a shot.

"Ooookay," Kara said. "You're right. This is too easy. Let's try it . . . upside down!"

"That's preposterous —" he started, then watched her with glee. He couldn't help himself. The challenge was too, too tasty.

Kara began a cartwheel and stopped when she was balanced on her hands, upside down.

She urged the d'flies to form the letters: DOOWSNEVAR. The Skultum stood on his head and read it: RAVENSWOOD!

His upside down was: GNOSLLEPS: SPELL-SONG.

Kara was ready. She snapped her fingers and winked at the flies — they knew. "One last word — and this one's for the money."

"One for the money, two for the show — this show is over, and I get to go!" He giggled, standing on his head and watching carefully as the dragonflies formed their last word.

At the top of his lungs, he shouted, CIGAM!

His jaw dropped, his eyes bugged. Too late. He realized what he'd done.

Magic flew from the fairy, covering Kara in light. Now back in its true and horrid form, the Skultum stood frozen. Its reptilian scales glistened as it faded away.

The last words he heard were Kara's: "You won! You won!" Like a Cheshire cat, the Skultum disappeared, leaving only its surprised face. With a *Pop!* it vanished.

Kara rounded up the dragonflies. "Great work, guys."

They chattered and squeaked, twirling happily in the air.

"There's just one more thing I need," she said.

The d'flies stopped in mid-twirl. *"Ooooo!"*

Chapter 16

Emily brushed her damp hair back as she stood in the center of the three crystals. The familiar feeling of hopelessness welled inside. It was mixed with a new feeling — dread. Then Emily felt something else. The room lurched and started shaking. Emily knew what it was. The wave was getting closer, rising into a crest that would crash into the crystals, washing away everything in its path.

"You did it before, Emily," Ozzie stayed behind her, close on her heels. "Remember little Vela and the elves."

Emily nodded. She had been sick, her jewel infected with the dark poison. A hundred mistwolves were infected now. This was different . . . Or was it? She could feel the pull of the Black Fire, reaching for her. But she had healed herself and in the process, she realized, had formed an immunity of sorts, a shield. Another gift from her friend, the fairy creature called Phel. Was that a dream? Had

Phel really come to her? She believed with all her heart that he had and she carried her shield like a weapon, striking at the Black Fire.

Zach stood to her left, dragon stone raised, pulsing with red power. "They're getting stronger!"

"There are too many of us!" Moonshadow called. *"Save yourselves!"*

"Keep quiet, Brother," Zach said, "You sound like a squeaky mouse."

"A mouse?! When I get out of here, I'm going to show you who's a mouse!"

"You are, that's who!" Zach goaded his wolf brother on.

Suddenly, the crystals began to pulse together in a unified rhythm.

Emily pushed harder, her stone flashing with incandescent intensity.

A second later, the massive wave of magic slammed into the room.

Emily tumbled back, overwhelmed by its power. The magic sparkled and glowed as it swirled into the crystals. Cries of agony rose from the mistwolves as magic began filling the crystals, crushing everything in its way.

There was a loud *CRACK!*

The base of one crystal had cracked! It forked and snaked its way upward. Flaming green liquid spurted from the gaps.

"Look out!" Emily screamed, dousing the poison with blazing blue light.

Flaming green droplets escaped from the glittering tower, splattering at their feet. Ozzie screamed, leaping back to avoid the burning poison.

"Healer! Run!" Moonshadow called out.

"No!" Emily shouted back.

If the enormous crystal blew apart now, the Black Fire fallout would be worse than anything the already ravaged world of Aldenmor had suffered. But if she didn't do something, the mistwolves would die.

"Zach, when I say so, split open the crystal!" Emily shouted.

"Are you sure?"

"Yes! I've stabilized most of the wolves, I'll finish the job as they come out."

"You hear that?" Zach yelled into the crystals.

"Yes," Moonshadow called back.

Without taking her eyes off the first crystal, Emily held out her arm. The rainbow jewel was blinding. "I can do this." There was not a single shred of doubt in her voice.

Ignoring the deafening rumble and the glowing green flames erupting around her, Emily pictured the mistwolves, strong and whole. She stood, firmly holding up her shield of light. "Now!"

Zach fired his dragon stone at the crystal, covering it in red. The crystal shook violently and shattered, exploding upward as if hurled from the earth itself.

Thirty mistwolves leaped into the chamber. Some fell to the ground roiling in pain. Others shook, growling and snarling.

Ignoring his wounds, Moonshadow stumbled past them, herding the wolves into the light of the healer.

"Moonshadow!" Zach recognized his pack brother at once. The wolf was badly burned, toxic green lines crisscrossed over his charred skin. Emily rushed forward, ignoring the searing poison and placed her hands directly over Moonshadow's flanks.

A shudder went through her body as she felt the great wolf's pain. Then his heartbeat locked rhythm with hers, and Emily pulled the sickness from the wolf's body. Ever so slowly, the green lines began to disappear and the flesh started to heal.

Emily whirled, covering as many wolves in healing light as fast as she could. She moved like a dancer, reaching the mistwolves with the power of her healing.

Then Zach, Emily, and Ozzie ran to the next crystal. Dragon stone raised, rainbow jewel ready, fierce fuzzy ferret face steady.

"Ready?" Zach asked.

Emily nodded. "Go!"

❧   ❧   ❧

Something opened and something closed in Adriane's mind at the same time. She felt mistwolves — they were free! She searched frantically through the voices in her head. But she couldn't find Storm's. She wanted to scream but was suddenly knocked to the ground as the throne room shuddered. Chunks of rock fell from the high ceiling, smashing to the polished floor.

The sorceress was on her feet moving to the seeing pool.

Adriane stood against the shaking wall. Lyra paced back and forth snarling. The cat was okay, as far as Adriane could tell.

With a stir from her finger, the Dark Sorceress conjured an image in the pool — and her eyes went wide with rage.

The wave of magic had come, but one of the crystals had exploded, leaving a cloud of magic hanging over the lair. The mistwolves had been freed!

She whirled around to the star map, watching the oncoming wave. It was unbelievable — more magic than she'd even dreamed possible.

Then she turned to Adriane. "Your friends are destroying the crystals. They would trade the lives of the mistwolves for the destruction of Aldenmor!"

"Either way, *you* won't control the magic," Adriane said cooly.

"Such a waste." The witch raised her arm, magic spinning from her long fingers. "The mistwolves cannot stand against my armies."

"Think again, loser," Adriane spat.

The sorceress's eyebrow raised in suspicion. She suddenly snapped her head as if hearing incredibly bad news and stared more closely into the pool. Her body was shimmering in rage, magic fire radiating around her.

Adriane steeled herself and faced the evil witch calmly. "What's the matter? Your monsters having a little *dragon* trouble?"

With a screech, the witch hurtled magic at Adriane. Lyra knocked the warrior to the side as it hit the wall, ricocheting around the room. Adriane flung her arms and sent golden fire back at the witch. The sorceress held up her hand, but as Adriane pushed harder, Lyra roared.

The witch's feral eyes opened wide. She was being pushed back by Adriane's power! What had happened? Adriane howled as mistwolf power surged into her jewel. But it was not enough. They were at a stalemate and they both knew the witch was more experienced.

Suddenly, bright white light spilled into the chamber — a portal opened right in the middle of the throne room! Something horrible roared. The manticore stepped through.

Adriane gasped. It was more hideous than she remembered. Hunched over, the demon creature was enormous. Its huge apelike arms rippling with muscle hung down to the floor. Legs the size of tree trunks lumbered forward as it scraped its razor-sharp claws along the stone. Fire-red demon eyes scanned the room.

The sound and the beast's foul stench made Adriane cringe.

The witch laughed. "It seems my dark creature has eluded your dragon."

Adriane slowly backed away. There was no chance of beating this thing, she was just too exhausted. She stared at the monster and — did that thing just *wink* at her?

Adriane couldn't believe it. She looked to Lyra. The cat seemed to be — *smiling?*

The witch stepped next to the manticore as the portal glowed behind her. "Take them!" she ordered.

"Oookee-dookee."

What was that?

Something fluttered. Adriane looked closer.

Fiona, the red dragonfly, was sitting on the

witch's head! The little d'fly peered into the sorceress's face. *"Peeyeww!"*

"Ahhhhhh!" the sorceress screamed, waving the creature away.

"Ahhhhh!" The little red dragonfly freaked and popped out.

Pop! Pop! Pop! Pop!

Dragonflies!

"Oooo, Dee-Dee!" Fred landed on Adriane's shoulder, nuzzling into her neck.

"What trickery is this?" the witch screamed at the manticore. "Kill them all!"

The creature's eyes flashed. It opened its razor-toothed mouth — and spoke. "I don't think so."

It wasn't the voice of a monster. It was — *Kara's* voice.

Adriane could feel the strong magic of her friend inside the thing. There was no doubt the creature was Kara.

The witch stared in shock. "How . . ."

But Adriane was already in front of her, wolf stone raised.

"Would you like to do the honors?" the monster held its twisted claws out to the portal.

Adriane stepped forward, her jewel blazing.

Shock registered across the witch's face.

Adriane looked at her jewel and lowered her arm.

"What I think she needs . . ." the warrior began, "is a little human touch."

With that, she connected — with a right cross! The witch flew backward, straight into the portal.

The dragonflies gleefully whizzed around the portal, spinning and twirling.

The manticore transformed, its huge body melting away to reveal a slim blond-haired girl in its place.

"You!" The witch stammered.

Lyra howled.

Kara waved to the sorceress. "Buh-*bye* now."

For a moment, the sorceress' eyes remained visible, radiating hatred.

The dragonflies squeaked and chirped as the portal got smaller and smaller, until with a twinkle, it vanished — taking the sorceress with it.

Kara stood wiping her hands. "Pretty smelly, huh? What?"

Adriane looked at her in shock. "That was amazing! How did you do that?"

Kara smiled and waggled a sparkling jewel in her friend's face. "I got a jewel. I got a jewel."

Adriane raised an eyebrow. But before Kara could gloat some more, Emily called out, "Adriane, come quickly!"

Chapter 17

Kara, Adriane, and Lyra entered the crystal chamber. It was in complete chaos.

Mistwolves were everywhere, howling and growling, crystal shards littered the floor, sparking and crackling. The ceiling had been blown open, the sky was visible through thick clouds of green. It hung over them, covering everything in the room with a glittering, pulsing glow.

The mistwolves all called to Adriane, who ran into the fray, looking for Zach and Storm.

"Kara!" Ozzie called. "Over here!"

Kara and Lyra found an exhausted Emily, still working to heal the wolves.

"Kara, are you all right?" Emily ran her hand over a brown-and-gray wolf and sent it on her way.

"I'm fine."

"What happened?" Emily asked.

"Never mind about me. How are you doing?" Kara wanted to know.

"The mistwolves are well enough to leave."

Emily swept back sweat-streaked hair from her face.

"What's stopping them?" Kara asked.

"They *refuse* to leave!" Zach ran to them, giving Kara a quick nod, then looked to the ceiling. "They are holding the Black Fire from spreading from this place."

The roiling fire pulsed and glowed above them. The cloud continued to darken, becoming almost black.

"I don't know what else to do!" Tears spilled down Emily's face.

"Emily!" Kara held her friend's hands, looking deep into her eyes. "Remember when I asked you how far this thing would go?"

Emily nodded, sniffling.

"And why we were chosen?"

"Yes," Emily answered.

"We *weren't* chosen." Kara said. "*We* were the ones who chose!"

Emily looked at her friend. She was right. Emily had chosen to become a healer. Adriane had chosen to follow Storm on the warrior's path. And Kara had chosen to join them.

"Now we have to follow our path wherever it leads. We each do it our own way — with the help of our friends!" Kara turned to include everyone in the room. "And we choose now to finish this!"

"She's right!" Ozzie joined in. "The magic is sick and needs to be healed, just like all of you and the other creatures of Aldenmor."

"Gather around us," Kara shouted. "Feed your magic to Emily. We will heal the magic."

Suddenly, Emily, Kara, Adriane, Ozzie, and Lyra were surrounded by a hundred mistwolves.

Emily rolled up her sleeves and concentrated. The rainbow jewel began to pulse with blue-green light. But the light was duller than usual, dimmed by the ominous black cloud overhead.

"Concentrate on building the light," Emily told them.

Silence filled the room. The mistwolves used their magic, sending it into Emily's stone.

Ozzie's whiskers twitched as he hugged Emily tight. The rainbow jewel brightened, then pulsed.

Lightning flashed across the clouds, sending wild magic flying. The chamber walls shuddered as one collapsed, sending dust and debris everywhere.

"Stay together," Moonshadow ordered.

Kara turned to Adriane. "Are you ready?"

Adriane stood next to Kara and held out her hand.

Kara grasped it. "Ready, Emily?"

Emily nodded, placing her hand over those of her friends.

Emily raised her rainbow jewel, sending blue fire up and around her arms. Adriane raised her wolf stone, golden fire wrapping around her and twisting over Emily's blue magic into a tight bond.

Then Kara held up her stone. It blazed like a diamond.

Everyone watched in amazement as blue and gold fire raced around Kara, covering her in magic.

"Let's do it!" she yelled, and let the magic go.

Silver fire burst from the unicorn jewel streaming like a rocket into the clouds above.

The cloud formed into a whirlpool of power.

With all of their hearts, the three mages focused their will.

Suddenly, the clouds exploded upward and streaming rays of multicolored lights lit the sky.

The chamber rocked as another wall collapsed.

"Let's get out of here!" Ozzie yelled.

The mistwolves bolted, running from the chamber in a wave. Emily grabbed Ozzie, hoisting him into her arms as Kara and Lyra herded the final wolves out.

Dust flew and the rumbling grew louder.

"Adriane!" Kara screamed, grabbing the warrior and pushing her from the chamber.

"Storm!" Adriane called out, but heard no reply, only silence echoing from the emptiness in her heart.

"We have to go now!" Kara pulled Adriane from the chamber and into the hall.

With a thunderous boom, the chamber behind them collapsed in a pile of rubble.

The girls burst through the front doors and into the bright light of the Shadowlands.

The mistwolves fanned out to make sure no guards or monsters stood in their way. Nothing did. Word had spread fast. The reign of the Dark Sorceress was over.

"Zach!" Drake swooped down from the sky, stirring up a dust storm as he landed. Zach ran to his friend, hugging the dragon tight.

The group made its way to the top of the dunes and looked to the skies.

It was incredible! Bands of light drifted overhead, brightening to form giant curtains rippling with reds, blues, oranges, and purples. The entire sky seemed full of color and motion. Bright points of light swirled like pinwheels as magic rained from the sky.

The magic drifted through the air, over the Shadowlands, bathing everything in a fine, shimmering mist. The healing of Aldenmor had begun.

As the group watched, the land began to transform. Dry, blackened earth drank in the magic and sprouted tender grasses and wildflowers. Charred tree and shrub branches burst with lush leaves.

Emily felt giddy, hugging Ozzie tightly, laughing and crying at the same time. She let the rain wash over her, never wanting this feeling to end.

Kara sat next to Lyra, hugging her friend close. She took a deep breath, inhaling fragrant spring blossoms. In her hands, the unicorn jewel felt warm.

Zach stood next to Drake, the big dragon refusing to let the boy leave his side.

The mistwolves surrounded them, howling in song, reveling in the healing of their planet. But then the wolfsong grew somber, filled with sadness and loss.

To the side of the dune, Adriane stood alone watching the magical light show.

Kara, Emily, Lyra, and Ozzie went to Adriane's side.

Tears welled in Emily's blue eyes. "There was nothing you could have done," she said, as if reading her friend's mind.

"I know," Adriane said.

"*Storm saved us all,*" Moonshadow said, slowing approaching Adriane, Zach at his side.

Kara and Emily put their arms around Adriane as the warrior leaned into them.

"No tears." Adriane wiped at her eyes. "She wouldn't want that."

"*One mistwolf held a hundred of us,*" Moonshadow said. "*Do you know how she did that?*"

Adriane looked at the large black wolf.

"She held us until we were safe because she was thinking of you. Her love for you gave her the strength."

"Thank you," Adriane smiled.

"We weep for your loss, Warrior."

The group was startled at the new voice they heard.

"You have guided magic back to the fairy glen." The voices of the fairimentals echoed in their heads. *"And you have changed the future forever."*

Epilogue

W*arrior."*

Adriane stood in the meadow under the shade of the great tree, Okawa. Its branches glistened with greens as if it, too, rejoiced in the coming rains. But the bright rippling colors were in stark contrast to the rain that fell in Adriane's heart. Around her a hundred mistwolves, the entire pack, had gathered.

Moonshadow, Silver Eyes, and Zach approached her.

"Will you lead us in the wolf song?" Moonshadow asked. *"We will wish Stormbringer well on her journey to the spirit pack."*

Adriane was honored to lead the sacred ritual, reserved for members of the pack only. She threw her head back and sang the wolf song from deep in her soul as it had been taught to her by her lost friend. The pack joined, sending their voices echoing across the Fairy Glen.

Slowly, the mistwolves walked away. Adriane, Zach, Moonshadow, and Silver Eyes stood watching soft grasses and rainbow flowers wave under the light breeze.

"I can't say good-bye," Adriane whispered.

"You don't have to," Zach said gently.

"She is not lost to us, but a part of the spirit pack," Moonshadow said.

"If you listen, they speak to us still from within." Silver Eyes brushed Adriane's side.

Adriane ran her hand over her wolf mother's soft fur.

"Hold on tight to every memory, Little Wolf Daughter," Silver Eyes said. *"It is what makes your heart strong."*

Adriane closed her eyes and let the memories come — memories of her and Storm. The first time she realized they could communicate. The two of them wrestling across the hills of Ravenswood. Storm helping her understand the magic, and friendship. And their journey — together and separately — to Aldenmor.

"When does it stop hurting?" Adriane struggled to stay strong.

"Not for a long time," Zach said. "But you go on and you *hold* on! Think about what Storm would want for you."

"I don't know if I can," Adriane said truthfully. Her heart lay in pieces, locked away in a place she could not reach.

"Little Wolf," Silver Eyes said. *"You must not close your heart to those who love you."*

From the corner of her eye Adriane caught movement. Silver Eyes was nuzzling a fuzzy mist-wolf pup forward. *"It is time for the student to become the teacher,"* the wolf mother said.

Dreamer was in front of her, shifting shyly on his white paws. The wolf pup lifted his head to the warrior mage.

Adriane knelt and looked into the pup's deep green eyes. "I guess we're both alone now," she whispered.

Dreamer understood. He moved into Adriane's arms. Feelings flashed — anger, fear, sadness, and loss — but underneath, tenderness and beauty, the promise of hope, and a conviction to fight for love, the heart of a warrior.

Holding Dreamer in her arms, Adriane cried. Her tears fell with the rain from her heart.

"I'll always be with you."

Dreamer's wolf eyes filled with love. And the bond was forged like iron between the lone wolf and the lone warrior — forever.

The Fairy Glen was packed.

Pegasi, wommels, brimbees, jeeran, all the magical animals from Ravenswood had returned to a place they thought they'd never see again. The waters of the fairy lake sparkled and glistened, reflecting the bright colors of the sky and the shimmering white of the portal that hung open near the shore. The wondrous Fairy Glen, seen by so few, was renewed. The heart of Aldenmor beat strong once again.

Ozzie stood chattering with a group of wide-eyed elves, astonished to be at such an extraordinary place. Emily, Kara, and Lyra waited patiently as Adriane approached with Zach, Moonshadow, and Silver Eyes. Emily smiled as she noticed Dreamer walking protectively at the dark-haired girl's side.

No words were spoken. Just a warm embrace by each told Adriane how much she was loved, how much she was needed.

"The prophecy has come to pass." The wistful windy voice belonged to Ambia, an air fairimental. A thicket of twigs, brush, and leaves then tumbled together as Gwigg, an earth fairimental, appeared.

The entire glade hushed at the presence of such magical creatures.

"Three mages have come to our aid and healed

Aldenmor," Ambia said. *"One has followed her heart, and found strength."* The fairimental flitted over Adriane.

"One has seen in darkness and found light," Gwigg rolled by Emily.

"And one has changed completely and found —"

"A jewel!" Kara mouthed to her friends, holding up her unicorn jewel now secured to her silver necklace.

"— restraint!" Ambia twinkled.

"Oh, that, too." Kara said, smiling.

"You changed from the prettiest to the ugliest," Lyra teased.

"Yeah, but I'm back. And I'm still a princess!" Kara giggled.

"The rain falls, covering Aldenmor with glorious magic," Ambia continued. *"It is full of possibilities and also fraught with dangers."*

"The Dark Sorceress has been exiled to the Other-worlds," Gwigg rumbled. *"But even now, magic trackers and unspeakable creatures of evil are gathering to seek out and control the magic."*

"So it begins, mages," Ambia whispered.

The voices of the fairimentals echoed in the girls' heads. *You have the power. . . . Guide the magic along the right path.*

The portal shimmered as blue-green oceans appeared. Gusts of water erupted as sea dragons, with merfolk upon their backs, burst free and arched into the air.

"We stand with you, Mags!" Kee-Lyn called from the back of Meerka.

"As do we!" The picture changed to show hundreds of elves standing atop rolling green hills and raising their arms in cheers.

"*Ozymandius,*" Ambia called out.

Ozzie shuffled forward and kneeled before the wisp of wind.

"*For your heroism and loyalty, you are hereby decreed a Knight of the Circle. Rise, Sir Ozymandius.*"

A twinkle of light suddenly glowed in the ferret's hands. When the light faded, Ozzie held a glittering golden stone. His eyes widened. "A ferret stone!" he shouted, showing his jewel to the astonished elves nearby.

Everyone cheered at this amazing honor. Crusp and Tonin and the rest of Ozzie's relatives proudly puffed up their chests, patting their newly famous elf kin on the back.

"Thanks! But . . . can I change back to my real body?" Ozzie scratched his ear.

Ambia circled the ferret like a glittering breeze. "*If you choose to stay here on Aldenmor, you may return to your elf body and honor us with your service.*"

"Yes!"

"But if you chose to return with the mages, you must remain as you are."

"Oh." Ozzie looked to the elves and turned to Emily.

Emily bit her lip.

Ozzie shuffled back and forth, fraught with indecision. "What should I do?" he asked, clearly torn.

"What you've always told us, Ozzie," Emily smiled. "You have to follow your heart."

Ozzie's brow crinkled as he clutched his new jewel and walked to the elf clan.

The animals of Ravenswood were crowded around Kara, admiring her unicorn jewel.

"It is magnificent," Balthazar said.

"Yeah, it sure is!" Then Kara smiled humbly. "Thank you, but you guys are the ones who deserve this, not me."

"Nonsense," Rasha said. "Your magic shines from within, the jewel is just a reflection of your beauty."

"Thank you." Kara hugged the animals that had become so close to her over the past months.

"Kara." Gwigg tumbled to a halt near her feet. *"The blazing star faces the hardest lessons of all in the days ahead."*

"Right, but what about the Skultum's magic?"

Kara queried. "You know, that fairy stuff about absorbing its powers."

"It is hard to say if you will keep it. You are not skilled enough to sustain that level of power," Gwigg responded.

"I see," Kara scrunched her nose. The jewel warmed and flashed — and her hair turned bright purple!!

"Ooo!" the animals admired her choice of color.

Quickly, before anyone else could notice, she turned her hair back to blonde.

"The magic runs deep inside you now," Gwigg warned. *"It is a gift. To use your powers impulsively only makes you more and more dependent on them. You must stand strong lest you fall under its darker pull."*

"What do I do?" Kara asked, suddenly worried.

"Stand strong with your friends," Ambia advised, leading Kara to the bright light.

Kara walked to the portal next to Adriane and Emily. The three girls clasped hands.

Ozzie and the elves were in deep conversation, then did a lot of hugging and more hugging. Emily watched as the ferret moved away from the elves to stand next to her.

"I'm going to miss you, Ozzie," Emily sniffled.

"Why, where are you going?" Ozzie looked confused, then smiled. "'Cause wherever it is, I'm going, too."

Kara, Lyra, Emily, Ozzie, Adriane, and Dreamer stood before the portal that would take them home. As the rainbow of lights twinkled in the skies over the Fairy Glen, they knew one thing for sure. Their friendship would see them through any new challenges and adventures they would face in the struggles ahead. The magic of Avalon had been released. But the mages had learned that the power to triumph over evil was ultimately not in the magic itself, but something more powerful: the magic of the ties that bound humans and animals, nature, and all living things — that is the spirit of Avalon.